D1564891

"Blumenthal's graceful, wise, moving first n[ ] of academia and the literary word, then plunges into Weinstock's painstaking self-analysis. . . . Blumenthal, a poet and former creative writing director at Harvard, has written an engrossing narrative: death-obsessed, life-affirming and, like all good novels, resonant with meaning." —*Publishers Weekly*

"The satire of academia in *Weinstock Among the Dying* succeeds in the hilarious footsteps of Nabokov's *Pnin*. In the end, however, wit and cynicism join hands with grief and growth, and enable Weinstock to bury his despair. His journey toward emotional fulfillment was a pleasure to follow for this reader. In turns humorous and sad, but consistently engaging, Blumenthal has written an eloquent, compelling, richly textured first novel."
—Jhumpa Lahiri, recipient of the Pulitzer Prize in Fiction
for *Interpreter of Maladies*, in *The Harvard Review*

"Michael Blumenthal's *Weinstock Among the Dying*, is a glorious home run, gratifying on several levels. It's a funny, satirical story of a young guy grappling with the Harvard mystique—a writer smart enough to get into Harvard and teach but seemingly not smart enough to get out. . . . Weinstock has already been compared to the work of Philip Roth, but Blumenthal's playful, witty, effortless prose has none of the heavy, Nixon-like smugness of Roth. WATD ranks in the A-category of sophisticated first novels." —Steve Kykes, *The Boston Herald*

"The best of *Weinstock* is a devastating, idiosyncratic satire of Harvard, where Blumenthal formerly served as director of creative writing, the very post occupied by Weinstock. Mercilessly he bangs away at the pretensions of academe. . . . Blumenthal's Harvard is "the only place in America where you have to study for dinner," a temple of "Best-in-the-World" elitism that Jewish faculty—even if their Jewishness is considered "an ugly blemish on the smooth, homogenizing hide of intellectual achievement—would never dream of leaving, for it is their "one chance in life to become the thing every Jew, deep in his heart of hearts most wants to be . . . The Great Goldberg. . . . Blumenthal insists that Harvard is no more nor less than "a dusty archival tomb, in which the collected letters, papers, manuscripts and miseries of the dead were far more significant than the real, passionate, life-giving triumphs and tribulations of the living."
—Stuart Schoffman, *The Jerusalem Report*

"The book sports some of the broadest satire I've ever read of academic existence—Blumenthal would never stoop to calling it "life"—and is as fizzy with ʋne-liners as a George Carlin HBO special." —Mark Shechner, *Bookpress*

"To say Blumenthal's first novel proves he's no lightweight would be an understatement. It is a brave, soul-baring exploration of contemporary man's search for love in a cynical, over-rationalized society."   —Theo Huffman, *The Budapest Sun*

". . . This work is a splendid accomplishment by a man whose previous writing consists primarily of five books of poetry. His wit and sharp pen satirize Harvard, academic politics, psychoanalysis and Jewish family life. Love and death, his central themes, are not satirized but rather presented as poignant parts of Weinstock's life story. . . . Blumenthal is indeed a creative writer himself who has great talent and who has richly demonstrated that talent in this unusually fine first novel."
—Morton I. Teicher, Dean, Wurzweiler School of Social Work,
Yeshiva University, and author of *Looking Homeward:
A Thomas Wolfe Photo Album*

"An acclaimed poet, Blumenthal demonstrates his ability to write witty, satirical prose, while remaining sympathetic to his protagonist. *Weinstock Among the Dying* is well crafted and eminently readable."
—Ellen R. Cohen, *Small Press Review*

"The book marries the psychological to the satirical, poking fun at academia and exploring a twisted psyche and its quest for the meaning of life."
—Jon Sanders, *The News and Observer*

"Poet Blumenthal, former director of Creative Writing at Harvard, lampoons that university's hallowed halls and the oddballs who roam them in his fictional debut—a lascivious and witty but all-too-*entre-nous* and familiar tale of academic life."   —*Kirkus Reviews*

"*Weinstock Among the Dying* is the triumph of a voice growing from inarticulate parentage that moves from death to life, from loss to birth, from oppression to poetry. From unpromising beginnings, Weinstock turns the trick on death and dying and now lives among us."
—Dr. John Mack, Department of Pyschiatry, Harvard University,
recipient of the Pulitzer Prize in Biography for *Prince of Our
Disorder: The Life of T. E. Lawrence*

WEINSTOCK AMONG THE DYING

BOOKS BY MICHAEL BLUMENTHAL

Sympathetic Magic: Poems. NY: Water Mark Press; The Water Mark Poets of North America First Book Prize, 1980; Fifth Printing, 1999

Days We Would Rather Know: Poems, NY: Viking-Penguin, 1984; reprinted by Pleasure Boat Studio: A Literary Press, NY, 2005

Laps: A Book-Length Poem. U of Massachusetts Press; Winner of Juniper Prize, 1984

Against Romance: Poems. NY: Viking-Penguin, 1987; reprinted by Pleasure Boat Studio: A Literary Press, NY, 2005

The Wages of Goodness: Poems. U of Missouri Press, 1992

To Woo and To Wed: Poets on Love & Marriage (editor). NY: The Poseidon Press, 1992

Weinstock Among the Dying: A Novel. Cambridge: Zoland Books, 1993; Winner, Harold U. Ribalow Prize for Fiction, 1994, *Hadassah Magazine;* reprinted by Pleasure Boat Studio: A Literary Press, NY, 2008

When History Enters the House: Essays from Central Europe. Pleasure Boat Studio: A Literary Press, NY, 1998

Dusty Angel: Poems. BOA Editions, 1999; Winner of the Isabella Gardner Prize

And Yet: Selected Poems of Péter Kántor (translator); Budapest: Irodalom Publishers, 2000

All My Mothers and Fathers: A Memoir. Harper Collins, 2002

And: Poems. BOA Editions (forthcoming, 2009)

The Selected Poetry and Writings of Michael Blumenthal. Legal Studies Forum, U of West Virginia, 2007

WEINSTOCK AMONG THE DYING

a novel
by

Michael
Blumenthal

Pleasure Boat Studio
A Literary Press
New York

AUTHOR'S NOTE:
In view of the tendency to identify characters in fiction with
real people—and in view of the additional fact that parts of
this novel are set in actual places, including an actual
university, where the author has spent some of his life—it
seems proper to state emphatically that this is a work of
fiction. There are no real people, including Martin
Weinstock, and no real events, contained herein. Like any
artist, the author has had to make his work of the union
between the abstractable feelings provided by his life
experience and the factual particulars furnished by his
imagination. However, all of the characters, names, and
experiences are fictitious, and any resemblance to actual
events or to people, living or dead, is purely accidental.

Weinstock Among the Dying
Copyright 2008 by Michael Blumenthal

ISBN: 978-1-929355-43-3
Library of Congress Control Number: 2008920124

First paperback edition. This book was originally published in hardbound edition
only by Zoland Books of Cambridge, Massachusetts, in 1993.

Text design by Boskydell Studio, re-done by Susan Ramundo
Cover design by Steve Snider, re-touched by Laura Tolkow
Printed in the USA

Pleasure Boat Studio books are available through the following:
SPD (Small Press Distribution) Tel. 800-869-7553, Fax 510-524-0852
Partners/West Tel. 425-227-8486, Fax 425-204-2448
Baker & Taylor Tel. 800-775-1100, Fax 800-775-7480
Ingram Tel. 615-793-5000, Fax 615-287-5429
Amazon.com and bn.com

and through
PLEASURE BOAT STUDIO: A LITERARY PRESS
www.pleasureboatstudio.com
201 West 89th St., Ste. 6F
New York, NY 10024

Contact Jack Estes
Tel/Fax: 888-810-5308
Email: pleasboat@nyc.rr.com

FOR THE LIVING
&
IN MEMORY OF THE DEAD:

Betty Blumenthal
1907–1959

Berthold Gern
1905–1993

BOTH BLOOD IN THE END

Contents

We die with the dying:
See, they depart, and we go with them.
We are born with the dead:
See, they return, and bring us with them.

— T.S. Eliot,
"Little Gidding"

If you want to become whole,
let yourself be partial.
If you want to become straight,
let yourself be crooked.
If you want to become full,
let yourself be empty.
If you want to be reborn,
let yourself die.

— Lao-tzu,
Tao Te Ching

But what should a kind-hearted boy do who
hasn't yet learned to defend himself against all
his mothers and fathers?

— George Konrad,
The City Builder

WEINSTOCK AMONG THE DYING

Prologue

Somewhere in the middle of his life's journey, Martin Weinstock lost his way and found himself Burke-Howland Lecturer in Poetry at Harvard University.

He didn't really know how he had gotten there, having grown up in that German-speaking refugee family whose few syllables of spoken English were as stilted and awkward as Kennedy's famous *"Ich bin ein Berliner"* of 1963. But there he now was, surrounded by what were touted to be "the best minds" in this dear country of his — the Green Berets of the American intellect. And, at this citadel of intelligence and Brahmin restraint, he felt irrevocably out of place.

Before coming to Harvard in the summer of 1983, fresh from three years as a television cameraman for West German television network DDT (an initialism that seemed to him not entirely accidental), Weinstock had done the best he could to prepare for this sudden — and it seemed to him entirely unmerited — entrance into the world of higher intelligence. While waiting for his various *echt Deutsche* colleagues to create the prerequisite "atmo" into which to poke their zoom lenses and mini-Nagras, he would poke his rather unrefined gaze into volumes of Chaucer, Milton, Shakespeare and Pope in such picturesque American cities as Duluth, Ames, Gary, Cleveland, Milwaukee and Amarillo. He even tried reading Goethe and Rilke in the original German. *"Wie soll ich meine Seele binden,"* he implored one of the cameramen during a shoot in Bismark, North Dakota, *"dass sie nicht an Deine rührt?"*

Desperate for what he assumed to be a greater intelligence than his own, Weinstock even ventured into the terrain of what he was told were the "in" texts of an enterprise called Critical Theory (Lit-Crit, as the initiated called it) — writers with European names like Barthes and Derrida, Blanchot and de Man (the last whom he couldn't help but think of as some hip version of former St. Louis Cardinal slugger Stan Musial). But their attempts at something resembling prose so bored him that he quickly found himself regressing to his adolescent pastimes of excessive masturbation and random sexual desire. Hardly was the word "Derrida" out of someone's mouth than he had to hastily seat himself in order to hide that formidable revelation of his loosely tethered unconscious that once went by the horrific name "boner."

By the time he arrived in Cambridge that first summer of 1983, Weinstock had already assembled all the natural prerequisites of academic life — a crumbling marriage, a case of the intellectual heebie-jeebies, an inexorable preejaculatory lust for what he imagined would be his beautiful, brilliant, talented female students (brains by Virginia Woolf, bodies by Sonia Braga, glands by Georges Simenon) and the onset of that stifled *joie de vivre* that views the utterance of such phrases as "the iconicity of mimesis" as a cause for celebration.

But there would also, he was certain, be compensations. His poetry — so long relegated to the lustful stolen hours and interstices of his life — could now be embraced in the open, at center stage, without the artificial embellishments of secrecy and sinfulness. There would, he realized, be no more secret rendezvous by the river, no more stolen kisses along the railway trestles, no more lingering, dry-humped afternoons beneath the magnolias and Japanese maples.

So, on that fuzzy July morning when he first entered the white clapboard building at 24 Burdick Place and saw the words MARTIN WEINSTOCK, BURKE-HOWLAND LECTURER IN ENGLISH plastered to the door of Room 26, Weinstock felt the potential joy of having finally arrived at the pinnacle of intellectual life and the onset of a brilliant career. This joy, however, was mingled with anticipation, this sense of success with a certain guilt at his own fraudulent occupation of it. And as he — the second-generation son of uneducated German-Jewish refugees who suddenly found himself a professor at the world's greatest university — opened the door to his Harvard office for the first time, Martin Weinstock also felt a deep, ineluctable sadness, as if he had just been dropped down a black hole from which it would be a long, long time before he would be able to rise again into the living grace of light and air.

BOOK I

The Shallows

———————•———————

What does it mean to be in pain?
No more than that the rain is rain,
and flood flood. Deep we are, and deep
is where we have to go. As seed goes deep.
As rain goes deep to bring forth the flower.

As the worm must go deep to take us dustwards.

— MARTIN WEINSTOCK
"Laps"

CHAPTER 1

Abstract Minds

People not quite knowing what to say,
Smiling, shaking, turning up their faces,
Wondering: *how did I ever get this way?*
With form and content having traded places.

Frosted cubes all floating in the punch,
Glittered cookies looming near the dip,
Colleagues promising: We *must* have lunch,
Like guests embracing on a sinking ship.

Fearful, trembling, elbows near their wives,
Men in perfect shoes patrol the cheer,
Wondering — *Where did they go, our lives?*
And wishing that a younger girl were near.

Affable as pirates, holding forth like saints,
We cruise in galleons of the Christmas spirit,
Each pretending to be what he ain't
For fear the real thing might dissolve when near it.

Now the wicks grow dim, the carols finish.
We've all grown putrid with our sense of cheer.
We entered full, then watched ourselves diminish
As we slid snakily into the year.

— MARTIN WEINSTOCK,
"Christmas Party"

W einstock had always been possessed of a profound sense
that to penetrate too deeply into anything had something
vaguely to do with death. Even as a college student, he
had been drawn to the 101 course in every discipline, as if to delve
more deeply into any subject guaranteed the onset of boredom and
indifference. Exactly where this idea came from he didn't know,

but whenever anything approaching expertise began to threaten — whenever, for example, he felt himself growing too close to a woman or a profession — a vague, prethanatic trembling overtook him, a kind of weakness in the knees and shortness of breath which signaled the onset of prolonged periods of sleeplessness and anxiety.

Weinstock didn't exactly know the source of this sensation, but he *did* know that — as a result of several years of what he thought of as merely a kind of sophisticated fiddling in the parentheses of an otherwise fully occupied day — he suddenly found himself possessed of a "vocation." He had, he was astonished to discover (as part of what he initially thought of only as a brief reprieve from "real" life), arrived at the first stepping-stone to a brilliant career: He was on his way to becoming one of America's "serious" living poets.

But there was something that absolutely befuddled Weinstock from virtually the moment of his arrival at Harvard. Having lived on the outside of "the academy" (that terrible, military-sounding term) for so long during his vocationally lost years as a cameraman, journalist and lawyer, he had been encouraged in his first, tentative ventures into the world of "letters" by the fact that his work seemed to move the ordinary, intelligent people he considered his friends. "Martin," more than an occasional Washington lawyer or bureaucrat confided to him, "what I so admire about your work is that I actually *understand* what it's about." And Weinstock somehow felt an obligation to keep doing this thing that seemed to provide pleasure to those he liked.

Now, in the well-endowed and perpetually sanctified courtyards of Harvard, having arrived at the supposed heights of what he had rather innocently set out to do merely to unburden himself of his own life, Weinstock found that the simplicity and directness he had so arduously cultivated earned him little but disdain. In fact, it seemed to him that he was now a man entirely bereft of friendships and surrounded only by those neutered, dispassionate associations known as "colleagues."

There was something about the word "colleague," it seemed, that implied a license to slander, insult, berate and (in any way short of actual homicide) *undo* others in ways which "friendship" could never have tolerated. During his first year in Cambridge, when Weinstock's second slim volume, *The Possibilities of Human Existence,* was published, the reaction made him feel like an animal lured into a beautiful meadow by a sweet-smelling piece of bait, only to find itself strafed by rifle and shotgun fire when it entered.

"Intellectually banal," roared one of the colleagues who had most cordially welcomed him in the pages of the *Harvard Crimson.* "Insipidly erotic," proclaimed an unsuccessful rival for his job in the *Boston Phoenix.* "A well-intentioned failure," chimed in a member of the Composition faculty who, after fifteen years as an uninspired and unpublished fiction writer in Fairbanks, Alaska, had reemerged at Harvard as an up-and-coming young critic. "The rhythmic equivalent of the mountains of Holland," wrote Harold Blumberg, Charles Emery Eagan Visiting Professor of Deconstructionist Countertextualism, in the pages of Harvard's literary magazine, *Veritas.*

Weinstock wasn't so much hurt as confused by the negative reception his work received among the Harvard intelligentsia. What he couldn't understand, above all, was why, at the very same time, his mailbox at Burdick Place was crammed with letters from intelligent heathens like the young folklorist from Santa Fe, from whom he received the following epistle:

Dear Martin Weinstock:

I am a former Harvard student myself (I transferred to Reed College after a nervous breakdown at the end of my sophomore year) and am writing to encourage you not to let them destroy you, though they will do their damnedest.

Your work is incredibly moving and beautiful, and I know they will do their best to make you feel stupid and fraudulent and grateful and unwanted. They will make you feel as though, if you haven't read *Beowulf* twice a year since you were sixteen and know at least the first 200 lines of *The Waste Land* by heart, you have no right to live. They will try and convince you that being a living writer who is not himself a fourth-generation Harvard graduate or a direct descendant of Henry IV (or married to one) is about as worthwhile as being a Band-Aid on a seam of the space shuttle. They will try and make you into yet another piece of dead flesh with feet just like the rest of them.

But, dear Martin Weinstock, don't let them! Your work is gorgeous and important and full of soul, and a source of strength to those of us who — as it says in the Book of Job (if you'll pardon my sounding like a Harvard graduate) — "alone have escaped to tell thee."

So — *please, please, Martin Weinstock* — hang in there. And if things get really rough — which I can't help but believe they will as long as you insist on retaining the rich and life-affirming nature of your soul — you might just try doing what I did during my two absymal, life-threatening years in the Harvard English Department: Remind yourself that it is not your living betters you are among, but the vengeful dead, who have returned to earth in the guise of the powerful to avenge themselves against those who still insist on the world as a place of joy and hope and affirmation and love.

A devoted admirer,
Jennifer Cerny

This disparity — between his reception at the hands of those he thought of as his spiritual and human brethren, and the animus of those with whom he was suddenly encased in what increasingly seemed like an oxymoron: *academic life* — convinced Weinstock that he now sat, Januslike, on the cusp between life and death, between the passionate, rosy-cheeked relations of his pre-Harvard life and the increasing bereavement of his present condition.

He felt, in a way that Jennifer Cerny's letter only seemed to confirm, as though he had suddenly descended into a dusty, archival tomb, in which the collected letters, papers, manuscripts and miseries of the dead were far more significant than the real, passionate, life-giving triumphs and tribulations of the living.

All of his life in Cambridge, in fact, seemed summed up by the inscription he had seen on a T-shirt during his very first foray into Harvard Square. "LIVE FOREVER:" it read, "DIE YOUNG."

2

> TO MEMBERS OF THE FACULTY
> AND STAFF:
>
> With regret I inform you of the death of
>
> ARCHIBALD H. MURRAY
>
> Professor of Renaissance Literature, Emeritus, which
> occurred on the twenty-sixth ultimo, in the eighty-
> seventh year of age. His thirty-seven years of service
> to this community, and to academic and intellectual
> life in general, will ensure that his memory will be
> etched permanently into the walls of this institution,
> as well as in the hearts and minds of all who knew and
> shared in the pleasure of his active mind and generous
> spirit.
> A memorial service will be announced at a later date.
>
> Your obedient servant,
> DONALD W. ATTERTON

"One of this institution's more remarkable redundancies," Weinstock's fiction colleague Geoffrey Armitage, who had arrived at Harvard two years earlier, commented wryly as he watched Weinstock tear open the black-bordered announcement in the university mail.

"What's that?" Weinstock asked.

"A death announcement for a member of this faculty. Why, after you've been at *this* place for thirty-seven years, death is a mere formality."

Announcements like this one, their black-bordered card stock easily identifiable through the pale white envelopes and familiar mailing labels, appeared in Weinstock's mailbox daily, along with memoranda from English Department Chairman Lawrence Gentry bearing such headings as ADDRESSES OF WIDOWS OF DECEASED EMERITUS PROFESSORS, which led Weinstock to suspect that the diminishing ranks of the living would soon leave him and his junior colleagues alone at Burdick Place in the company of their dour secretary, Priscilla Brimmer.

Priscilla, a forty-five-year-old Berkeley graduate, had been living with her older brother in Duxbury since her husband left her for the twenty-three-year-old wife of the Sanskrit Department chairman in 1967. String bean shaped and inappropriately stylish for her daily rounds between the Xerox machine and the telephone, she had been taking classes in entomological drawing at the Harvard Extension School for some fifteen years, in the hope of eventually establishing herself as an illustrator of beetles for scientific textbook companies. Thus far, however, she had succeeded only in exacting the price of her humdrum and loveless existence from the lives of the English Department junior faculty in ways so convoluted and subliminally concocted that it would have taken an expert in the intimate workings of the neurotic personality to decipher them.

On many a Thursday and Friday, when he didn't have class or office hours, Weinstock found himself gazing at the reflection of oncoming traffic in one of Priscilla's postmodern earrings as he drove her to psychiatric appointments in towns with names like Revere, Billerica, Dedham (which he pronounced *Dead Ham*) and Woburn (pronounced *Woooburn* by the locals). "I don't think I can face the human race again today," she'd keep repeating, fastening and unfastening her earrings as they drove.

It wasn't merely the fact of being surrounded by the dead, the dying and those who aspired to those conditions that began to depress and confuse Weinstock upon arriving at Harvard. It was also the fact that they were, for the most part, so hard to tell from the pasty, expressionless faces of the living.

This realization grew particularly vivid whenever he met a colleague for lunch at the Faculty Club, known to most of the junior faculty and nonacademic staff as Club Dead. In the center of the Club's main dining room, beneath eighteenth- and nineteenth-century portraits of various deceased Harvard presidents and high Anglicans, was a long table around which many of the University's least decorous and most decorated chair holders, often in the com-

pany of President Atterton, convened for lunch. To get almost anywhere in the dining hall, one had to walk past this pasty-faced
battalion of blue and gray suits, many of them sporting the Harvard
crest on their dark burgundy ties. Passing them, Weinstock inevitably experienced a sensation vaguely related, yet somehow eroti-
cally opposed, to what he'd been told beautiful women felt when
walking a gauntlet of construction workers. All eyes, he sensed,
were upon him. But they were more like the eyes of turkey vultures
in search of road kill than like those of lustful young men looking
for some anonymous piece of meat to poke their members into.

And Harvard was certainly thick with members. Clubs and so-
cieties, centers and institutes, journals and committees, proliferated
like krill in the waters of the northern whaling grounds. "I sing of
myself and celebrate myself," Harvard ceaselessly intoned with Walt
Whitman. Wending his way between the death notices and health
benefits announcements in his university mailbox each day, Weinstock was certain to come upon at least one invitation to a reception,
opening, luncheon, cocktail party, lecture or publication party, addressed to him or addressed to Dean of Australian Studies Melvin
Wennstock and misdelivered.

Never much of a joiner, Weinstock found this chaotic circuit of
self-celebration and conviviality, with its endless demands of sched-
uling, RSVPs and refusals, more than he could manage. Finding
himself, one night, mistakenly attending a reception in honor of
W. S. Frazier Professor of Australian Studies Christopher Crabbe's
new book, *Sacred Cauldron: Familial Bonding and Transgression
in Aboriginal Culture,* he could do little but stammer his way
through an endless series of toasts and vodka tonics while a brigade
of faculty spouses and chair holders with Australian accents bom-
barded him with snippets of conversation like "Don't you think
Hopgood's theory of the social reinforcement of group incest tri-
angles is terribly controversial?"

One evening, however, Weinstock found himself at an occasion
he *had* been invited to — a reception (which just happened to coincide with T. S. Eliot's ninety-fifth birthday) for new members of
the literature faculty at the home of one of Harvard's most prestigious and tradition-bound private clubs, the Pink Rose. Most of
the great figures in what was simply known in Cambridge as Amer-

ican "letters" had been members of the Rose, one of whose many Byzantine customs was to require each member to mail in a pink rose, which was, upon publication of his first book, framed and mounted above an inscription from the author. (There were, Weinstock couldn't help notice, apparently no female alumnae of the Pink Rose.) This created a veritable museum of luminaries such as Eliot himself, John Masefield, Somerset Maugham and, yes, even nasty old Robert Frost, their framed and deracinated petals threatening to rain down onto the fading blue encomiums of their collective gratitude.

Weinstock had been invited to the reception by a particularly sallow-faced undergraduate poet who introduced himself on the phone as "Anderson Whitfield III, secretary of the Pink Rose." Having not yet mastered the art of the premeditated excuse, Weinstock could do no better than to mumble a quick, unenthusiastic "Why . . . sure, I'll be glad to," and so found himself, on the evening of the reception, both sartorially and psychologically unprepared for the elite company into which he had miraculously entered.

Nor had he yet entirely appreciated the convention among Harvard faculty of being paid and treated like academics in private while conducting themselves like aristocrats in public. Dressed in his usual brown corduroy sports coat, washed-out jeans and burgundy cowboy boots, Weinstock found, literally, all eyes upon him as he entered the Pink Rose's ornate, antique-ridden living room.

"Gentlemen," young Anderson Whitfield III announced to the gathering of large, pudgy men with cigars seated around the fireplace, "I'd like to introduce Professor Martin Weinstock. Dr. Weinstock —"

"Mister," Weinstock corrected him.

"Pardon me." A cloud of irritation drifted across Whitfield's face. "Mr. Weinstock is our new Burke-Howland Professor of Poetry."

"Lecturer," Weinstock corrected Whitfield again.

"Ah, yes, lecturer. . . . I beg your pardon." Hundreds of pupils suddenly moved in unison from Weinstock's toes to his midsection, as — in what seemed the direct physical expression of a collective wish to mold a suit and tie out of the air around him — a small circle of wing-tipped men slowly rose to greet the usurper of their sartorial symmetry. There was what seemed like an endless silence, during which everyone seemed to be waiting for the wished-for garments to materialize. Finally, the last to rise from his seat, a balding, elephantine gentleman who introduced himself simply as "Barton Haxton, Bank of Boston," broke the silence.

"A poet," Haxton boomed into the smoky living room. "Well, well." Convinced that his hostly duties had been successfully accomplished, he reseated himself in the thick, leathery chair in front of the fireplace. "Ahhhh," he boomed, exhaling a long flotilla of pipe smoke into the midst of their small circle, "poets. . . . Do you gentlemen know that I heard John Masefield read in this very room in 1928?"

An inescapable sense of reverse peristalsis entered Weinstock's body. Never had he been so aware of wearing the wrong shoes. Dinner was served — rack of lamb, filigreed green beans, Chateauneuf-du-Pape 1981, *mousse au chocolat*. Only Dorothy, the pallid undergraduate seated on Weinstock's right, made even the slightest attempt to engage him in conversation.

"Did your father go here?" she asked as the assembled dignitaries of the Pink Rose raised their glasses in honor of T. S. Eliot's ninety-fifth birthday.

3

Juli 3 '84
Pine Hill, N.Y.

Dear son Martin!

We arrived here at 9:00 in the evening on Tuesday the 28th of June; we left N.Y. at 5:00. also 4 hours. We have here cold, cold weather, so that is why my cold. Just now we are coming from the Doctor Sunday 7.3. He decided it is bronchitis (acute) blood pressure 140/80 ist good — He gave me right away a prescription to take but the Drugstores are closed — Sunday. I think in few days it will be gone. When will you come up? Our phone number is 1-254-4937.

Ilse Metzger has bad news. She wanted on 7/13 to go to Switzerland and Germany for some weeks — now some bad news, she is total broken COLON TUMOR MALIGNANT also part on the

PANCREASE very very sad we were outside ourselves — so everybody has that what they get — who has it has it — Do you understand dear Martin what that means? Whatever you don't get in the old years is profit!!

Our neighbor Jack Greenberg is Dying. . . . The Golden Age!! — thank the LORD — We are feeling fine. . . . except for the sudden cold and AIR CONDITIONING DRAFT — PLEASE TAKE YOU ALSO GOOD CARE of yourself — precaution is always better than healing — TUESDAY the 5th of July our good Betzele remembrance of her 82nd Birthday. May her good Soul rest in Sholem and the good LORD reward the good Deeds in the other WORLD.

Today 7/5.84

DEAR SON. Please forgive me that I write you delayed due to my sickness. I am again a little bit better. Today is Mama selig's Birthday the 82nd. So dear son the letter must go away — the box will soon be emptied.

LOVE,
DADY

Weinstock had always loved reading his father's letters to friends and lovers. Doing so seemed to relieve the boredom of the repetitive events they described, and others seemed to find them far more entertaining than he did.

"Well, here's Issue 236 of *The Morbidity and Mortality Newsletter*," he'd say, and then go on to recite the inevitable list of deaths, illnesses and diagnoses described in his father's heavily misspelled, comical "Gerglish." It had always seemed to Weinstock that some psychoanalyst with an abiding interest in such matters could have made an interesting diagnosis based on his father's graphics alone. But he personally had lost interest, the diagnosis having long ago ceased to matter.

Yet this latest epistle from his father, coming directly after a two-hour staff meeting with Director of Creative Writing Morton Gamson, somehow depressed Weinstock more than usual. And now — off to lunch with Siegfried Marikovski, Samuel W. Worthy Professor of American Literature and his one real friend in the English Department — Weinstock resolved to try even harder to get to the bottom of his malaise.

"I don't know what it is, Siggy," he said over an iced cappuccino and raspberry croissant, "but I've kind of had a bad case of the *blahs* ever since coming here. . . . Yet everyone and their mother keeps telling me how blessed I should feel."

"Well, what do you think's the problem?" Marikovski, despite his senior standing and international eminence as an expert on Thoreau and Henry James, had always taken a sincere interest in Weinstock's well-being. "Do you think it's the insecurity about your future here?"

"Well, yeah." Weinstock rotated the wooden stirrer in his cappuccino as he pondered the question. "At least in part. But I think it's something more. . . . I can't seem to stop thinking about death. It's as if there's something about this place that reminds me too much of home — too much of my father."

"Your father?" Marikovski didn't seem to get the connection. "I thought he was an uneducated man who doesn't even speak English."

"He is. But he's so damned preoccupied with death and the dead — and he himself simply won't die."

"What's so terrible about that? You seem very attached to him."

"Well I am, in a way. Why, when I was a kid, after my mother died and I really needed him, he was always having heart attacks and the like, and I was sure he was going to keel over any minute. I used to wake up every morning and first thing I'd do was run into his bedroom just to make sure he was still alive."

Marikovski seemed moved, albeit puzzled. "Yes," he murmured as if talking aloud to himself, "I can certainly see how that must have been upsetting. . . . But what's the problem with his being alive *now?*"

"Well, you see, back then — when I wanted so badly for him to live — he was always dying. And now — when I'm really kind of ready to get him and all his death and dying the hell out of my life — he simply refuses to die. It kind of makes me feel like poor Watson waiting around for Wellberry to kick off." Marc Watson, for seven years the junior medievalist in the English Department, had been encouraged in the belief he would be granted tenure after the death of emphysemic Atherton Professor of Medieval Literature Simon Wellberry.

"Yes" — Marikovski spoke as if from direct experience — "they never *do* die when you're ready for them to, do they?"

"I'll say," Weinstock agreed. "I'm sick as hell of running my life as if it's this fragile little chrysalis hanging from a thread right in front of me and I'm about to sneeze."

"That's not the way to go about it." Marikovski's tone shifted to one of well-intentioned sternness. "Besides, *every* son wants to kill his father sooner or later. . . . You've read Oedipus. The best thing to do is exactly what you want — that'll kill him faster than anything else."

"Yes, I suppose you're right. But what *I* want to do most of the time is just get my ass the hell out of this thanatic, life-denying place."

"People like you and me" — Marikovski smiled knowingly — "simply *can't* leave this place."

"Oh? Why's that?" Weinstock's tone betrayed a sense of disbelief.

"Because it's our one chance in life to become the thing every Jew, deep in his heart of hearts, most wants to be."

"And what's that?"

"The Great Goldberg."

"The Great Goldberg?" Weinstock couldn't help laughing as he pronounced the words. "What the hell is that?"

"It's you and me," Marikovski replied with utter seriousness. "Right here. Right now. *We're* the Great Goldberg — merely because we're Jewish and we're here."

"Oh yeah? What does that mean I'll be when I get kicked out? The 'Formerly Great Goldberg'?"

Marikovski paused for a moment as though seriously pondering the answer. "You will be" — he inhaled deeply — "though I think it's unlikely that will happen, just like everyone else who gets kicked out of this place."

"And what's that?" Weinstock inched forward on his chair, suddenly oozing curiosity.

"A mere mortal, just another face among the living. But why don't you forget about leaving here and about your father for a while and come over to this conference at the Center for Literary Studies this afternoon. I think you'll find it right up your alley."

"Oh yeah? . . . What's it about?"

"It's called 'Representations of Death: An Interdisciplinary Conference.' I'm one of the sponsors."

Weinstock must have blushed slightly, for Marikovski merely repeated the invitation. "If you'd like to, you're perfectly welcome to walk over with me after lunch. You might even find it inspiring."

Weinstock had been planning a drive to Crane's Beach on what seemed like it could well be the last warm afternoon of Indian summer. Yet for some reason he felt drawn to join Marikovski at the conference, and, after lunch, they headed across the Yard toward the Center for Literary Studies, where the meeting, chaired by Constantine Cavafy Professor of Modern Greek Studies Stella Zaradapoulous, was just coming to order.

Weinstock took a seat near the back of the room while Marikovski shuffled through the tightly knit gathering toward the front, where Professor Margot Lightfoot and the other cosponsors were already seated.

"I want to welcome you all to this First Annual Conference on Representations of Death," Zaradapoulous — taking periodic puffs from a cigarette — began, "a topic of, alas, common interest to us all." Two seats to Weinstock's left, a no more than two-month-old infant, looking somewhat dead himself, was sleeping in his mother's arms.

"We have a full, but I hope not a killing, program ahead," Zaradapoulous continued, "as we discuss what has been described as 'life's one sure thing' — the subject of which Philip Larkin said: 'Most things may never happen: this one will.'

"Above all, it is my hope that, by the end of the day, we will have succeeded in that noblest of enterprises — keeping the eloquent dead fully employed."

"As I would like to reserve ample time for discussion and questions following each paper, I would, without further ado, like to introduce Professor Loring Rogonnet of the University of Bridgeport, whose topic will be 'Blood-letting on Paper: Death of the Poet as a Literary Ambition.' Professor Rogonnet's presentation will be immediately followed by Professor David Donnelly of Bates College speaking on 'Dead Flesh, or the Smell of Literature,' following which there will be a question and answer period. Professor Rogonnet . . ."

Loring Rogonnet, a statuesque, sallow-looking woman with

caved-in cheeks, wearing a dark green dress beneath a pearl-embroidered black sweater, rose and took a seat at the front of the room. Stopping to light a cigarette, she directed a penetrating gaze at the audience, pausing briefly as her eyes met Weinstock's.

" 'The prospect of death,' " she began, "as Samuel Johnson wrote, 'wonderfully concentrates the mind.' This in many ways echoes the sentiments of Giacometti, who — on being hit by a car while crossing the Place d'Italie — reported his first feeling, in the state of a lucid swoon, as 'Something has happened to me at last!'

"The goal of my own brief remarks here today will be to present to you the thesis that in order for the poet — that ultimately childlike figure — to do his or her best work, we must perpetually remind him of what Jean-Paul Sartre so well knew . . ."

Rogonnet now seemed to be staring directly at the young mother and child seated in Weinstock's row. "We must remind him," she continued, nearly shouting, "in Sartre's words, that *all children are mirrors of death.*' "

The infant, perhaps intuitively aroused by the mention of his premature demise, stirred slightly in his mother's lap, letting out a brief, scarcely audible cry. Weinstock looked up at Marikovski, who was lighting a cigarette.

"We must remind him," Loring Rogonnet continued, "that — to paraphrase Emily Dickinson — 'Tis dying he is doing, but he's not afraid to know.' We must remind him — as the Hungarians have quite literally testified to in their recent reburial of the body of Béla Bartók — that it is the artist's task to die over and over again so that he may give life to the world of his readers. We must remind him that he must write, in the words of South African novelist Nadine Gordimer, *as if he were already dead.*' "

A familiar sense of ennui passed through Weinstock as Rogonnet spoke. He felt a sudden craving for light and air, a need to escape from this tightly packed room of cigarettes and dyings. Staring half apologetically and half angrily at Marikovski, he rose and tried to make his way inconspicuously toward the seminar room door. His movements, however, woke the infant, who began wailing as Weinstock slipped out into the aisle. Rogonnet paused, as all eyes directed themselves at Weinstock's premature departure.

Flushed with embarrassment, Weinstock averted his gaze from

the small gathering of onlookers and rushed down the stairs. Within seconds, he was out the door, running toward his car at 24 Burdick Place. A warm, near-summery breeze was furling a full spectrum of leaves into the fall air.

Weinstock quickly opened all the windows and started the engine. He wanted to head toward the North Shore as fast as he could, toward air and light, toward a place where none of the deaths being whispered about would be his own.

4

Even before coming to Harvard, Weinstock had never much liked the word "serious." Seriousness was, in fact, something he had struggled hard to keep *out* of his life. Like truffles or expensive French wine, he had always found it a vastly overrated experience. As far as "art" went, he agreed with the painter Ad Reinhardt: It was too serious a matter to be taken seriously.

But here at Harvard, to his naive astonishment, the word "serious" took on new and nearly religious dimensions. The highest compliment that could be paid was to append someone's name to that ominous objective. "Dr. Havisham," Department Chairman Lawrence Gentry said, introducing the University's Getlin Lecturer in the Humanities, "is one of the nation's most *serious* Chaucerians." Weinstock hadn't read much Chaucer, but the little he *had* read he had always found an absolute scream. He therefore found it particularly strange that seriousness in pursuit of such matters should suddenly seem so virtuous.

On the subject of seriousness, Weinstock preferred the attitude of former Assistant Professor Sidney Darn, who had left Harvard for a job at a state college in New Jersey: "We must take the somber out of the serious," Darn wrote in an article many felt was directly responsible for his being denied tenure. Yet, in Cambridge, the somber and the serious were like Siamese twins connected at the scrotum: No one was interested in even *trying* to separate them. "Dr. Wicklow," a colleague said, turning to Weinstock at a faculty luncheon, "is the most *serious* candidate we have for our Renaissance vacancy." Weinstock's response — "It seems to me we'd be better off trying to hire someone funny" — somehow failed to elicit the sympathetic resonance he had hoped for, and he suddenly found himself stricken from the monthly luncheon list.

Most serious among all those who roamed the somber, ivy-covered halls, however, was Acting Director of Creative Writing Morton Gamson, a short, melancholic Pirandello scholar and would-be novelist described by Armitage as "like six depressive characters in search of a smile," the kind of man whose worship of the somber was surpassed only by the tenacity of his adulation for its practitioners.

Not without a certain twinge of sadness, Weinstock had to agree with Armitage's assessment. Gamson, whose profoundly melancholic air seemed all too closely at times to mimic a certain melancholy of Weinstock's own that he longed to disavow, epitomized the sense of *"la vie manquée"* that dominated the Department. About to retire after thirty-five years as an untenured Adjunct Professor, he had been named acting director following the retirement of Weinstock's previous boss, a kindly, self-effacing, marginally talented novelist named Donald Radbush.

This past year, Gamson's first novel — a massive, eight-hundred-page opus entitled *The Lost Years of Marvis O'Callahan,* which he had been working on since graduate school — had been published to such universal disapprobation by critics and writers that it was clear to everyone but Gamson himself that he'd been handed the Creative Writing job as a consolation prize for the shattered hope of his late years, the novel he dreamt would vindicate his never-realized promise as a scholar.

To make matters worse, Gamson's wife, Penelope, a child psychologist and ceramicist of some repute, had recently published a wildly successful memoir entitled *There and Back,* recounting her supposed abduction by extraterrestrials during a sabbatical year in San Miguel de Allende. Gamson had been going through a serious depression at the time, in no small part due to the harsh reception of his novel. Now, as Penelope moved like a starlet from talk show to talk show, her book flagrantly decorating the window of almost every bookstore in Cambridge, Morton's own long years of failure and ennui were cast in stark relief by his wife's seemingly effortless success.

Gamson himself had been a Harvard graduate student in the '40s and had, according to some, shown considerable promise as a scholar in those heady, robust years after World War II. Yet, for reasons known only to psychoanalysts and other students of the human spirit, he had been unable to extricate himself from the deep melancholy that now seemed to have entirely enveloped him. The author of six increasingly unsuccessful works of criticism since his first book, *Ravages of Darkness: The Dark Veil of Contemporary European Theatre*, had surfaced to only faint praise in 1951, he now patrolled the halls of Burdick Place, soaking up levity wherever he went, while the other writers, Weinstock among them, lived in a kind of terror lest they flunk Gamson's Monday morning "quiz" on the contents of *The New York Review of Books* and *The New York Times Book Review*.

Occasionally Weinstock would see Gamson crossing Harvard Square in midafternoon, looking like a disoriented patient who had strayed from a psychiatric ward. "Whenever I see him," Armitage would say, "I hear Peggy Lee in the background singing 'Is That All There Is?' " *That,* Weinstock had to admit, was much the same music *he* was starting to hear as he surveyed the rapidly closing portals of midlife in the rocky boat of the Harvard English Department.

Gamson also epitomized the odd predicament of the self-styled "rebel" at Harvard — "rhetoric by Camus, life-style by Donald Trump," as Weinstock's friend Claudia, who taught Latin American Studies at Brandeis, put it. Though vociferously proclaiming his alliance with the young, "creative" members of the Department against the Old Guard, who took him seriously neither as a scholar nor as a novelist, Gamson acted — whenever any of the writers proposed a minor change in the way things were done — as if some sacred rite were about to be violated. "I don't think it's a good idea" was his response to any such suggestion. When anyone asked, "Why not?" the answer was always "Because it's never *been* done."

"Scratch any one of these guys very hard," Weinstock mumbled to Armitage and their nonfiction colleague John Corliss after one such episode, "and you're sure to find another Old Boy."

"Yeah," Armitage countered, "and scratch any of the Old Boys and you're almost certain to come up with a corpse."

"Pure pornography" was Gamson's description of every book

Weinstock had ever loved, until finally — in a gesture whose irony seemed to escape him totally — Weinstock, Corliss and Armitage presented their boss with what they privately referred to as "The Thanatos Quartet" for his sixty-fifth birthday — hardbound copies of The *Tibetan Book of the Dead,* the *Dead Sea Scrolls,* Thomas Mann's *Death in Venice,* and a book of Holocaust poetry entitled *The Death Mazurka,* wrapped in black and bearing the dedication: "For Mort, who brings such life to our writerly clutch."

It was not, of course, that Gamson was mean-spirited or ill-motivated. But nearly forty years of watching younger scholars and writers succeed in measures he no longer even dreamt of had exhausted even his soldierly resilience for Oedipal defeat. Along with the encroaching realization that he was a man entirely unsuited for the creative life, they had slowly and inexorably eroded his capacity for humor and self-mockery.

The truth was that Weinstock liked and felt sorry for Gamson. But he also — as his own supposedly brief tenure at Harvard began to take on the appearance of a life sentence — felt sorry for himself. He had, after all, never before lived in a place like Cambridge, "the only place in America," he told his old friend Trevor, "where you have to study for dinner." And there were times when, like a deranged, psychopathic geyser, Weinstock simply felt like running into Gamson's office, up and down Harvard Yard and into the Faculty Club, jumping into the midst of the blue-suited, ghoulish faces seated at the *Stammtisch* and screaming — in his loudest, most unserious voice — *cunt, prick, sphincter, rice pudding, fellatio,* just for the pleasure of uttering these early icons of his libidinal netherworld into the air once more.

"When do you think the last time old Gamson really put it to Penelope was?" Armitage asked Corliss one afternoon over at Burdick Place. "Probably at the John Donne tercentenary?"

"Nope," Corliss said. "I think it must have been right around the invasion of Normandy. But think of it this way — things could've been a helluva lot better for Mort if only he hadn't been so short."

Armitage looked up. "Short? — What the hell does *that* have to do with anything?"

"Well" — Corliss smiled — "just think of what they must've called him during that year he spent in Paris on a Fulbright."

"What's that?" Armitage seemed perplexed by this non sequitur in their conversation.

"They must have called him" — Corliss chuckled, closing the door behind him as he spoke — *"le petit Mort."*

5

One morning late in the spring semester, Weinstock heard a knock on his office door. One of his favorite students, a dark-eyed, Sephardic-looking sophomore from Saddle River, New Jersey ("Nixon country," she called it) named Alexis Baruch, stood smiling at him from inside a loosely fitting T-shirt bearing the inscription "A woman without a man is like a fish without a bicycle." In her right hand was a copy of the *Selected Poems* of Adrienne Rich, in her left a copy of *Pure Lust* by Mary Daly.

"Hi." She smiled from the doorway in a way that made Weinstock wish fish were in greater need of bicycles. "How are you?"

"Oh . . . ah, swell." He hesitated, not quite knowing the answer. "And you?"

Although his immediate predecessor had been exiled to Kansas State after being accused, by fifteen undergraduate women, of offenses ranging from "suggestive leaning" to "innuendos over lunch," not even the best efforts of Weinstock's rather Germanic superego had been able to restrain him from occasionally, as he put it, "dipping into the archives" during his first year at Harvard. An added incentive to his sexual meanderings, he liked to think, was his rapidly crumbling marriage to Deirdre MacAllister.

But there were limits. Weinstock had quickly come to realize, to the pre- and postcoital stimulation a thirty-six-year-old man could derive from a twenty-year-old, even one who had spent semester breaks in Florence and summer vacations in the Dordogne since she was two. So he had quickly come to console himself with the less intoxicating but safer pleasures of physics graduate students, visiting junior faculty and divorced colleagues.

And now, as this intellectually and physically vivacious undergraduate stood before him in all her predisillusionary splendor, Weinstock's mind, despite the small flicker of temptation that burned there, thought of little else than what he would do that night to avoid having to attend yet another departmental lecture with a title like "The Bioethics of Dickens's *Our Mutual Friend.*"

"Oh . . . I suppose I'm OK," responded Ms. Baruch (whom Weinstock always referred to in the privacy of his ruminations as *Atoh Adonoi*). Her tone was that of someone eager to reveal the deeper truth behind the polite answer.

"You suppose?" he asked cooperatively.

"Well, you know, Martin, it gets awfully lonely here at Harvard. . . . Especially around exam period, when everyone's trying so damned hard to capture the presidency by the time they're forty-two . . . just to beat out dear old JFK, if you know what I mean."

"Yeah," Weinstock murmured sympathetically, "I think I do. . . . But I always thought *you* were someone with a lot of friends."

"Friends?" Alexis moved with a quick combination of incredulity and flirtation into the chair beside him. "People in Cambridge don't have friends — they have appointments."

Weinstock's own little black pocket calendar — thick with an armada of luncheons, receptions, readings, lectures, faculty meetings, conferences and collegial coffee breaks — bore out Alexis's reply, and he felt a sudden sense of solidarity with the young woman seated before him, who had spent the summer between her freshman and sophomore years plucking chicken feathers at Kibbutz Ravnosh near the Sea of Galilee. "Well," he commiserated, "if it's any consolation, it's not any different for the faculty."

"I know," Alexis replied with a tone of utter self-assurance. "I was good friends with this Government professor last year, and he used to complain about it all the time. . . . I sense from what you say in class sometimes that you're kind of lonely here too." She was now leaning forward so intently that Weinstock could almost count the thin wisps of hair at the base of her neck.

Oh God help me, he thought. A long silence flickered between them.

"Oh . . . not really," he replied lamely. The last thing he needed at this point was a sexual harassment complaint on his hands, particularly as the University's guidelines on the subject made virtually every form of interaction between a student and a professor beyond a conversation about "The Wife of Bath's Tale" into an act of aggression. Uninspired as his life at Harvard was, Weinstock suspected it might be worse at Buckholtz State, where not even the perpetually expanding aura of his curriculum vitae would offset his ever-diminishing sense of self.

"Oh, no," he repeated, his eyes starting to cloud over with incipient tears. "I'm not really lonely here. . . . I just like to joke about it in class."

"Sure. But you know what Freud said . . ." Fully psychoanalyzed by her sixteenth birthday, Alexis, he could tell from their previous conversations, possessed a psychological fervor bordering on the prosecutorial.

"No. . . . What did Freud say?" Weinstock was genuinely curious.

"He said that people never kid. . . . Somewhere in *The Psychopathology of Everyday Life,* I believe."

What the hell, Weinstock suddenly thought. Hadn't Charles Bukowski said somewhere that even an eighty-year-old man could temporarily defeat death by making love to eighteen-year-old girls? (Reading Bukowski, like going to Club Med or applying to law school, was something he was certain at least half the Harvard junior faculty did secretly, but no one had the nerve to admit.)

"Listen, Alexis." Weinstock swiveled his desk chair so that he was gazing right into his student's incendiary brown eyes. "Would you consider it terribly inappropriate if we had a drink somewhere? . . . We could just call it," he added, not quite intending the pun that slipped, to Alexis's bemused delight, from his lips, "an extension of my office hours."

Alexis's right hand discretely made its way onto Weinstock's left kneecap. She looked at him with a patronizing gaze, flirtatious and pitying.

"Why, no. Not at all, Martin," she replied demurely. "I thought you'd never ask."

6

"I feel like a fraud," Siegfried Marikovski confided to Weinstock in the basement of the Harvard Faculty Club. "I live in dread of the fact that I'll sooner or later be discovered as an ordinary nincompoop who stumbled into writing a couple of mediocre books that happened to get way too much attention from the fifteen or twenty people who bothered to read them."

Weinstock was incredulous. Marikovski, author of some twenty-seven books, more than 300 scholarly articles, the object of an intense and lucrative bidding war between Yale and Harvard, had always seemed to him to be sitting securely at the very pinnacle of American academic life. And now this incredible confession.

"That's funny," Weinstock offered collegially. "I feel like a fraud too — only I *am* one."

"You!" Marikovski seemed amazed. "One of the country's leading young poets?"

"Oh, sure." Weinstock couldn't help but be amused by Marikovski's sincere air of astonishment. "Why, I've never even read *Ulysses* . . . not to mention *The Divine Comedy*."

Even before coming to Harvard, Weinstock had been told that it was a place where the living had hardly any status, that his only hope for staying would be to exercise a nearly religious devotion to the lives of the dead. The facts seemed to bear this out: of the 394 cocktail parties, openings and receptions he had been invited to thus far — not counting the 114 in celebration of Harvard itself — 186 had been to honor the dead, and almost all the remaining 94 were for the infirm or dying. He had counted.

"Ah, yes," admitted Marikovski. "But *you*, at least, are among the creators. It's people like *me* who are the true frauds."

Weinstock somehow couldn't muster the conviction to counter Marikovski's argument and simply continued swirling the olive in his vodka martini. "Yeah," he responded rather lamely. "It's tough here, isn't it?"

"It certainly is. Why, just this week I turned down an invitation to spend a month in South America so I could stay here and work . . . just because I felt too insecure about using part of my sabbatical for something that would seem so frivolous."

"You *what*?" Weinstock, who had been dreaming of a trip to Brazil and the Galápagos for years, was utterly incredulous.

"Yup — I turned down a trip to Rio to present a short paper and then take a two-week cruise down the Amazon. I felt I needed to stay here and finish my Thoreau book." Marikovski shook his head sadly as he spoke, like a man disappointed by the limited exercise of his own will.

"Siggy," Weinstock protested, "Thoreau's dead. And who, for that matter, would have been more in favor of your going than him? Meanwhile you — Siegfried Marikovski, sitting right here before me in living flesh — why, you're alive."

"We're all dead." Marikovski took a sip of his diet Dr Pepper. "You know what Borges said — 'We are all dead men speaking to dead men.' Some of us are just here playing at this brief ellipse of living, trying to pretend it's not so."

"I'm not pretending." Weinstock felt he needed to make a small addendum to Marikovski's statement. "I'm *alive*. I don't see any reason in the world to start playing dead until I have to." Much as he liked his elder colleague, Weinstock had long been aware that Marikovski was at heart a deeply melancholic man. After losing both his parents at age eight, when they were abducted by the S.S. from the Vilna ghetto, he had hidden for three years in the forests and railcars of Poland and Austria before being taken in by an Austrian family near Salzburg at the end of the war. When his adoptive family was finally able to locate a pair of distant cousins in Palestine, Marikovski, at age twelve, was sent to live with them in the small town of Afoulah. But the father was killed in the War of Independence, and his wife committed suicide shortly thereafter, and young Siggy soon found himself on a boat headed for America, sent to live with another set of cousins, who owned a dry-cleaning store in Valley City, North Dakota. There, as the one Jewish kid — a fragile, asthmatic boy — in a school full of Swedish and Norwegian Lutherans built like linebackers, Marikovski spent a painful adolescence, from which, given the other unenviable facts of his biography, he had never recovered.

"I had a worse childhood than you did" was a game Marikovski and Weinstock often found themselves engaged in — one Weinstock's older colleague always won hands down. Weinstock knew that, despite the decency and generosity of his conscious intentions, Marikovski, in the darkest corners of his merely human heart, was thrilled at the thought of Weinstock's winding up in the same lethal, tenured academic trap (chaired and chained, publishing and perishing) in which he now found himself.

"Did you hear the news?" Weinstock picked up the phone one Saturday night to the off-bright sound of Marikovski's voice.

"No . . . what news?"

"They've concluded that urban academics are the happiest of all professionals."

"Whaaat?" Weinstock was only half amused at being roused from his habitually early bedtime by such an unlikely piece of news. "Who the hell concluded *that,* Siggy?"

"It was in this morning's *New York Times.* They did a survey, and it shows that professors at urban universities think they have more satisfying life-styles than any other group."

"Yeah," Weinstock grumbled sleepily, "but did anyone ask them if they have better *lives?* Who the hell else did they ask — undertakers and trash collectors?"

"Don't be so cynical, Martin," Marikovski cautioned. "I think there's a good chance it's going to work out for you here, you know. . . . The Department needs someone like you . . . and Gamson's going to retire at the end of the year."

Images of the powdery faces at the Club Dead *Stammtisch* or the turdlike, lethargic body of Morton Gamson resurrected themselves before Weinstock's eyes whenever Marikovski mentioned the possibility of things "working out" at Harvard.

"That's great, Siggy." He yawned into the receiver. "I know you're doing everything you can to help."

"Believe me, Martin, I am . . . . It's not a bad place, you know, Cambridge. . . . You can get a lot of work done here."

The thought of Marikovski's passed-over trip down the Amazon raced through Weinstock's mind like a bevy of corpses heading for a funeral pyre in Benares.

"Yup," he agreed. "It's a great place to get work done."

❖

The following afternoon, Weinstock found himself once again at the Faculty Club, walking by the pasty *Stammtisch* faces on his way to lunch with Leonard Hapgood, chief of psychiatry at Cambridge Hospital. Hapgood's research involved some of the same issues in the Oedipal struggle between fathers and sons that, according to the critics, Weinstock so exhaustively confronted in his poems.

"Sometimes, Martin, I have to tell you," Hapgood confessed over his second glass of Pouilly Fumé, "I feel like a terrible fraud."

"A fraud?" Weinstock stared up from his Poland Springs in disbelief. "You? How could *you* possibly feel like a fraud?"

"Oh, it's easy." The look of soporific sadness Weinstock had begun to associate with the Harvard senior faculty suddenly descended over Hapgood's face. "Two of your colleagues down the hall win the Nobel Prize for Medicine, a student you once gave a B− to gets a MacArthur and two people you voted against for tenure get the National Book Award and Pulitzer respectively, and you just start saying to yourself: 'Who am I? — Leonard Hapgood, author of fourteen measly books that no one but other psychiatrists and a few patients who are college professors have ever read, a chief of psychiatry whose only real distinction from his patients is that he's the one with the keys,' and you think to yourself: 'I'm nothing but a goddamned fraud.' "

Weinstock, the author of two slim blue volumes of poems and two articles in *Sports Illustrated,* could hardly believe his ears. "Leonard, Jesus Christ, if *you* feel like a fraud, how can *anyone* in this place feel good about themselves?" he blurted out. Several of the until then seemingly dead occupants of the *Stammtisch* interrupted their reveries of Chablis to glare angrily at the usurper of their collegial tranquillity.

"Don't you get it?" sloshed Hapgood from the cusp of his Pouilly Fumé. "That's the very idea of this place. No one's *supposed* to feel good about themselves. . . . Do you think they'd keep driving themselves nuts if they were actually happy?"

Weinstock was momentarily stunned by Hapgood's logic. He gazed across the table at his friend, who seemed to have sprung to life by having so accurately described his predicament. "Yeah. . . . I suppose you're right. I sure haven't been feeling too good about *myself* since I got here."

"And *that,* my young friend" — Hapgood gazed over his shoulder in a kind of semicircle whose radius swept up virtually all the occupants of the dining room — "is why we all love and need so much to belong to clubs here at Harvard. Because a club, at least, gives you a way of feeling good about yourself. A club is one way of saying to all the world: 'Hey, I'm all right. I'm special. I belong.' "

A sudden shimmer of nausea ran through Weinstock's body as he watched Hapgood revel in his own entrapment, his own undeserved self-hatred. Somehow the chef's special of the day chicken Kiev no longer interested him.

CHAPTER 2

Husks

Once there were twelve bodies
where we now sit. I know it,
because there are still husks
where those bodies once were,
empty carapaces
overtaken during the mind's coup,
begun as a benevolent
   dictatorship
but now gone wild
(as all power does)
with its sense of itself,
and so we are all seated here,
   captives
of bad wine and too much to eat,
and grow quietly to hate one
   another

for the pure tedium of what we
   have become —
repeating the word *tenure*
as if it were a mantra,
while the body,
that old anthropologist
(the one true scholar among us)
stirs restlessly
in its prison of pomp and
   conceptions,
as if to remind us
how brief its tenure is,
how transient its publications.

— MARTIN WEINSTOCK,
"Academic Suppers"

To say that Weinstock's predecessors and colleagues at Harvard were an intimidating group was to understate the matter. The very folding chair which he, Martin Weinstock, now occupied, had previously been held by such great American poets as James Mendelberry, author of the famous 477 Sheep Songs, written in the voice of a Renaissance lamb, and Richard Lovell, who, only a decade earlier, had supposedly bedded hundreds of Harvard undergraduates on the same fleecy, discolored carpet on which Weinstock now held office hours.

Chair holders, in fact, surrounded Weinstock in flocks and droves. Not since his college summers as a waiter in the Catskills had he seen so many varieties and permutations of chairs — "folding chairs," "endowed chairs," "rotating chairs," "lifetime chairs," "interdepartmental chairs," "emeritus chairs," "distinguished chairs" and God knows how many other kinds of chairs just waiting to be filled by the serious buttocks of some scholar soon to be exiled from Seoul or Bialystok.

"Jesus Christ," Armitage exclaimed during Weinstock's first semester, "I haven't seen so many goddamned chairs since the Salvation Army came to a building demolition in Detroit in 1967."

"Yeah," Weinstock replied, "but I have a feeling that Harvard gives out chairs the way parents who don't know how to love give out music and sailing lessons, if you know what I mean. . . . It's what the psychologists call a 'bad holding environment.'"

" 'Bad holding environment'? What's that? Sounds like a sixties rock band."

Weinstock chuckled. "No, it's just a place where no one really feels safe, where you can't let down your guard and relax."

"Relax?" Armitage almost fell off his chair. "The only way you get to relax around here is to wind up inside one of those little black-bordered announcements from Atterton telling everyone what a great contribution you've made to the University and how they'll never ever forget you."

"Yeah," Weinstock suddenly humorless, agreed. "Sometimes I have the uncomfortable feeling we already have."

❖

Down the hall from Weinstock's office, in Room 22, sat that great icon of contemporary literature, exiled Polish poet Tadeusz Klavicki. Klavicki, an early associate of Lech Walesa, had recently been appointed to the long-vacant Cookston Professorship of Rhetoric, four of whose previous occupants had won the Nobel Prize. A rotund, convivial man of prodigious talents and equally prodigious appetites, he could imbibe vast quantities of Russian vodka without blinking an eyelash while Weinstock sat nursing a single Amstel light. Expelled from Poland during the suppressed Solidarity uprisings of the late 1970s, Klavicki was immediately invited to Harvard by the Departments of English and Comparative Literature, who were well aware that, though a prophet might be unwelcome in his own country, he attracted extraordinary amounts of prestige — and dollars — to someone else's.

"Amanda Wayland, bless her heart, says he's The Best in the World," Armitage explained to Weinstock regarding the esteem in which Klavicki was held by Harvard's well-known critic of contemporary poetry. "An essential title to hold around here."

"What's that?" Weinstock wasn't exactly sure what title Armitage was referring to.

"Best in the World. . . . If you want to stay around this fucking place your whole life, they've gotta be convinced that you're The Best in the World."

"Who, may I ask are 'they'?"

"Why, the other Best-in-the-Worlders — who else? That's what Wayland is, isn't she? — The Best Critic of Contemporary American Poetry in the Whole Fucking World. That's how it works around here, don't you know? Somebody *up there*" — Armitage pointed across the Yard to University Hall — "decides that you're The Best in the World, and then when — every once in a blue moon — someone from inside is brought up for tenure, all The Best-in-the-Worlders from everywhere are brought together in some dark room with a bunch of sherry and stale Brie and asked if that person, too, is enough of a Best-in-the-Worlder to join their elevated ranks. . . . This *is*, after all, *the* Best Fucking University in the World, don't you know?"

"I suppose so."

"You have to realize," Armitage continued, "that, as far as dear old Harvard is concerned, there are only two kinds of people on the planet."

"Oh? And *who*, may I ask, are they?"

"There are the people *Harvard* needs — let's call them type A's, like Klavicki — and then there are the people who need Harvard — Type B's, like you and me. If you're a Type A, people ask, speaking of Harvard, 'Hey, isn't that where Klavicki teaches?' But if you're a Type B — like you and me, old buddy — well, then people are always saying, 'Hey, isn't he the guy who teaches at Haaarvaaaard?' What's more, once they've decided you're a Type B, there's no fucking way on earth you can ever become a Type A — except, that is, by dying or by getting the hell out of here and getting famous somewhere else, so that they can finally ask you back when you're too goddamned old and fucked up to enjoy it anyway, and can just be paraded around the country like a mascot to raise more bucks for dear old *Veritas*.

"And *that*, my dear friend," Armitage droned on, "or, at least, the conviction on the part of wealthy alums — mainly Type B's like us appended to the name Harvard for so long it's become tattooed on them like a foreskin — is why this university is so goddamned loaded with shekels while every other university in the country spends all day scratching its balls looking for a way to keep the Xerox machines running."

"All I know," Weinstock replied, a sinking feeling settling into the pit of his stomach, "is that this whole damned conversation is making me long for dear old Roman Hruska."

"Roman *who?*" Armitage looked up, a befuddled expression on his face.

"Roman Hruska. . . . Don't you remember him? He was that senator from Nebraska who, during the Carswell Supreme Court nomination hearings, said the Senate should confirm Carswell because mediocrity should be represented on the Court just like everything else. Well, that's about how I feel about all this Best in the World shit. Why *can't* they have a couple of plain old human beings who happen to have a little bit better than average talent or brains represented here too?"

"You don't for a minute think they don't, do you?" Armitage seemed somewhat amused by what he considered Weinstock's innocence. "Why, there's plenty of mediocrity around here, like anywhere else. The only difference between the mediocrities here and the mediocrities everywhere else is that the ones here devote their whole lives to making sure no one but themselves knows how truly mediocre they really are. I mean, let's face it, how much more mediocre can a person *get* than dear old Gamson or some of our other colleagues? It's just a matter of marketing, my friend."

"Marketing?"

"Yeah, you know — Kleenex tissues, Heinz ketchup, Thomas' English muffins, Coca-Cola, Harvard. Just keep telling everyone you're The Best in the World and — whammo! — sooner or later everyone believes it. Who the fuck *knows* who's The Best in the World, anyway? I mean, Jesus Christ, Martin, all those fat alums don't need to go repossess their checkbooks just because a couple of guys like us happened to sneak in through the back door."

Money, in fact, was a thing not much talked about openly at Harvard but clearly a fuel which silently and efficiently lubricated the ever-turning wheels and clanging pistons of the University's machinery. With the exception of an occasional quote from Wallace Stevens to the effect that "money is a kind of poetry" (virtually the only kind of contemporary poetry Harvard embraced), the green stuff, like death itself, was never mentioned among the faculty and administration. Yet the place was crawling with legal and illicit tender, testified to by the periodic miniparades of mink and chinchilla into the Faculty Club and the ubiquitous presence of stretch limos parked just behind President Atterton's office in Massachusetts Hall. The University's alumni questionnaire, for that matter, listed no fewer than forty-seven titles by which alumni could choose to be addressed, by far the least regal of which were Mr. and Ms.

"Why, I can't fucking believe it." One of Weinstock's favorite former students, a talented young writer now working as a disc jockey at an all-night rap music station in Pasadena, called after receiving the form. "They've got a box here you can check marked 'Most Reverend Archbishop,' right below another one that says 'His Royal Highness!' And if none of those quite fits, you can also check 'Right Honorable Lord' or 'Chief Justice.' Jesus Christ, it's enough to make a fella downright ashamed of being a mere *magna cum laude!*"

Princes, princesses, kings, archbishops and lords, indeed, constituted a not-too-small pantheon among Harvard grads, and there were rumors galore about the vast infusions of wealth and priceless memorabilia that poured into the Harvard coffers from the bulging pockets and estates of friends and alumni. Corliss's description of a Harvard diploma as "the most lucrative adjective sale in the world," Weinstock was convinced, was merely to call the largely economic exchange carried on in the language of euphemism and high-mindedness by its rightful name.

The fact was that, as in Weinstock's own modest case, the adjective "Harvard" appended to one's name could be worth real dollars on the open markets of commerce and promotion. One could, in fact, dangle forever quite comfortably above the safety net of being "Harvard graduate so-and-so" or "Harvard Professor this-and-that," and it seemed not at all illogical to Weinstock that, given the widely marketable aura which the adjective lent its bearer, humble citizens from all over the world would gladly fork out thousands of hard-earned shekels for a rectangle of forty-pound paper with the words "HARVARD UNIVERSITY" etched above their ornately calligraphed names. As it was, a popular T-shirt spotted around Cambridge eloquently addressed the subject: The word "HAR-VARD" was printed in large block letters on the front, while the reverse side read, "This T-shirt cost my parents $70,680."

In light of the odd and often subterranean nature of these prevailing currencies, someone like Klavicki, given the charm and sincere generosity with which he dispensed his literary and ambassadorial skills, quickly established himself as one of Harvard's best citizens. Moving from banquet to banquet "like" — as he himself put it — "a high-priced Polish whore," he had so endeared himself to the Harvard administration and the American literary world that he seemed like a piece of carrion on whom all the vultures of literary ambition periodically descended to feast.

In the enormous shadow cast by Klavicki — a poet of profligate energies, a critic of dazzling intelligence and luminous prose, an imbiber of limitless capacities, a host of inexhaustible generosity — Weinstock quickly became the beneficiary of a lack of attention so resounding that he could move like a ghost through the hallowed halls of 24 Burdick Place. If he was ever sorely in need of attention and acclaim such as Klavicki received, he consoled himself, he could always move to Poland.

The other side of the equation was that, in comparison with so imposing, talented and likable a presence as Klavicki, Weinstock felt . . . well, he felt — how else could he say it? — he felt like a fraud.

2

Weinstock was preparing to have lunch with Amanda Wayland, Norton Professor of English and, as previously mentioned, the country's most powerful critic of contemporary poetry. Wayland had also been a prime mover in Weinstock's coming to Harvard, having reviewed his first book, *Love's Tent,* in terms so glowing that he almost instantaneously went from being an anonymous cameraman at West German television network DDT to the Burke-Howland Lectureship and the center (which he more accurately thought of as the armpit) of contemporary American poetry. "With the appearance of Martin Weinstock's first book, *Love's Tent,*" Wayland wrote, "a new and deeply melancholic voice has emerged on the American poetry scene, a voice both bleak and disconsolate, yet ravenously in search of the small happinesses and erotic interstices which make this pain- and death-ridden life tolerable."

Weinstock remembered the unabated terror he felt when he was informed that not only Harold Blumberg and Gamson but Wayland herself — described as "the anointer and dethroner of the gods among American poets" — would be there for his interview at the Faculty Club that snowy February afternoon. Wayland's review of his book hadn't yet been published, so he had anticipated with unrelenting dread and sleeplessness what he, a second-generation literary autodidact from Washington Heights, might possibly have to say to the woman who, according to one of his friends, "can recite *The Norton Anthology of Poetry* back to you word for word like a floppy disk."

But Wayland turned out to be a consoling, almost maternal, presence at the luncheon. "You absolutely *must* have some soup" was the first thing she said to Weinstock, "or else you'll catch cold in this terrible weather." Weinstock had never understood, given the elevated and discerning nature of Wayland's tastes, what it was in his own easily accessible and intellectually humble oeuvre that interested her to begin with, but he remained deeply grateful for her confidence and support. Though they had, since that first nervous, wintry afternoon, become friends of a sort, Weinstock remained secretly terrified of Wayland, dreading that she would discover that — like most everyone else at Harvard — he felt himself a fraud, an impostor from the libidinal netherworld who had somehow managed to "pass" into this world of higher intelligence.

Wayland herself had always remained a mystery to Weinstock. A woman of harsh, seemingly inflexible judgments and impeccable integrity, she nonetheless sometimes based her affections and dislikes on what seemed to him rather superficial criteria. "I detest his work," she once said of a famous Czech poet mentioned for the Nobel Prize. "He never showers." Wayland had once described a younger American poet — one whose poems frequently made mention of her children's genitals and were permeated by none-too-oblique references to the Nazis — as "purely and simply, the worst poet in America," a distinction Weinstock felt was open to a great deal of competition. "Besides," Wayland added, "she looks like an ostrich."

As inflexible as Wayland's literary judgments sometimes were, she was even more adamant on matters such as family life, which she considered a form of unmitigated torment. Whenever Weinstock mentioned his desire to have children as a way of rectifying his own confused paternity, Wayland acted as if he'd suggested mating with a sea cucumber. "Why in the world do that?" she would ask, only to answer her own question. "The family is a gulag."

Wayland, who had grown up in a strictly Irish Catholic family in Boston (her maiden name was O'Callahan), was no less unequivocal on the subject of religion. "It has never brought so much as a *scintilla* of happiness into the world," she told Weinstock one night after a reading by an Israeli poet who described religion as "a good thing to have had . . . in the past." "As far as I'm concerned, they should all be abolished — *period*. Their only function in civilized life is to rationalize hatred and stupidity."

"Don't you think," Weinstock ventured timidly, "religion contributes something to the texture of life?"

"Nonsense," Wayland replied. "Religion contributes to the texture of life the way Hitler or Mussolini contributed to the texture of life. . . . It adds nothing of aesthetic value, only death."

Intimidating and unrelenting though she could be, there was something Weinstock found genuinely likable about Wayland, above and beyond his debt of gratitude. So he was looking forward, albeit with the usual trepidation, to their lunch that day.

"Why, hello Martin," she greeted him from a corner table at Casablanca, "you're looking marvelously well. . . . And how's your work going?"

Weinstock always dreaded these inevitable questions about his "work," having heretofore regarded writing as pure, unadulterated play. He gave his usual response. "Fine. I'm working on this villa-nelle I keep hearing a line from. I just can't seem to get any further on it."

"Oh. What is it?" Wayland, though she often chided him about his lack of discipline, was always interested in anything formal Weinstock was up to. ("It's lovely," she remarked about almost every poem he sent her, "but it doesn't scan.") Weinstock, by con-trast, had trouble admitting to her (or to his students) that, before being hired, he had thought "prosody" was the name of some small-town contra dance.

"Oh . . . it's nothing serious — just something that keeps flashing into my mind."

"Well, why don't you tell me? You know how interested I am in your formal experiments."

"It goes, 'The dead are dead and lovers love to kiss.' Nothing very original, as you can see."

"Not really." Wayland, though often harshly critical of others, was always, Weinstock felt, unduly generous toward him. "I think it's rather catchy, as a matter of fact — and even true."

"What do you mean, true?" Weinstock hadn't thought of the line as having any objective veracity.

"Simply that my friends are dropping all around me like flies, that's all." Wayland sighed. "Why, I just came from visiting my friend Eleanor, who's racked with cancer, and yesterday we buried my former colleague at Brandeis, Morris Feinstein, and my sister Beverly in Braintree is sick with bronchial pneumonia, and every-where I look someone is dead or dying or afflicted with some terrible illness."

"How awful." Weinstock was genuinely moved by Wayland's air of beleaguerment. "I guess we're lucky just to be here and in good health."

"Well, *I*, for one, certainly don't intend to remain here any other way." Wayland spoke with the air of certainty that usually accom-panies statements of fact.

"Well," Weinstock hesitated, "I guess it's not up to us to decide."

"Of course it's up to us." Wayland was virtually scolding him by now. "Why who in the world *else* should it be up to?"

"The gods, I suppose." Weinstock realized, too late, that he was barking up the wrong tree.

"The gods! Oh, Martin, I forgot what an innocent you are! Well, *you* may decide to leave such matters to the gods, but as for myself, I've got this small capsule hidden behind my *Concordance to the Complete Works of Shakespeare* that I won't hesitate to make use of when my time comes."

"Capsule?"

"Yes, capsule. Pure cyanide — it's quick, it's painless, and you don't have to hang around asking for help from those who would just as soon you were gone anyway. . . . Why, as soon as I have the slightest inkling that I'm about to be dependent on anyone, I'm going to remove myself permanently from the human comedy."

Weinstock was taken aback, never having heard anyone speak so openly of their own suicide. "Why . . . Amanda, you're always so helpful to the people who need *you* — why in the world wouldn't you want to ask for the same thing?"

"Because I see how they suffer and how wretched they are for having to ask for help, and I'll be damned if I'm going to stick around just to wind up in the same position. Once you're on the way out and lucky enough to know it, why hang on?"

Weinstock had to admit there was something irrepressibly unsentimental about Wayland's reasoning. Yet the thought of his decent, warmhearted colleague removing her *Concordance to the Complete Works of Shakespeare* from one of her bookshelves and popping a capsuleful of poison into her mouth depressed and distracted him.

The dead are dead and lovers love to kiss. The line reverberated again through his mind as he munched silently on his Caesar salad and thought about Alexis Baruch.

"Well, I suppose I can understand your reasoning," he confessed, "but I think I'd prefer to go out like that baritone at the Met who dropped dead singing in *La Forza del Destino* . . . or like Nelson Rockefeller."

"Nelson Rockefeller?" Wayland seemed surprised to hear the late vice president's name brought up in a place where the only person publicly acknowledged as presidential was Atterton. "How in the world did *he* die?"

"Don't you remember?" Weinstock blushed at having brought up the subject. "The joke about him was that he came and went at the same time."

"Oh yes, now I remember." The thought of Rockefeller's rather poetic death brought a smile to Wayland's unusually somber expression. "With that young secretary of his, wasn't it?"

"Yes, Megan Marshack, bless her heart." Weinstock was astonished by the ease with which he remembered the prurient details.

"Well, Martin. I suppose there's more of a chance of *your* exit occurring in that manner than mine. I think I'll stick with the more reliable method, thank you."

Weinstock realized that he might have embarked on a somewhat sensitive subject. Wayland's amorous life, if one could call it that, seemed primarily occupied with the likes of Shakespeare, George Herbert, John Donne and Wallace Stevens. "The dead," she'd once confessed to him, "are more reliable company. One's heartbreak with them is only on paper."

The rest of the meal passed without further mention of suicide, Wayland having originally asked Weinstock to lunch to discuss who should be asked to read in next year's Morgan Watson Reading Series, whose committee she chaired. Although the force of Wayland's opinions allowed for little debate, her generosity toward Weinstock was such that she liked to provide him with at least the illusion of having some say in the matter. When he actually took the liberty of suggesting someone, however, as he did on this occasion, her dismissal of his candidate was usually uncategorical. "The most sentimental man in America," a title Weinstock felt he himself could lay claim to, she scoffed at the mention of the poet from Berkeley.

As they walked back toward the Yard, Weinstock couldn't help thinking of Wayland's pre-planned suicide. "I sure hope your friend Eleanor and your sister are better," he said, placing a hand tentatively on her shoulder as they crossed the street.

"Oh, they won't be — but thank you anyway, Martin. It's too late for such thoughts, so why get all sentimental? . . . One does what's necessary and gets on with one's work."

There was no arguing with Wayland's position. So Weinstock

simply shrugged his shoulders and waved once more as she rounded the corner onto Dunster Street.

The dead are dead and lovers love to kiss. He walked over to the pay phone next to Out of Town News and dialed.

"Hi, Alexis," he whispered into the receiver. "Wanna have a drink?"

3

Death, as you may have noticed by now, was hardly a new subject for Weinstock. Ever since Heinz Weinstock silently and uncomplainingly slithered out of his own mother's dying body in Frankfurt am Main on September 10, 1905, death was — as Weinstock was fond of putting it — "the great aphrodisiac in our family, the grease that keeps all the bearings lubricated."

"In my family," he would explain to those who questioned the source of his ironic disposition, "we had the shiva stools out so often, visitors thought they were the regular furniture."

Sitting, on the afternoon of his thirty-eighth birthday, among the stacks of Widener Library ("those actual or potential urns," as Mayakovsky Professor of Russian Literature Josef Brunoshevski described them, "containing the remnants of someone's rustling ashes") for the first time since coming to Harvard, Weinstock realized it was anything but unfitting that he should have wound up here, at a university and in a profession whose thanatic nature reflected his own.

Outside, on the lawn in front of founder John Harvard's brooding statue as he walked toward the densely columned, grayish building, a small faction of The Harvard Pro-Life Society was conducting a protest against the University's refusal to take a public antiabortion position. Among the protesters was Alexis Baruch, wearing a brightly pigmented orange-and-green T-shirt on which were emblazoned the words "YOU DON'T HAVE TO BE ANTI-HARVARD TO BE PRO-LIFE," a sentiment whose veracity Weinstock was not entirely convinced of. Alexis waved to him cheerily as he walked up the stone stairs.

"Hey, Martin," she called out to his acute embarrassment, "it's been a while since our last drink. Why don't you come picket with us? It'll do you good!"

"Uh . . . no, thanks." Weinstock waved back. "I think it's a bit more life than I can handle right now. But see you later, I hope."

Weinstock, never much of a fan of his own birthday, had decided to break his long-standing vow against entering Widener to read Kafka's *Letter to My Father,* a document he had of late developed an acute interest in. As he sat completely engrossed in the darkened PT 2621 section of the stacks, he suddenly felt the flicker of the Library's lights being turned on and off and heard a raspy, authoritative voice call out, "THE LIBRARY WILL CLOSE IN FIFTEEN MINUTES. PLEASE RETURN ALL BOOKS AND PREPARE TO VACATE THE BUILDING. THE LIBRARY WILL CLOSE IN FIFTEEN MINUTES."

Damn, he thought, just as he was beginning to forget about celebrating that odd and purely accidental event, his life. He rose from the carrel and headed toward the light switch between the stacks.

"Hi, Martin. What were you reading so intensely back there?"

Weinstock turned his head to find the life-affirmingly emblazoned figure of Alexis Baruch staring over his shoulder.

"Well, well . . . Alexis. Hi there. Just catching up on a little Kafka to cheer myself up on my birthday. What happened to your demonstration?"

"Oh, that's been over for about an hour now. Too bad you couldn't join us. Abortion *is* murder, you know."

"Yes. I gather lots of people feel that way. I'm afraid I'm not one for demonstrations. Never have been."

"Yes, I can tell. You're kind of the introverted, brooding type, aren't you? But, hey, happy birthday." Weinstock had turned his back to the shelves to face Alexis. Suddenly, without warning, he felt her musk-scented body pressed against him as she planted a lascivious kiss directly on his lips.

Perhaps it was the unexpectedness of this turn of events or the deathlike trance from which he had so suddenly been aroused by the librarian's bellowing and Alexis's sudden appearance, but Weinstock felt himself irrepressibly aroused by the scent of Alexis's hair and the moist, riveted contour of her lips. His right hand shot toward the light switch as he pressed his enlivened body forward against his former student's and ran his left hand upward along the back of her right thigh, where he could feel the smooth, fleshy moon of her left buttock obediently fall into his palm. At the same time, he forced his tongue up into the roof of her mouth.

"Oh, Jesus . . . . Martin . . . . Oh God." Alexis's eager hands were soon unbuckling his belt. He could hear the sweet metallic sound of his zipper opening. With her other hand, Alexis hastily yanked her yellow skirt and lace underpants free from her hips until they fell against the tops of her white basketball sneakers, then guided his eagerly throbbing cock toward the tuft of curly black hair at the confluence of her thighs.

"Wh . . . what about . . . what about birth control?" Weinstock could hardly get the words out in his preejaculatory frenzy. "Wasn't that *you* out there at that anti-abortion rally?"

Once again a raspy voice, this time from somewhere not far away, rang out: "THE LIBRARY WILL BE CLOSING IN FIVE MIN-UTES. PLEASE RETURN ALL BOOKS AND PREPARE TO LEAVE THE BUILDING."

"It's OK, Martin. . . . It's all taken care of." Like a football referee signaling the flight path of a successful field goal, Alexis's right hand continued to guide his cock toward those moist, quivering lips which, by now, Weinstock was gently massaging with his fingers.

"THE LIBRARY WILL BE CLOSING IN TWO MINUTES. PLEASE PREPARE TO VACATE THE BUILDING," the voice droned on.

By now there was no stopping Weinstock. Closing his eyes to the blurred title of Joyce's *Dubliners* staring out from above Alexis's left shoulder, he felt his hungry organ slush and slide like a happy eel into her deeply greased vagina. There — at precisely 4:59 P.M. on the first day of his thirty-ninth year, surrounded by the collected works of Joyce and Kafka — Martin Weinstock shot his living seed into the damp, dark, welcoming orifice of Alexis Baruch.

4

"Amidst such plenty," Weinstock's old friend Trevor Johnson, visiting from D.C., remarked to him one afternoon as he sat listening to Weinstock bemoan his fate, "how could such ingratitude exist?"

And, as Weinstock reflected on the subject, the question seemed a good one: *Amidst such plenty, how could such ingratitude exist?*

Perhaps, in fact, this had become the central question of his life: *Amidst such plenty, how could such ingratitude exist?* How could a man with a great teaching job at a wonderful institution, with fantastic students in a beautiful city, with marvelous friends and a history of sweet, generous, interesting lovers, be so glum? How could someone like himself, Martin Weinstock — young, attractive, intelligent, desired — be so filled with his own disdain? What was so *wrong* with a life which the vast majority of mankind would gladly have given the final sagging chromosome in their bored, uninspired bodies for even a small snippet of?

The answer, of course, was *nothing*. Nothing was wrong with this life that some small corner of Weinstock's uninspired imagination could not have corrected, that some small relinquishment of greed and obsessive self-interest might not have rectified.

There was a long silence as Trevor's question hung unanswered in the air, transmogrifying itself slowly into judgment. *Amidst such plenty, how could such ingratitude exist?*

Perhaps, Weinstock thought, as Trevor sat slowly pirouetting his plastic spoon around in his coffee cup, perhaps plenty itself was a heavy burden whose weight only grew when it wasn't shared, dispersed, dissipated, *energized* by the joy of its own use? Perhaps such ingratitude couldn't die until something living, something other than himself, had been born in its place?

"Well, what about it, Martin?" Trevor seemed to be growing impatient with the weight of his unanswered question. "Why isn't someone like you happier, with all the great shit that's come his way and that just keeps on coming while you sit there with your long face and sad poet's eyes and spit in its face as if it were a turkey vulture coming after you like a piece of carrion?"

Again there was a long silence, filled with the heavy weight of Weinstock's long-delayed reply.

"I don't know, Trevor," he mumbled, amazed at the depths of his own self-deception, "I just don't know."

5

There was, nonetheless, something amusing about life at Harvard which, in its better moments, offset the deathlike pallor that shrouded Weinstock's existence. For example, an oddly consistent military vocabulary penetrated the place, as scholars in the English Department pursued with almost religious devotion an enterprise they referred to as "canon formation."

From what Weinstock could understand of it, canon formation involved a periodic sifting and resifting through the works of what Professor of Medieval Literature Warren Jessup Bolder called "the noble dead" to determine what the great "texts" (a word used as religiously by the Harvard faculty as "pussy" had once been by Weinstock) of Western literature were and save it from the follies of unenlightened mortals like Jennifer Cerny.

Weinstock was tremendously amused by the fervor and frequency with which this task was approached, and by the ease with which a sense of disarray and conflict could be injected into the enterprise. Recently, for example, when a Feminist Revisionist Medievalist Deconstructionist (more consecutive "-ists" than Weinstock thought the English language could safely accommodate), a hyperbolic young scholar from the University of Massachusetts named Katherine Sedgewick, delivered a series of lectures entitled "Chaucer as Rapist: Eroticism and Misogyny in The Canterbury Tales," a group of women graduate students in the Department, along with most of the faculty of the newly created Women's Studies Program, demanded the convening of an interdepartmental conference to consider "removing Chaucer from the canon," an emotional predicament for the dead poet Weinstock considered vaguely analogous to being evicted from a rent-controlled Cambridge apartment.

It seemed there was always some crisis in the academy about the formation and re-formation of the canon, the most recent of which had taken place the preceding spring, when a huge hoard of pro-Nazi propaganda was found by a Harvard professor on a Guggenheim Fellowship among the archives of recently canonized French scholar Henri Ronsignard. A high-level conference of Francophiles and Christian scholars was convened to decide "what to do about the Ronsignard problem" and to debate the issue of whether a writer's moral and political beliefs should be considered in determining his eligibility for canonization.

Somehow this very idea of "canon formation," and the acrimonious debates doused in cream sherry and cheddar cheese fish crackers which it engendered, made Weinstock think of a platoon of twitching, blinking and gesticulating men and women puttering around with some out-of-date military hardware. He himself had always sided with the third part of a Taoist maxim he was fond of quoting: "The intelligent speak, the fools argue, the wise are silent." He had not (he reminded himself) fled the acrimony of one profession — the law — just to get caught up in another whose pettiness was rivaled only by the depth of its insecurities.

So Weinstock coined for himself the following useful and, he thought, humorous maxim: "I'd rather be a spray gun than a canon," and went on fiddling, as best he could, with the sound of things. There would be a price to pay for his frivolity in the end; it was, he also knew, one that would be collected from them all sooner or later anyway. But he didn't, for the immediate present, want to be included in the broad sweep of a line by a young Irish poet he had recently seen quoted in a review by Klavicki.

"The dead," the Irishman wrote, "have been seen alive."

❖

At Harvard, it seemed, the dead *had* been seen alive. Weinstock had recently read that the suicide rate among junior faculty who had fallen from the University's Olympian heights was twenty-five times the national average. Among the saddest such documented cases was that of a former assistant professor in the History Department, Askold Doxbinder. Doxbinder, after winning the Pulitzer Prize but being denied tenure by a narrow vote of his department, had chained himself to the steps of Widener Library on the coldest night of the year and died of exposure. Scrawled in the snow directly beside his partially frozen body the next morning were found the words "Give me Harvard or give me death." Only after a full investigation by the Cambridge police (which the University tried to suppress) was it revealed that the two members of the Department who cast the deciding votes against the young scholar were historians whose own books had been unsuccessfully submitted for the same prize.

That such intense examples of personal unhappiness could be translated so artfully into professional success had baffled Weinstock almost from the moment of his arrival in Cambridge. He had always loved Theodore Roethke's line "the right thing happens to the happy man," yet it seemed that the only thing that happened to the happy man in Cambridge was six or eight years of economic and professional insecurity followed by a one-way ticket out of the place — wham bam, thank you, ma'am!

Rumor had it, in fact, that a full third of the *senior* faculty checked out of the exclusive psychiatric wards of McLean Hospital in nearby Belmont every morning. Quite recently, one of Harvard's most prestigious behavioral psychologists, Norman Kinsolver, whose professional life had been devoted to formulating what became known as The Kinsolver Index of Spiritual Development, had taken his own spiritual development so far as to check out of McLean one sunny afternoon and plunge into the icy waters of Massachusetts Bay, leaving his car parked at nearby Logan Airport.

"This place," Weinstock's former lover Rae Beth Shintow, now a punk rock star in Cleveland, remarked when she came to Cambridge during his first semester, "feels like the academic equivalent of a Leonard Cohen album — most of the folks around here look like you'd have to check them twice to make sure they're still breathing! . . . Why, Jesus Christ, Martin, you ought to get your sweet little poetic ass out of this place before you turn into one of them."

As Weinstock sat thinking of Rae Beth's words, there was a knock on his office door. It was Gamson, looking like a stale cheese with legs.

"Have you seen *The New York Review of Books?*" Gamson was clearly on the verge of tears. Weinstock had never in his life read what Armitage called *The New York Review of Each Other's Books,* but, since coming to Harvard, he had bought a copy every two weeks and placed it on the edge of his desk to prepare for conversations like the one he sensed was about to take place.

"Why, I just this minute got it." He motioned to the untouched periodical neatly folded before him. "What's the matter?"

"A godawful review of my book by yet another illiterate SOB from California." The nonacclaim which had greeted the publication of Gamson's novel had been so dramatic that both Armitage and Weinstock, along with their junior colleagues, had stopped reading even the daily papers for fear that yet another trashing of their colleague's late-life oeuvre would need to be confronted. Weinstock himself had tried on seven separate occasions to read the massive opus, each time retreating once again to the cheerier pages of Bukowski or Henry Miller, until he finally grew so bored and embarrassed by his inability to endure the book's unabating torpor that he paid one of his undergraduates seventy-five dollars to write a three-page plot summary.

Now, with Gamson's turgid, downward-sloping body standing beside him, he slowly opened the cover of *The New York Review*. On the first inside page was a headline reading "DEATH OF THE NOVEL: AN EXEMPLAR," followed by a review so scathingly negative that Weinstock couldn't even bring himself to utter his usual practiced attempt at consolation ("Don't take it too seriously, Mort. . . . History will redeem you").

"Geez." Weinstock felt somehow relieved to be confronted by a situation that seemed beyond the remedies of feigned sympathy. "It's really pretty bad, isn't it?"

"That ignorant sonuvabitch obviously didn't understand the book at all . . . . I have the growing sense that my kind of sensibility just isn't for these times." Gamson was a man who — enviably, it seemed to Weinstock — possessed a Miniver Cheevyesque ability to find the source of his failure everywhere but within his own passionless characters, most of whose idea of a fun afternoon was chancing upon a first edition of *Hard Times* in an antiquarian bookshop.

"Don't take it too seriously, Mort." Weinstock's repugnance at his own mealymouthed duplicity was so intense he felt his entire body threaten to go into a state of rebellion. What he really wanted to say — wanted to *scream*, in fact — was "*Listen, Mort, your stupid book sucks and you know it and I know it and everybody who has read or tried to read it knows it, and the damned truth is the whole world, including you, would be better off if you left the goddamned trees standing and donated your word processor to the Salvation Army, and didn't inflict any more of those tedious, peck-*

*erless characters of yours on us. Do you hear me, Mort? YOUR
BOOK SUCKS! IT JUST PLAIN SUCKS!"*

But, after three years of walking among the dead and near-dead
of the Harvard English Department, Weinstock felt nearly dead
himself. So he merely looked up at Gamson once more, the lame
expression of a lobotomized sheep passing over him, and repeated
what had by now become, for better or worse, part of his own small
litany.

"Don't take it too seriously, Mort." He heard the awful, transparently insincere, words coming from his mouth once again. "History will redeem you."

6

Since arriving at Harvard, Weinstock's most memorable student
had been a young wisp of a girl named Melissa Wainwright, daughter of Economics Department Chairman G. Gordon Wainwright
and his sociologist wife, Brenda. Weinstock's affection for Melissa
covered both ends of the spectrum, from those first, terrifying weeks
when she had inadvertently "rescued" him from his almost para-
lyzing sense of fraudulence to his present relationship with her as
a source of his own enlightenment and pleasure.

Melissa had been a member of Weinstock's first poetry seminar
during the fall of 1983, when he felt it would be only a matter of
weeks before he would be "discovered" as the only Harvard English
professor in history who hadn't read the *Divine Comedy,* much less
Ulysses. As it was, this sense of his inadequacy had only been rein-
forced in his other writing section, when, just seconds after the first
meeting ended, a young man named Eric Monsky knocked on his
office door.

"May I speak with you a moment?" a self-consciously sophisticated voice, reeking of entitlement, asked.

"Sure." Weinstock sensed that the conversation was not going to
be a pleasant one. "What can I do for you?"

Monsky, as if to make it unmistakably clear that it was he, rather
than Weinstock, who was in the position of authority, wandered
around the room, gazing at the various prize announcements taped
to the walls, before sitting down.

"May I have a copy of this?" he asked, pointing to an announcement for that year's Pulitzer.

Somewhat taken aback by this first private conference with a Harvard student, Weinstock sat for a moment in stunned silence. "Why, uh . . . sure," he finally stammered. "You wanted to talk about something else, didn't you?"

"Oh . . . yes." Monsky continued to gaze at the wall as Weinstock spoke. "I just wanted to say that I think I'm going to drop your course."

"Oh?" Weinstock knew that he hadn't exactly seemed like the heir apparent to Mendelberry and Lovell during the first class meeting, but, then again, he didn't feel things had gone all *that* badly. All he had done, in fact, was talk briefly about the syllabus and "ground rules" for submitting work and have the students introduce themselves.

"What seems to be the problem?"

"Well, I simply don't think I have anything to learn from the other students in the class." Monsky spoke with the conviction of someone stating a fact rather than expressing an opinion.

"Oh? Don't you think that might be something of a premature conclusion? We haven't even discussed any of the poems yet." Weinstock was certain by now that Monsky's halfhearted attempt at politeness consisted solely of his substituting the words "other students" for "you."

"No, I don't at all. I looked over the poems in your mailbox, and it's clear to me that I'm much more sophisticated than the other students. It would just be a waste of my time to take the course."

"You mean to tell me that you took the poems out of my mailbox?" Weinstock had been forewarned about certain Harvard students, but this was simply too much of a strain on his still naive credulity.

"Of course I did. You see, this is my last year here, and I'm tremendously busy as poetry editor of *The Muse* and applying to graduate schools and really feel that I don't have any time to waste on courses that won't really challenge me. . . . I hope you understand — it's nothing personal. I just feel that I'd be better off in Klavicki's advanced section."

"Of course." Intimidated at first by Monsky's arrogance, Weinstock felt his blood begin to boil as he stared at the smug, self-satisfied adolescent seated before him.

"You know, I've been at this much longer than most of the other students. . . . Both my parents are well-known writers, so I've been working at poetry for over ten years now. I've just had a poem accepted by *The New Yorker,* in fact. You don't publish there, do you?"

"No, I don't. Listen, I'm terribly busy right now. I'm sorry the class seems like such a disappointment to a published person like yourself. But I've really got quite a bit of work to do."

Monsky shot to his feet, clearly astonished at Weinstock's lack of interest in his lineage. "Well — I hope your class works out OK. Maybe I'll stick a few things I've written in your box during the semester. I'm sure you'll find them interesting."

"Sure. I may even learn something." Weinstock's sarcasm was clearly lost on Monsky, who leveled yet another self-confident smirk at his now former professor and shut the door behind him.

"Arrogant little fucker," Weinstock mumbled to himself as he tossed Monsky's first submission, a rhymed sonnet entitled "At Keats' Grave," into the trash.

Luckily for Weinstock, however, his experience in Melissa Wainwright's section the next day proved a delightful contrast. The class had been under way some fifteen minutes when the door opened and Melissa, in a state of dishevelment and confusion that rivaled the average bag lady's, poked her head through the crack.

"Oh . . . excuse me," she said in a voice so birdlike Weinstock was stunned to find it belonging to anyone more developed than a six-year-old. "Is this English 2B . . . the poetry-writing seminar?"

"Why, yes. Come on in." Irritated at first by the young woman's lateness, Weinstock couldn't help but be humored by her untidiness, a welcome contrast to Monsky's robotlike impenetrability.

"I'm terribly sorry," Wainwright whispered almost inaudibly, staring down at a hieroglyph of smudged, multicolored ink on the back of her left hand. "I had it written down as Room Thirty-three by mistake. . . . This *is* Tuesday, isn't it?"

"Yes" — Weinstock could hardly keep from joining the undercurrent of laughter that seized the rest of the class — "it's Tuesday. Why don't you have a seat?"

Melissa's entrances over the next four weeks were always variations on the same theme. Arriving fifteen minutes late, she maintained the disheveled, ethereal air of some deranged Ophelia who had simply stumbled into the room en route to throwing herself in a pond or sleeping on a subway grate. Weinstock couldn't help but notice that she was, in fact, rather pretty, but it was also clear that the utter absentmindedness of her self-presentation left little room for attention to such matters as the cultivation of physical beauty. Nonetheless, he felt an immediate gratitude for her presence, having made the understandable mistake of equating her air of confusion with a lack of intelligence, and therefore feeling he had found a "soul mate" to his own sense of fraudulence.

As the weeks passed, without the appearance of any further Monskys, and having grown accustomed to the fact that his sense of being an impostor was widely shared (though better disguised) among the Harvard faculty, Weinstock also became aware that behind the birdlike voice and rag-doll figure of Melissa Wainwright lurked an extraordinary intelligence. If he intended to look to his students for relief from his sense of mediocrity, he soon realized, he would have to look elsewhere.

Melissa, in fact, was a kind of reeducation for Weinstock concerning the disparities between form and substance. After he finally stopped focusing on the high, sparrow tones of her voice and actually began listening, what struck him was Melissa's absolute self-assuredness and intelligence as she disagreed with what was often a class consensus.

"Noooooo" — she would pout and pucker her syllable of dissent into the air after discussion of a student poem — "I absolutely don't agree." And then, inevitably, in the same birdlike voice, followed an alternative interpretation so cogent and intelligent as to be virtually irrefutable. Struck not only by the force of Melissa's intelligence but by her utter heartfeltness, Weinstock soon found himself spending more than an occasional hour discussing some literary or psychological question with her during office hours at 24 Burdick Place.

One afternoon, while discussing one of her poems, the subject of how to portray the tragic in narrative form came up. "The reason we no longer write the kinds of tragedies Shakespeare wrote," she explained, "is that we no longer have the kind of secrecy people had in his time. We're besieged by openness and confessionalism," she added. "Why, today, if Othello believed Desdemona was cheating on him, they'd probably wind up at the family therapist's instead of his getting all suspicious about Iago. It's impossible to have that kind of tragedy in our culture. . . . It depends too much on what's left unsaid."

"The girl's fucking brilliant," Weinstock confessed to his soon-to-be-former wife. "She has more soul in her little pinkie than most of the English Department has in its whole goddamned body."

"That would still leave plenty of room for the pinkie, wouldn't it?" his wife added in a moment of clarity Weinstock would look back on nostalgically years later.

"The only way we upper-middle-class kids have to avenge ourselves against our parents," Melissa informed him one afternoon, "is to be unhappy. That's *our* version of the Oedipal triumph we have everything, have been successful at everything, so what else can we do but try and convince our parents that there's some deep disorder in our souls which all their caring and generosity and intelligence have failed to penetrate?"

At the end of her sophomore year, having twice more taken his seminar, Melissa arrived at his office door with a surprising announcement.

"I'm taking next year off," she informed him in her usual timid voice.

"Oh — why's that?" Weinstock was trying hard to hide his disappointment at the prospect of losing one of the few bright spots in his otherwise pained existence.

"I've decided I need to spend a year doing something else — something a little less self-centered and cerebral than being a student."

"What do you have in mind?"

"I'm going to North Dakota to work in this home for orphaned young women from rural areas. I think it's the kind of place where I could really contribute something. It's so different from the kinds of experiences and people I connect with here at Harvard."

"I know what you mean," Weinstock countered, perhaps a bit too enthusiastically. He noticed that even the sound of Melissa's voice — that intentional subterfuge designed to discourage all but the truly interested — now seemed filled with intelligence. "I'll miss having you around here, though. I hope you'll write."

"*Of course* I will," she almost scolded him. "I've learned a lot from you. I'm really grateful for that."

Weinstock found it hard to hide his astonishment at the thought of his having taught this precocious creature anything. "Why . . . thanks," he stammered somewhat embarrassedly. "I was kind of getting the feeling that, if either of us was learning anything, it was me."

Melissa blushed as she backed toward the door. "Well, listen," she more instructed than asked, "you'll be here next year when I get back, won't you?"

Weinstock felt a twinge of sadness, both at the thought of her leaving and of his remaining. "Yeah . . . I suppose so. That is, unless they discover how stupid I am or I die."

"I don't think there's any danger of the former" — she smiled — "or of the latter."

"I don't know about that," he half-joked. "Sometimes I feel like it's the only way to really fit in."

7

It was almost a year later, on one of those few genuinely springlike days in Cambridge when the lilacs are blooming and the damp, prolonged chill of winter seems finally to have exhausted itself, that Melissa Wainwright again appeared at Weinstock's office door. He had just come from a memorial service for Milton Hirschfeld, Charles W. Emery Professor of Languages and Literature Emeritus, the first Jew ever tenured by the Harvard English Department and a man for whom Weinstock had harbored a particular affection. Hirschfeld, a kind, prematurely senile, nearly deaf gentleman, had always confused him with other members of the junior faculty, an error in identification which Weinstock took more as a sign of Hirschfeld's affability of spirit than as an affront to his own individuality. "It's a pleasure to see you again, Mr. Barnes," Hirschfeld had greeted him the last time they met.

Weinstock was sitting at his desk thinking about his recently departed colleague, soon to be immortalized in one of Atterton's black-bordered announcements, when he heard a soft rapping on his office door.

"Come in," he ventured eagerly, glad to have his thoughts distracted from any further contemplation of the noble dead. For a moment he didn't recognize the thin, rather drawn young woman who stared in at him through the crack in the door.

"Why, Melissa — is that you?"

"Yes," a familiar birdlike voice answered. "I'm back."

"Well, come in, come in. It's *great* to see you!" Weinstock realized he had genuinely missed the presence of this one seemingly kindred spirit among his students. "How the hell *are* you?"

"Well, if you really want to know, I'm not so good."

Weinstock immediately saw that his initial impression of a somehow diminished spirit had been accurate. "What's the matter?"

"Why, haven't you heard?"

"No. Heard what?" He had received several characteristically melancholic letters from North Dakota but had no reason to suspect anything unusual had gone wrong during her months away from Cambridge.

"About my friend Richard?" Weinstock remembered Melissa having frequently mentioned her old high school classmate and closest friend Richard Lorenz, now a medical student at U.C. Davis.

"No. . . . What about him?"

"He's dead."

Weinstock momentarily caught his breath. "What do you mean he's dead?"

"Exactly that — dead. . . . Murdered in fact."

"By whom?"

"They don't yet know. They think it may be this guy Larry he had an affair with at Berkeley a couple of years ago and who was insanely jealous about Richard's getting involved with a woman. I'm surprised you haven't read about it. It's been in all the papers. I went out to San Francisco for two weeks to help look for him after he disappeared, but my mother just called last night to tell me they found the body floating in San Francisco Bay near the Golden Gate Bridge . . . strangled."

"Oh God, that's awful." A wave of nausea passed over Weinstock. He knew what a blow the loss of yet another friend through violent means (Melissa's freshman roommate had been raped and knifed to death on a New York City rooftop) would be to the fragile-seeming young woman standing before him.

"I'm so sorry," he commiserated. Then, almost as an after-thought, "Are you coming back to school next semester?"

"Well, I thought I was. But now I feel so depressed and exhausted that I think I'm going to try taking some more time off and write about Richard — kind of as a way of remembering him to myself, if you know what I mean. I don't want this to be just another sensational story people read about in the papers and then forget. . . . He really *meant* something to me, you know."

"Yes." Weinstock knew how seriously Melissa took her attachments. "I know."

Write Melissa did — so well, in fact, that when, six months later, a 600-page account of her ten-year friendship with Richard Lorenz entitled *Contra/Dictions: The Life of a Friendship* appeared on his desk, Weinstock found himself so moved that he sent it to his editor in New York. Three weeks and a $500,000 advance later, Melissa Wainwright's moving testimonial to her longtime friend — now re-titled simply *The Missing Corpse* ("a book with the word 'diction' in the title will never sell in America," Weinstock's editor assured her) — was on its way to becoming the most talked about first book by a young writer since Norman Mailer's *The Naked and the Dead*.

Happy as he was for Melissa and her book, Weinstock felt the disparity between the lack of recognition (or money) accorded his own work and the sudden fame, wealth — and, best of all, *read-ers* — that were his former student's at least temporary possession. He felt, in fact, a sudden, curmudgeonly kinship with Gamson, who had so often been eclipsed by the dazzling success of former students, while he himself plodded on unrecognized in the dark kingdom of the somber and serious.

"Let's face it," Weinstock remarked to Armitage, leaning into the latter's office the day after the contract was signed, "nothing sells like death."

"Except sex," Armitage added.

"But, as we all know," Weinstock reminded him, "they're inextricably intertwined. You know how Harold Bloom puts it? — *'that old oxymoron: sexual life.'* "

"It sure is around here." Armitage shook his head sadly. "Why, this place feels to me like the living embodiment of the return of the repressed."

"It's the *revenge* of the repressed, isn't it?" Weinstock was suddenly lost in thought as Armitage spoke.

"Return, revenge — what the hell's the difference?"

Weinstock sat silently for a moment, drumming his fingers on the desktop.

"Could be there's a big difference," he answered, not without a twinge of sadness. "Could be there's a helluva big difference, it seems to me."

BOOK II

Beginnings

———————•———————

The tragic hovers in the corners
of the house. It shivers
in the pillows and the sheets.
It winds its slender rope around
the half-completed and complete.

— Martin Weinstock,
"The Happy Nihilist"

CHAPTER 3

Births

It is a gift if one is born happy. Those who are born
unhappy are incurable.

— HENRY MILLER

When my grandmother's life came to a sudden halt after my father's birth in Frankfurt am Main, Germany, on September 10, 1905, my father, Heinz Weinstock, was hardly left alone in the world.

Before dying — perhaps from the fatigue of uttering this last child into the world — my grandmother had managed to go to the well seven other times. She had issued forth six daughters and another son to keep her surviving infant company in the cruel, heartless world into which she had sent him as her final act among the living.

My grandfather, a small-time kosher butcher in the Jewish ghetto of Frankfurt, must not have had a light load to bear as the newly widowed father of eight children. Max Weinstock, as anyone in his shoes might have been, was not in a position to make many demands on any woman who came along to help him lighten the burden of his progeny. So, when a neighbor introduced him to Janette Lissauer, an eager Jewish widow from the neighboring town of Oberursel, it was only a matter of months before my father's motherless infancy was blessed with a new stepmother.

Janette Lissauer was clearly a woman whose interests were dominated more by the need to find a husband for herself — and a father for her two fatherless children — than by any wish to become a stepmother to the eager, needy brood of eight onto which my grandmother closed her eyes for the last time in the bedroom of Number 12 Kesselstrasse. And it must have been my father — the youngest, most vulnerable, most needy of the lot — against whom she vented the lion's share of her rage at having found herself in so difficult — and, in her own mind, so clearly *unchosen* — a predicament. "My schtepmutter, she never luved me, bis auf de End von her life," my father frequently told me while I was growing up, "venn she could finally beleev what ein wunderbahrer son I was."

So it was surely not a random event that caused my father, at the ripe age of fourteen, to apprentice himself to the reputable German fur wholesaler Meyer und Vogel, GmbH, in Nuremberg, thereby escaping the confines of his wicked, domineering stepmother and following in his beleaguered father's footsteps (it being hardly a large leap to go from selling meat to selling furs).

If you look at the early photographs of my father, the ones taken in the early 1930s after he was promoted to traveling salesman, you can see that he might have passed for a German matinee idol: His jet black hair, slicked down with pomade, shimmers in the light, and, in his gray, wide-lapeled suit and a shirt so white it makes the gray seem almost charcoal, he has that thin, tightly strung look frequently associated with romantic men, coupled with a seductive, sideways glance in which his gaze — ever-so-slightly androgynous, vulnerable and charming — never quite meets the camera head-on.

These were the years when Julius Streicher and his henchmen were already parading down the streets of the Jewish ghetto in Frankfurt with whips and clubs, shattering the windows of Jewish shops like my grandfather Max's kosher butchery. They were already the years when it was suspect, if not downright dangerous, for a young Jewish male to be seen in the company of an Aryan woman, just a few years before the Nazis actually passed the laws that made such liaisons illegal. My father — passing through the beautiful Bavarian countryside with his chauffeur when he offered Claire Haas, a lovely, blond-haired opera singer and innkeeper's daughter, a ride at a bus stop in Baden-Baden in 1934 — may, of course, have been too removed from all this to pay much attention. He may already have been a man too needy, too mired in his own doomed fate, to be wary of falling in love with someone his life would never allow him to possess. Or he may have merely wanted to strike back at his father for marrying a woman he hated. He may have wanted to wound the man who had wounded him.

What I *do* know is that my father lacked the will (or the courage) to claim what he most wanted. He allowed the one true object of his passions and desires, the one *chosen* woman of his life, to elude his grasp: After a three-year romance conducted in hotel rooms, the backseat of my father's limousine and the first-class compartments of trains — the Nazis hot on her trail and her lover incapable of defying either them or his father to claim her — Claire Haas boarded a plane from Frankfurt to Santiago, Chile, to join the Stuttgart Opera's South American tour. There she remained until 1986, when she died of cancer, my father never having seen her again.

2

Nor does it seem likely that *I* was born happy. My real mother, Meta, a rabbi's daughter from a small Polish town near Minsk, met my biological father, Berthold Loeb, on Kibbutz Ravshan in Armageddon, some fifty-five miles north of Tel Aviv, shortly after escaping Nazi Germany in 1938. Their first child, a son named Yitzhak, died of infantile leukemia when he was ten days old. All the evidence points to the fact that, having then given birth to another son and a daughter, my mother wasn't that wild about uttering a fourth child into the world, particularly under the circumstances into which I was born on April 2, 1949.

It's likely that I wasn't even conceived in America but on the dust-filled, not yet fully irrigated fields of the kibbutz, which my parents left less than nine months before my birth. They had come to the States for what was to be a two-week visit in the fall of 1948, just after the outbreak of the War of Independence. The purpose of their trip was to celebrate the seventieth birthday of my father's mother, Johanna, at the home of her daughter and son-in-law, Heinz and Bettina Weinstock, with whom she resided in the Washington Heights section of Manhattan.

The Weinstocks, unlike Bettina's slightly more adventurous brother, but like most German Jews who managed to get out in time, had left Nazi Germany in 1938 for the economically and politically safer terrain of America. After several years working as a busboy at New York's Waldorf-Astoria, Heinz Weinstock had managed to work his way back into the only profession he had known since entering the doors of Meyer und Vogel, GmbH, in Frankfurt at age fourteen — the fur business. Within a few years — thanks to an unending supply of charm and flattery (*"Gnädige Frau,"* he would say to every woman who entered his showroom, "in this coat, you will *schtop* the traffic.") — he was able to build a fairly successful business as a retail jobber on Twenty-ninth Street, allowing him, his wife and his nearly blind mother-in-law to move into their sunny, five-room apartment at the corner of 181st Street and Fort Washington Avenue.

So it was with a great deal of anticipation (and a certain amount of envy) that my parents-to-be set out from Tel Aviv with their four-year-old daughter, Rachel, and two-year-old son, Aharon, one afternoon in early September for what they thought would be only a brief reunion with their comparatively worldly and successful New York relatives. But, as fate would have it, just after Berthold and Meta Loeb's arrival in New York and the celebration of Johanna Loeb's seventieth birthday at Cafe Geiger on East Eighty-sixth Street, the Israeli war against the British intensified. And Heinz Weinstock, whose life's motto was *"Es ist nicht nötig dass man lebt, sondern dass man seine Pflicht tut"* (It isn't necessary that you live but that you do your duty) quickly decided he simply couldn't allow his wife's brother's family to go back to such an insecure, dangerous existence.

Turning the obituary pages of the German-Jewish weekly *Aufbau* one morning just after my parents' arrival, he noticed in the "For Sale" column an offering of a five-acre, ten-coop chicken farm in the small, heavily Jewish community of Millville, New Jersey, some three hours from New York. Leaving the house for what he said was an appointment with a customer, he drove 120 miles south on the New Jersey Turnpike the next morning, plunked $12,000 in cash on the table of J. Willis Realty on Memorial Drive in Millville, and returned that night to proclaim his brother- and sister-in-law proud new owners of a three-bedroom fake-brick house, five acres of land, and a purchase-and-sale agreement for 7,500 five-day-old baby chicks, to be delivered a week from that Monday to their new home at 1066 East Delancey Drive, Millville, New Jersey.

"I don't know how we will ever make it up to you," Berthold Loeb, on the verge of tears, told his brother-in-law.

"Jawohl," Meta Loeb concurred, "it is so generous, I don't know what we could ever give you in return."

"You would, I know, do the exact same for us," Heinz Weinstock assured his relatives. "After all, *es ist nicht nötig dass man lebt, sondern dass man seine Pflicht tut.*"

And so, with a quick flick of Heinz Weinstock's eager pen and an overnight trip to Montreal to apply for visas, my no-doubt-already-pregnant mother, Meta; my father, Berthold; my brother, Aharon; and my sister, Rachel, packed themselves into the burgundy 1946 Chevy Heinz Weinstock bought them and headed south on the New Jersey Turnpike. There, in the company of several thousand other eggs incubating their way toward life or the pan-fried extinction of some family's breakfast table, in the burgeoning belly of Meta Loeb, I made my first, tentative motions toward the light and air of this world.

<h1 style="text-align:center">3</h1>

I will never know, I suppose, at what point in my mother's pregnancy it was decided that I was to be adopted by my aunt and uncle. Maybe — as they drove south that afternoon on the New Jersey Turnpike, thinking gratefully of the generosity of their childless relatives and of the burden of having yet another mouth to feed on the income generated by a small family chicken farm — the idea first hatched in my parents' minds. Or maybe it was only months later, when Bettina Weinstock looked down one morning to find a small brownish lump on her left breast and a radical mastectomy was performed on my father's hardly forty-year-old sister, leaving her in a state of weakness and depression for which the most effective therapy, according to her doctors, would be "to give her something new to live for."

What a convenient solution it must have been! On the one hand, a childless woman dying of cancer who had, in some sense, "nothing to live for"; on the other, her newly arrived immigrant brother and sister-in-law with two young children and a chicken farm they were uncertain would provide them with even a subsistence living. So, on April 10, 1949, just eight days after I uttered my first uncertain cry in this world, I was handed from the nurturing breasts of Meta

Loeb into the arms of Bettina Weinstock and took my place among the dying of the world.

"The day vee picked you up in Millville," my parents would say throughout my early years, "we was so happy." Throughout the beginnings of my burgeoning consciousness, the answer to that ever-present childhood mystery — "Where did I come from?" — seemed to me to be that babies most certainly were "picked up" somewhere, like special delivery packages or diseases.

And, meanwhile, here were these two families for whom death, like a pair of bookends, had entered from opposite directions: the one husband poor, unskilled, soon to be the father of a third child, shards of a war's bullet still implanted in his arm; the other charming, middle class, perhaps even impotent, faced with a dying wife and a blind, aging mother-in-law. The perfect solution must have presented itself: they would exchange death for life, barrenness for hope, the farm of thousands of unfertilized eggs for a single, fertilized egg.

And with that trade — carried out as cleanly as the trade of my boyhood hero, Duke Snider, from the Dodgers to the Mets — I, too, exchanged "uniforms," and Berthold and Meta Loeb, my natural parents, became my aunt and uncle . . . and Heinz and Bettina Weinstock became my father and mother.

CHAPTER 4

Fathers

I hold a candle to your face:

In the light, the lines of you
are a latticework of loss —
three mothers, two wives,
an uncertain son
who thrashes about
in the brine of your eyes,
calling you *father, uncle . . .*
mother.

If all men want mothers,
what might we,
having none, want?
We could break
from that design —

take back the stolen rib
and the fig leaf, take back
the diaphanous heart,
take back the fluttering eyelids.

Father,
hermaphrodite,
mermaid and minotaur,
read this
in any language:
Lese dieses
in jede Sprache.

Be water, Father,
be blood.

— MARTIN WEINSTOCK,
   "Father"

If you believe, as I do, that most of life's incidents are merely metaphors lying in wait for the lives that contain them, you'll also be interested to know how my father met my mother, Bettina Loeb, in the small German town of Georgensgmünd just outside Nuremberg, in August, 1937.

My father must, of course, have still been depressed about his lover Claire's departure, frightened by the ominous march of Julius Streicher and his S.S. troops through the streets, terrified for his own life and future. And his stepmother, too, must still have been deeply wounded by the death of the only son from her first marriage in an automobile accident just a year before. So, stopping, at his stepmother's request, at the widow Loeb's house to pick up the key to the small Jewish cemetery where his stepbrother lay buried, my father must have been pondering his own death as well. He must — his true love gone, his real mother dead, the Nazis already hard on his heels — have felt a terrible emptiness . . . a fear, a longing for comfort.

I picture my mother — a shy, pretty young woman of thirty — on that day my father first came by to pick up the cemetery key to lay some flowers on the grave of his stepmother's son. I imagine her standing in a back room, peeking out from behind a curtain, then shyly entering the foyer, eyes down, to where her eager mother had summoned her to introduce her to the dashing young Jewish furrier from Frankfurt.

There were, no doubt, not many men for a young, fatherless woman like my mother (whose only brother, my biological father-to-be, had already fled Germany for Palestine) in a small town like Georgensgmünd, not many opportunities for romance or escape. When she saw the handsome, dapper, charm-oozing figure of Heinz Weinstock at her door, a deep glimmer of hope must have passed through her. And finding this shy, pretty, available girl and her widowed, ambitious mother, both eager to welcome a man like himself into their home and hearts, Heinz Weinstock must have suddenly felt fate smile down on him. For here, finally, he could have both a loving mother and a shy, devoted wife.

So, arriving to claim on behalf of his miserable stepmother the key to death — the cemetery key — my father must have felt instead that he had found the key to a new life. *What did it matter that he felt little of the passion he had felt for Claire Haas for this pretty Jewish girl who shyly reached her hand toward him, hardly daring to look up?* It wasn't, after all, passion he was after any longer but safety — not really a wife he had been looking for all these years of kissing women's hands but a mother, a mother like the one at whose living breasts he had never fed, into whose living eyes he had never looked.

So, on February 1, 1938 — not even a year after the love of his life had fled forever to South America — in a small, private ceremony in the southern German resort town of Konstanz, Heinz Weinstock married Bettina Loeb, acquiring both a wife and a new mother with whom to soothe his wounded, grieving heart.

2

One of my first memories of my father, just after my third birthday, is going downtown to make a recording of Mario Lanza's "Golden Days." It was a time when a dollar bill could still buy things: a pound of Horn & Hardart's rice pudding, a whole pepperoni pizza, a silk tie, a two-minute recording of anything you could eke out, recorded in the quiet anonymity of a green-curtained booth somewhere near the Garment District, where my father peddled minks, Persian lambs, raccoons and Alaska seals in the showroom he rented from Jack Klug and Samuel Rabinowitz at 231 West Twenty-ninth Street, telephone number Lackawanna 4-1294.

Among my father's great loves were Mario Lanza and his *Student Prince,* loves he maintained with the same fierce, undivided loyalty with which followers of Callas and Caruso, Tucker and Peerce, Domingo and Pavarotti would love their heroes. Along with the dulcet tones of Eddie Fisher singing "Oh, my papa, to me you are so wonderful," it was the voice of Mario Lanza belting out "I walk with God, from this day on," "Drink, drink, drink" and, of course, "Golden Days," that filled our five-room apartment at 801 West 181st Street in Washington Heights, just across the street from the forbidden *goyische* pews of Cabrini Church, and just down Fort Washington Avenue from not sufficiently orthodox Fort Tryon Jewish Center, where most of my more assimilated friends were bar mitzvahed.

I should, I suppose, have been amazed at the time to discover that, beyond the two words of the title, my father didn't know a single syllable of "Golden Days," a song he must have heard, played and sung several thousand times during the years of my childhood. Even now, the scratched and warped forty-five, with the words "Martin and Dady, GOLDEN DAYS, 5.1.52" scrawled on the label in red ink, reveals — along with the birdlike, contorted chirpings of a three-year-old boy — my father's commendably cantorial voice belting out the words "Golden days . . . da *da* da da da da da *da* . . . Golden days . . . da da da da da da da *da* . . . Golden days . . . da *da* da *da* da da da *da* . . . Golden days . . ."

It didn't occur to me then that there was any *meaning* to this lapse on my father's part — to not knowing the words to the song he most loved, a song he had heard and played thousands of times. I didn't, for that matter, yet know that listening meant much of anything, that listening said something about both listener and speaker. I didn't yet know that listening — like gifts you bought people, like the way you honored their choices in life, their griefs, their happinesses — reflected a kind of *attention*.

I didn't yet know, in fact, how difficult — how nearly impossible — it was for anyone to listen to anyone if no one had ever listened to them.

3

Another strong visual image I have of my father from early childhood is of our car being pulled over into the breakdown lane of a highway, with my father standing behind it talking to some Smokey-the-Bear-looking state trooper.

"Good day, Officer Tumilinsky," my father would say, reaching into his breast pocket to remove the small plastic wallet containing his business cards as he struggled to read the officer's nameplate. "My name is Heinz Weinstock . . . a great pleasure to meet you."

While other boys I knew had fathers who often got tickets for speeding or failing to come to a complete stop at stop signs, it was only *my* father, it seemed, who was perpetually being stopped for driving too *slowly* in the passing lane, entering via the exit ramp or failing to drive with his lights on after dark. The reason, no doubt, was that we were usually lost: In the twenty-odd years he had been vacationing at the Pine Hill Arms Hotel in Pine Hill, New York, my father had never once been able to find the place without first wandering off toward far-out-of-the-way New Paltz or Buffalo.

"I have chinchilla, silver fox, Peruvian mink, Alaska seal and — this month only — some very special leopard coats . . . the best prices in New York," my father, handing the trooper a fifty-cent costume jewelry necklace he had bought from some panhandler in the Fur District, would be saying as I rolled down the car window. "Come down to my showroom with your wife, and — I guarantee you — we will find something that will *schtop* the traffic. . . . Believe me," he would continue, "I will sacrifice something for you."

Time and again, to my utter incredulity, the trooper and his wife *would* show up at 231 West Twenty-ninth Street the following week, always leaving with no less than a mink boa or a remodeling of some dilapidated old Persian lamb stole. "You see," my father would say, kissing the woman's hand as he led her to the elevator, "I told your husband I would sacrifice something for you. In this coat, Mrs. Tumilinsky, you will *schtop* the traffic."

It was, no doubt, the utter onslaught of his verbiage — the faltering English, the old world, gentlemanly charm — that did it. But, one way or another, I don't remember my father *ever* actually getting a ticket. The more traffic violations, illnesses, wrong numbers and missed coin tosses at tollbooths he was able to accumulate, the more sartorial splendor, it seemed, the wives of state troopers, surgeons and tollbooth attendants were able to display.

Within minutes, we would be back on the road, cheerfully headed for my father's next mishap, singing "*O Jugend, O Jugend, was warst Du so schön*" (Oh youth, Oh youth, how beautiful you were) or an old Bavarian beer-drinking song, *"Trink mir noch ein Tröpfchen,"* along the way.

"A pleasure to meet you, Officer Tumilinsky," I would hear my father saying as he started the car, simultaneously squeezing a few more business cards into the officer's hand. "God loves you, and so do I."

4

I had only one dream insofar as my parents were concerned: *English*. Like Jason longing for the Golden Fleece, like Tantalus thirsting for his beckoning grapes, I, too, ached — not for balm or salvation but for the sweet syllables of my native-born language, the language (as I saw it) of life.

"Such a pleasure to see you, gnädige Frau Frölich," my father would greet my elementary school principal, a tall, statuesque woman by the name of Frohlich, in his few syllables of the national vernacular. "God loves you, and so do I."

Our house, insofar as I was concerned, was a kind of leper colony of the wrong tongue. *"Du, Du, liegst mir im Herzen,"* my father would invariably be singing just as a friend of mine — or, worse yet, a potential *girl*friend — would call, *"O Jugend, O Jugend, was warst Du so schön."*

I begged. I pleaded. I prostrated myself on my knees before them. "Please, please," I whelped like a wounded dog, holding one hand over the receiver, "can't you talk English just this *once?*"

To their credit, they sometimes tried. "Good day, young Mr. Wortman," my father would say to my friend Richie as he walked into our house. "And how is your dear mamama, and the rest of your family?"

No sooner was a friend comfortably ensconced in my room, no sooner did I allow my relentless guard a moment's reprieve, than my grandmother's voice would cry out from the kitchen, *"Martin, kannst Du mir bitte ein Moment in der Küche helfen?"*

Everywhere I looked, shame, my loyal servant, waited. My creeping, blind, obituary-eager grandmother, whom I loved — what possible social credit could she bring to the life of a twelve-year-old boy? What small emoluments of allure and sensuality? My crazed father, cruising the neighborhood with his dead carcasses and kissing the hands of widows and widowers, what possible competition was he for the likes of Donna Reed's fly-fishing husband or Beaver's father, or for the guitar-strumming family of Ozzie Nelson?

"Please, dear God, please," I went to bed murmuring under my breath while my father made me recite the German litany *Heile heile Segen, morgen gibt es regen, übermorgen Schnee, dann tut's Martin nimmer weh,* "please let me wake up normal and ordinary, in a world without umlauts and accents."

Then, of course, there was their age. "What a beautiful grandchild you have." People would stop them on the street, pinching me on the cheek. "You must be so proud."

"How come your parents are so old?" my friends would ask. "Were you a mistake or something?"

"I *had,* of course, been a mistake, and so, at times, my whole life seemed — the wrong parents, the wrong language, the wrong anatomical constellations filling the house. Why, oh why, couldn't we just be like everyone else?

Like it or not, however, I was wedded to this constellation — wedded to walking my grandmother, on warm summer nights, up the hill to Bennett Park, where, while other kids played stickball and a game called ring-a-lievo, I read to her aloud from the bold-faced, exuberant letters of the German-language obituaries.

"Inge Heinemann, nee Bendauer," I would sing, like Goethe. *"Geboren 7.2.04, Karlsruhe, gestorben 9.13.58, Bayside, Queens."*

When I wasn't sitting in Bennett Park, or walking up Fort Washington Avenue, with her, I might be — just as, to my unwavering embarrassment, my two elementary school crushes, Cathy Honigsberg and Barbara Meinstein, walked by — unfolding a folding chair to sit her down beside the red-painted concrete facade of L. CHIAO CHINESE LAUNDRY, whose mingled scents of laundry starch and Chinese food seemed to me as exotic and alluring as the jungles of Madagascar, and in whose even more pronounced divergence from the prevailing culture I rejoiced with what small sense of triumph my situation allowed.

Wrapped in blue-and-pink twenty-pound paper of the kind that, I was to discover later, would eventually enfold the sanitized toilet seats of low-priced motels, our sheets — so firmly pressed down and ironed that they were more like layers of phyllo dough than German linens — emerged from L. Chiao's every Friday morning to the interwoven mumblings of my father's or mother's broken English and Grandmother Chiao's Chinese, the combination of which sounded like the disparate melodies of Fauré's *Requiem* and the Talking Heads issuing from a single set of speakers.

But what I longed for was the local patois, the language of Kennedy and Stevenson, Frankie Valli and Dion, Robert Young and Walt Disney. To be young and free and truly American, I thought, *that* was the Edenic condition! "The world is an awful place," a poet had once written, "with room for tennis." And it was something very much like tennis I wanted — tennis, whiskey sours, the *Daily News,* and a home where no one would be singing *"In Salzkammergut, da ka' ma' gut lustig sein!"* America, I thought, was the place of life and light. Germany had been the place of death. It was life, after all, I wanted — in any language I could get it.

There were also moments of reprieve — moments when I could penetrate the legitimate English-speaking world of my countrymen, as on that Sunday afternoon when my parents took my grandmother and me to Lindy's on Fifty-third Street for an afternoon of cheesecake and celebrity gazing. Lindy's was famous at the time — if not for flesh-and-blood celebrities, at least for their signed black-and-white portraits decorating its window, which suggested (at least to the so-called bridge-and-tunnelers who came into the city on weekends) that, by merely sitting down at one of the tightly clustered, deadly uncomfortable tables, they could rub shoulders with the likes of Frank Sinatra, Tony Bennett, Ed Sullivan, Lawrence Welk or — if they were among the truly chosen — Milton Berle.

Milton Berle, along with Lawrence Welk and Ed Sullivan, was one of my parents' few English-speaking heroes. Every Tuesday night, we sat transfixed before our black-and-white Emerson console as first Uncle Milty and then diminutive, birdlike Arnold Stang strode onto the stage. "Hi, Uncle Milty," twittered Stang, who couldn't have been much more than four foot ten, making chirping sounds as he stood beside Berle, who, by comparison, looked like Charlton Heston doing a nightclub routine.

Hardly had we been ushered to our seats — my parents and grandmother chattering away in their usual *Frankfurter Deutsch* while I tried as best I could to distance myself from the humiliating foreignness of my clan by scanning the room to make sure no one I knew was around — than the door opened from Seventh Avenue and in walked, smoking a big, fat cigar and leading his mink-clad wife on his arm, none other than Milton Berle himself.

I was ecstatic. Here, in the flesh, seated, literally, a few feet away from me, was both an embodiment of America and a potential escape from my parents' table. Hardly had Berle and his wife been served their slices of Lindy's Famous New York Cheesecake, to the awestruck gazes of half the population of Teaneck, New Jersey, than I was out of my seat and standing beside Uncle Milty, trying hard not to inhale lest one of his wafting curlicues of thick cigar smoke enter and clog my already asthmatic lungs.

"Hi, Uncle Milty," I ventured bravely, doing my best Arnold Stang imitation. *"Cheep cheep cheep."*

There was a prolonged silence as Berle, clearly irritated by my premature invasion of his cheesecake break, exhaled a blackish cloud of cigar smoke toward my nine-year-old face.

"Hello there, young fella," he said, after what seemed an interminable pause, reaching out to place a cold hand on my face. Then, grasping a chunk of my left cheek between his thumb and forefinger in the same way my deceased Uncle Fred (whom I had hated) had always done, he turned and twisted the small nodule of flesh, causing me to wince in pain as he said — as if for the benefit of everyone else in the room — "Great to meet you, son," then patted me on the shoulder like a third-grade teacher sending a disorderly student back to his seat, and redirected his attention to his cheesecake.

Deeply embarrassed at having failed to make a more enduring impression on one of my family's few American icons, I again seated myself at my parents' table.

"*Solch ein massel,*" my father said, using the Yiddish word for good luck. "Milton Berle."

"*Und,*" he added, before I could even respond, "such a beautiful coat, his wife has on . . . cerulean mink. Something, let me tell you, that *schtops* the traffic."

I realized, to my relief, that I could barely hear what my father was saying. I was too busy trying to hide my face in my cheesecake. I was too busy rubbing my burning cheek.

5

The names on our buzzers in the lobby of 801 West 181st Street had little in common with the Welches, Johnsons, O'Briens, Whites and Athertons of nearby Hudson View Gardens. Ours, rather, read like a *Who's Who* of Holocaust survivors: *Marx, Engel, Fleischmann, Fleishhaker, Hertz, Monat, Strauss, Pollack, Lilienfeld, Katzenstein, Baumwoll, Bergmann.*

The native tongue, as I've said, was German — so much so that I remember coming home from my first day at kindergarten and announcing to my parents that all the kids in the class were speaking a foreign language. In fact, the first pun I remember hearing — well before I knew what a pun *was* — was a reference to our neighborhood as "*kein Ton English,*" pronounced so as to confuse the German words for "not a word of" (*kein Ton*) with the Swiss-German word for district (canton).

There was, however, one glaring dereliction from the otherwise *goyischerein* register of tattered, scotch-taped names posted beside our apartment buzzers. It was in the space marked Number 41, where — calling out to us with the conspicuous self-consciousness of a ham sandwich at a Hasidic wedding — was printed the foreign-sounding, bifurcated name del Monaco.

The del Monacos — as God, in her infinite humor, would have it — had a daughter: a fire-engine-red-haired, tightly jean-clad, voluptuous, athletic creature named Linda, who was whisked off every morning by bus to some school with the word "Saint" in its name and who we would periodically find necking in the elevator with her boyfriend, Brad Mitchell, who lived in attached but "integrated" 815 West 181st Street, across the courtyard. Torrid rumors about Linda spread through our solemn, Kaddish-saying crowd, including that her father, whom we would occasionally see wearing grease-stained overalls, actually worked *with his hands,* a possibility as exotic and unspeakable to us as being one of the Great Wallendas.

We, of course, all lusted for Linda, who became a kind of prototype of that "forbidden shiksa" we were all to covet — and many of us marry — later. Wild, flamboyant, disobedient, she stood for all the things we wanted that seemed forever denied us: sex, sports, scallops, Sunday school, screwdrivers.

The other *goy* in the building — much better disguised behind his classically German name (we kids originally assumed that all "New World" Germans were Jews) — was the superintendent, Mr. Süess, a tall, dour, laconic man whose well-known heart condition we would do everything possible to exacerbate by playing what we called "imaginary" baseball in the courtyard between our building and Brad Mitchell's den of sex and seduction. Having been sternly rebuked by Süess on several occasions for breaking Mrs. Laupheimer's second-story window with one of the pink rubber Spaldings we used for punchballs, we sought to entice our ailing and mean-spirited superintendent from his ground-floor apartment (from which he would emerge, Hiawathalike, brandishing the long, spearlike rod he used to change light bulbs in high places) by going through all the motions (and sound effects) of a full-fledged game as we hit and tossed what were no more than pocketfuls of air between us.

"You damned boys," Süess would emerge from the service entrance screaming. "If you don't get the hell out of here, I'm going to have the whole bunch of you thrown out of the building . . . I swear to God!" Assured by my parents that an anti-Semite lurked behind every corner — not to mention every sharp-edged wooden pole — I took it for granted that "the whole bunch of you" meant us Jews, just as I had taken it for granted that my parents were right when they insisted that my cousin Aharon's rejection by the Phi Epsilon Pi fraternity at Rutgers (which, I later found out, was almost exclusively Jewish) was also an illustration of rampant anti-Semitism.

Like the quintessential *goy* who, by now, lurked both in my mind and in the nationally broadcast households of the Cleavers, Nelsons, Robertses and others, Süess did one other thing I dreamt, throughout my childhood, my own father might do: *He went fishing.* Every Sunday morning, often as early as 5:00 A.M., he would leave the building for some deep-sea-fishing charter boat that went out on the Hudson, inevitably returning later that day, like a kind of urban Captain Ahab, a bounty of huge fish danging from his wrist. Much as we all hated Süess, these mysterious marine exploits on the Hudson — as contrasted with the various cardiac emergencies, diabetes, angina pectorises and other illnesses of our own fathers — endowed him with a near-legendary quality which I, for one, dreamt — no, *begged* — my father would one day partake of.

One morning, indeed, the day arrived. To my utter shock and amazement, my father came into my room one Saturday night to inform me that "I won't be home venn you wake up tomorrow morning. . . . I am going fishing with Süess."

What prompted him I will never know. All day, like an expectant father cruising the maternity ward, I waited on pins and needles, imagining my father, Heinz Weinstock, the Mario Lanza of the chinchilla cape, engaged, Cousteaulike, in mortal, hand-to-hand combat with the demons of the high seas. "My father," I boasted to my astonished friends Raymond Fleishhaker, Frankie Engel, Steven Fleischmann and Ronnie Baumwoll over imaginary baseball, "is out fishing with Süess."

Agog with anticipation, I waited and waited until — finally — beaming from ear to ear and carrying five of the largest fish I had ever seen, my father, accompanied by our ever-saturnine superintendent, emerged from Süess's dilapidated station wagon. *"So, da,"* he, suddenly halo-bedecked, announced, *"ich habe sie gefangen,"* I caught them.

For what seemed months (though it was only a matter of days), I was ecstatic. *My* father — *my* maladroit, hand-kisses, traffic-schtopping, God-blessing, shiva-sitting father — was a fisherman! *Good-bye, Arnold Stang!* I shouted happily, *Hello, John Wayne!* Possessed and exuberant, for the first time in my life my fantasies of my father extended beyond the halls of Congregation Beth Hillel and Bloch & Falk's Kosher Delicatessen to the deep antarctic waters, the Great Barrier Reef off the coast of Australia, the gorilla-dense jungles of Rwanda and Uganda.

My fantasies, now weighted with tangible possibilities though they were, were short-lived. For, sometime about a week later, while rummaging around on my father's desk looking for a pen, I found the bill: $114.65, payable to Wolf's Fish Market on Amsterdam Avenue.

I never said anything, though I suspect — from his rather depressed reaction to the sudden diminution of my filial enthusiasm — that my father must have known. In any event, I consoled myself, he had tried. And there wouldn't, thank God, be any other opportunities. Because the very next week, while reaching up with his infamous spear to change a blown bulb in the rooftop elevator shaft, Süess had a heart attack and died.

6

There were two movie theaters in our neighborhood — the RKO Coliseum on 181st Street, where, for seventy-five cents, you could catch a double horror feature such as *The House on the Haunted Hill* and *The Tingler,* and that "other" theater, The Heights, off the beaten track on 183rd and Audubon, where my parents would occasionally take me to see "our" kind of — i.e., a German — film.

It was at The Heights that I saw my very first movie — a German classic of the 1950s entitled *Der Hauptmann von Köpenig,* based on the true-life story of an early-twentieth-century ne'er-do-well and panhandler. In the movie at least, he looked like a cross between Hitler and Charlie Chaplin. On his appointed rounds of pawnshops one day, our hero bought himself a German captain's uniform, in which he proceeded to sneak into a German army training facility

just before the outbreak of World War I. Undetected by either the
troops or other officers, and armed with the sheer — how else can
I say it? — *balls* of those with nothing more to lose, he somehow
managed to impersonate his way into an actual captain's position,
was transferred to the front when the War started, and, by the time
he was finally found out, had distinguished himself as a widely
decorated military hero.

I went to see the film — usually accompanied by both my parents
and our close family friend Helen — whenever it came to our neighborhood, completely enthralled by what a mere change of uniform
could accomplish. *"Kleider machen Leute,"* (clothes make the man),
I had often overheard my parents say. Here, indeed — in the person
of our beloved Hauptmann — it seemed true, though my actual
experience (armed with the example of my father's profession and
that of my seamstress aunt, Tina) had taught me the opposite: *Leute
machen Kleider.*

Yet Hauptmann — in all his half-comic, half-tragic splendor —
gave me hope for the future: *Anyone,* I realized, could get away
with being an impostor, a fraud. You could pretend to be something
you were truly not — a sea captain, a poet, even a Harvard professor — simply by being convincing enough in your performance
of the impersonated one's role, simply by wearing the right uniform.
Even someone like me, Martin Weinstock — a second-generation
boy from a gulag of German-speaking, panic-stricken parents —
could ultimately triumph. By the use of my wiles and imagination,
I, too, could escape from the domain of dead furs. I, too, could
"schtop the traffic."

There was another traffic schtopper in the life of my family's all-
too-rare cinematic forays — this one capable of being seen on the
echt English screen of the RKO Coliseum — Maurice Chevalier.
The one time I remember my father stepping into that theater was
on a night shortly after my ninth birthday when he took us to see
Chevalier, one of his heroes, in that great French precursor to *The
Sound of Music* — *Gigi.*

There's a scene early on in the movie in which Chevalier is walking
down a street in Paris. Some boys — playing what I assumed to be
a rather traditional French prank — plant a black top hat, beneath

which they've placed a large stone, in the street in front of him. Chevalier, not suspecting what's underneath, stops to kick the hat out of his way and stubs his toes on the stone, a moment in cinematic history which my father found so hilarious that he burst into a roar of laughter so uncontrollable that one of the ushers appeared, flashlight in hand, to ask him to get a grip on himself.

But there was no stopping my father, whose periodic outbursts of this kind were so heartfelt and beyond the control of either will or decorum that he had no choice but to let them run their gamut. Three more times, as I slunk farther and farther down in my seat to avoid being noticed, the usher politely asked my father to cease and desist, until, finally — accompanied by both the house manager and two more ushers wielding humongous flashlights — my parents and I were led ignominiously down the aisle like a bunch of drunken rowdies and asked to vacate the theater.

There was also a third man — a cinemalike figure, a kind of Hauptmann — whom my father and I were perpetually in wait for: *the messenger Elijah.* Every Passover, following an endless litany of *hahgadyohs* and *dayenus*, we would reach that to-me-melancholy portion of the Seder in which it was my duty, as youngest and only, to go to the door and admit that long-awaited harbinger of a kinder, gentler world for whom we each year reliably poured an extra glass of wine and who, equally reliably, always disappointed us with his nonappearance.

Elijah was the messenger whose coming, according to the Old Testament, would herald the coming of the Messiah, and upon whose arrival babies and snakes would embrace beneath the willows and maples, and our endless "next year in Jerusalems" would, finally, take place in Jerusalem, where we would all be Hauptmänner and Chevaliers in some happy Eden of schtopped traffic and relentless singing.

By the time I was ten, however, the potential but too often repeated drama of this moment, the longed-for gaze of the Chosen One as I opened the door onto a more hopeful world, had brought me to a state of resignation which must, I suspect, have accounted for the unusual heaviness of my footsteps toward the door this Passover. Hadn't I, after all, in good faith poured Elijah a glass of Manischewitz Concord grape year after year, Seder after Seder? Hadn't

I gone — at first eagerly, then with an increasing premonition of defeat and disappointment — to the door each year and opened it, only to gaze out into the long corridor of black-and-white tiles and green, institutional walls, a world of grit-caked, opaque windows and abandoned fire escapes?

It must, then, have been with a particular sense of defeat and betrayal, a sense of once more repeating a ritual whose fruitless outcome was predestined, that I lumbered, this Passover of my eleventh year on earth, to the door of Apartment 53 and opened it to find *not* nothing but a man in a black suit and gray felt hat carrying a leather attaché case, his thumb planted on our buzzer.

"He's here!" I went racing back into the living room, where my parents and assorted aunts and uncles were devouring the rest of their boiled chicken, bitter herbs, haroseth and matzohs. "It's Elijah! He's here! The Messiah is coming! It's really him!"

Certain, no doubt, that his melancholic son had finally crossed the threshold into derangement, my father slowly rose and followed me back into the hallway, where the rather astonished, no doubt terrified man in the black suit had placed his attaché case on the floor and was staring perplexedly into space, trying to make sense of his far more enthusiastic than usual reception.

"Hallo," my father greeted him with his usual affirmative salutation, "my name is Heinz Weinstock. *Good yontef.* God loves you, and so do I."

"Maybe I have come at a bad time," the man, noticing what must have been a starry-eyed expression on my face, said shyly. "I have some things here you might be interested in." Before either my father or I could say another word, he set his attaché case down on its side, popped open the latches and lifted the cover to reveal *not* the sacred garments and offerings of the Messenger Elijah but the assorted brushes, pastes, pomades, shoehorns and tie clasps of that other great harbinger of the twentieth century, the Fuller Brush man.

7

They are still in their original metal canisters, the old eight-millimeter films my father shot in the years between 1949 and 1959, still labeled with their original, now browned, Scotch-taped labels: MARTIN LEARNS TO WALK, 1950. GOLDEN DAYS, 1952. FAMILY PICNIC, MOHANTSIE PARK, 1954. MILLVILLE: AHARON, RACHEL, OMA & MAMA, 1956. FARM LIFE, 1956. OUR LAST FILM FROM OUR DEAR MAMA, 1959.

When I go to watch them, however, the figures are almost always cut off, dismembered by the cameraman's poor aim, his frenetically moving the camera from place to place, scene to scene. It is, in fact, almost impossible to splice together a narrative from all this: things seem dissociated, random. Persons appear for a brief second, then are never seen again. If there's any thread of consistency, in fact, it's the repetition itself: yet another brief segment of my grandmother and mother walking arm in arm in Fort Tryon Park; yet more footage of me with an earache, yet another hello and goodbye at my aunt and uncle's chicken farm in Millville.

The only person, in fact, who seems captured in any essential way is the cameraman himself — my father — in those rare scenes in which someone more tranquil and focused must be holding the camera. What's constant about him — what seems, at least, to constitute some kind of "Portrait of the Father as a Middle-aged Man" — is that he is constantly in motion, agitating, running, lifting, singing, playing the harmonica, waving his white handkerchief. He seems — to my own more tranquil, middle-aged eyes — like a kind of human maelstrom: lifting, cajoling, kissing, hugging, entertaining anyone and everyone he can get his hands on, incapable of letting any action (or, more precisely, any *in*action) take place without his dominating it. Not even the respite of melancholy seems able to contain him as he moves — with an energy so relentless and manic it exhausts even the viewer — through friend and family alike, stooping occasionally to lift me into the air before setting me down and moving on to the next person in line.

If, it occurs to me now, there's any unevenness at all to the attention he distributes so evenly and energetically to all around him, it's the somewhat diminished level of it he directs toward the melancholy but kindly-looking woman carrying a black pocketbook who is almost always off to the side of the action. She seems, in a way, like the date he might have arrived at the party with, only to have someone else in mind when it comes to the dancing. Sometimes she gazes off to the side, and I could swear — or am I imagining it? — that I see a slightly exasperated, though patient, look come over her face, a faint expression of tedium and ennui. She is, indeed, the least flamboyant of the women, most of the others being my father's sisters.

But, then again, why should she be all that cheerful? She doesn't have that much longer to live. She's my father's wife, my soon to be dying mother.

8

I don't remember anyone ever saying the word "cancer" — or the word "dying" for that matter — during the last year of my mother's life. I only remember, that fall after my tenth summer, returning to Washington Heights from our usual two-week vacation in Pine Hill and having my mother enter the hospital for some "tests."

What exactly these "tests" were, nobody said. I only remember, the morning after my mother entered the hospital, asking my father what she had gone in for and watching the cup suddenly tremble in my grandmother's hand as she burst into tears and I felt my father's foot gently kicking her under the table.

"Why are you so depressed?" I would ask my mother repeatedly during the next several months as she bent over the Biedermeier dresser in my parents' bedroom to brush her hair. "What's the matter?"

"I'm not depressed," she'd reply, feigning an obviously forced cheerfulness. "Nothing's the matter."

To all my various questions there were no answers, as doctors appeared and disappeared, my mother vanished into various hospitals and came back, and my grandmother's cup continued to tremble in her hands, spilling coffee-drenched challah all over the table. I had only words for hints — occasional, strange-sounding English words like "pleurisy," hospitals with odd, sometimes otherworldly, names like Doctors, Harkness Pavilion, St. Luke's, Mt. Sinai — and the uncanny ability of a child to sniff out the truth, no matter how many lies and omissions were created to mask it.

My father seemed, somehow, almost entirely absent during these months — a kind of mythic figure who came and went, schlepping furs and various delicatessen items from Max Ehmer's and Horn & Hardart, kissing his customers' hands and *schtopping* the traffic. It was only the presence of my grandmother Johanna and our ubiquitous family friend Helen, along with the progressively more solicitous attentions of the other mothers in the building, that served to fill in a landscape suddenly rendered barren by the progressively withdrawing, depressed figure of my mother.

Where *was* my father during these months? I now wonder. Somehow relentlessly present, yet, as an emotional figure, almost entirely erased from my memory of that time, so that there is not a single conversation of any kind I remember having with him between that morning my mother first went into the hospital and the morning of her death some twelve months later.

Perhaps, I imagine now, he was already launching a kind of "preemptive strike" to make sure that he would not be, once again, the abandoned child reaching up toward the breast of its living mother to find only a void. Perhaps he was merely teaching me, in the enacted life of his fears and disappointments, the Golden Rule that I was just at that time beginning to hear of at school: to do unto others as others had done unto you, to disappear before someone else disappeared, before someone who desperately needed you could learn to hold on.

CHAPTER 5

The Eight Days

I rise
by my own power
and remember her:
how she faded
into the deep, quiet pool
of her own evening, how
like a swimmer setting out
to swim to a place
she will not be returning from,
how she fluttered her eyelids
beneath the blue water...

— MARTIN WEINSTOCK,
"Laps"

I was ten years old. She was sitting on the large bed with my father. It was late September. The bedspread was a dark burgundy, the sun hovering like a lozenge over Fort Washington Avenue. I had walked down the hill from my aunt's house and was sitting alone in the living room reading. Suddenly I heard a sound like a stifled bird's cry coming from the bedroom. I went on tiptoe and opened the door.

She was sitting there, on the bed with my father. They were holding hands. In the other hand, my father was holding a white pail. It was the same pail my grandmother used to urinate in. But now it was my mother, her head held like a spigot over the white porcelain, who was using the pail. A strange light was shining in her eyes. She was holding her face above the pail, vomiting into it.

I didn't want to look, yet I felt a strange fascination with what I was seeing. The vomit was deep green, like pea soup. I couldn't help myself and kept standing there, watching my mother's throat heave like a clogged garden hose over the pail. Suddenly, my father looked up and saw me. He asked me to go get my mother some mints. I walked out into the living room, where the mints were where they had always been — in a small, silver tray behind the glass door of the Biedermeier cabinet my parents had brought from Germany. They were white, like the pail.

I took the tray and went back into the bedroom. My mother had stopped vomiting now, but the vomit was still there in the pail. She smiled and took some mints from my hand. *Thank you, darling,* she said, *thank you, darling.* She spoke in English.

I turned to walk out of the room. She was still there, on the bed, holding my father's hand. *Thank you, darling,* she said again. *Thank you.* It was the last time I ever saw her sitting up.

2

The men came early in the morning — two of them, dressed in white and black. They wheeled the large bed silently into the corner of the room. It stood there like a huge, white dinosaur, silent as sleep. It stood in the same place I had slept as a child and dreamt of falling. But now it was my mother who was falling, who fell into the fresh sheets, white as the pail had been white, clean as snow.

Suddenly, the house began filling with people, strangers in dark suits carrying small black bags, relatives I hadn't seen in a long time. I walked into the room, like a comma within the long sentence of intruders who had been in and out of the apartment all morning. I wanted to turn the large crank at the foot of the bed and make my mother's head go up again. There was something fun about turning it, like yanking water from a very deep well, helping it to rise.

But my mother wouldn't rise. It seemed as if all the rising had gone out of her, and she just lay there, like an old boxer too tired to get up after being knocked down for the last time. I turned the crank and cranked her head up until she nearly looked right into my eyes.

Leaves were falling from the trees outside on Fort Washington Avenue. It was Monday, September 21, 1959.

3

I woke, sick in my own flesh with the thought of her. I got out of my bed. I felt like a fever carrying a body and walked back into her room. She lay there, perfectly still, a large spider's web of tubes running from all sides of her like cables out of some celestial battery.

I stood at the door and stared, as if I were scouring the heavens in search of a galaxy. I waited and waited. Nothing rose. Nothing except a small armada of bubbles rising into the glass bottle they had hooked up beside her. They rose into the dense liquid like the last breath of a drowning swimmer, like words trying to say: *I am still here, son. I am still here.*

4

For weeks after she died, I asked everyone who had been near her those last days when they last heard the sound of her voice. I must have already known that the voice was the heart's harp, and I wanted to know what chord, in the end, had issued from hers.

All day, we had eked, the two of us, our illnesses into the feverish air. Now it was nighttime. All day I had stayed in bed, mimicking her. Now I rose, opening the door to the bedroom, and stood there watching. I felt as if I were standing on a threshold to somewhere I had never been. I felt as if I were *her* mother, as if I myself were a woman. She just lay there on the high bed, cranked nearly down, her eyes half open.

I went in and stood beside her. I could hear her breath rising, like a wounded bird's, from beneath the blanket. I could see her right arm extending into its circuitry of sugar. I placed a small, warm hand on hers. Her eyes fluttered. I whispered, as softly as I could, as if not wanting to wake someone: *Good night, Mom.*

There was a long silence. It seemed like my words were passing to somewhere very far off. She opened her eyes, as if she had suddenly been called back from somewhere she was eager to get to. I felt two fingers curl, ever so lightly, around my own.

At first she said nothing. Then, as if by a heroic effort, her lips began to move. It seemed like hours passed before a word finally

came. *Good night, darling,* I heard her say, *Good night darling* —
words that would echo for years through my silenced life.

5

All morning I begged them to let me enter the room. *Later,* they
kept saying. *Later, later.* All morning I listened to the sound of the
bedroom door opening and closing, opening and closing. I could
hear them all descending on her — the neighbors; her brother, Berthold; my father's sisters; a flotilla of doctors with their little black
bags; the rabbi with his assorted *brochas.* Our house was a garden
of death, and, like bees arriving to gather pollen, they all came to
gather around her.

After I had begged all morning to enter, someone — I can't remember who — came and led me to the bedroom door. I remember
looking at the hallway clock. It was 2:00 in the afternoon. Opening
the door, I saw the burgundy bedspread again. I felt afraid, at first,
to turn my head toward the large ghost of the bed where she lay.

Finally, though, I did turn my head. What I saw terrified me: Her
eyes, glazed as if they were coated with shellac, were wide open,
staring up at me. Years later, in my hunger for the mock coherence
of metaphor, I would watch two Chinamen pull a Northern pike
from the St. Lawrence River and, in the death struggle of that huge
fish, would see again those eyes as I saw them now. But now I had
nothing to compare them to, and, looking as if into a deep, bot-
tomless well, I looked for the first time, Death in its very face and
called it *Mother.*

But she didn't answer. Like a trapped fly dissolving into a spider's
web, she lay there, the mute syllables of another country issuing
from her. *Mother,* I called out again, *Mother. Mother.*

Twenty-five years later, I would still be speaking whatever words
came to me into the long silence of what she answered.

6

I woke to a commotion of rabbis and the scent of dying. Death
itself had slunk through the halls like a serpent during the night,
choking the breath from her. Now, returned to her original inno-

cence, she was merely a body again, and I couldn't overcome the desire to kiss her. I wanted to go into the room where her body lay — body from which I had never fed, body whose naked breasts I had never seen — and kiss the body good-bye. I wanted to hold her, mother of no milk, one last time, to place my mouth against her mouth and breathe the life back into it.

I started toward the room. Hands restrained me. Voices said: *Not yet. Not yet.* What could I do? I waited, listening to the sound of doors opening and closing, wheels rolling down the hallway, the whispered voices of strangers. I knew what they must be doing but couldn't believe it. *Wait,* they told me. *Wait. We'll let you in.*

No one knew what they were doing. No one knew how long a man mourns, mutely, for a child's missed mourning. Suddenly, the small concertina of wheels and doorbells stopped. The whole house grew terribly silent. Someone came into my room to get me. It was my friend Raymond's father, Kurt, our family's accountant. I was crying. *You can go in now,* he told me. *You can go in now.*

Slowly, I turned the knob to the bedroom door. I turned my eyes from the burgundy bedspread to where I hoped I would find her. The bed was still there. The sheets were still perfectly white, as though not even death had been able to dirty them. But she was gone. They had taken her away while holding me prisoner in the back room. Now she wasn't even a body anymore.

For the next twenty-five years, I would blow kisses into the emptiness I found there.

7

All day I watched the playoffs on TV. Small processions of grief echoed like commercials through the house. The low stools were being recalled from their closets like pinch hitters. For months, I had emptied my sadness into her. Now that they had taken her body, I no longer wanted to know the grief of bodies. I wanted, merely, to think of strikeouts and passed balls, the living heroics of the great catch.

That night, the ball game over, my father called me into the room where she had died. I stood before the Biedermeier dresser, eyes to the ground, as he bent to open the bottom drawer. There — neatly folded as if waiting, still, for her body — was her pink nightgown. I watched it rise like a loaf of bread in my father's trembling hands, moving toward me.

Slowly, my father lifted the nightgown to his own lips. He whispered a blessing in Hebrew. Then, instead of the body I had so wanted to kiss, my father held the empty nightgown against my face and whispered in German. "*Gib unsre Mama einen letzten Kuss,*" Give our mother one last kiss. Terrified, I closed my eyes and made the puckering sound of a feigned kiss as I felt the cold silk pressing against my lips.

Ever since then, I have turned my face away from women's eyes.

8

It was a beautiful day. I was at my friend Raymond's, where they had sent me. I could hear the church bells ringing along Fort Washington Avenue. I looked out the window and saw a serpent of black cars lined up along the curb, a procession of shoulders wrapped in fur entering them. I couldn't keep myself from watching as they drove off. I tried to look into the windows of each of the cars. I didn't want to miss, again, her body.

Suddenly, I found myself sitting on the floor with Raymond, laughing wildly. I laughed and laughed, until my whole stomach hurt but couldn't stop. *Your mother has just died,* I said to myself. *How can you be laughing this way?*

I've forgotten everything else about that day, though I tried for years to remember. I've forgotten when they came home, what they said, whether or not the rabbi took me into my room again to say it was all for me. But I remember, always, that long, wild, bellyaching laugh and the long serpent of black cars, and wonder whether, had I wept then, I might have been spared the long, silent weeping since.

I wonder whether, had I wept then, I might have wept for real.

CHAPTER 6

Muses

She knows the darkness
is only a passage
between light and light,
that the wisteria
climbing the house
are real, and lust
only tenderness gone wild
in the wrong field.
She is the one who is
always fertile in times
of barrenness, the one
with the silver hair
carrying a candle
through the long tunnel.

She is Halcyone,
calming the waters
after all my deaths;
she is Eurydice,
refusing to fade
when I look behind me.
She is the one
who wakes
with her arms around me
when I wake alone.

— MARTIN WEINSTOCK,
"The Woman Inside"

It was several months after my mother's death that I stopped my father in the hallway leading from my childhood bedroom to our apartment door and asked him the question that — from the moment I first heard of being "picked up" as a young child — had remained unanswered.

"Dad," I asked as we stood between my room and my father's fur-filled showroom, "what do you mean when you talk about 'picking me up' in Millville?"

Standing a few feet from the door through which my mother's body had been taken from the house, my father then told me the strange, abbreviated, no doubt edited story of my entrance into this world.

"Vee loved you mit our whole hearts," he said to me, "und vee was so happy to have you here mit us. . . . Your mama she was like someone who had a whole new hope. . . . You were our million."

"But why didn't you ever tell me?" I remember asking. I remember feeling only moderately surprised. I remember feeling that this piece of rather momentous news — this news by which my father was no longer my father and my dead mother no longer my mother, by which my uncle was no longer my uncle and my aunt no longer merely my aunt, by which my cousins were no longer my cousins and I was no longer an only child, by which blood was water, and water blood — was of no great weight.

My affections, after all, had been long fixed. I didn't, it seemed to me, love my dead mother any less for having suddenly become my aunt, or my aunt Meta (whom, if the truth be known, I had never been able to *stand*) any more for having become my mother. What more was birth, I remember thinking, than a physical thing — a chance, mechanical event that shook you out into this world of living and dying, of lies, deceptions, secrets and half-uttered truths? What did it matter who you were born to, where you came from, whose act of love or hate had brought you into this half-lit world or dark hallway where a man who, moments before, had been your father suddenly whispered to you the truth of your life?

"Vee *did* tell you," I remember my father answering that afternoon, "venn you was a little boy. . . . You don't remember?"

2

I didn't remember (and I doubt they had ever told me directly), but what I *do* remember is that my father — with a bad heart, a grieving ten-year-old son and a blind mother-in-law in tow — was suddenly among the newly widowed. From the moment my mother's cancer-ridden, twice-mastectomized body was lowered into the ground, my father's six surviving sisters, dreading that they might have to lend a hand in caring for us, began a frenzied search for a wife for their widowed brother.

I remember the sudden arrival in the mail of plastic models, children's books, polo shirts and Erector Sets from someone who went by the mysterious name of *"die Witwe Hertz"* (the widow Hertz) and to whom — when she finally made an appearance some weeks later — I took an instant, visceral dislike.

To say that Ilse Hertz was not the kind of woman who could easily endear herself to a ten-year-old boy who had just lost his mother is to possess a mastery of understatement. Hunchbacked, a dour grimace perpetually pasted to her face, accompanied by a yapping, overweight, twelve-year-old English fox terrier inappropriately named Ami, she had recently been widowed by the sudden death of her second husband, Fritz (her first husband, too, had died of a heart attack . . . on Thanksgiving Day). Fritz had been an industrial glove tycoon of sorts who — like the legendary shoemaker who bought enough leather for one pair of shoes, then sold them to buy two, and so on — had gone from selling a shoe box worth of cheap mechanics' gloves to running a miniempire out of the dimly lit confines of his basement in Jackson Heights, where, some eight years earlier, his first wife had hung herself from one of the rafters with the cable from their TV antenna.

"I think both her husbands died voluntarily," I would later say to my friends, "just to avoid the prospect of staying married to her."

Ilse Hertz, indeed, was every maudlin story's archetype of the wicked stepmother. Thanatic, fearful, parsimonious beyond the gravest necessity, she was so transparently incapable of anything even bordering on genuine human affection that her very presence — the *possibility* that she might be brought on as the "replacement" for my genteel, loving, always-dying mother — sent me into a fear and depression so violent that, but for the certain knowledge that I couldn't abandon my also-dying father and blind grandmother, I might easily have considered fleeing to the chicken dust- and flee-ridden confines of Millville, where at least (I now knew) my true flesh and blood dwelt and wouldn't (or so I hoped) abandon me again.

"Wem hättest Du am liebsten dass ich hierate?" my father asked me. "Whom would you like most for me to marry? — Helen," he began, referring to the dear family friend who had been like a second mother to me during my childhood and the final year of my mother's life; "Giesella," his long-suffering and never-married seamstress, whom I had always liked; "oder Frau Hertz," this twice-widowed, childless purchaser of children's toys whose interest in me, I immediately sensed, extended no further than as a door into my wid-

owed father's vulnerable heart — to be used for that purpose and immediately slammed shut.

"Helen oder Giesella," I replied, referring to the two women already reliably ensconced in my affections. The third alternative, I felt, was too unspeakable to name.

I still don't remember what, if anything, my father said in response. But one thing I *do* know for certain: On October 5, 1960, just over a year after my mother was lowered into the ground, he presented me with the third mother of my not-yet-twelve-year-old life.

Her name was Ilse Hertz.

3

My stepmother, it became immediately clear to me, was inordinately devoted to prayer. From virtually the day she moved into our apartment from her deceased second husband's house (a move she agreed to only under great duress, I having convinced my father that, having just lost my mother, I didn't need to lose my friends as well), she would sit in a corner, her little black German-Hebrew prayer book conspicuously opened to the page marked "*Morgensgebet einer unglücklichen Ehefrau*" — Morning Prayer of an Unhappy Wife.

It had never occurred to me that the Jewish religion — or the attentions of the Deity in general — could be so responsive to special needs. Daily — indeed, several times a day — there was my stepmother, invoking the particulars of her situation to the god of Abraham, Isaac and Jacob, then proceeding, as soon as the door closed behind my father and her yapping English fox terrier, to torture me to the point of tears with innuendos and accusations that it was I, that mournful little troublemaker, on whose behalf she had been forced out of her attached, two-bedroom minicastle a stone's throw from La Guardia Airport.

As soon as I started sobbing, she would be down on her knees, both arms wrapped imploringly around my upper calves as she literally — tears running in big dollops down her abundantly freckled cheeks — *begged* me not to say anything to my father about what she had done, lest he send her packing to her former domicile off the Eastern Air Lines runway. Indeed, I *didn't* say anything — having already sensed that my father's role in my life was fundamentally one of a betrayer, and not wanting to edge my way any closer to the orphanage doors by further exciting his already diseased heart.

By the time my father and the yapping little mutt returned home from the Fur District, my stepmother had independently worked her way back into a fervor over the subject, and within minutes — foaming at the mouth like a rabid dog, his face red as a cooked beet — my father would be hurling invectives into the air in German and trembling with a rage at once so inappropriate and so terrifying that I felt I had no other recourse but to place myself, tearstained and begging for all I was worth, between my by now nearly hysterical parents, pulling desperately at my father's pant legs in the hope that I might restrain him sufficiently to avoid having yet another one of my parents' bodies dragged, this time openly, through our apartment door.

By the time the uproar ended — my stepmother cowering, prayer book in hand, in a corner, my father wiping the saliva from his lower lip with a cologne-soaked handkerchief — the damage was done. It was usually only a matter of a day or two before I — at the ripe, sophisticated age of eleven — would be off with my father to the office of Dr. Leon Werther, cardiologist, where I would watch, terrified, while a vast webwork of metal nodules were pasted on my father's chest and connected to an electrocardiograph.

Paralyzed somewhere between awe and desolation, I watched the small, electrified needle hump and stagger as it charted the series of peaks, troughs and straightaways that signified the perpetually worsening condition of my father's four-chambered organ. Some twenty minutes later, having been told that my father's condition was "not quite a heart attack, but a substantial worsening of the cardiographic picture," we were back home, where my father was put, immediately, to bed, under the watchful eye of his sobbing, prayer-book-toting, wife, the book no doubt opened to "Prayer of an Incipient Widow."

From then on, I was so certain each ensuing night was going to be my father's last that I would wake every morning, until the day

I left for college, run to my parents' bedroom door and — even before making sure the sun had risen — listen for the faintly consoling sound of my father's breathing.

4

When I was fourteen, an age at which little else occupies the minds of adolescent boys but thoughts of hot, initiatory nights with the opposite sex, my father decided to take me on a midwinter cruise to the Bahamas aboard one of the widow- and widower-packed ships of the Greek-American line.

"It is life's greatest dream," he insisted, all my protestations that I would rather stay home and go to spin-the-bottle parties with Elissa Frei notwithstanding. "A cruise. . . . You will never forget it."

My father had always loved cruises. "My dream," he perpetually repeated, "the greatest *simcha* in life." When he had married my stepmother — her tales of lifelong seasickness notwithstanding — he had talked her into taking a two-week cruise to Jamaica and the Virgin Islands for their honeymoon. Armed to the gills with Dramamine, sleeping pills and sedatives, they departed from the West Side Pier — or, rather, they boarded the ship. For it took little more than a step onto the deck of the 1,600-bed cruiser for my stepmother's constricted spirit to manifest itself by sending her body into a reverse peristalsis so severe that half the ship's crew were soon running all over deck, terry-cloth towels draped over their forearms and buckets of all sizes and shapes ready to lurch forward in their trembling hands.

But it was too late to turn back, my father having already forked out some $10,000 in 1960s currency for their little adventure. For two solid weeks, my stepmother, her yapping fox terrier, Ami, loyally at her heels, puked and gurgled a compost of eggplant, spanakopita and stuffed grape leaves seaward, cursing the gods that had brought her into the cruise-loving arms of *Heinz Weinstock, Fine Furs.*

"F-Harry-Stow" — my father mumbled the Greek sounds for "thank you" to the small flotilla of stewards and deck masters who nervously awaited the next eruption of his wife's stomach. "God loves you, and so do I."

But now, some three years later, it was I, with a stomach to rival

Captain Ahab's, who was my father's cabin mate, and, instead of rolling over onto the imagined palpitating carcass of Elissa Frei or Linda del Monaco, I had to devote all my bodily energy to *not* rolling off the three-foot-wide upper bunk of our bargain-rate compartment onto the heart-diseased, diabetic shape of my father.

"F-Harry-Stow," my father greeted every creature with an even marginally Greek face. "This is my dear son, Martin, taking a cruise with his daddy. . . . God loves you, and so do I."

As I'd expected, there wasn't, with the exception of the crew, another being under the age of sixty-five on board. As we sat down to dinner that first night, I was greeted, to my utter nonamazement, by a group of rag-necked widows and spinsters with names like Lisbeth, Emma, Molly and Friedel, arrayed like a cluster of secondhand pearls around our necklace-shaped table.

"What a handsome young man!" each greeted me in turn, stroking the pomade-slicked crest of my simulated pompadour, "and what a lucky father, to have such a handsome son."

"F-Harry-Stow," my father replied to each one. "I told him he will never forget this cruise, so long as he lives."

After four days of at least six meals a day and no exercise beyond a game of shuffleboard with a retired jeweler named Alfred Ostrich from Poughkeepsie, we arrived in Nassau, by which time my disdain for my father — or, rather, my guilt at being the unappreciative son who wasn't having a better time — had reached such epic proportions that I was actively contemplating patricide or suicide. By the time we finally stepped ashore, my only remaining fantasy was to be with a young, dashing, athletic father who would rent a Harley-Davidson and whisk me off to the bars and discotheques, where we would find a couple of well-stacked blondes and male-bond into the night together.

Instead, my father, tossing his "F-Harry-Stows" and "God loves yous" left and right like a man tossing crumbs to pigeons, bought us two tickets on a tourist bus to Paradise Island, where he rented a deck chair, wrapped himself in a thick padding of blankets and fell asleep on the beach (he couldn't swim), while I summoned what little masculine bravery I possessed and stroked my way toward the horizon.

Slightly aquaphobic from youth — when I had wrestled with periodic bouts of asthma amid abortive swimming lessons at New York's Hotel Paris — I suddenly turned to find myself farther from shore than I had realized, where, seized by a soul-gripping panic, I began thrashing wildly in an effort to navigate my way once more into the shallows.

"Dad!" I screamed at the sleeping figure back onshore. "Dad! Save me! I'm drowning!" I must, for a moment, have imagined that my father, like legendary Clark Kent of that great metropolitan newspaper, would suddenly throw off his glasses and emerge, a kind of refugee Johnny Weissmuller, rushing into the water to rescue me, his Jane. But my father couldn't have heard my desperate cries even had he been awake — and certainly couldn't have done anything to help. Sure that I was about to meet my Maker, here, some 2,000 miles from kissing parties, Chubby Checker and the long-held-out hopes for my lost virginity, I began bobbing beneath the surface, taking small gulps of sea brine into my already congested lungs as my father snored on into his dreams of lost youth and angina pectoris.

As I rose for the last time into the light and air of this world, gasping for breath and feeling at least half grateful that I would be spared the return trip in the company of Emma, Lisbeth, Friedel and Molly, I felt a fluid but nonetheless solid sensation at the tips of my toes. Having already begun reciting the mourner's Kaddish on my own behalf, I suddenly recognized a familiar texture — sand! Allowing my wildly thrashing feet to fall by their own weight, I found myself standing, only half gratefully, in what was no more than three feet of water.

Realizing that the gods were not yet prepared to claim me, here on Paradise Island amid the loneliness-inducing company of my father, I walked slowly, rather shamefully, toward shore. My father had just surfaced from his nap when I reached his deck chair. "Well, son," he asked, sitting up and staring out to sea, "did you have a good swim?"

"Great, Dad," I replied, stonefaced. "The water's terrific."

And so went the one great adventure — aside, that is, from beating Alfred Ostrich again at shuffleboard on the way home — of my Caribbean vacation with my father. When we got back to New York three days later — I having gained at least ten pounds and no longer able to fit into any of my clothes — we opened the apartment door to find my stepmother, a rental nurse from Jewish Family Services at her side, in bed, tears streaming down her cheeks.

"*Ilselein!*" my father cried, running to her side, "*was ist denn los?*"

"I hope you both had a good time." My stepmother lifted her head from the pillow to stare at us, her face contorted in pain and anger. "I haf been lying here all week in *terrible* pain. . . . You should never haf left me alone."

"What happened?" I interrupted from the doorway.

"It seems she's broken a vertebra," the nurse explained.

"How'd she do *that*?" I was still naive enough to think of my parents' lives from a causal perspective. "Did she fall?"

"No," the nurse said. "It's strange — it seems she broke it without actually doing *anything*."

"Such a *Schlemassel*," my stepmother chimed in.

"A miracle," said my father. I thought I saw tears running down his cheeks as he spoke.

5

The first actual woman I kissed was Harriet Lieberman of the East New York section of Brooklyn.

It was 1964. I had met Harriet at an outdoor skating rink in Lakewood, New Jersey, where my parents were spending their usual one-week winter vacation at a hotel populated mostly by diabetics, arthritis sufferers and victims of angina pectoris. Over my stepmother's violent objections and relentless sulking, my father had taken me — bored, by now, nearly to distraction after two days in this Magic Mountain of stress and high cholesterol — to Lakewood's one source of amusement for the under sixty-five set: the ice rink.

There — unwaveringly supervised by her widowed mother, Milka, an old customer of my father's, and wearing a short pink skating skirt and tight halter top that made her prematurely bulbous breasts look like small hot-air balloons — was Harriet Lieberman, cruising along on the ice at breakneck speed while I mustered every ounce of my fourteen-year-old will to keep my severely bent ankles from breaking as I supported myself in a quasi-upright position along the railing.

"Gnädige Frau Lieberman," my father said, dragging me over to the other side of the rink and bending to kiss Harriet's mother's hand, "what a *simcha* to see you again. You remember me? Heinz Weinstock — you bought a beautiful Blackglama mink from me a few years ago, which schtopped the traffic. This is my dear son, Martin. . . . And what a beautiful young daughter you have. God loves her, and so do I."

Milka Lieberman did, of course, remember (how could she possibly have forgotten?), and, to my father's delight, it turned out that she and her daughter were staying at the same Sunnyside Hotel where I was ensconced with my parents. By that evening, my father had already arranged with the maitre d' ("Come see me in my showroom downtown. . . . I will have something for your wife what will schtop the traffic.") to have the Liebermans moved to our table, where, for the next three days, I sat, virtually tongue-tied, gazing at the beckoning full moons of Harriet's generously protruding breasts.

Miraculously enough — and with what seemed little effort on my part — Harriet and I wound up kissing behind the elevator our last night at the hotel, and — armed with the tremblingly scrawled integers of her phone number in my dungaree pocket — I returned to Washington Heights confident that (hardly a year after the bar mitzvah that declared me, unambiguously, a man) I, Martin Weinstock, was firmly in possession of that sacred rite of passage into puberty: a girlfriend.

Once home, I devoted myself to my new enterprise with an almost religious fervor. I quickly found myself — over the strenuous objections of my father and the unexpressed but obvious delight of my stepmother, who no doubt hoped the worst might befall me — descending from the downtown train at the New Lots Avenue station every Saturday night and, the one white boy in a crowd of blacks and Hispanics, taking a bus through the most dangerous section of Brooklyn until I found myself staring at buzzer 14F at 228 New Lots Avenue, from whose little metallic rectangle the name Lieberman beckoned like a sexual holy grail.

The pop cultural icon of the time was the Beatles' hit single "I

Want to Hold Your Hand," which had every adolescent in the Western world cruising the streets humming:

> Hey, hey, I'll tell you somethin'
> I think you'll understand
> Well you've got that somethin'
> I wanna hold your hand . . .
> I wanna hold your haaannnnnd
> I wanna hold your hand.

It wasn't at all, however, Harriet Lieberman's *hand* I wanted to hold but those bulbous, scrumptious, globular, beckoning, initiatory, *real* breasts — those nearly hallucinogenic-looking, generous tits. Weekend after weekend, her mother having gone to bed, I would back Harriet against their dining-room wall and shove the quivering serpent of my tongue more than halfway down her throat while reaching, like a drowning passenger in search of a life raft, for the steel-rimmed barricade of her D-cup bra.

Beyond the occasional split second of what we referred to in those days as a "dry feel," however, the best efforts of my wildly jabbing left and right hands got me little more than a clutch of polyester and a sternly reprimanding "not yet." Fatigued and frustrated, wanting at the very least to see close-up the twin objects of my fervor, I finally suggested that we go for a swim one Sunday afternoon at the Highbridge Athletic Center, located near our apartment in Washington Heights. The idea was that — stimulated by the refreshing rush of water in and around the various orifices and protuberances of her body, aroused by the sight of me in a scrawny little bathing suit bolstered by a jock strap — Harriet would be unable to resist later submitting to the clutch and sweep of my efforts in my parents' hopefully empty (they usually went to funerals on Sundays) apartment.

Everything went as planned until we got to the pool, where Harriet emerged from the girls' locker room wearing a two-piece sequined lavender bathing suit whose top enticingly surrounded a pair of boobs significantly larger than even my rapacious imaginings had been able to conjure up. No doubt realizing that I was by now in a state of mesmerized, utterly subservient titillation sufficient to render me virtually possessed, Harriet must have decided to milk my erotic subjugation for all it was worth. Walking coyly to the diving board, she proceeded to stand at the edge for what must have been a full minute, bouncing lightly into the air on her tiptoes so that her breasts juggled playfully into the filtered light while I waited, moon mouthed, at the shallow end.

Finally, having apparently had enough of reducing me to a throbbing pulp of tumescent flesh, Harriet bounded lightly into the air and, executing what seemed to my aquaphobic gaze like a swan dive worthy of Aphrodite herself, disappeared below the neatly sliced surface.

On the verge of my first real-life orgasm, I waited breathlessly for the shimmering reemergence of Harriet Lieberman's body into the beatified light. To my utter amazement, and the raucous delight of everyone gathered around the pool, what emerged from the depths and rocketed skyward to the surface was not the ample, coveted flesh of my incipient conquest but two off-white, eerily familiar-looking pillows of peaked cloth, which proceeded to bob and dance on top of the pool like small circular dories.

Momentarily shocked — indeed, stupefied — by what I was seeing, I was virtually the last person around the pool to catch on to what had just happened. With an amazement bordering on horror, a sense of betrayal both painful and familiar, I suddenly realized that what I was seeing — floating serenely as two sunbathers toward the sides of the pool — were the at-last-unmasked, lifeless, cloth breasts of Harriet Lieberman.

6

In the six years between my father's remarriage and my finally leaving for college, there was one thing my stepmother was always glad to do for me: *help me find jobs.* She was so good at it, in fact, that — undeterred by the child labor laws — she managed, in the summer of my fifteenth year, to find for me the much-coveted, seven-day-a-week, fourteen-hour-a-day position of waiter, busboy, bellhop, poolboy, handyman, and children's counselor at a booming thirty-bed resort hotel in Hunter, New York, known as Lustig's Lodge.

The job paid sixty dollars a week, straight cash, and — under the malevolent, gulaglike gazes of my stepmother's friends Irma and

Julius Lustig — I and the hotel's only other employee, a twenty-five-year-old, voluptuously endowed German by the name of Ursula Prehn (also hired illegally, without working papers, and whose job description, as best I could tell, was cook/chambermaid/dishwasher/girl Friday) worked our little fingers to the bone, finding our few moments of respite, as might be expected, in the pleasure of each other's company.

It began, of course, innocently enough — with (for a fourteen-year-old, at least) "deep" nightly conversations about the meaning of life, the limited possibilities of altruism and — of course — the Nazis, about whom Ursula's most memorable comment, it seems to me in retrospect, was how enraged her parents were at the reparation payments being made to the Jews. She was a small-town girl, from a little dot on the map named Dangensdorf, located between Hamburg and Hannover, sporting the kind of large, muscular legs and (after a glass of wine or two) slightly tipsy swagger that must have made her attractive bait for American servicemen stationed not far from her house, and in one of whose company she was not reluctant to show me a rather suggestive photograph she kept tucked in her wallet.

Almost nightly, a forged draft card and an unimpedable hard-on in my pocket, we would make our way "downtown" past the darkened cemetery to Hunter's only bar, the Dog's Tooth Inn, where I would, with all the suavité and panache I could muster, order the one drink I knew the name of — an old-fashioned — and wait, ever-patiently, for Ursula to make her move, to please-oh-please teach me something about the art of love, to help me make with her *Eine Kleine Nachtmusik*. In the interim, egged on by my earlier close call with Harriet Lieberman and my rising scatological fervor, I would raid her room at midday, while she was off making beds, and — like a bloodhound on a fox's trail — inhale in large, buoyant, intoxicated sniffs the mingled odor of crotch and anus that wafted with the aphrodisiacal power of expensive perfume from her soiled underwear.

Weeks went by with little more than this in the way of "action," until one night — obviously moved to a state approaching heat by my latest insights into the ethical imperatives of the ill and dying — Ursula thrust her large, fully salivating tongue into my mouth on the bench behind the hotel swimming pool and — kaboom! — before I knew it, there it was, in my very hand — *not* a piece of fabric, *not* some little adolescent's padded brassiere, but the real thing — a breast!

I was ecstatic. Despite all my stepmother's efforts to avenge herself on the Nazis by incarcerating me in the work camp–like confines of Lustig's Lodge, I had done it: I held, there in my very palm, the thing even my panicked, fur-ridden father couldn't seem to land, the real, authentic, life-giving, *Deutsch-geborene* item: *tit*.

I was so happy I felt like weeping, and for the next month — always somehow waiting for what I expected would be the "next step" that never came — I wildly and exuberantly massaged the robust, initiating breasts of Ursula Prehn. Everywhere — from the kitchen to the boiler room to the still-unmade bed of longtime hotel guest and famed psychoanalyst Theodore Reik — Ursula and I smooched and grunted and petted, until I was certain that I had reached, if not the pinnacle then certainly one of the summits, of sexual satisfaction.

Unfortunately for us, however, one of our tumescent interludes happened to take place in the hotel kitchen on an afternoon when we were mistakenly certain the wicked witch Irma had retired to her quarters. Hardly four hours after she found us (my arms clasped lovingly around Ursula's breasts from beneath the armpits), my father and stepmother marched into Lustig's Lodge, ordered me to pack up my belongings and — with my stepmother mumbling something in German about all the money I could have made if only I weren't so oversexed — trucked me off, virginity intact, to spend the rest of the summer in Pine Hill reading stock market quotations out loud from *The New York Times*.

My father, no doubt shocked and distraught by my attempted re-creation of his aborted love for Claire Haas, went into a flurry of activity, calling various German embassies and consulates around the country in an effort to have Ursula deported for sodomizing his son, but without success. I did, however, see her one more time — almost a year later at the Port Authority Bus Terminal in New York, the day she again arrived from Germany and was about to board a bus for a summer job at the Concord Hotel in Kiamesha Lake. She had written to me in care of a friend, several times during the year, but, when I briefly saw her that day at the gate, the previous summer's heat had all but been replaced by my infatuation with Elissa Frei, and I felt but a tepid flow of the exhilarating juices that had socked through my fourteen-year-old body the summer before.

I tried to see Ursula only one more time — several summers later when, thanks to my stepmother again, I had gotten a job waiting on tables at Grossinger's. One night, overcome by nostalgia and lust, I climbed the wire gate behind the Concord, snuck into the dining room and — on what I thought was a lark — asked to see Ursula Prehn.

"Today's her day off," the headwaiter told me obligingly.

"Do you know where I can find her?" My heart was racing, my skin perspiring.

"I don't know. . . . She's probably with her husband."

"Her husband?"

"Yeah. . . . Mario. He's one of the waiters, a Brazilian guy. You want his number?"

"No, thanks. . . . I'll catch her another time."

"Wanna leave a message?"

"Uh, no . . . that's OK. Just an old friend who wanted to say hello."

I turned and headed off, back over the fence and into the chilly Catskill night. Ursula Prehn — the unconsummated, Aryan love of my pubescence, the scent of whose turgid underwear shall be with me forever — was never seen by me again.

7

Money — along with prayer and illness — was the one other subject perpetually occupying my stepmother's niggardly and beleaguered consciousness.

"Phillips Petroleum?" she would call out from the kitchen.

"Fifty-eight and three-quarters," I'd reply.

"Bethlehem Steel?" came next, in double trochees.

"Thirty-nine and five-eighths."

"*Oy veh . . . das ist furchtbar.* . . . Ohio Edison?"

"Twenty-seven and a half."

So it went, I seeming to have graduated from reading obituaries to my grandmother only to arrive at this. When I wasn't reading to my stepmother from the stock market quotations or going to school, I spent every spare hour trying to figure out how to earn some of the precious legal tender she so arduously preoccupied herself with. One might have thought all this would have turned me into one of those adolescent stock market moguls I had occasionally read about in the financial pages. But the very idea of such a venture, being tainted by its association with my deranged praying mantis of a stepparent, made me sick, and I could turn my entrepreneurial zeal no farther than the downstairs storefront of Julius Hoffman Dry Cleaners on 181st Street, for whom, every afternoon between the hours of four and six, I delivered dry cleaning to various apartment buildings around Fort Washington Avenue and Cabrini Boulevard in a frenzied effort to raise enough money to pay for college.

Among those buildings, rising majestically over the grassy banks of the Hudson, stood the matched set of five red-brick high rises that were Hudson View Gardens, well known as inhospitable to (and largely unaffordable by) the neighborhood's merchant-class German Jews. Awed by the sight of the elegantly clad doormen, and by names like Welch, Fox, Crane and MacAlpine taped to the buzzers (not to mention the generous tips usually forthcoming from behind those doors), I would scud eagerly down 181st Street, often stopping on the way to treat myself to a malted and a pack of baseball cards in anticipation of my bounty.

Perhaps most amazing of all were the *women* who often answered the door to claim their freshly laundered garments, many of whom were unlike any member of their gender I had ever laid eyes on. Tall, blond, wearing long pink nightgowns and jewelry — yes, jewelry! — in midafternoon, they wafted long trails of perfume out into the hall ahead of them, their white-toothed, Ozzie-and-Harriet smiles and perfect English often leaving me with a longing to be American and *normal* — yes, normal! — so profound that I would remount the hill toward Fort Washington Avenue literally praying to die and be reincarnated in some not-far-off East Hampton as a Barkley or Gardner.

By now, of course — the disappointments of Harriet Lieberman and the greased lucubrations of Ursula Prehn still fresh in my mind — the ideal of the golden shiksa was firmly entrenched in my consciousness, only aided and abetted by the tall, luscious, clean-smelling, middle-aged women — think of it, *mothers* all of them! — who, like a flotilla of Rapunzels, came to the doors of Hudson View Gardens to deposit their coins and freshly printed dollar bills in my eager hands.

My senior year was approaching, and I had — between the Lustig Lodges, Grossinger's, Julius Strauss's and snowed-in cars of the world — stowed away enough precious legal tender to *almost* pay for the first year of college at the state university for which I was inevitably destined. So it was with great delight, not to mention relief, that I arrived home one afternoon to find a letter addressed to me from the local chapter of B'nai B'rith informing me that, on the basis of my outstanding scholastic record, I had been awarded a $400 scholarship (the full annual state university tuition in those days) for my first year of college. The check, I was told, would be in the mail shortly, and I was to be congratulated on my fine academic performance and the great promise I held out, for both myself and the Jewish community, for the future.

Having been blessed with a stepmother who would send me out with a quarter for a twenty-three-cent head of lettuce and then ask for the change, the thought of four hundred *free* dollars suddenly descending on me — dollars which would liberate me from having to say any further thank-yous to the father who (I was told) "has sacrificed everything for you" — sent me into paroxysms of near ecstasy, and I found myself whispering a blessing to the illusive and inscrutable gods as I waited for the precious shekels to descend and help free me from the dark tabernacle of Dow Jones and electro-cardiographs.

Months went by, with — to my surprise and growing suspicion — no mail addressed to me beyond the usual renewal notices from Reader's Digest Condensed Books and Stamps of the World. Finally, with but a few weeks remaining before the due date of my tuition bill, I came home one afternoon to find my father alone in the house.

"Dad," I said, "you didn't happen to see that check that was supposed to come from B'nai B'rith for my scholarship?"

"Oh, that," my father answered rather glibly. "Jawohl . . . it came, and I sent it back."

"You *what?*" For one who should, by now, have been accustomed to betrayals, I had retained, it seems to me in retrospect, a remarkable innocence.

"Ja," — I could feel what seemed almost like a hint of pride in my father's voice as he spoke — "I sent it back to the B'nai B'rith."

"Why on earth would you do *that*? I *earned* that money with my grades in school. What right did *you* have to send it back?"

"No son von Heinz Weinstock is going to take charity from the B'nai B'rith." My father by now was oozing a kind of fierce, uninhibited pride. "Anyway," he continued, kissing me a bit too tenderly near the lips for my own comfort, "with a father like me, who would sacrifice anything for you, why in the world would you need the B'nai B'rith?"

8

How could I dispose of her, the wicked witch of Dow Jones and *davening?* I dreamt, I prayed, I flirted with thoughts of matricide and dismemberment, I petitioned the fickle gods nightly for relief from my and my father's ordeal.

There was, in fact, no cruelty I didn't imagine inflicting upon my deranged, death-dealing stepmother. Trembling with rage, my fists clenched into tightly humped nuggets beneath the sheets, I fantasized about tying her to a chair, then kicking her so powerfully and repeatedly in the face that her features themselves would be splattered all over the plastic- and sheet-swathed furnishings she so religiously guarded from the defilements of human touch. I could send away for a gun through the mail, I thought, then pump dozens of bullets into various parts of her and watch her bleed to death while I smoked a cigarette and — like my favorite fictional detective, Mike Shayne — suavely imbibed a schnapps. Or I could, like a misdirected Oedipus, gouge her eyes out and doom her to a life where not even the small scobs of dust, not even the five droplets of orange juice remaining in my glass and for which she lived, would be able to summon her attention from the netherworld where her panicked, humpbacked consciousness no doubt dwelt.

My father, as I saw it then, was merely a victim: He had never loved her. He hadn't wanted to marry her. He had been forced, by his overzealous and manipulative sisters, the Sirens of our tragedy, into a marriage with a penny-pinching, despondent widow who had robbed him, and us, of all our *joie de vivre,* who had changed the presiding melody of our house from "Oh, what a beautiful morning" to the words of that famous, heartbreaking Schumann lied: "*Ich grolle nicht, und wenn mein Herz auch bricht,*" I don't complain, although my heart is breaking.

I asked the gods: Hadn't my poor father already suffered enough? — a mother dead before he could even get his mouth to her nipple; a wicked stepmother who detested him; Julius Streicher and the S.S. patrolling the streets of his city; his true love fled forever to some far-off Chile; exiled to a new country at the age of thirty-three; a wife dead of cancer before he was fifty-five? I wanted to save him — to return him once more to his life of cruises (without me) and singing, of harmonicas and Mario Lanza . . . to his "Golden Days."

There was yet another fantasy I had — a safer one, less satisfying but less messy. I would first poison the bitch, something quick but, hopefully, painful. Then I would dig a hole in her beloved six-by-eight-foot backyard — which, if one took the intensity of her rhapsodizing about it seriously, might as well have been the gardens of Versailles — and bury her there, heaping shovelfuls of dirt on her as the last gasps of painful asphyxiation spread over her pouting, malevolent features.

I imagined the trial if I were found out: I would, of course, argue in my own defense. I would simply explain who I and my father were, what she had done to us, how she had made of our once relatively happy home a dungeon of doused lights and orisons of an unhappy housewife. No jury, as I imagined, could possibly convict me, an innocent child whose life had been joined to that of a wicked witch as unjustly and haphazardly as the lives of Hansel and Gretel had been led to the gingerbread house by bread crumbs.

I dreamt, I fantasized, I hoped and hated, but did not — *could not* — act. Like a young Hamlet, strung out between vengeance and indecision, I paced and fretted, wept and railed, dreamt and hoped. Could not some benign natural force, some dramatic intervention from above, remove her from our lives? The Good, after all — my mother, my father's mother — had died young and easily. Why, now, could Evil not perish? Why, powerless once at keeping the Tragic out of my life, did I now feel powerless again at removing the Daemonic from it?

So, a child filled with a man's hatred, I raged and fantasized, waited and deliberated. And — like all rage not acted upon, like every killing instinct that cannot find its rightful object — my rage went where I wished, above all, to place my stepmother's wretched and tormented body: *underground*.

BOOK III

Purgatory

———————•———————

Life cries out to us: *diversify,*
And love calls back: *to specialize.*

— MARTIN WEINSTOCK,
"Bleibtreustrasse"

CHAPTER 7

Merciless Loves

And when she says,
night, love, night frightens me, you know
she does not mean darkness.
And when she says, *I love you,*
she means *watch your step,*
the rest of your life.

— MARTIN WEINSTOCK,
"Freudian Slip"

Shortly after his late-afternoon tryst with Alexis Baruch in the stacks of Widener Library, Weinstock met Laura Bromwich, an attractive young visiting Petrarch scholar from Beloit College in Wisconsin.

"I've got just the woman for you," his friend Nourit, a lifelong graduate student in psychology, said one night as Weinstock bemoaned his lack of an amorous life. "She's smart, beautiful, kind, loving and almost available — what more could you want?"

"What do you mean, *almost?*"

Nourit couldn't help notice that the penultimate word in her list seemed most to arouse Weinstock's interest.

"Well, she's kind of been going out with someone. But she doesn't much like the guy, and I think she's looking around for someone else. Someone who's smart, sensitive, funny, a good cook, an athlete in the rack — you know what I mean."

"Someone like me."

"Exactly."

Laura Bromwich indeed *was* smart, beautiful, kind, gentle and available, all of which qualities (especially the last) were enough to fill Weinstock — on the morning after their first night together, when they went for a walk around Walden Pond — with an immediate desire to create some distance.

"I don't think we should be in a hurry to establish any kind of a narrative," he said, as she hooked her arm affectionately into his.

"What do you mean?" Laura seemed taken aback by having their just begun relationship already framed in literary terms.

"Well, you know, I think we should take it day by day — no story, no labels, no chapter headings, just get to know each other."

"I thought that was what we *were* doing." A slight look of alarm spread over her usually disarmed features. "Are you afraid of something?"

"Afraid?"

"Well, I thought maybe the idea of getting close to someone after your divorce might be a bit scary."

"Not at all," Weinstock lied. "I just don't think we should write a whole story before we have one."

"That's fine with me." She unhooked her arm and continued walking beside him, apparently lost in thought.

"Anyway," she added, "you don't have to worry — I'm only here for the year before I have to go back to Wisconsin. . . . It's all very safe."

"That's not what I was worried about," Weinstock lied again, putting his arm around her this time. "I just want to let the story unfold naturally, not squeeze it into some sort of box it doesn't yet belong in."

"I couldn't agree more," she said, as they rounded the far end of the pond and headed past Thoreau's former homesite.

2

They were lying in bed, in the spoons position. He could feel Laura's back against his chest, the twin moons of her buttocks against his thighs. Her hair tickled his nose. Her head and shoulders smelled like perfumed milk. His right hand was cupped around the nub of her firm, girlish breast. He felt safe and warm. He didn't want her to turn around. He didn't want her face to meet his face.

But there was something more she wanted from this, something else she needed. Though he wanted to sleep, though he wanted to forget the sight of her living, womanly face and relish the anonymity of her motherly warmth, she turned around. She turned around and began to touch him in that place where so many virtual strangers had touched and excited him. She began to touch him in that fallen kingdom of his desire, which lay like a sleeping pup against his thigh, unable to respond. She began to touch him, and, when he wouldn't respond, she lowered herself between his legs. She lowered her soft, saddened, unexpectant face until her lips were against him.

He couldn't help himself and closed his eyes. He closed his eyes and thought of some other woman, perhaps some stranger he had passed that day on the street. He imagined some place of no real affection, some slightly violent place, and, when he half-opened his eyes, he gazed down at the top of her gray-blond hair moving rhythmically up and down over him. He imagined himself anywhere but here — anywhere but in this bed, this bed of life. He imagined himself anywhere but where he would have to open his eyes and look a living woman in the face and say *you*.

He thought of things he might have done, things he had done when they first met. He wanted to say to his body: *go;* to his eyes: *open*. But this body wouldn't go, his eyes wouldn't open. Instead, he closed his eyes and thought of someone else, of someplace else. Instead of a living woman he could open his eyes to and name, he thought of someone he could only close his eyes to and desire. Someone, maybe, like a dead woman. Like someone else he hadn't been able to look in the eye.

And though he couldn't give and receive pleasure with a living woman, with his eyes open, it was still pleasure he wanted. It was pleasure she wanted, too — though she wanted it from him, with his eyes open.

He closed his eyes and imagined himself somewhere else. He imagined it wasn't a real, breathing, flesh-and-blood woman with skin smelling like milk whose head was moving up and down over him, but some unknown, exotic woman named Rachel, Dania, Lima, Galápagos, Kenya, Tanzania. He imagined it would be great to be somewhere else.

He closed his eyes and felt himself rise into her mouth. He felt the pleasure and the sadness of it, the sadness of being somewhere else, the sadness of holding life in his very hands and being unable to grasp it, of violating what he most needed by calling it by the wrong name. And when his seed — the life-yearning, replicant-hungry, eager, lovesick seed — shot out and entered her through the tunnel that could give voice but not life, he shuddered through his entire body and let out a moan, like someone suffering with a long illness who had experienced a moment of relief, like someone tired of his own pain.

He heard a small, birdlike, swallowing sound from below him on the bed and felt her rising toward him again. He smelled the warm milk moving toward his face. Once again, she lay in the spoons position in front of him, this time with her hand between her own legs, moving it up and down. "Just hold me," she asked. "Hold me so I can come too."

He held her, she who was responsible for both their pleasure, with his eyes closed and his breathing heavy and his sadness so nearly tired of itself that he fell asleep, dreaming the morning would come when he would be able to open his living eyes onto a living woman's face. He dreamt that she would no longer need to be the source of her own pleasure, that the gone faces of the dead and departed would no longer call out to him from the living face of someone who loved him.

They fell asleep that way, like two souls in separate ships trying to find each other in a fog-decked sea.

3

"You're not going to get sick now, are you?"

Weinstock was in Chicago for the weekend, giving a workshop for medical students entitled "The Embalming Word: Poetry as Elegy," and he had asked one of the students, an attractive young blonde named Anne Bristol, for a tour of the Anatomy Lab during the morning coffee break.

Dressed in a short denim skirt with a zipper running down the back and pink high-heeled shoes, she turned toward him as she opened the latch on one of the large aluminum vats in which the corpses were stored, revealing a plastic sack floating in what looked like slightly hazy bathwater.

"Sick?" Weinstock bristled. "Why in the world should I get sick?"

"Just thought I'd ask." Anne untied a coil of string from the top of the plastic sack as he rolled the plastic surgical gloves farther up onto his wrists. "This isn't exactly everyone's cup of tea, you know."

"Well, I'm not exactly everyone — in case you haven't noticed." Weinstock felt dismayed at having been so readily classified with the rest of the human race.

"Yeah. . . . I've noticed. . . . Why *do* you want to do this, anyway?" An odor like stale baking soda filtered toward him. Anne rolled down the top of the bag to reveal the scooped out insides of a human cranium.

Weinstock gulped as he stared down at a flap of almost translucent flesh that resembled the top of a kettledrum. "Because I've never really seen a dead body before, and I thought it might be about time."

"Uh oh." Anne paused for a moment as she pulled the plastic bag down over the cadaver's ribs. "I guess they really haven't gotten to the internal organs on this one yet. So you're not really going to get to see that much. But *look* at those lungs, will you! Take a look at the tag down here" — she pointed to a small white card dangling from a string at the base of the aluminum vat — "and see what the cause of death was."

Weinstock ducked under the sweetly perfumed fragrance of Anne's body and turned the white card up toward him. ABRAHAM CARDONA it read. AGE: 70. C.O.D.: EMPHYSEMA.

"Emphysema." Weinstock couldn't somehow resist staring up at the beautiful olivy skin at the apex of Anne's thigh as he spoke.

"That was an easy one." She smiled self-satisfiedly, poking a gloved finger into a bluish mass of lung above the dead man's ribs. "These fellas are supposed to be pink. Can you imagine how many cigarettes this guy must have smoked? . . . Here — poke your finger into it and feel how soft this lung is."

Trying to seem intrepid for his attractive host's benefit, Weinstock plunged an index finger into the moldy-looking blue mass. "That's awful — I can't imagine why anyone in their right mind would smoke."

"Neither can I," Anne concurred. "But some people don't seem to be all that wild about living, if you know what I mean."

"Yeah . . . I know." Weinstock stood silently gazing at the twin masses of spongy blue surrounded by what looked to be tubules of string. "The whole thing looks amazingly like a turkey carcass, doesn't it?"

"Yup," Anne responded matter-of-factly, continuing to roll the bag downward to reveal the long, muscular sinews of the arms and fingers. "It *is* a lot like one, to be perfectly honest. . . . Wanna take a look at the brain now?"

"Uh . . . sure." Weinstock tried to appear nonchalant as he gazed down into the dead man's skull. "Where is it?"

"I think it's somewhere in here." Anne reached into Abraham Cardona's postmortem bathtub and pulled out a small plastic sack tied at the neck. A lump of gray matter vaguely resembling a rotted Osage orange sat inside. She untied the string and placed the brain in her palm, extending it in the direction of Weinstock's rapidly withdrawing face.

"Here. Why don't you hold this in your hand and see how it feels?"

He extended his right palm, into which Anne placed the brain. It felt like a waterlogged softball.

"Now, this is the cerebral cortex — what they call the gray matter." She pointed to he spongy gray top. "Right back here" — she motioned toward the lower base — "are the two lobes of the cerebellum, which coordinate voluntary movement and equilibrium. . . . Pretty neat, huh?"

"Yeah." Weinstock handed the brain back to her. "Fascinating. Sometimes I have the feeling that this is what my colleagues *really* mean when they say they're 'working on' Henry James."

"It's too bad they haven't gotten any further on these." Anne put the brain back into the plastic bag and started poking around in Abraham Cardona's lower torso. "It would be great if you could see some of the inner organs opened. . . . They're the best part."

"Maybe next time." Weinstock's air of disappointment must have seemed almost genuine. "Meanwhile, what do you with all these bodies when they're through cutting them up?"

"We have a funeral."

"A funeral? But I thought these people have all been dead for over a year."

"They have. But, because the families have never actually been through any formal service, we decided to have a small ceremony for them after the dissections are finished. So the families all come here to the hospital and we have a group funeral in the chapel, led by the students. It's really very moving. And it provides a kind of closure, I think — not just for the families, but for the students too."

"Yes," Weinstock said, staring vacantly across the room of sealed metal vats. "That makes perfect sense to me."

"Well — unless there's something else you want to see — I think I'll close old Abe up, OK?"

Weinstock gazed at the dead man's blue, puffy lungs once more, then at the beckoning blue eyes of the soon-to-be-doctor standing beside him. "I think that's plenty." He placed a hand lightly on her shoulder. "Thanks."

Anne lifted the bottom end of the vat over the body and fastened the latches. When she turned back toward him, her face juxtaposed against the dead, ghostly, dissected body of Abraham Cardona seemed so beautiful that Weinstock stood for a moment, overcome by a profound sense of emptiness and longing he all too eagerly mistook for desire.

Hardly realizing what he was doing, he reached out both hands and placed them on either side of her neck, pulling her face toward him and placing his lips solidly against hers just in time to squelch the gasp about to echo from them. He could hear the swish of embalming fluid around the remains of Abraham Cardona as he pressed her body against the metal vat. Oblivious to the actual woman who was too shocked, overwhelmed, and intimidated to resist, he forced her body onto the Anatomy Lab floor and lowered himself on top of her. In the gleaming lab, among the freshly polished vats containing the cut-up, dissected bodies of the dead, he felt a force he mistook for life run through him with irresistible urgency.

"Ohhh God," Anne Bristol begged as he forced her underwear below her knees and slid his eager, extended organ into the parched valley between her pubic hairs. "Ohhhh Goddddd . . . please don't fuck me . . . please . . . Ohhh Goddd."

As the warm, disinfected air of the Anatomy Lab mingled with the perfumed scent of Anne Bristol's body and the lubricating odor of sex, Weinstock imagined for a moment that he saw a lid open onto the long-sealed sight of his mother's body. He turned his head sideways to avert the confused, frightened, overwhelmed stare of the woman still struggling beneath him. A seemingly endless, unstoppable stream of seed issued, like a long weeping, from him. His eyelids suddenly seemed to be supporting an unbearable weight and fell shut.

There, at the base of the dead, dismembered body of Abraham Cardona, his penis still lodged inside a violated woman he neither knew nor loved, Weinstock fell into a brief, sad, nearly comatose sleep.

4

The place was almost entirely filled with women — women alone, women with other women, women attendants, doctors, nurses and counselors who floated in and out of the large waiting room, occasionally calling out for a "Miss Dyer" or a "Miss Doyle," then accompanying their clients down a corridor to what the Clinic's literature delicately referred to as "the procedure."

To Alexis Baruch's and Weinstock's left, in a dark corner of the room, an Indian-looking couple, the man madly puffing on an endless chain of cigarettes, were whispering to each other. Weinstock detected a thin track of tear-smudged makeup on the woman's cheeks. Directly across from them, a large pregnant woman and what looked like her younger sister were sitting on a sofa, staring off into space. Opposite them, a young black woman in a brown leather jacket and long dangling earrings sat nervously tapping on the coffee table with her fingers.

Weinstock had been here before. Not to this particular clinic, but to one just like it (not once, but twice) some six and seven years earlier. He remembered now, with a sense of shame and embarrassment, how — in a haze of anger and self-involvement, terrified of his own neediness, overwhelmed by his own disappointment at not being man enough to give life to what was begging to be born — he had turned away, first from his girlfriend and then from another, more casual lover who needed his support. This time, he had promised himself, it would be different.

He had tried, from the moment the results of the lab report had issued from Alexis's lips at a restaurant in Lexington, to participate in this unpleasant but (they finally agreed, Weinstock convincing her that an abortion would be a lesser crime than the murder of her own future) necessary ritual. As each of his progressive attempts at including himself in what he imagined to be her depression and loneliness was rebuffed, he had begun to realize that the pain of suddenly finding themselves at an abortion clinic was a different matter for a twenty-one-year-old undergraduate and a thirty-eight-year-old man. It was *he,* he began to realize, who was depressed and lonely.

And now, offering to accompany her to the preabortion interview and then upstairs for "the procedure" itself, he was politely but cursorily rebuffed. "Why don't you wait here, Martin?" Alexis only half-smiled. "I'll come right back down when it's over."

So he sat there, puffing on a cigarette without inhaling and browsing through a copy of *People* magazine. Unable to concentrate, he began to think of what he had read in the various embryology texts he had been browsing over the past couple of weeks: After one month, a beating heart, cells that were beginning to differentiate themselves into the first, shy whisperings of spinal cord and organs. After two months, buds forming the tentative beginnings of arms, legs, fingers, toes. After three months, he conjectured — perhaps at this very second — the first wisps of a soul, the first half-formed dreams uttered out into the dark, wet cavity of the womb.

Contemplating the glaring contrast between his original complicity and his present superfluousness, Weinstock felt a wave of anger well up inside him. "The ways we miss our life *are* life," a poet had once written. So, perhaps, were the ways we missed our deaths. And he was beginning to feel that he had already missed more than enough of both.

Some thirty-eight years earlier, he realized as he sat blowing trains of smoke into air, he himself might have come close to being the subject of "the procedure." Some thirty-eight years ago, had this possibility been available, a vacuum hose might have been inserted into Meta Loeb's womb and the power turned on. And he, Weinstock, would have been earlier, and more irrevocably, among the dying.

He was roused from these reveries by the sudden reappearance of the attendant, who informed him that "your friend is doing fine. She'll be down in a few minutes." Unseen by him, untouched by him, the deed was done. What might once have spoken was now forever silent. What might have dreamt had now been sucked back into the darkness of no dreams. What might have issued out and turned its living face toward the light of the living had now been claimed forever by the already overpopulated villages of the dead and dying.

Alexis entered the waiting room and walked toward him.

"How'd it go?" he asked.

"Fine," she replied, as though he had asked about a visit to the dentist. "I'm starving. . . . Can we get something to eat?"

Heading back toward Cambridge, they stopped at the International House of Pancakes conveniently located just a quarter mile from the clinic. "They must do a helluva business," Weinstock joked unsuccessfully as they entered.

Alexis ordered blueberry pancakes. He ordered French toast. They ate in silence, Weinstock continuing to puff on cigarettes as he ate.

"I didn't know you smoked." Alexis looked up from her blueberry pancakes, wearing an expression that made him feel as if she wished *he* had been the subject of "the procedure."

"I don't. . . . Just something I do to keep my hands busy."

Back in Weinstock's apartment half an hour later, Alexis made a beeline for the sofa to pick up her violin and shoulder bag. "I think I'll go practice awhile before my lesson." She shrugged, heading for the door.

"Well," Weinstock offered weakly, caught off guard by the abruptness of her departure, "don't you want to come back and take a nap later? You might be feeling kind of lousy."

"No thanks," Alexis chirped lightly. "I think I'll go back to my room."

"Well . . . can I call you later?"

"Nope" — she shook her head — "I think I'll want to sleep for a while." She opened the door and disappeared into the bright, breezy Cambridge morning.

CHAPTER 8

The Dead and the Old

It was at this time that Gertrude Stein and her brother gave a lunch for all the painters whose pictures were on the wall. Of course it did not include the dead or the old.

— GERTRUDE STEIN,
The Autobiography of Alice B. Toklas

"I'm so worried about my thesis," Nourit Goldman complained to Weinstock as they were having lunch at the Hofbrau, a local Cambridge watering hole. Nourit had come to the Ed School as a psychology graduate student in 1974 and was madly trying to finish her doctoral thesis, a cheerless, massively researched opus entitled "The Lame Shall Enter First: Pathologies and Adult Trauma as a Product of Interrupted Mourning During Adolescence."

Over a ten-year period, Nourit had interviewed some 450 adults in Israel and the United States who had lost one or both parents during adolescence. For the past four years, however, she had been so paralyzed by writer's block that she had decided to occupy herself more productively teaching introductory Hebrew courses at the Extension School. Now, with the famous Harvard "eight-year-rule" about to go into effect, she had no choice but to commit her reams of data to paper or be banished forever from the thanatic corridors. She had asked Weinstock to lunch on this dreary Tuesday to advise her on how best to overcome a terrible case of what was known in Cambridge as *thesistius paralystritus*.

They had been sitting at the table for some twenty minutes, without even a hint of a waitperson to take their order. "Jesus," Weinstock moaned, invoking the name of his least favorite religious figure, "the service sure stinks here. We've been here for half an hour and no one's even poured us a glass of water."

"Oh, I hadn't noticed." Nourit had been gazing distractedly into the air, thinking about the aborted mourning of adolescents. "I'm too busy worrying about my thesis."

"My friends Margie and Jack warned me about this even before I moved to this living mortuary," Weinstock said irritatedly.

"Warned you about what?"

"The service. . . . They always kept saying to me, 'Don't move to Cambridge, move to Boston. Everything's better in Boston . . . more grown up. In Boston,' they said, 'waiters and waitresses are really waiters and waitresses. . . . In Cambridge they're all Sanskrit scholars and physics graduate students worrying about translating the Upanishads or the implosion of atoms in a vacuum.' And they were right. . . . I can't believe how crummy the service is. Why, a person could *die* waiting for someone to take their order in these crummy joints full of waitroids who can translate Aristophanes from the ancient Greek but can't recognize an ice dispenser when they see one."

"My, my. Aren't we a tad hostile?" Nourit opened her briefcase to reveal a pile of computer printouts so thick the table sagged under their weight, along with a thin paperback volume with the boldly red-lettered title TOUT ANIMAL POST THESUS TRISTE: IMPOTENCE AND WRITER'S BLOCK IN ACADEMIC LIFE.

"Have you been helped?" Weinstock turned to see a thin, bedraggled-looking creature dressed in a white smock, her hair rising in smoky curlicues of light blue.

"Are you, perchance, our waitress?" Weinstock seemed to have thoroughly exhausted his residual charm within his first six months in Cambridge, thereby having forsaken his reputation as — in Trevor's words — "the only man I know who eats the waitress and leaves the food."

"Uh . . . yes. I'm sorry I didn't notice you sooner. . . . We're terribly busy today and I'm the only waitress." As he turned to count only two other occupied tables in the largish room, Weinstock noticed a paperback copy of Gogol's *Dead Souls* peeking out from the sallow-looking girl's apron. He shot a self-satisfied glance at Nourit.

"That's OK," he murmured. "I'm getting used to it."

"Can I tell you about today's house specials?"

"Nope." Weinstock was in no mood for a recitation of various béchamels and fettuccine sauces by a Gogol scholar.

"Certainly," countered Nourit, glaring at him disgustedly.

"Well . . . uh, if you'll excuse me for a moment, I'll have to run into the kitchen and get the card I wrote them on. . . . I don't have them all in my head yet."

"Yeah." Weinstock was hardly a fountain of sympathy. "It must get awfully cluttered up there. . . . Just bring me a rare tofuburger and a small salad — with the house vinaigrette — and an Amstel light."

Nourit smiled commiseratingly at the fatigued girl. "I'll have a grilled Reuben with potato salad and a glass of white wine, thank you."

"Martin, you don't have to be such a damned prick all the time," Nourit scolded Weinstock as the young Gogolite headed for the kitchen.

"I'm not a prick. . . . I just get damned sick of all the intellectuals around here who can't put their cerebral cortexes back into their craniums long enough to take your order."

"What is it that makes you so damned angry at 'intellectuals' all the time? Maybe you're afraid that *you're* really not one. . . . Maybe you're feeling a little bit like a fraud here at Harvard yourself, no?"

"Of course I feel like a fraud here, thank God. Everyone with an intact soul and a pecker that can still tell the living thing from Madame Bovary feels like a fraud here, don't you know that? Why, every damned one of these so-called intellectuals you admire so much, whether they admit it or not, goes to bed nightly praying, '*Dear God, please, please let me find some way out of this terrible sickness, this compulsive mindfulness of mine. Please let me wake up happy and stupid again.*' But I thought we were going to talk about *your* problems, not mine."

"Yes . . . my thesis."

"Yes, your thesis. . . . What about it?"

"I can't write it."

There was a small commotion at the table behind them as a pallid-looking man in a blue blazer sat down to join a woman reading *The Annotated Canterbury Tales.*

"Hello, Marjorie," the man greeted her, an air of condolence in his voice. "Making any progress on your thesis?"

"See." Weinstock felt the first chink in his increasingly icy disposition as he began to marvel at the humor of it all. "You're not alone. The whole damned town is sitting at their word processors trying to rouse themselves into some state of epiphany that will allow them to make something living from the dead objects of their affection. Cheer up, Nourit — you're right there in the mainstream."

"Very funny, Martin. You're so damned smug and self-satisfied because *you* managed to sneak into academic life through the back door without ever having *really* put your mind to anything for more then fifteen minutes at a time, and then you exorcise your resentment and sense of inferiority by making the rest of us feel as if *we're* inadequate for working so hard."

"Working hard?" Weinstock seemed truly incredulous, rather than merely ironic. "From what I can tell, all you so-called serious scholars do is spend eight or ten years around here agitating over how you *should* be working harder or you *can't* write or you *don't* have enough data or some other such serious and incredibly boring piece of nonconversation. If that's what you call 'working hard,' my dear, I feel rather fortunate to have missed it."

"Well, what would you suggest I do?" Nourit placed her right arm forlornly on the huge stack of data next to her water glass. "That's why I asked you to lunch, you know . . . for advice. Especially since all this 'hard work' you so contemptuously look down upon seems to be something you've so successfully avoided in your own life thus far."

"What I'd suggest, Nourit dear, if you really want to get this silly thesis of yours written, is that you do something else."

"Something else? What do you mean?"

"Exactly what I said . . . something else. Go swimming. Take a hike. Study Spanish. Get laid."

"Especially the last, I'm sure. . . . But how the hell is doing something else going to get my thesis written?"

"Well, you know what Hamlet said?" Weinstock hunched forward on his left elbow, placing his right hand on Nourit's small mountain of data.

"Hamlet? No . . . what did Hamlet say?"

"He said, 'The hand of little employment hath the daintier sense.' "

"Oh yeah? Well, from what I can tell around here, all the hand of little occupation has is a one-way ticket to Eastham Community College."

"Maybe. But from what I can tell, at old Bait-and-Switch U the only thing all you Hands of Too Much Cogitation have is a one-way ticket to the same place, plus ten wasted years waiting for inept waitresses while you piss and moan about the fates of your various theses. Maybe, if you would get out of those musty cubicles in Widener Library for a couple of minutes and go for a walk, you'd actually have an idea interesting enough to write about."

As he spoke, a hand reached over his right shoulder and lowered a plate onto the table in front of him.

"Medium cheeseburger, a Bass ale and a Reuben with white wine. . . . Will that be all?"

Weinstock turned his head in disbelief. "I ordered a rare tofu-burger and an Amstel light. Don't you think you could take your mind off of the dead long enough to get a still-breathing person's order right?"

"Martin! You really don't need to be so uptight. She made a mistake. I don't see what the one thing has to do with the other." Nourit was growing increasingly irritated that what had been initiated as an attempt to get a bit of friendly advice had grown into yet another occasion for one of Weinstock's harangues.

"I'm really sorry." There was a penitent twinge bordering on confusion in the young woman's voice. "I — "

"I know," Weinstock interrupted. "You're terribly worried about your thesis."

"How did you know?" The girl stared at him as though she had just encountered a clairvoyant.

"Oh . . . just a hunch," he answered nonchalantly. "I know how it is around here. . . . Leave it. I'm not that hungry anyway."

"Well . . . uh, gee, I'm terribly sorry," the young scholar stammered, backing away from the table toward the swinging doors.

"No problem," Weinstock reassured her. "We really came for the conversation anyway."

"Oh, Martin." Nourit kicked him lightly in the shin underneath the table. "You really are one arrogant, cynical pain in the ass."

"Oh, Nourit," he rejoindered, a sudden tone of high sobriety in his voice, "let's get down to something really interesting, OK?"

"And what would that be?"

"Let's talk about your thesis."

2

"My friends," proclaimed Dean of Undergraduate Studies Gustavo Lopez to the thousands of proud parents, students, friends and dignitaries assembled for the University's three-hundred-fiftieth Commencement Exercises, "without your money — I mean, your support — we could not be here today."

It was a bright, indelibly clear June day in Cambridge. Weinstock was relishing the warm late-spring air and the play of light against the tower of Memorial Church as he sat among the crowd gathered for the oldest continuous civil ceremony in the United States, a rite which — from the first words of the university marshal asking the sheriff of Middlesex County to "Pray give us order" to the sheriff's resonant cry some three hours later to the effect that "the Meeting is adjourned" — had remained virtually unaltered for 350 years.

"The debt we all owe to Harvard," the dean continued, holding to his accidental metaphor of monetary exchange, "has enriched our lives. And we will, really, never get away from here. . . . Harvard will not let us."

Weinstock had always enjoyed the figure of Dean Lopez — a rotund, light-skinned Spanish aristocrat with a seemingly endless collection of bow ties and a pronouncedly Elizabethan accent whom, several years earlier, one of the students had dubbed Refrigerator Lopez, after a 325-odd-pound tackle for the Chicago Bears. To Weinstock's eternal amusement and delight — and to the dean's everlasting chagrin — the name stuck: To undergraduate students and junior faculty members alike, Lopez was known simply by the convenient shorthand Refrigerator.

"Mr. Weinstock," the dean, sporting a brown-and-burgundy-striped bow tie and wool jacket, once addressed Weinstock en route to Burdick Place, "I read your piece last weekend in *The New York*

Times." The dean was referring to a story Weinstock had written about having escaped from the Vietnam War by inhaling tent dust in a factory in upstate New York. "Very interesting."

Weinstock had always liked the dean, whose regal bearing and Oxford don's accent cut an amusing and idiosyncratic figure around Cambridge. But he had also always seen him as a kind of logical cog in Harvard's ever-turning promotional wheel. "Why, it's absolutely amazing," Weinstock said to Geoffrey Armitage over a martini at the Faculty Club. "Where in the hell do you think they even get guys like Lopez to begin with? Why, I can see the ad now:

> HELP WANTED: Third World upper-level administrator for prestigious New England University. Oxford or Cambridge educated. Light skin and British accent preferred. White wife a plus, along with a certain sartorial panache. Mexicans and Caribbeans need not apply.

"Why, you certainly are one mean-hearted bastard," Armitage scolded him.

The truth was that there was a certain enjoyable irony and openness about all this window dressing at Harvard. There were, Weinstock had to keep reminding himself, often genuinely likable and decent human beings such as Lopez beneath the surface. So that now, as he watched an undergraduate in a THIS SHIRT COST MY FAMILY $70,680 T-shirt dart through the crowd, Weinstock redirected his attention to the dean's elegantly tinted presence amid a flotilla of gown-and tassel-bedecked dignitaries on the podium.

"There are, of course," Lopez continued, "all sorts of displays of devotion and fidelity to this institution on the part of its students and alumni, ranging — as I'm sure many of you know — from the unbridled enthusiasm of the young undergraduate who shaved a large H into his chest hairs several years ago during the Yale game to the more quotidian but equally valued gifts of time and generosity which so many of you have contributed. And we must, of course, realize that students at Harvard aren't exactly normal or average — or else they wouldn't be here.

"For that reason, the student I am about to introduce as this year's recipient of the Charles Emery Gomes Award for Distinguished Service to Humanity is anything but a normal or average young man. Taking a year off from his premedical studies in bio-chemistry at the end of his junior year, he traveled throughout Central America, observing poverty and injustice, and wrote a deeply inspired and moving chronicle of those months entitled *The Other Side of Life*, which will be published shortly by Harvard University Press. Now, he is about to pursue his medical studies at Duke University, but he will always remain to us an expired — pardon me, an *in*spired — example of the possibilities of compassion and generosity, and of the commitment on the part of so many of our students and alumni to participate in lives less privileged and more troubled than their own. It is my great pleasure to present this year's Charles Emery Gomes Award to Daniel W. Peabody III of Atherton House."

Still chuckling at the thought of an *exemplar moribundum* being introduced to receive the University's award for humanitarian service, Weinstock allowed his gaze to wander among the elegantly dressed crowd, filled with what the University's Latin hymn una-pologetically referred to as "*Lagiantur donatores*." It alighted upon none other than the Sephardic features of Alexis Baruch, dressed in a crimson and black graduation gown, in the row in front of him. Weinstock had neither seen nor spoken to her since she walked out of his apartment door after the abortion, she having refused either to answer his phone calls or to respond to his repeated notes asking her to lunch. Alexis was seated between a stunningly at-tractive middle-aged couple — the woman, to accent her elegant waves of frosted blond hair, dressed entirely in black; the man wearing over his tennis-anyone body a cream-colored summer suit that was so perfectly fitted as to convey the appearance that every fiber had been individually stitched on.

Alexis had turned to survey the crowd while Daniel W. Peabody III droned on from the podium about the sufferings of displaced Honduran refugees seen through the eyes of a Hasselblad 240. Much to Weinstock's surprise, she immediately directed her parents' at-tention toward him with a bilateral squeeze of their shoulders.

"This is my former poetry professor, Martin Weinstock," she yelled across the applause that greeted the end of Peabody's acceptance speech. "These are my parents, Martin — Justin and Bella Baruch."

"Pleasure to meet you, Martin." Justin Baruch's large hand and cuff-linked wrist reached over the back of his chair to grasp Weinstock's.

"Yes indeed," Mrs. Baruch concurred. "I think I remember Alexis speaking very enthusiastically of you. Didn't she study Joyce with you — or was it Kafka?"

Weinstock felt a vermillion tide surge onto his cheeks as he saw the humored, if not sadistic, twinkle in his former student's eyes. "Why . . . uh . . . no," he stammered. "A poetry workshop, as I recall."

"Ah, yes," Bella Baruch corrected herself. "It must have been someone else I was thinking of. In any event, a pleasure to meet you, Professor Weinstock. Alexis is graduating today, so — as you can imagine — we're very proud."

"Yes. . . . It's remarkable how quickly time passes," Weinstock said pensively. "Congratulations."

"My dad went here too." Alexis beamed. "Class of 'fifty-four, Law School class of 'fifty-seven. Isn't that right, Dad?"

"Yup," Justin Baruch confirmed, "and this ceremony hasn't changed one syllable, I'm happy to say. . . . Only the professors have gotten younger." He slapped Weinstock fraternally on the shoulder.

"And the students," Weinstock added, to the delight of his rather resplendent-looking former student. Their small convivial gathering was hushed back to attention by the admonishments of a deeply bejeweled neighbor dressed — to Weinstock's amazement, on this tepid June day — in mink.

By this time, President Atterton had risen several times from the large Jacobean chair used since the eighteenth century at Commencement Exercises to welcome graduates of the various schools "to the fellowship of educated men and women" and was in the process of conferring honorary degrees on several distinguished persons, ranging from the heir to the British throne to a leading South African novelist, thereby welcoming them to the ranks of fifteen U.S. presidents and the leaders of thirty-seven other nations.

Immediately following this, the congregated assembly broke out into a chorus of the Harvard Hymn, singing the collective praises of

> *Deus omnium creator*
> *Rerum mundi moderator*
> *Crescat cuius es fundator*
> *Nostra Universitas.*

Weinstock soon found himself at the back of a proud procession of dignitaries, university officials, graduates and parents moving through the 350-year-old Yard "from the Age that is past, to the Age that is waiting before," and toward the University's gates.

As they passed the statue of the University's illustrious founder, John Harvard, Weinstock saw a large, pastily madeup, middle-aged woman in a pillbox hat pressed up against the statue. She was motioning wildly to a man crouched in front of her with a Polaroid camera.

"Move back a bit, for God's sake, Mason!" she ordered the defeated-looking figure squatting before her. "I want to make sure you get the whole statue into the picture this time."

3

"The only difference between the living and the dead around here," Weinstock remarked to Armitage, "is that they give better parties for the dead. . . . Why, the last hundredth birthday party I went to was for my deaf grandmother Selma. But she, at least, was *alive* at the time."

T. S. Eliot was turning one hundred, and you could have sworn Christ himself had risen from the dead to mark the occasion.

"Why, if they could turn out this many rich folks in gray suits to help the living," Weinstock remarked to Marikovski during one of the University's infinite number of cocktail parties and lectures to mark the occasion, "they'd drive Mother Teresa right out of business."

The University, indeed, had gone hog wild in celebration of its favorite son's centenary. "A tattered coat upon a stick if I ever saw one," Weinstock whispered to Laura while looking up at a Wyndham Lewis portrait of the poet during the opening reception at the

Pink Rose. "Why, whoever described that old fart as having 'a face that had never been young' sure as hell had it right."

"Oh, Martin," Laura chided him, "why don't you relax and have a little fun for a change? Who knows — maybe they'll have a hundredth birthday party for *you* someday."

"Oh sure." Weinstock smiled, placing a palm discretely on her left buttock. "That's about as likely as their naming a new building after Attila the Hun. . . . Ummm, Hun Hall — has kind of a nice ring to it, matter of fact."

"Martin Weinstock" — Laura couldn't help chuckling as she threw her hands up in the air — "I don't know why you ever came to this place to begin with if you hate it so damned much."

"You know damned well why I came. . . . It's why *everyone* comes. As a friend of mine put it: 'When Harvard calls, the dead and the nearly dead answer.' But come here for a second," he said, pulling her toward a far corner of the room. "There's something I want to show you. . . . Look."

Unbuttoning the three middle buttons of his blue shirt, he pulled Laura toward him so she could see the bright red lettering on the T-shirt beneath his dress-up garb. T. S. ELIOT IS DEAD the Day-Glo letters boldly proclaimed.

"Martin!" The usually unflappable Petrarchan seemed unable to decide between laughter and embarrassment. She stood in front of Weinstock to shield him from the others in the room while he refastened his shirt buttons. "You are an utterly, utterly impossible person! Tell me you don't have even the slightest thought of unveiling that thing at this party tonight, oh please tell me," she implored.

Delighted by now at the incipient terror his prank seemed to have struck in his girlfriend's heart, Weinstock pulled her even farther into the corner. "My dear," he said, "you haven't seen all of it. . . . Weinstock himself has written a little poem for the occasion as well."

"A poem?"

"Yup. A duet, in fact. I was hoping you'd be willing to sing it with me. Here it is."

Weinstock reached into his breast pocket and took out two carefully folded sheets of paper, handing one to his date. On it was typed the following words:

DUET FOR THE CENTENARY OF T. S. ELIOT AT HARVARD
after Roethke

He: He wrote real good, he wrote real well:
          He heard the ringing of the bell;
She: But I'm so sad to have to tell
Both: — We're sick of T. S. Eliot.

She: He had a face to greet a face.
He: How they adore him at this place!
She: But's it so hard to just keep pace
Both: — With their love for T. S. Eliot.

He: When he was young, he sure seemed old:
She: They say he wore his trousers rolled,
Both: But we're quite sick of being told
         — How great was T. S. Eliot!

He: I'm Puerto Rican
She: I'm half Jew.
He: I wonder if he ever knew
          Some types whose blood was less than blue,
Both: — Old tight-assed T. S. Eliot.

She: An oil-skinned girl, I'll rub your back,
          In windblown water, white and black,
He: And we'll withstand the cold attack
Both: — Of thoughtful T. S. Eliot.

He: Today his birthday came and went:
          You'd think their passions had been spent.
She: Let's just go home and pay the rent;
Both: — To hell with T. S. Eliot.

Both: — Oh far beyond, dear Thomas Stearns!
He: To where your gyre turns and turns,
She: Their love still grows, although I burn
Both: — For no more T. S. Eliot.

Both: Oh T. S. Eliot, you're dead,
He: A votive candle at your head

She: So let's go home and go to bed
Both: — Enough of T. S. Eliot.

"Martin" — Laura was trying hard to contain herself — "I really think you're starting to lose the few marbles you have left. You don't *really* think I'm going to stand here and make a fool of myself by singing that ridiculous thing with you, do you?"

"Don't worry," Weinstock reassured his by-now-incredulous date, "I'm saving it for a truly special occasion. . . . You are utterly safe here with Weinstock, I assure you."

"Well" — Laura breathed a sigh of relief — "thank God for small blessings. I really don't know, Martin, why you simply can't enjoy being at this place for a couple of years, no matter *what* you think of it. . . . There are tons of people, you know, who are absolutely dying to be in your position."

"They'd fit right in, wouldn't they?"

"What do you mean?"

"Well, what better way to fit in among the dead than to join them? — After all, there's no surer avenue to Harvard than a little *Lebensschuldigkeit.*"

"*Lebensschuldigkeit?* — What in God's name is that?"

"You know — guilt about living. Why else do you think this place throws ninety-five percent of its birthday parties for the dead? It's simple: Make people feel bad enough about the mere fact of being alive, deprecate all their life-affirming, spontaneous, noncerebral impulses as pagan or adolescent — or simply "not serious" — and sooner or later you're bound to wind up in a place whose celebratory instincts gravitate toward the one permissible avenue of achievement: *death.*"

"Martin! Give me a break! That's the most cockeyed, insane theory I've ever heard. I think you've spent too many years on that psychoanalyst's couch."

"You think so, huh? Look at where we are tonight. Here I am, about to turn a robust, life-affirming thirty-nine to a cacophony of silence, and we're standing around with a bunch of old farts in gray suits and crested ties drinking to the memory of some pockmarked, scrawny corpse who wrote probably the most unreadable poem in all of literature and whose life ambition it was — and if this isn't a form of death, I don't know what is — to become a Brit! Why, the most interesting and revealing thing that guy ever said was '*I am afraid of high places and cows.*' That says it all, doesn't it? Air and meat and shit! The great components of human life. And that little midwestern nerd, who wrote his Ph.D. dissertation at this mortuary on something called 'Meinong's *Gegendstandstheorie* Considered in Relation to Bradley's Theory of Knowledge,' was scared, no pun intended, shitless of them all. Jesus Christ, Dr. Bromwich, give me a break, will you?"

"Martin, I think it's time for us to leave. You're obviously not enjoying this. I don't know why you wanted to come in the first place."

"I *love* coming to these things," Weinstock, though not ungrateful to be heading for the door, exclaimed. "They always reaffirm my conviction that I am one of the few still living, hot-blooded creatures around this place. But if you insist, I'd be glad to go home and have you read to me from 'The Pardoner's Tale' in Middle English."

"That might not be a bad idea," Laura quipped, perhaps more sardonically than she had intended. "You might even *learn* something for a change."

4

"Hey, Martin," Armitage announced at Weinstock's door one afternoon not long after the Eliot Centenary, "the Dean's Office called. . . . Sounds important. Thought you might like to know."

"Podolskiy's office?" Weinstock could hardly disguise his amazement. "For me?"

"Yup. 'Professor Martin Weinstock, please. Dean Podolskiy would like to speak with him' is how her secretary put it. Maybe they're calling to offer you Gamson's job. He's retiring at the end of the year, you know. . . . And you're *soooo* much like him."

"Thanks, pal." Weinstock grinned at his smiling colleague. "I'll make sure the first thing I do if they offer me the job is to offer you one-year renewable appointments until you rot. . . . By the way, sport, there is at least *one* big difference between Gamson and me."

"Oh yeah." Armitage paused on his way out. "What's that?"

"I believe," Weinstock said, in a tone of feigned gravity, "that

God paused on the seventh day to get laid. Gamson thinks it was to catch up on *The New York Review of Books*. . . . Anyway, I think Gamson has had his heir apparent picked out for years."

"You mean that little worm Pawley?" Armitage asked, referring to Gamson's favorite former student, John Pawley, who had recently published a lugubrious but critically acclaimed novel entitled *The Secret Life of Ferdinand Pizarro*, written entirely in the voice of the 16th century Spanish explorer.

"Sure. After all, where else could Gamson possibly find a successor who would make him look almost cheerful?"

"You've got a point there," Armitage admitted. "I couldn't believe that shit of his about wanting to have an allergy to the sensual world he published in *The Globe*'s Christmas wish list. But I still think they're going to offer it to you. After all, Gamson is the only person in the world, Pawley's mother included, who can stand the little creep. Why, even Klavicki, who barely ever admits to hating anyone, turns purple when you mention his name. He says Pawley has the kind of personality that makes General Jaruzelski seem like a matinee idol."

"Yeah" — Weinstock couldn't help but laugh at the thought of diminutive, grim-faced Pawley being compared to the former Polish dictator — "but personality has never exactly been the big prerequisite for staying on in the Harvard English Department."

"True," Armitage confessed. "Believe it or not, I think Pawley may even be too depressing for this place. They need someone like you around — kind of a little affirmative action program for the lighthearted."

"And the light-minded, I think Gamson would say. But thanks for the thought anyway, though I'm sure what the dean really wants is to remind me to hand in my ID card at the end of the semester so I won't sneak any books out of the library."

"We'll see," Armitage rejoined. "Just don't forget to ask for the Big T when she offers it to you, OK?"

"The Big T? What the hell is that?"

"Security. You know — tenure. Tell her you've been here for five fucking years, that you've published more than all the so-called serious scholars in the department put together, and that it's time for the University to lay the Big T on you if they want you to stay."

"Are you nuts?" Weinstock was genuinely amused by his colleague's fantasies. "First of all, the dean isn't going to offer me anything more than that new filing cabinet for my office I've requested for the past three years. Second of all, you know by now that this University gives out security the way a dog trainer gives out biscuits — enough to keep you perpetually hungry, and not enough to ever allow you to start misbehaving. Unless, of course, they decide you're The Best in the Fucking World, which, as we all know, they *never* decide about anyone who needs or wants them enough to already *be* here.

"Why don't you say *that* to Podolskiy then? You know the old saying? 'The truth will set you free.' "

"Oh, sure." Weinstock looked at Armitage incredulously. "The only way the truth sets you free around here is that you lose your job."

Weinstock had, in fact, been looking for a permanent job, without success, throughout the first half of this last year of his no-longer-renewable appointment. Having spent the prime years of his academic "career" at Harvard, however, he now found himself both too far along to accept a tenure-track appointment somewhere else and not having put in the requisite time at another university to be considered for a permanent job.

"It's the old psychological catch-22 of this place, I'm telling you," Marikovski warned him one afternoon at lunch. "The perfect trap for a nice second-generation Jewish boy with a mother complex."

"What do you mean by that?" Weinstock asked.

"Simple." Marikovski's insight into psychological matters always astounded him. "You can't leave on your own, since it's too cozy and prestigious and seemingly secure, but they won't let you stay either . . . so your only solution is to fall in love with someone else who never quite matches up to that wonderful mother who won't keep you, yet who makes it almost impossible for you to leave."

So it was with mixed feelings, that afternoon, that Weinstock sat in the waiting room outside Dean Podolskiy's office, wondering why — for the first time in five years — the dean had sent for him.

"Professor Weinstock" — the dean, wearing a dark lavender business suit with a large diamond brooch pinned to her lapel, emerged some ten minutes late for their scheduled appointment — "forgive me for being late. . . . How nice to see you." The dean, a statuesque, elegant woman whose maiden name was Sparks, had been married for over thirty years to Romanian psychoanalyst Anatol Podolskiy, whom she had met on a Fulbright to the northern Romanian province of Bukovina in 1956, while still a Harvard graduate student.

"Nice to see you too," Weinstock echoed. "I don't think we've ever actually been introduced."

"No, I suppose not. I'm, of course, aware of your fine work, and you *did* get my note congratulating you on your Guggenheim, didn't you?"

"Why, yes . . . I sure did. Thanks so much for that." Weinstock felt an uncomfortable air of concordance beginning to settle over his personality.

"Well, Professor Weinstock, I suppose you must be wondering why I was wanting to talk with you."

"Well, uh, yes . . . I *was* kind of wondering." Weinstock felt a pronounced distaste for his own amenability as he sat demurely nodding at the dean.

"Well, as you know, Professor Gamson is retiring at the end of the year as director of the Writing Program."

"Yes, I know. . . . We're going to miss him terribly," Weinstock lied.

"Well, the Department would like you to stay on as his replacement. We are prepared to offer you a promotion to associate professor if you're interested."

Something Weinstock's predecessor Robert Wellingham had told him before leaving for Berkeley two years earlier suddenly came back to him as the dean spoke. "A promotion at Harvard," Wellingham said when Weinstock asked him why he'd left before the end of his appointment, "isn't a promotion — it's a stay of execution."

"Why, I'm tremendously flattered." Weinstock was trying hard to hide his suspicions beneath a patina of gratitude. "But I'm not exactly certain what that would mean in terms of my future here . . . if you know what I mean."

"Of course. I understand perfectly." The dean uncrossed and crossed her legs on the large burgundy sofa and clasped her hands in her lap in a kind of neoclerical posture. "What it means is that the Department is willing to offer you a promotion to the associate level along with the directorship of the Program for three more years."

"And then?" Weinstock felt a bit like someone who was having the card read to him when what he really wanted was the gift.

"Well, Professor Weinstock, then" — the dean drew out the last syllable — "depending, of course, on the Department's recommendation and your work as director — a further decision will have to be made."

"If you don't mind my saying so, Dean Podolskiy, by then I'll be forty-two and will have been here for eight years. . . . What if the Department suddenly decides it doesn't want me to stay on, or that it wants someone more famous to direct the Program? What am I supposed to do then, get an accounting degree?"

"I can perfectly understand your position, Professor Weinstock, but I see no reason at the present time why this won't work out. As you know, we'll be needing *someone* to direct the Program at the end of that time."

Weinstock felt his anger and disgust rise as the dean spoke. If the dean didn't see any reason "why this wouldn't work out," why couldn't she offer him a permanent position right now and get it over with, instead of putting him on trial for another three years? He had, after all, published three books in five years, gotten distinguished teaching awards every year, received more fellowships and prizes than anyone else in the Department. What in the world *else* was a person supposed to do?

"I appreciate how you must be feeling, Professor Weinstock" — the dean leaned away from Weinstock as she continued — "and I don't want you to think that both I and the Department aren't aware of your accomplishments, which are part of the reason we're making this offer. But, as you know, *this* University has a slightly more irregular way of handling promotions than most institutions." The stressed syllables of the dean's voice suggested she was testifying to the divinely ordained rather than the humanly premeditated.

"Yes." Weinstock couldn't disguise the rueful tone of his voice. "I know."

The dean gazed at her watch as he spoke. "You'll have to excuse me, Professor Weinstock, but I have to be at another meeting. What

I would suggest is that you think it over a few days and then get back to me with your decision . . . which both I and the Department hope will be affirmative. How does that sound?"

"That's fine," Weinstock relied lamely, rising to shake the hand extended toward him. "Thanks very much."

"I'm very pleased at the thought of your staying on," the dean offered, striking an upbeat note as she showed him to the door. "Congratulations."

"Thanks," he muttered again as the door closed behind him. "Thanks a lot."

As he walked down the long, carpeted corridor from the dean's office toward the front door of University Hall, a line by one of Weinstock's favorite novelists, a Czech writer now living in Paris, kept reverberating through his head: "But where was that sad funeral music coming from," it went, "the brass band that sounded so real?"

5

"I don't particularly care if the person we get is a nice person, or easy to get along with, or any of that," said the new chairman of the English Department, Paul Weitzel. "The only thing I care about is that it's The *Best* Person in the World."

Weitzel and Weinstock were discussing the new opening for a fiction writer in the Writing Program. The chairman, recently chosen to succeed Lawrence Gentry, a man Weinstock had been inordinately fond of, fidgeted nervously in his swivel chair as he passed an expensive-looking fountain pen between his hands.

Weitzel, as opposed to Gentry (a gentle, soft-spoken man who, it was rumored, spent parts of every summer and midsemester break at a Zen monastery outside Toronto), was the kind of person Weinstock most hated — "institutionally ambitious," as Marikovski described him — someone whose face was a living testimonial to God's dictum (as paraphrased by Emerson) that one can have power or joy, but not both. Unlike Gentry, who belonged to that well-born and comfortable Harvard caste who were the most secure (and therefore in many ways the most trustworthy) members of the University community, Weitzel was one of those most dangerous of men: an escapee from his own past. The third-generation son of German-Lutheran coal miners who emigrated to West Virginia, he had attended merely Princeton as a graduate student, during which period emerged the only two real ambitions of his life — chairing the Harvard English Department, and becoming a German.

Having spent his last four sabbaticals at various *Wissenschaftskollegiums* and *Freie Universitäts* in Berlin, Hamburg, Dresden and Munich, and half his adult life reading Goethe, Hölderlin, Rilke, Lessing and Brecht, Weitzel wanted nothing more intensely than to be able to say, along with John F. Kennedy, "*ich* auch *bin ein Berliner.*" This second metamorphosis had eluded him, however, and he therefore had to content himself with slinking suspiciously around the English Department offices, his pince-nez mounted triumphantly on his small, Germanic nose, mumbling "Harvard, Harvard über alles" under his breath to assure himself that he had, indeed, reached at least one pinnacle of his narrow aspirations.

Sporting a wispy, gray-and-white goatee and a paranoid, furtive gaze, Weitzel suggested in both face and manner the sort of insecurity that, while it always gravitated toward power, was highly uncomfortable with its exercise, reminding Weinstock of the words of Isabella, describing the presumptuous and mortal Man in Shakespeare's *Measure for Measure*:

> Dressed in a little brief authority,
> Most ignorant of what he's most assured,
> His glassy essence, like an angry ape
> Plays such fantastic tricks before high heaven
> As makes the fragile angels weep.

Since taking over as chairman, Weitzel had set about zealously revamping the Department according to the latest vicissitudes of academic politics. Among this first acts had been the hiring of Harry "Suitcase" Gibbs, the country's most eminent — or at least its most notorious — scholar of what was known as the "New Historicism." (How, Weinstock had often wondered, did it differ from the "Old Historicism?") Gibbs's nickname had originated with former major league baseball player Harry "Suitcase" Simpson, a journeyman outfielder traded so many times during his career that he was dubbed

Suitcase in honor of the fact that he could never quite get around to unpacking his bags before being traded again. Much like his namesake, Gibbs was the incarnation of the now-fashionable, globe-trotting academic, a man so adept at soliciting new (and more lucrative) offers from each successive university it was rumored that no landlord could ever get him to sign even a one-year lease.

"Jesus Christ," Armitage remarked to Weinstock on hearing of Gibbs's appointment, "they must have to buy a minivan every time they hire that fucker. He comes with a whole goddamned entourage by now." Gibbs, it was rumored — in addition to attending to more fund-raisers and fewer students with each successive appointment— also habitually arrived as part of a "package" deal, typically including several concurrent chairmanships (English, Comparative Literature, etc.), the editorship and funding of a major journal and the hiring of several associates (including, rumors went, his gay lover, a chauffeur and a full-time publicist). "The Michael Milken of academic life," *The New York Times Magazine* had dubbed him in a cover story earlier that year.

"He's an extraordinary asset to Harvard," Dean Podolskiy extolled to a reporter at a reception in Gibbs's honor at The American Academy of Arts and Letters. "His charm and network of connections are unequaled anywhere in America. All you have to do is open up the newspaper and you see his name."

Not everyone, however, concurred with the dean's appraisal. "He's like a little academic Napoleon," a Harvard colleague of Gibbs, asking to remain anonymous, was quoted as saying. "If you say a bad word about him anywhere in the profession, you're digging your own grave. Why, there's not a damned prize or fellowship in this country anyone in my field might want that he's not on the committee of. . . . It would be like cussing out the Pope in the Vatican."

"That sonuvabitch has more voices that the Vienna Boys choir," Weinstock told Armitage after first meeting Gibbs. "One minute you could swear he was Jack Kerouac, the next he's Jacques Derrida. And anyway, I *hate* anyone who calls me buddy the first time they meet me," he added. "And that asshole uses the word with all the sincerity of George Bush using 'gentle.' "

"He's the type of person," Marikovski, not one easily to bad-mouth a colleague, remarked about Gibbs one evening over dinner, "who, once upon a time, would have gone straight into investment banking. But these days, sadly enough, you can do pretty well as an entrepreneur in academic life as well. The days when the academy was a place where good-hearted, honorable people with fine minds hid out and quietly did their work are over, *kaput.* It's Wall Street now, with a more duplicitous face."

In addition to Gibbs, Weitzel had used his ascendancy to the chairmanship to have his former student — a fiery, blond-streaked feminist literary theorist by the name of Hannah Trouble, who dressed habitually in maroon — lured away from the English Department at Duke, along with assurances from Dean Podolskiy that she would be provided with a magnificent office overlooking the Charles. "I smell Trouble" quickly became, behind Weitzel's back, the battle cry of the junior faculty. When the dean, just before Trouble's arrival in Cambridge, hedged on her promise, Trouble quickly further immortalized herself in the annals of Harvard folklore with an angry phone call to President Atterton. "*Mr.* Atterton," she allegedly told the president, "I want that fucking office and I want it *now* . . . or else I'm staying in Durham and you can take your silly little offer and shove it."

Harvard loving no one more than those possessed of the hubris and sense of personal power, justified or not, with which to resist its allures, Trouble had her new office virtually overnight and was soon ensconced along with Weitzel — in her immaculate maroon clothes and elaborately painted red and black fingernails — among the Department's power elite. Within a month of arriving (during which time she reluctantly cohabited with her long-time lover, former chairman of Latin American Studies Antonio Cabral, not believing, she maintained, in what she called "shared domiciles" between men and women), she bought herself a house in which, according to Armitage, "even the toilet paper holders and doorknobs look like they were designed by Oscar de la Renta."

Trouble was the type of person the academy, and especially Harvard, loved — someone with an articulate and seemingly elegant opinion on every issue, from whether the University should continue its involvement with ROTC to whether kosher luncheons should be subsidized by the Faculty of Arts and Sciences. Indeed, if there was any truth to Weinstock's beloved Taoist maxim concerning the wisdom of silence, wisdom was certainly not an attribute Trouble could be easily accused of. Within no time, the minutes of the Faculty of Arts and Sciences' monthly meetings were replete with paragraphs beginning "Professor Trouble commented," "Professor Trouble pointed out" or "Professor Trouble argued."

"I'm not sure why the *best* person for the job can't also be a decent human being who's easy to get along with," Weinstock said to the chairman. Weinstock had come, in his five years at Harvard, to feel toward the word "best" roughly the same antipathy the Jews must have felt toward the word "*heil*" in Nazi Germany.

"I'm not saying that." Weitzel seemed somewhat taken aback by his untenured colleague's attempted resistance. "I'm merely saying that we are trying to build the *best* department we can here, and I don't think that personality and character are the criteria of utmost importance."

Weinstock's hatred of Weitzel intensified as he sat staring at the chairman, though he tried hard to rouse some scintilla of compassion by remembering what a friend in the Philosophy Department, whose father had been a colleague of Weitzel at BU, had once told him. "You have to understand," his friend explained on an occasion when Weinstock was complaining about Weitzel's contemptuous attitude, "what an uptight, uneducated Lutheran family he came from . . . and the whole business with his father."

During Weitzel's undergraduate days at Oberlin, Weitzel's father, laid off from the mines and suffering from black lung disease, had apparently walked into a bank in Charleston with a sawed-off shotgun and escaped with some $500,000 in cash, before being apprehended some weeks later at a brothel in Las Vegas. "I don't think he's ever gotten over trying to distance himself from what his old man did," Marikovski had once told Weinstock. "He's simply the kind of guy who, as soon as he feels what he's achieved being even slightly threatened, sees the abyss yawning all around him."

Weinstock, having felt the abyss yawning all too often himself, stared at the chairman and tried to arouse an even momentary sympathy for the constricted bundle of near-humanity that sat before him. Unlike Gamson, with whom he felt both a certain identification and a certain repulsion on account of it — Weitzel aroused in him only a feeling of disgust at his angular, daemonic impenetrability, his dark evocation of that life principle Weinstock so hated: the triumph of the will to power over the hunger for goodness.

"Well," Weinstock said, trying his best to mimic the chairman's habits of stress and accentuation, "I'm sure the *best* person will turn up, and — when he or she does — will be *dying* to come . . . . But it seems to me," he added with an air of resignation, "that we ought at least to be open to the fact that he or she might be a decent and affable human being as well."

"I *am* open to that possibility," the chairman replied, rising from his chair and moving toward the door to indicate that he considered their meeting at an end. "But I very much doubt it will turn out that way."

CHAPTER 9

Words

So, he lay, for years,
on the cold couch,
and, brick by brick,
tore down the house
of his illusions, he tore down
the walls and the floors,
the roof and the windows,
he tore down the doors,
and, finally, he tore
at the foundation itself,
hoping a place without illusion
would reveal itself there . . .

— MARTIN WEINSTOCK,
"The Analysand"

"Just say whatever comes to mind, Mr. Weinstock."

Weinstock paused for a long time, as if to remind himself that something *had* to be coming to his mind, blank as it often seemed.

"I feel for some reason as if I'm surrounded by death — I mean, by the dead and the dying. It's as if I can't even breathe . . . can't come up for air. Like I'm choking or something."

"As you often feel that you can't breathe here . . . that the analysis is choking the life out of you. Isn't that so?"

"Yes . . . I suppose so."

Weinstock felt as though he were being lured into admissions he wasn't sure he was prepared to make, as was often the case in his ongoing psychoanalysis with Dr. David Greenblatt. On this day, he felt particularly uncomfortable on the couch of Greenblatt's subterranean office. What he wanted most was to jump to his feet and liberate himself forever from eighty-dollar-an-hour nonconnection to the small, bearded man seated in a brown leather chair behind him.

"Sometimes I really hate this shit, you know." He spat the words out as if he were aiming at the cinder-block ceiling above his head.

"Yes," Greenblatt's ever-composed voice came puttering back from behind his right shoulder, "I know. . . . Perhaps it reminds you of something?"

"You bet your ass it reminds me of something. It reminds me of my stupid, death-dealing, mock-religious father and of all those other death-dealing bastards at Harvard whose idea of a good time is an open reading of *The Waste Land* on a beautiful day."

"And you, on the other hand, really *know* how to have a good time — don't you, Mr. Weinstock?"

"What do you mean by *that*?" Weinstock turned his head to glare at the nearly invisible figure sitting behind him.

"Exactly what I said. . . . I mean, after all, if you're so angry at all of us — at myself, at your father, at your colleagues at Harvard who don't know how to have fun — I suppose that must mean that *you* do. . . . Or am I mistaken?"

"Well, I certainly do better than you." As he spoke, Weinstock thought guiltily of his tryst on the Anatomy Lab floor with Anne Bristol of only weeks before.

"Can you say more about that?"

"What more would you like me to say?" Weinstock's voice by now must have been an equal blend of boredom and irritation.

"Well, you must have some fantasies about how little fun I have when I'm not here with you."

"I'm not all that sure it's worth fantasizing about, if you want to know the truth. I think you're probably so damned comfortable in that nonparticipatory voyeurism of yours that you sit in a stuffed chair behind your wife while she fucks someone else."

"Someone else?" Greenblatt seemed suddenly interested. "Anyone particular you have in mind?"

"Now what in God's name do you mean by that? . . . Why should I give a damn about who else your wife is screwing?"

"I simply thought you might have some thoughts about who it might be." A pregnant silence filled the room as Greenblatt paused. "I wonder if you happen to know what my wife's first name is."

"Yeah, I know." Weinstock was beginning to feel belligerent in the face of what he experienced as a kind of cross-examination. "Laura. . . . What of it?"

"Well, it's also the name of the woman you've been seeing, isn't it? I wonder what you make of that coincidence."

"What I make of that 'coincidence,' Dr. Greenblatt, is that probably half the women in the Western world are named Laura. . . . What do *you* make of it?"

"Well, I must admit that your fantasy somewhat reminds me of the movie *Dona Flora and Her Two Husbands*. I wonder whether you've seen it?"

"Yeah, I've seen it." Weinstock was suddenly feeling on the defensive. "What does that have to do with you and me?"

"I wonder if you remember the scene where the first husband comes back to life and watches Dona Flora and her second husband make love."

"Yeah, I remember it . . . pretty funny scene. Kind of like Henry Miller watching his wife make love to an accountant."

"Yes." Greenblatt donned that frequent tone of knowing bemusement Weinstock so detested. "Just as you see yourself as a kind of Henry Miller to all of us accountants and orthodox Jews and serious scholars and Freudians who are suppressing your natural *joie de vivre*."

The turgid, lifeless body of Abraham Cardona, accompanied by the imploring voice of Anne Bristol, stammering "please don't fuck me," rose out of Weinstock's unconscious as the psychoanalyst spoke. "Listen" — Weinstock nonetheless felt both the end of the hour and the end of his patience rapidly approaching — "if you're trying to suggest to me that I have some sort of fantasy about screwing your wife or that I'm merely going out with Laura because she happens to have the same first name, I think that that's the most utterly ridiculous, narcissistic pile of crap I've ever heard . . . and I resent your even suggesting it."

"It was *your* fantasy, if I remember correctly." Greenblatt's tone of voice resembled a creditor's reminding a debtor of a long-forgotten loan.

"Yeah," Weinstock confessed, "but it's *your* stupid, self-serving interpretation. Which only serves to illustrate my point that if you'd just go get laid or *do* something instead of sitting in that stupid brown chair of yours all day long doing a bad imitation of Sigmund

Freud, you'd probably be capable of some more interesting thought than that everyone in the world spends their life with no other purpose than trying to be you."

"Yes, your world does seem oppressively full of dull, death-dealing people who want you to be exactly as boring and lifeless as they are, doesn't it? — myself, your father, the members of the English Department."

"Yeah." Weinstock felt a trace of sadness as he spoke. "Freudians, deconstructionists and orthodox Jews."

"All so terribly oppressive to your pagan and joyful Henry Miller. . . . Yet you can't seem to get yourself up from the couch, where you lie — as you put it — like Philoctetes stranded on Lemnos, unable to wrest yourself from among the dying, of whom you consider me one." Weinstock had long been fascinated by the protagonist of Sophocles' play *Philoctetes,* one of the original Greeks who, en route to Troy with Agamemnon and Menelaus, was bitten by a serpent and abandoned on the island of Lemnos, where he remained stranded for ten years waiting for his wound to heal.

"Maybe so." Weinstock was beginning to feel defeated by the persistence of Greenblatt's reasoning. "But I think that bit about my going out with Laura just because she has the same first name as your wife is a complete crock."

"Well, you yourself are somewhat well versed in psychoanalytic theory, aren't you, Mr. Weinstock? You must have some feelings of your own about transference."

"I feel about transference, Dr. Greenblatt, the same way I feel about tofu."

"Tofu?"

"Yeah . . . tofu. I like it, but not in every dish."

Weinstock heard a slight chuckle coming from over his right shoulder, then the familiar refrain. "I'm afraid our time is up for today. See you tomorrow."

2

Weinstock had been reading travel books. Rome and the Amalfi coast. The Isle of Skye. Tanzania and Rwanda. Scotland and the Hebrides. Lisbon and Madeira. The jungles of New Guinea.

"Somehow, I must confess" — he sat gazing at Greenblatt one afternoon (having moved, for a time, off the couch and onto a chair) — "my own inner Amazon doesn't seem nearly as interesting as the rest of these places. I somehow don't feel like saying, when people ask me what I did with my Guggenheim year, 'I ventured deep into the Manaus of my soul.'"

"Then what keeps you here?" Greenblatt seemed impelled by genuine curiosity.

"Well, I think, in part, *you* do."

"*I* keep you here? . . . How do I manage to do that?"

"Well, you're the one who's always saying, every time I want to go anywhere, that its' 'resistance' . . . that I need to be here in order to do 'the work.'"

"So what keeps you from defying me? Are you afraid it's going to kill me?"

"No." Weinstock shifted a bit uncomfortably on the couch. "That's not it. It's just that I can't seem to allow myself much in the way of pleasure."

"Yes." Greenblatt nodded almost imperceptibly. "You might say that you're a kind of *killjoy* to yourself, don't you think? That you're able to make any situation the source of your own defeat."

"What do you mean?"

"Well . . . I haven't, for example, had many patients who have ever *suffered* from their analysis as much as you seem to. Nor have I known many people who work at your university who have needed, for some reason, to make it into such a deathlike experience . . . which I gather is what your novel is about, isn't it?"

"Yes . . . in part."

"You even occasionally refer to Harvard as Thanatos U in your book, don't you?"

"Yes."

"But it seems to me that there's much that's life giving about the University as well. Yet you somehow don't seem interested in focusing on that."

"That's not what my book is about," Weinstock protested.

"That's a choice, isn't it?" He felt Greenblatt smiling slightly as he spoke.

"I suppose so."

"And it seems to me — at least from the way you describe him — that your friend Gamson, whose depression so angers and terrifies you, has something of the same attitude."

"What attitude?" Weinstock shifted again on the couch at the thought of being compared with Gamson.

"That everything the University and his life have given him is a source of disappointment and defeat — his family, his financial security, his writing . . . and now even his secure and dignified retirement."

Greenblatt paused for a moment before continuing. "Just as this analysis, too, could become a source of defeat if you choose to make it into one."

"Yes." Weinstock felt something in his chest tighten as Greenblatt spoke. "I suppose so."

"So I wonder what it is inside you that — rather than defeat me, or defeat your father — chooses to always defeat yourself . . . and that then gets filled with rage and blame at its own defeat. . . . Some part of you, perhaps, that *prefers* Lemnos to Troy."

"Who in his right mind would prefer Lemnos to Troy?"

"Who do you think?"

"Well" — Weinstock paused once more before speaking — "only someone who preferred dying to living, I suppose."

"Or staying home and killing himself to venturing out and slaying Paris."

The knot in Weinstock's chest suddenly grew so tight that he felt himself growing short of breath. "Yes."

"As sometimes you, too, have thoughts of killing yourself, if I'm not mistaken."

There was what seemed like a long silence before Weinstock responded. "Yes. . . . Sometimes."

"But there's also another force within you — the one that's wanted for so long to get off that couch." Weinstock turned his head as Greenblatt spoke.

"Yes." He felt the tightness in his chest suddenly loosen as he spoke. "Something that wants to live."

3

"You have the worst case of applyomania I've ever seen," Laura said to Weinstock a few weeks before she was scheduled to leave Cambridge for Wisconsin. "Sometimes I think you just keep applying for things — jobs, fellowships, graduate schools, women — so that you can relive your stupid childhood situation of being the chosen one again.

"And then," she added, "you simply get your revenge by turning the chooser away, like you've kept doing to me."

It had been months now since, with the end of her time at Harvard rapidly approaching, Laura and Weinstock had been "negotiating" about what to do with their relationship as the time for some sort of decision neared. On no fewer than three occasions, he had either asked her to stay in Cambridge and move in with him or, with his fellowship year approaching, offered to move to Wisconsin for the year. Each time — within a few days of making the proposal — he would succumb to a feeling of intense, irremediable panic (much like the kind that inevitably struck during his travels) and retract the proposal.

"Sometimes you seem to have absolutely no center," Laura, no longer hiding a considerable degree of disgust, said. "You approach, then you turn away, and then you turn back again, always expecting the person or thing that's the object of your ambivalent feelings to stay put waiting for you to finally come to rest somewhere. . . . That is," she again appended her statement, "assuming you *ever* come to rest anywhere."

Indeed, it seemed to Weinstock that what Laura said, painful though it was, was not far from the truth. Who shall be the chosen, and who the chooser? seemed the central question of his existence, as he muddled through the obscure and indiscernible pathways that had become his life.

It was a question he often thought about as he applied to law schools, graduate schools, psychology programs, business schools and fellowship programs throughout the world — usually succeeding, but deciding at the last moment not to go. He had to admit that Laura was probably right: "When in doubt — apply" might well have been the motto of the first thirty-nine years of his life.

"Has it ever occurred to you," she'd once asked him, "that you may already, against all your inclinations, *be* something — that you don't need to keep applying to *become* something else?" What was it, he wondered, about someone who was always applying, petitioning, asking to be selected, to be numbered among the chosen? Maybe Laura was right: *He had no center.* He was always shooting his seed, sending off his applications, distributing his petitions for love and travel and a place of rest into the wind, not knowing what it was he would actually *choose* had he a center from which to do so. Instead, he consoled himself time and time again by becoming the chosen, the selected, the one who was wanted by someone, someplace, something.

"He has no self," Keats wrote of the poet's identity, and that seemed to be his problem: *He had no self.* How could you possibly choose anything, want anything, be applied *to* for anything if you had no self?

"What would it be like for you simply to hold still and do nothing until you *knew* what you wanted?" Greenblatt had once asked him.

Weinstock deliberated a long time before answering. "But what if I *never* found out what it was I really wanted? What if I simply waited and waited and did nothing, and then *nothing* came to me?"

"You're terribly frightened of that, aren't you?" Greenblatt responded with an unusual degree of gentleness. "You're terribly afraid that if you don't act, if you just sit in your room and wait as you did that morning your mother died — if you don't hurry up and apply for something — you'll fall into some awful abyss which you won't have the inner resources to get yourself out of again."

"Yes." Weinstock felt a flood of tears well up inside him as he answered.

"And yet when you *do* apply for things, when you actually *are* among the chosen, you become angry and bitter and anxious and disappointed at having been chosen by something you didn't choose — like having once again been 'adopted' by someone who couldn't nourish you. You begin to feel — instead of like someone with options and choices — like someone trying to get himself home through great adversity and danger."

"Yes."

"So you make out of what to others might seem like a pleasant choice between attractive alternatives a heroic struggle — a kind of Amazon, full of strangler figs and dangerous serpents, a Lemnos of struggle and isolation."

"Probably." Weinstock was growing more uneasy with each reply.

"So that Troy, for you at least, might actually be a place of still-ness, of not petitioning anyone for anything. . . . Which must," Greenblatt said, falling into an afterthought mode much like Laura's, "seem to you like a terrifying place . . . a place where a bloody battle would need to be waged."

4

"I don't know why I seem to be so obsessed with these oracles," Weinstock muttered into the air above Greenblatt's couch the fol-lowing week.

"Oracles?"

"Well, you know, the way Oedipus goes through all that damned grief and trouble to avoid Teiresias's prediction, and winds up killing his father and marrying his mother anyway. Or poor old Croesus, who — when he's told by the oracle that his son Atys would die from a wound inflicted by some swordlike weapon — banishes all swords from his palace, just to have him killed by a stray javelin intended for a wild boar. Or Sleeping Beauty's father, banning all those spinning wheels from his kingdom only to have his daughter prick her finger on one anyway. . . . The whole thing kind of gives me the creeps."

"Can you say more about that?"

"Well, I suppose that, in many ways, I think of my birth, my childhood, as a kind of oracle — something I keep fighting against, but can't defeat."

"Sort of like that line of Henry Miller's you're so fond of quot-ing — the one about those who were born unhappy being doomed?"

"Yup."

"So you often think of yourself as being doomed — as someone who is fighting and struggling against hopeless odds?"

"Well, yes, I suppose I do. I suppose that sometimes I think I ought to simply throw in the towel and submit to those terrible powers we don't seem to have much of a chance against."

"Just as you must, as a child, have felt that you didn't have much of a chance against the 'powers' that surrounded you — your dying mother, your panic-stricken father, your overpoweringly willful aunts, your neurotic and stingy stepmother."

"Yes . . . like that, I suppose."

"Which doesn't, of course, give you much of a chance of defeating those 'dark gods,' or of coming out of all this better than what made you. . . . Or, for that matter, of waking up one day in bed with a woman you won't need to call Mother."

Weinstock suddenly realized that there were tears running down his cheeks as Greenblatt spoke, that he was shaking with sobs.

"Let's put it this way," he said in hardly more than a whisper, afraid the dark gods might overhear him. "I don't think the odds are all that good. In fact, I don't, in my heart of hearts, think they're very good at all."

BOOK IV

The Dead More Than the Dying

Why should we celebrate
These dead men more than the dying?
— T. S. ELIOT,
"Little Gidding"

CHAPTER 10

Bungled Actions

the placid decencies a day extracts from us
are purchased at a price some darkness pays for.
— MARTIN WEINSTOCK,
"Civilities"

A
s far back as I can remember, my father and stepmother
had been masters of what Freud called "bungled actions" —
those frequently comical, always entertaining, slips and mis-
haps which, on occasion, lead to embarrassing results.

"You vill never believe vat happened mit us, dear son," my father
informed me as my parents entered through the garage door during
a visit I paid to their house while attending a conference in New
York.

"Jawohl," my stepmother seconded. "To make such a terrible
mistake. . . . I was red in the whole face."

"What happened?"

"We was sitting in the Hirsch Funeral Home," my father began,
"und I was saying to Ilse what a surprise it is that no one von the
family looked to be around — "

"Und your father was introducing himself to everyone and saying
to them all what a wonderful woman she was, and may she rest in
Sholem like he is always doing," my stepmother interrupted.

I had always described the Hirsch Funeral Home, located on
116th Street and Audubon Avenue, to friends as "the bar mitzvah
factory of the high end." On any particular Sunday, some dozen
funerals — mostly of German-Jewish refugees with names like Dingfelder, Hertz, Monat, Berger, Schwartzschild and Katzenstein —
took place simultaneously in its interchangeable chapels of elegy
and adieu. "My parents' version," I explained to Laura (who was

forever astonished that, whenever I called, they seemed to be just getting back from a funeral), "of Monday night football . . . a way of keeping themselves busy in old age."

"Jawohl," my father continued. "Und then, all of a sudden, the Rabbiner was standing up and giving the sermon and schpeaking about the family, und he started talking about 'the deceased Gretel Lisberger.' Und we suddenly realized that we was in the wrong funeral."

"Such a *Schlemassel*," my stepmother said, invoking the Yiddish word for misfortune. "The Katzensteins were such good customers."

❖

Then there was that cold, unforgettable night some twenty-five years earlier, when, after a series of frantic late-night phone calls, my parents and I had to rush down to the Main Post Office at Thirty-third Street in Manhattan to retrieve the sympathy letter my father had just written to Hugo Baumgartner.

Having heard that very morning that Hugo's wife, my parents' fifty-six-year-old friend Lotte, who had been fighting a losing battle with breast cancer, was close to death, my father immediately sat down and uttered forth that venerable staple of his literary repertoire, the condolence letter. "My dear Hugo," the letter began,

> I cannot tell you how shocked and saddened my wife und I are by hearing this terrible news of the dead of your dear and beloved wife and our great friend Lotte.
>
> We know, of course, what you und your family haf suffered in the months of your dear wife's sickness, und she has been every day in our prayers and thoughts. This past Shabbos, I said a special prayer for her and for your family in the Synagogue, in the hope that dear God Almighty should hear our prayers and bring to her and to you in your suffering relief.
>
> As you know, it is only one year since I lost my dear beloved Betzele, also to this terrible cancer, so I know from the buttom of my heart what terrible suffering you have lived, and pray for you that she may rest in Sholem. It is only good that she was blessed for God in her life mit two such wonderful children as your two

boys, who will grow up I know in loving memory of their dear beloved mama Lottchen.

Und I know — as was the case mit my beloved Betzele who passed away more than a year ago 9.25.59 — that you see in your heart what a good und loving husband you have been to her, may God bless and keep her, and what two wonderful boys she has brought into the world mit which to keep her memory.

My wife and son join with me to say Kaddish in memory of your dear wife und our beloved friend Lotte whom we will remember only mit the best und loving memories, may she rest in Sholem, and for whom we will say this Shabbos a special Hallelujah that her suffering is finally over and for the good memories and special friends she has left on this world.

God bless you and your family. Our thoughts and prayers are mit you in your sorrow.

Yours,
Heinz Weinstock & family

I'll never forget the expression on my father's face when, later that long-ago evening, a neighbor casually mentioned that she had just been to visit Lotte Baumgartner, who was feeling much better. Nor will I ever forget the frenzied search and rescue mission that followed, as our whole family piled into the car and headed down to the Main Post Office.

I had never seen so many bags of mail piled in a single place. The thought of having to retrieve the small white envelope addressed, in my father's nearly hieroglyphic scrawl, to "Mr. Hugo Baumgartner & family" seemed, even to an eleven-year-old boy, an insurmountable task. Yet retrieve it we did, after hours of sifting through thousands of letters destined for postal district 33, though it was only recently, thinking back on the contents of that never-delivered letter as my parents returned from the wrong funeral, that I became aware of the strange quality of my father's eagerness.

I've often wondered, since that panicked late-night rush and mad search through stacks of not yet sorted mail, what might have happened had the letter marking the passing of Lotte Baumgartner (who, following a remarkable recovery, recently celebrated her eighty-fifty birthday) actually been received. I wonder what it would have been like for a still-living woman to read a letter of condolence for her own death. I often wonder why my father was so eager to pronounce a woman dead, while a not yet completed life still blazed within her.

2

februar 26, '88

Dear Son,

Wir haben viel happiness mit your visit to us . . . wir danken you for all your LOVE STAY ONLY HEALTHY WITH US FOR MANNY YEARS TO COME. I hope that you had a *good* trip on Sunday — PLEASE TAKE CARE OF YOU ON ALL YOUR WAYS — enclosed a POEM from our Rabbi's wife which she made to Viola (lady which I introduced to you in Temple on Friday evening . . . she was sitting on the table with us too . . . Remember her?)

Mama und I found last week an unbeliefable Koincidence . . . YOU WILL NOT BELIEVE IT, it is a mirakle. I was going through my old papers — death announcements from the AUFBAU from this time when our dear Mama Betzele passed away 9.25.59 may she rest in Sholem, und Mama and I discovered that the announcement of the dead of her dear husband #2 Fritz who died in the same week was on the *SAME PAGE* in the AUFBAU right next to our MAMA. . . . IS IT NOT A MIRAKLE??? IMagine, that these two people who had in the same week such a Schlemassel — such a bad luck und tragedie — would come to be married. . . . I think it is AMAZING.

Enclosed I have made for you a Kopie of the dead announcements. . . . I think it will be very interesting for you. KEEP IT PLEASE AS A MEMORIAL of our dear Betzele, und of this strange Koincidence. Mama she was *amazed* by this discovery . . . jawohl, the life is funny, is it not so dear son?

PLEASE REMEMBER: 3–7–88 Helen's 90th birthday. Please take *good care of* her wonderful *KIDDISH CUP* — hold it in honor, ein present it was for you from her . . . we owe to her many, many thanks — CUP has a great value, about $1,000 — she was our dearest friend — *MAY SHE REST IN PIECE.*

SORRY — you forgot to take with you the whole big ENVELOPE filled with all LOVELY MEMORIES from Miss Lieberman's time (you remember her??? she was your first girlfriend love. . . . O

JUgend O Jugend was warst Du so schön!!), and of many many other lovely MEMORIES. ALL LOVE FROM MOM . . . she is too busy with cleaning . . . you know how she is if she has a cleaning women? *Mechuge* . . . let her work.

LOVE,
DADY

I unfolded the tattered piece of paper contained in the envelope. On it was Xeroxed the obituary page from the Friday, October 9, 1959, edition of the German-Jewish weekly, *Aufbau*. Staring up at me, in large boldfaced letters, was the following black-bordered announcement:

On October 1, 1959, following a brief, severe illness shortly after the completion of his 60th year of life, my dearly beloved husband, son-in-law, our dear brother-in-law, uncle, nephew and cousin

FRITZ HERTZ
(formerly of Mannheim)

passed from us. In deep mourning:

ILSE HERTZ verw. Dingfelder
geb. Fleischhaker

45–15 37th Avenue
Elmhurst 70, L.I., N.Y.

I simultaneously wish to thank those who sent them for their much-appreciated expressions of sympathy.

Directly catty-corner from it on the same page, was the following piece of ancillary news:

Pain-filled, we wish to inform you that our dearly
beloved wife and mami, our faithfully caring
daughter and sister, sister-in-law, aunt and cousin

BETTINA WEINSTOCK
geb. Loeb

was forever taken from us.
All who knew her will be capable of measuring
our loss and pain.
In the name of the grieving survivors:

HEINZ WEINSTOCK

801 W. 181 Street
New York 33 N.Y. — Millville, N.J.

We wish simultaneously to thank all those for the
innermost evidence of their shared grieving.

I stared silently at the twin obituaries for some time before folding
and replacing them in my father's envelope. By now, there was little
amazement left in my father's unearthing of various "unbelievable
Koincidences," and "mirakles." There was, in fact, beginning to be
a terrible logic to it all, a kind of order.

I opened the bottom drawer of my desk and dropped the letter
into the long-festering pile of letters and obituaries my father had
sent me over the years. Then I did the only thing I could think of
as I surveyed the long history of coincidences and miracles I had
inherited as the birthright of that early exchange. I put my head
down on the desk and began to laugh uncontrollably.

Then I started to cry.

3

Thanks to the diligent removal of their bodies in order to protect me from trauma, I have never actually *seen* the dead body of anyone close to me. I have seen the dead on occasion, but always in the form of someone from whom I've had a certain emotional distance, a consoling remoteness.

The first such person was one of my guests at Lustig's Lodge, where I first encountered the initiatory breasts of Ursula Prehn during the summer between my sophomore and junior years in high school. The man was the eighty-five-year-old father and father-in-law of a middle-aged couple, the Kellers, who descended promptly every morning at 7:45 for breakfast. A ruddy-faced semiinvalid who, his daughter informed me, had had a pacemaker implanted in his chest after suffering a nearly critical stroke earlier that year, the old man sat placidly at the table making a sequence of low, moaning sounds, always in fours, while I set his customary breakfast of prune juice, poached eggs, whole wheat toast and Sanka on the place mat in front of him.

Uh uh uh uh he would intone in an abbreviated code of gratitude and conviviality that I was beginning to grow rather fond of. *Uh uh uh uh* he repeated with an iambic lilt. *Uh uh uh uh.*

On the final morning of the Kellers' stay, as the limousine that was to take them back to New York pulled up at the hotel door, I sensed all was not quite right with the old man.

Uh uh uh he went as I placed the prune juice in its usual position directly to the left of his fork. *Uh uh uh* he went when I returned moments later with the poached eggs and toast. *Uh uh uh. Uh uh uh.*

Suddenly, as I bent over to put his cup of Sanka in its usual position between the prune juice and the whole wheat toast, the elderly gentleman's trisyllabic complexion went from a pale pink to a deeply crimsoned red. A prolonged and unaccented *uh uh uh* echoed from his lips, and his head fell to the side, like a ball knocked from a pedestal.

"Daddy!" screamed his distraught daughter. I stood in startled amazement at the split-second transformation I had just witnessed.

"I'm afraid he's dead," the physician seated at the next table whispered calmly.

Indeed, the old man *was* dead, just like that, his four beats having been reduced to an inauspicious three. When the ambulance finally came to take him away some forty minutes later, the drivers carried the dead man out just as he was — still seated, head to the side, in the wooden chair directly beside his nearly hysterical daughter and speechless son-in-law.

Years later, teaching an introductory prosody course whose subject matter I knew little or nothing about, I would tell the story of the old man's passing as living proof of the fact that "when you lose your rhythm, you lose your life," a principle whose truth I'm not entirely unconvinced of to this day.

The second, and last, dead person whom I had the displeasure of encountering was Penelope Dekmejian, the daughter and stepdaughter of my good friends Eudora and Richard. The twenty-year-old, deeply troubled girl had taken an overdose of antidepressants while visiting her father, an Armenian investment banker, in Houston during her senior year in college. I had only seen Penelope once during her lifetime but remembered her as a lithe, pale-faced, ectomorphic creature who aspired to be a jazz dancer in New York. So I was all the more shocked to find a bloated, hair-bedecked, roseated corpse staring up at me from the coffin at Zweig's Funeral Home in Long Island City.

"My God, she's changed," I, much to my embarrassment, found myself muttering out loud as I stared down at the puffed, painted body of the once beautiful twenty-year-old.

"She certainly has," replied the girl's grief-stricken aunt, who was standing behind me in the viewing line.

These two rather close-up, if not highly personal, experiences with the physical afterlives of the deceased led me to believe that the body is, indeed, inherently opposed to any prolonged immortality on the part of the soul. I began to suspect that I had been spared a great deal of pain and disillusionment by having my mother's body removed before I could pay it my last respects that blustery fall day in 1959, a sequence of events that had also been true of the first death that touched me intimately — that of my parakeet Jerry, in March of 1956.

The poor bird — much like old Mr. Keller that summer morning at Lustig's Lodge — turned bright red one night on its perch, its eyes shut and trembling helplessly. I futilely attempted to rouse it with a combination of whistles, simulated parakeet noises and German beer-drinking songs, all of which proved equally unsuccessful.

"Promise to wake me if anything happens to Jerry during the night," I implored my father in exchange for agreeing to go to bed. But the next morning, when I rose and ran to the kitchen pantry, where Jerry's cage had hung for the past seven years, there was only an empty next of filigreed metal where my dying parakeet had been hours before.

My father — ever eager to insulate me from the traumas of grief — had taken the dead bird from its cage during the night and thrown it down the kitchen dumbwaiter, so that I would be spared the sadness of finding my most treasured living attachment dead the next morning.

Clearly the dead were different — cold, unconvivial, monolithic — and my lifelong fascination with them was not without its ambivalence and sense of disapprobation. If the dead were merely the good citizens of the next life, then why, I asked myself, had they been removed so secretively and quickly from my ministrations of adieu? If the body was merely the soul's worn and recyclable old shoe, why had it always been taken so stealthily away after it had outlived its usefulness to its original wearer? If the dead were of no further use in this life, why did so many of my colleagues pay such a prolonged homage to them? Why were they so capable of drowning out the voices of the living?

4

I have always loved making lists. For me, lists are a hedge against chaos, a way of organizing my passions. During an early period of depression, I made an unusual list, one that still hangs over my study desk to remind me of less hopeful times. WAYS TO DEFEAT DEATH it proclaims:

1. Sleep with young women
2. Change jobs frequently
3. Travel

4. Get up off Greenblatt's couch
5. Don't look a woman in the face while making love.
You are staring at death.
6. Write short. Avoid prose.
7. Pray for a better life.
8. Make lists.

I've always felt a kind of odd satisfaction in gazing at this list, though, of late, its contents seem less and less appealing. I experience a kind of sadness these days as I survey this short list of my possibilities, particularly number 3 — "Travel" — which caused me such torment in the past.

I have always collected travel catalogs. "51 GREAT GALAPAGOS ADVENTURES" one blares from my living-room coffee table. "WILDERNESS TREKKING IN NEPAL" calls out another. "THE WILD GORILLAS OF TANZANIA" beckons a third.

"I don't understand why you don't find the exploration of yourself — a kind of 'journey into the interior of Martin Weinstock' — as interesting as a trip to Borneo," Greenblatt would protest whenever I brought up the subject. But I simply didn't find the terrain of my own overanalyzed interior nearly as fascinating as the jaguars, pumas, sloths, anteaters, coatimundis and wild boars of the tropics.

Yet, in the actual lanes and flight paths of movement, I have always been something of a failure. A terrible homesickness comes over me virtually every time I confront the exotica of another country — so much so that I have never once managed to remain abroad even until the return date of my original ticket. Instead, I usually find myself in a panicked flight for the nearest airport, where I try to convince some poor, befuddled airlines clerk that I urgently need to change my return date because "my father is in critical condition in a New York hospital."

My father *had* been in critical condition in a New York hospital on any number of occasions, the one I remember best being the day before my first wedding, when he was at Mt. Sinai having a pacemaker implanted to rouse his twenty-nine-beat-per-minute heart.

I remember sitting there, in the hospital's postsurgical "family only" waiting room, half-wishing my father's long ordeal of mock dyings would finally come to an end, when the surgical nurse, carrying a clipboard and her most professional look of controlled compassion, emerged from the elevator doors.

"Is there a Mr. Weinstock here?" she called as she marched into the room full of potential widows, widowers and orphans. My heart leapt into my gullet. I made a beeline for the elevator.

"*I'm* Martin Weinstock."

"Could you wait over there in the corner, Mr. Weinstock?" The grim-faced young woman motioned to me. "I need to talk with you alone when I'm done here."

A sudden, all-consuming chill overtook my body as I headed for a corner of the room while the nurse conveyed her various pre- and postmortems to the assembled relatives. *How appropriate,* I thought as I lit a cigarette and collapsed into a chair. *How perfectly fitting:* my wedding and my father's funeral on the same day.

Finally, after what seemed like hours, the nurse — wearing a suddenly lighthearted expression — came walking toward me.

"He's dead, isn't it?" I asked half hopefully.

"Why, no," the nurse answered to my amazement. "On the contrary, he's doing fine. . . . We don't usually allow relatives into the recovery room, but your father is *soooo* charming. He begged me to let you in so he could talk to you. I just didn't want the other patients' relatives to hear."

I felt a sense of shocked disbelief. "Uh . . . yes . . . he's very charming, isn't he?"

"He sure is. So, if you'll follow me, Mr. Weinstock, I'll take you down to the recovery room. . . . But you have to promise you'll only stay a minute, all right?"

"I swear." I was still trembling.

A few minutes later, the green swinging doors marked RECOVERY ROOM. HOSPITAL STAFF ONLY swung open to reveal a large, disinfectant-soaked room filled with perhaps two dozen blood and towel-draped bodies attached to a vast webwork of intravenous devices and life-support systems. Somewhere from the middle of this carnage I head an all-too-familiar voice singing the overture from *La Forza del Destino.*

"Just follow me, Mr. Weinstock." The nurse motioned with an almost inaudible whisper. "He's right over there."

In a surreal daze, I followed the sound of that familiar voice to the center of the room. There, his head propped up on a set of pillows and a blood-spattered white surgical towel wrapped around his chest, my father was holding the hand of yet another nurse, whom — in a kind of grogged, postsurgical stupor — he was now serenading with Mario Lanza's "Golden Days."

"Here's your son, Mr. Weinstock," the nurse whispered. By now, she had almost lost her own sense of recovery room decorum as her eyes met the blushing gaze of her co-worker.

"Ach, my dear son." My father's head turned away from the nurse to look up at me.

"How are you, Dad?" I asked halfheartedly.

"Everything ist *wunderbar*," my father replied. "I am in wundervoll hands here." My father was grasping both the by now nearly hysterical nurses by the hand.

"He's a marvelous patient . . . so incredibly cheerful." The surgical nurse smiled at me. "He even tried to sell me a fur coat. You're lucky to have such a wonderful father."

"Will you call Mama for me and tell her everything is fine?" my father asked, referring to my stepmother.

"Sure," I replied. "But if you're really all right, I have to go back to Washington. I'm getting married tomorrow, you know, and we're leaving for Italy the next day."

"Ja, of course, I know," the suddenly serious patient replied.

"Mr. Weinstock, I'm afraid you'll really have to leave now." The nurse, still trying hard to contain her laughter, was tugging at my shirtsleeve.

"I'll call after the wedding to make sure you're all right — OK, Dad?" I placed a tentative hand on my father's shoulder.

"Jawohl. . . . Don't worry — your daddy vill be fine."

"Yeah. . . . I'm sure you will be." I turned toward the recovery room door.

"Und, Martin. . . ." My father's head turned once more toward me as I began to disappear through the swinging doors.

"Yeah, Dad?" I stopped in my tracks and waited for my father's parting words.

"Have a wonderful trip."

CHAPTER II

Eggs

What comes first, the chicken or the egg?
— ZEN KOAN

All my life, I've felt a deep attachment to eggs. As far back as I can remember — in the deepest frost of winter, in the stifling humidity of summer, in times of grief and in times of contentment — eggs have always been there.

I remember the black grader in the damp, mildewed basement of my aunt and uncle's chicken farm; the constant hum of its small motor; the dull, insulated thump of eggs onto the slightly inclined rubber runway as they rolled to the bottom and were loaded into cardboard containers and cartons.

I remember the babies and pullets and mediums and jumbos, the browns and the whites, the tiny pinprick of focused light that surged, laserlike, from the candler to illuminate those mysterious interiors of white and yellow, and that elusive four-leaf clover among eggs, the double yolk. I remember that even rarer find — the calcium-deprived egg that emerged without even a shell to hold it in place. Sometimes, in fact, I felt that I *was* that egg — without a hard shell, a convincing poise, to hold myself in place, — soft, vulnerable, yearning for cover.

I remember the warm feel of eggs freshly out of the hen's body, the sweetly familiar smell of chicken shit. Best of all, I remember the gleaming black blob of bullet still lodged in my uncle's right tricep, how it glistened in the morning light as he carried buckets of eggs from the chicken coops into the basement.

I remember the egg auction, and the egg prices right there on the front page of the *Millville News* (of equal stature with the erecting of the Berlin Wall). I remember the smeared, yellowy coils of chicken shit on my uncle's worn boots. I remember the twice-yearly arrival of hundreds of madly squawking yellow chicks; the proud, libidinal strut of the roosters; the huge bags of chicken feed stacked in the barn, onto which my cousin and I would bound in a mountain of dust; the blond, balloony ticks we would pick out of the scruffy hairs of the farm dogs, Micky and Fips, and splatter in tiny star bursts of blood against the porch.

I also remember loading my uncle's station wagon with carton after carton of eggs each Sunday night to prepare for the three-hour drive to New York to sell his eggs door to door the next morning. It occurred to me, with an ironic sense of symmetry, that my uncle delivered eggs in the same refugee-laden apartment buildings of Washington Heights through which my father carried the dead carcasses of mink and Alaska seal, the lifeless boas of chinchilla and mouton. And there, at the same time, was my uncle, calling out: *Life! Life! This is the life of eggs!*

Something in these earliest of memories of my aunt and uncle must have said to me: *yes, this is man and woman, this is life and death, this is the long labor of the body.* I must have already known — in that deep, subliminal, unimpedable knowledge that is a child's — that *this* was the place of my true blood, that this man with the bullet in his arm carrying eggs, and *not* the man carrying those dead carcasses, was my true father. I must have known all along that it was with the living egg, and not with the dead mink, that I would need to reclaim my life.

But I didn't simply want to step from one rotten egg into another. I wanted to be a man with all his eggs in the same basket, his yin and yang under a single roof.

2

So who were they — these people who bore me, my flesh and blood? This mysterious "aunt" and "uncle," who — I knew from those whispered secrecies, those taut innuendos of mystery — were something more, but didn't know exactly what? The six-years-older girl whose tightly drawn underwear wrapped like a transparent shroud around her buttocks introduced me for the first time to the allures of an intact female body, the three-years-older boy with whom I would frolic between the chicken coops, wrestle on top of the musty feed sacks, whom I would follow around the various baseball diamonds and football fields of Millville, trying to learn how to be a man? Who were they — this family whose fake-brick-and-shingle house Heinz and Bettina Weinstock and my grandmother Johanna at least thrice annually pulled up to for "vacations," from whose brightly wallpapered attic windows I would watch the shining black bullet still lodged in my uncle's tricep from the 1948 war glisten in the morning light as he dragged large metal baskets of eggs from the coops?

I look, now, at the home movies my father made during that period, their images moving frantically from face to face in an ill-sequenced narrative so scattered and disassociated as to seem postmodern, and what I see could, clearly, be the events of any "normal" extended family: My parents, my grandmother and I, in all our comparatively "urbane" splendor, getting out of my father's maroon 1948 Chevy; my aunt and uncle — lumbering, "farmy," dressed in overalls and Millville Egg Auction sun visors, throwing open the screened door to greet us; my two cousins, running from the yard or chicken coops, grabbing their little cousin — or should I say their brother? — by the hand, eagerly awaiting the packages of food and gifts they're well aware their "rich" uncle has brought from the big city. It all seems — and, as I remember it, *felt* — rather cozy and familiar. Who could possibly know what strange subtext lurked beneath these surfaces? What wild convolutions of biology and destiny?

Looking at them now, these four grown-ups and two children — the aunt who is my mother, the mother who is my aunt, the uncle who is my father, the father who is my uncle, the two cousins who are my brother and sister — I can't help but notice how much more attractive "we" are. My father cuts a downright dashing figure — handsome, energetic, animated, well-built. My mother — though she already exhibits some of the melancholic, doomed attributes of the dying — is well-dressed, reserved, feminine, unmistakably European. My aunt and uncle, by contrast, still look like a couple of Israeli kibbutzniks: beak-nosed and peasanty, their bodies a testimony not to grace but to endurance, not to style but to hardship. To say that they — particularly my aunt — are not exactly beautiful would be, I think, to substitute generosity for mere tact. So why not say it? They, particularly my aunt — this woman who bore me — are downright unattractive, could easily be typecast as migrant workers on a Romanian dairy farm. Perhaps more significant, they have a certain look not very attractive to a young child — the look of those who have had a difficult life.

Yet — given the obvious strangeness that must have lurked just below the surface of all this conviviality — little, in fact, seemed strange. Summer nights, surrounded by a potpourri of brightly glowing pucks and coils designed to keep mosquitoes away, the eight of us — along with the two farm dogs, and a rotating menage of stray cats, kittens and fireflies — would sit in the front yard without a word about either dyings or exchanges, and it might — yes, indeed, it *might* — have been like any other extended family of immigrants in America . . . cousins, uncles, grandmothers, hooked noses, another tongue.

Was it only my imagination, I wonder now, or did I always have a sense that there was, somehow, more to it? That my aunt, in particular, always wanted something very disturbing from me, wanted me to *fail?* It began, I think, when my success in school — my terrific report cards, my excellent exam scores, my skipping several grades — slowly began to distinguish me, even, from my almost equally successful cousin Aharon. Or was it the fact that I — now the "son" of a better off, more successful father — had nicer clothes, better opportunities for summer camp, the company of more urbane, ambitious friends? Did she, I wonder now, sometimes have the feeling that they might have given away the Good One? Could it have been, I wonder, that this woman — this woman whose body, whose act of love, had borne me, and who should, by all rights, have been the one person on this earth unambivalently on my side — didn't, in fact, *want* me to be happy?

The truth was I never liked her, this aunt who was really my mother, this woman who, for whatever inscrutable reasons, had given me life. Trapped with her, from time to time, in the cold, clammy basement beside the egg grader, I felt somehow jeopardized, unwelcome, unloved. As for my cousins, what — from all these accumulated years of visits and embracings — was my most vivid memory of them? My cousin Aharon, having climbed a tree in the front yard that I was afraid to climb, is looking down at me, goading me on. Suddenly, I see his face retch forward — not unlike the way I would see my mother's face over the white pail several years later — and a huge wad of spittle arches through the air and lands in my eye. I remember wiping the spit from my eye, how wet it felt, how slimy, mucuslike, cold. I remember it as if it had been a voice saying: *This is not your place, your life, your family, here among the living. This is not your flesh and blood.*

3

There's an African folktale I've always loved:

A hunter takes his young son on a deer hunt into the forest. While they're walking in the woods, the father shoots a forest rat and gives it to his son.

"Hold on to this," he says to his son, "in case we need it later."

But the son throws the rat away. Later that night, having failed to kill any other game, they come to the spot where they are going to camp for the night. The father makes a fire and turns to his son. "Give me the rat," he says.

"I don't have it," the son answers. "I threw it away." Furious, the father hits him with an ax handle, leaving him unconscious in the woods.

The next morning, the son wakes and goes back to his father's house. He takes his belongings, puts them into a sack and starts walking through the woods away from his father's house. Finally, he arrives at a kingdom whose king had recently lost his only son. When he wanders into the king's tent, the king says to him, "From now on, you will be my son." At first the elders of the village don't believe the boy is the king's son. After a while, though, he slays a horse and seduces some maidens with the other boys, and is accepted by the court.

Years later, the boy's real father, the hunter, wanders into the village during a festival. He sees his son riding a horse, immediately recognizes him and says, "Get down from that horse! You are my son and must return to your home with me."

The king rushes out of his tent and — on seeing that the boy's real father has come to claim him — has his servants saddle up some horses. The boy and his two fathers then leave the village and ride out into the bush. Suddenly, the king produces a sword from his sheath, gives it to the boy and says, "Now. Me or your father — which one will you kill?"

Maybe that, too, was *my* question: *Which one would I kill?*

I remember those Monday nights in Washington Heights when — like the father in the African folktale — my uncle came to our house and slept in my room between long days of delivering cartons of eggs door to door. I remember sitting at the kitchen table with both my living fathers — the father of the fur and the father of the egg — as he sat drinking beer from a tall glass.

As my uncle and I got ready for bed, he would always take two quarters from his pocket and push them toward me. Each time, I would refuse the two shiny George Washingtons moving at me from my actual father's hand. Each time, my uncle would push them back, until, finally, I gave in to what I had wanted to begin with, and this strange ritual of insistence and refusal would come to an end.

Thinking about it now, I wonder what the meaning of that often-repeated event was. I wonder what was behind the persistence of my refusal, that repeated play whose ending was known at the outset, that conversation in which "no" meant "yes" and "don't" meant "do," in which "I don't want" meant "I want," and "no, thank you" meant "yes, please."

"The death of a man's father," Freud wrote somewhere, "is the most significant event, the most decisive loss, of a man's life." Yet here I was, with the most significant event of my life not yet having happened . . . *not once, but twice,* with both my uncle and my father still alive and kicking, solid as bookends around the unrelenting story of my search.

"If there is no longer a father, why tell stories?" But what if there are *two* fathers? What if you are a man who not only hasn't been blessed, like Sartre, with his father's early death, but is stuck with the crazed chorus of two living fathers, both refusing to die?

Maybe, I realize, thinking back on those Monday nights of beer and reverberating quarters, all I have uttered since has been an effort to imbue that sequence with an actual sincerity, to take the sword from the hand of my adopted father and drive it homeward toward the true coinage of my actual paternity.

CHAPTER 12

MALHEURS

But something remained wrong —
a dull ache whispered from below his voice
where his heart should have been, a seed
rumbled in the pit of his stomach as if to suggest
a tree that had never grown, a stone skimming
the surface of water once and then sinking.

— MARTIN WEINSTOCK,
"The Man Who Needed No One"

The first undressed body of a woman I ever saw was that of my blind grandmother, Johanna. I remember it, in the moonlight of the fifth-floor bedroom I shared with her as a child. I remember its vast folds of flesh, sagging like an old turtle's when she rose from the high, creaky bed in the corner of the room to urinate into the rusted bedpan. I remember — with the inner, still inarticulate voice of a three-year-old boy — looking out toward the ghostly, naked, drooping figure that stood before me and thinking to myself: *So this is a woman.*

She couldn't, of course, have known I was looking — that blind, dazed, groping, confused creature who rose from the bed to the tinkly crescendo of hairpins falling from her night table, who lifted her pink nightgown and stretched her other hand out into the vague unspecificity of the room to find a place to relieve herself of the burdens of her own body. She couldn't have known how each night I watched her open the small green bottle of pills she took for her chronic constipation, watched her unfasten the pins from the bunion at the back of her head so that a gray waterfall of hair plummeted down her back and she became, to my still-questioning eyes, a kind of old girl of near death, a corpse disguised as a windup doll that could defecate and pee. Nor could I have known, as she stood in the middle of the room five flights above the streets of Washington Heights, that I was staring the naked body of life and death in the face through the moonlight of early childhood.

There was also my mother's body, which I never actually saw (or, if I did, somehow erased from my memory) but which was known to me primarily as something appended to the small pillow of cloth I would sometimes see lying inside her brassiere on my parents' bed. A white omelette of false flesh, it suggested to me a place where no questions could be asked, and no answers would follow.

But I know that my grandmother's body, my mother's never seen but known to be disfigured body — the bodies of these two largely unknown, moribund creatures — were the images of woman I have carried with me for almost half a lifetime. So that now, whenever the breathing, life-hungry body of a younger, healthier woman becomes familiar to me, the scarred and defaced bodies of those first-loved women rear their ugly heads once more and cry out: *No.*

2

There was also a third woman's body in the house — a nearly perfect one, in fact, except for its knobby head of brass and lower torso of mesh and steel grating.

I remember staring long and hard at the firm, neatly stitched breasts of my father's mannequin (whom I named Lucretia) whenever the endless parade of stoles, coats and boas were periodically undraped from her shoulders. I remember sneaking into the fur room to embrace the cold, unyielding, partial, yet somehow seemingly perfect creature. I would stand on my tiptoes to kiss the long, brass neck, which, in my ravenous imaginings, responded like a ripe avocado to the ministrations of my lips and tongue. I remember thinking to myself: *Yes, maybe somewhere there is a woman's body like this — a tight, firm, unstained, undefecating thing with a face, with a living face and eyes.*

I also remember — whenever I would hear the click of the front door behind my departing parents — making a beeline for the fur-room door and swaying Lucretia's body from the brass wheels connected to the steel mesh of her lower torso. From there, I would lower her onto her back against the rug in front of my father's full-length showroom mirror, then throw myself in a fit of passion onto her cloth-and-metal body.

It was on one such afternoon not long after my mother's death, when I must have been no more than eleven, that I remember feeling a strangely unfamiliar, tingling sensation at the center of my body. It felt as if I were going to pee, yet somehow different, more pleasurable. I didn't quite know what to do as a strange, seamy, viscous discharge suddenly oozed onto Lucretia's stitched cloth belly. Afraid that I was about to urinate onto the most sensuous of my father's small harem, I ran for the bathroom, leaving a trail of small, thick droplets in my wake.

Over the next several years, my romantic interludes with my father's stitched, metallic, passive, yet somehow beautiful mannequin — with or (I hoped) without my parents' knowledge — continued. Continued, that is, until the day I was scheduled to leave for college.

That morning, with a combined sense of nostalgia and lingering desire, I stuck my head through the fur-room door, hoping to catch a final glimpse of my beloved. There, in the exact spot where the object of my most tender ministrations once stood, now sat only the snarling shape of my stepmother's English fox terrier. They had obviously removed her during the night, no doubt in the same surreptitious manner in which they had taken my mother's body away years before. Perhaps, I consoled myself, they suspected that, in the excitement of leaving home, I wouldn't notice. Or maybe my father had, once again, wanted to spare me the pain of a final good-bye.

Yet it seems to me now that — with Lucretia's sudden banishment from the playground of my lonely adolescence — my childhood came irretrievably to an end. The last symbol of my private triumph had been eliminated, as if my entire childhood had been reduced to a bit of padded cloth and an unanswerable moan, as if everything I had ever loved had been taken from me during the night.

3

I have always seen my life with women as divided between the cunt and the womb.

"Every man," my friend Claudia lectured me one night, "wants a cunt and a womb — passion and slippers. Just like every woman wants a good hard fuck and a good soft baby. But the men," she added, "never have the guts to find both in the same place."

Yes — cunts and wombs, pricks and babies, all that was stiff and erect, and all that was soft and yielding — these were the stuff of my morbidly and falsely divided life. Like a starling trapped between shut windows, I had imprisoned myself in their locked rooms throughout my years. After talking to Claudia that night, I again made a list of the artificially dichotomized world I had so relentlessly formulated for myself and, gazing at it, saw before me the doomed, divided, abstracted pathways of my own strivings:

CUNT	WOMB
life	death
light	darkness
air	earth
passion	suffering
conqueror	victim
pleasure	comfort
man	child
achievement	loss
play	work
yielding	consuming
happiness	sadness

There it was — stretched out like the scorecard of two teams playing in different arenas, two travelers heading in similar directions but never meeting, two potential lovers unable to overcome their own images of adversity.

I also knew there had to be a thread, a passage, between these two deeply running tributaries. I knew that the sweet, playful, beckoning opening of the cunt invariably led to the dark, moist, consoling cave of the womb. I knew that, below the surface of the man who longed for and needed the happy conquest of the former was the child who forever mourned his weeping expulsion from the latter . . . and longed to go back.

I knew that — between the dark, dead, stifling carcasses of fur which draped and decorated the dying bodies of my mother and grandmother and my father's mannequin Lucretia, and the living, light-beckoning eggs of my uncle's New Jersey chicken farm — there was a road longer, wider, far more dangerous to cross than the New Jersey Turnpike. Along that road were places more odiferous than Newark, uglier than Trenton, more terrifying than the powerful fists of New Jersey's own former middleweight champion, Reuben "Hurricane" Carter.

It was the road between the cunt and the womb, between living and dying.

4

I met my wife, Deirdre MacAllister, while sitting at a café in Washington, D.C., reading Italo Calvino's *Italian Folktales*. I was still working as a cameraman for West German television network DDT, and it was one of the only times in my adult life I wasn't actively looking for a woman.

The second she walked into the café and sat down beside me, though, I was a goner. Green eyes, a wide, gap-toothed smile, L. L. Bean duck boots, blue jeans, and an embroidered white Mexican-style blouse that made her look like she had just been out horseback riding with Sam Shepard.

She had, in fact, done virtually all the things I'd dreamt of, and lacked the courage to do: five years of salmon fishing in Alaska, bicycling alone through Poland and Hungary, sailing with a Greek sea captain in the Mediterranean, organic farming in rural Ohio, the triathalon in Honolulu. The antithesis of that burdened, ever-thinking, inert self I so wanted to be rid of. Who knows but that I may have been the same to her.

By midafternoon, we were in bed. Over the next six months or so, until our wedding, we hardly ever got out. If we did, it was only in order to assume a new position *en plein air*. From the banks of the Tidal Basin to the hills of the Shenandoah Valley, I shot my eager, desperate seed into her, hoping, like Proust pondering his grandmother, to find in her lovely midwestern face, the entrance to another soul.

What beautiful dirty words we used during those months of our courtship! Like reporters, we took down, in the blissed syllables of cunt and asshole, in the sweet hyperbolic life of prick and sphincter, every minute perambulation of our roiled, rolling, oiled, blissed-out bodies. "Ride me into the moon, you beautiful cunt!" I would scream at her, contorting my lips into the curled grimace of a crazed leprechaun. "Fuck me until I turn blue!"

"Talk dirty to me, baby, suck my asshole dry as a desert," she would reply. "Eat me until I disappear. Sit on my face till I can't breathe."

"Life! Life!" I inveighed along with Flaubert, "to have erections!"

Though, years later, I would design for myself the small, talismanic motto "Never speak in heat," it was almost entirely in heat that I spoke during those months, as I explored with her the life of the cunt. Until, one afternoon on a friend's secluded deck in Sperryville, Virginia, from a position too intricate and unspeakable to name, I asked Deirdre MacAllister to marry me.

My father, who was suffering from his twenty-nine-stroke-per-minute heartbeat and a terrible case of shingles at the time, reacted with uncharacteristic brevity to my fiancée's acquaintance. "Es ist nothing but sex," he spat at me with cobralike viciousness at the counter of a small coffee shop in Pine Hill, New York. "Vergisse mich" (forget me). He slammed down his spoon, then turned to me on the sidewalk to which I had tearfully followed him, adding the classic survivor's curse: "If anything happens to me . . . it's your fault."

We were married on that same deck in Virginia four months later, the rabbi and I being the only Jews at the ceremony, the *huppah* held up at each corner by a lapsed Catholic. My father had taken note of the occasion by having the pacemaker implanted near his heart the previous afternoon, and my Jungian analyst made me promise to take the phone off the hook during the wedding, because — as he indiscreetly put it — "I wouldn't put it past the sonuvabitch to die just as you were saying 'I do.' "

But my father didn't die, and I did say "I do," and I spent the next four months — that is, whenever I wasn't maneuvering Deirdre into some new position from which I could squirt my desperate seed into her body — in complete and utter terror of her abandoning me, of her one day discovering what an empty accordion of longing and seed had sent that litany of cunt and prick into the air around her.

Until, one morning, shortly after receiving the call from Harvard offering me the Burke-Howland Lectureship, armed with the convenient excuse that I was "too good" for my midwestern Puella of the lustful flesh, I turned in our bed and woke to find a mere human being — a human being onto whom I could heap the anguish of my accumulated self-loathing and emptiness, a face that was not my face, a soul that was not my soul, a body that had become merely yet another urn of death and disfigurement, another way of neatly dividing the domains of the womb and the cunt.

I turned, and, in my wife's thin but shapely body, saw once again the sagging flesh of my grandmother; the disfigured breasts of my mother; the sad, diminished, divided language of darkness and wombs. I felt again the hunger for which no mere mortal could ever be enough, the emptiness no other human being could ever cure. And so — to the extent that I had been present to begin with — I disappeared, like a late-night flight taking off for another continent, like a spent prick.

CHAPTER 13

Abnormal Griefs

It is almost night
when the joys of this life
finally find you again:
looking for tulips beneath the ice.

— MARTIN WEINSTOCK,
"Melancholy"

A
ll my life, rabbis have frightened me. They seem to me to represent a punitive, moralistic authority, a somberness of black robes and judgment. Rabbis, I observed from the earliest years of my childhood, were also the only sort of man my father could seem to get close to. *Guten Abend, Herr Doktor Rabbiner,* he would greet the rabbi, who occasionally came and sat in my parents' living room drinking a kosher schnapps. In my family, it might be argued, the rabbi was a kind of chair holder, a sort of emeritus professor.

But there was something about these rabbis I never much liked — a certain excessive sobriety perhaps, a kind of humorlessness. Judaism, religion and God, in their eyes, were a kind of T. S. Eliot whom they were always celebrating but about whom no possible irreverence was permitted.

"A man buys a Cadillac and goes to see an orthodox rabbi," I, an eight-year-old boy, told Rabbi Dr. Leo Arnstein, seated on my parents' living-room sofa. "And he says to the rabbi: 'Rabbi, would you please say a *brocha* over my Cadillac?' The rabbi thinks about it awhile, then looks up and says to the man: 'What's a Cadillac?'"

"So the man takes his Cadillac and goes to see the conservative rabbi," I continued, as white-bearded Arnstein listened attentively. "He says: 'Rabbi, would you please say a *brocha* over my Cadillac?'

The rabbi looks up with a confused expression on his face, scratches his head and says to the man: 'What's a Cadillac?'

"Finally," I continued, "the man takes his Cadillac and goes to see the reform rabbi. 'Rabbi,' he says to him politely, 'would you please say a *brocha* over my Cadillac?' The rabbi looks enviously up at the Cadillac, scratches his head and says to the man: 'What's a *brocha*?'"

I had — from the time I first heard it from my friend Raymond — found the joke hilarious. So it was much to my amazement that a stern, punitive expression moved like a dark cloud over Arnstein's Moseslike face.

"You stupid boy," the rabbi scolded me. "Don't you know that even a reform rabbi knows what a *brocha* is?"

Devastated by my first failure as a stand-up comic before a rabbinical audience, I retreated sulkily to my room. It was the same room where, some two years later, my family's new rabbi (Dr. Arnstein, to my unabashed delight, had died), a deeply religious, salt-and-pepper goateed man named Dr. Hugo Vronsky, came to talk to me the day after my mother's death.

"It is not a good idea for you to go to the funeral," Vronsky informed me, followed by an illustration whose oxymoronic logic no ten-year-old boy could fathom. "Your mother wouldn't want you to be there if she were still alive."

The idea that my mother wouldn't have wanted me there to say good-bye as she was lowered into the ground — like the idea that she wouldn't have wanted me to say good-bye before she was taken out of the room the morning before — nonetheless came as a shock to me.

"I *want* to go," I wailed. "She was my mother."

"Yes," the rabbi answered. "I know. . . . But you will do her memory more good by staying here."

Four years later, as the flag-draped casket of John F. Kennedy stood on the caisson before the Capitol in front of the riderless black horse, I watched the president's three-year-old son salute his slain father's body and thought again of Rabbi Vronsky seated beside me in my room, telling me I couldn't go to my mother's funeral.

"We get over mourning," Greenblatt would say to me almost thirty years later, "but we never get over not mourning."

Never, I had begun to realize, was a terribly long time. Never was too long to live in a world where the egg and the fur, the funny and the serious, the living and the dying, were constantly divided. Never was too long not to be able to look a woman in the eye and say: *you.*

Arnstein was dead. Vronsky was dead. Kennedy was dead. T. S. Eliot was dead. My mother was dead. Soon, no doubt, my two fathers — the father of the fur *and* the father of the egg — would be dead too. And the most difficult step in learning how to be dead, Italo Calvino (who was also dead) had written, is to become convinced that your life is a closed whole, all in the past, to which you can add nothing and could alter none of the relationships among its various elements.

But I saw myself as still among the living — among that ever-smaller percentage of those who could add to their own past, who could fight a battle against their own oracles. Never, it seemed to me, was too long a time to do without that satisfaction. Never was too long a time not to be able to look a dead woman in the face and say good-bye.

2

On the morning my mother died, after finally opening the bedroom door and seeing the empty white hospital bed, I remember going into the kitchen and sitting at the table.

There was a commotion in the house, people coming and going, and — though it didn't occur to me at the time as an actual question — I must have pondered it anyway: *Now* what do I do? What's supposed to happen after your mother's dead body has been carried out of the house?

So I did what my family always did — and still does — in times of overwhelming grief or anger: *I ate.* Baby-food custard, the kind I'd always loved. I don't remember if it was Gerber or Beech-Nut, but I remember its creamy consistency (the consoling marriage of cream and eggs), like the Horn & Hardart rice pudding my father brought home from the Fur District, whose intrusive raisins I used to scatter on the ground like little pellets of scat.

I don't exactly remember who sat there at the table with me while I ate. I think it was Helen, the "adjunct" member of our family, and my uncle and grandmother. I remember stirring the custard for a long, long time before eating. I remember the hiss of air from the lid when I opened the jar, and the circular motion of the spoon as I stirred. I remember how good the custard tasted, how — in moments of grief, even thirty years later — I still think of eating custard.

"She was so young," I, already an archivist of utterances, said to my uncle a bit later, while trying to determine my mother's last words. "She was only forty-two."

"No," my uncle corrected me, "She was *fifty*-two. . . . She lied to you about her age. She thought you would love her more if she was younger."

Two thoughts crossed my mind: The first was that — with one magical swoop of my uncle's tongue — my mother had been given ten extra years of life. The harsh injustice of a woman being plucked so young from the earth had been somehow mitigated, made less painful. The voice, I realized, could give gifts. Then, close on its heels, came the second thought: How terribly insecure she must have been about my love, this woman whose own body couldn't nourish me, who hadn't borne me, who was too ashamed of her scarred and dying body ever to take off her clothes in front of me, because she must have known that what would be revealed would be what no young boy wanted to see.

"I love Helen more than I love you," I remembered saying to her once in a moment of anger. I thought to myself now that she must have believed me, must have believed that I loved that other woman — that woman of the intact body, that woman who had been able to bear children, that woman who was not so visibly among the dying — more than I loved her. Maybe, it suddenly occurred to me, I had.

I sat at the kitchen table and ate my custard, and thought of what they had done with her body — of where I might still find it, how I might still kiss it good-bye, how I might touch it for the last time — that body which, as I recalled, I had little memory of ever having touched, aside from clinging to her skirt when my mother would leave me at school every morning after walking me there.

After eating my custard and walking by the bedroom again to make sure they hadn't — in a moment of remorse, a moment of mercy — replaced her body, what did I do? What does a ten-year-old boy *do* after his mother's dead body has been carried out of the house? Go out and play baseball? Watch the playoffs? Stick a piece of bubble gum on a string and fish for change beneath the subway gratings?

No, he doesn't do any of those things. What he does is he goes looking for sympathy, for someone who will tell him the truth, someone who will allow him to grieve.

I realized now what I must have always realized, must have always known the way only a child knows the unspeakable and the unspoken: That our house was not a place of truth, not a place of sincerity. I must have known early on that in my family — especially in the case of my father (that kisser of women's hands, that flatterer of women's bodies) — no one really meant what they said, or said what they meant, that the place of the fur was a place of untruth. I must have decided very young that what I most wanted to be was a man who *said* and *meant* at the same time.

So what did I do after eating my custard, after checking once more for my mother's body, after determining as best I could that the last words to have issued from her lips were the "Good night, darling," she had whispered to me from her deathbed that Wednesday night? What I did was walk up the stairs to the sixth floor of the building, to Apartment 61, where my friend Ronnie Baumwoll lived, and ring the doorbell.

Months before — when no one had said a word to me about what was really wrong with my mother, when no one had told me she was dying — Ronnie's mother, Molly, had asked me how she was. And because I *knew* — because a child, in the deepest recesses of his heart and soul, *always* knows — I fell sobbing into her arms. So her home, her arms, her body, became for me a place of truth, a place of the sincerity I had always longed for.

There was something else that must have been terribly attractive to me about the Baumwolls' apartment, that must also have imbued me with the sense that their home, if not my own, was a place of truth. It was *Mr.* Baumwoll. He was, as I remember him, a man completely without charm. In fact, as I have said about my colleagues at Harvard, he was terribly "serious." A disc jockey for a classical radio station in New York, where he hosted a weekly German-language music and talk show, he was a man who worked with words. Words, I sensed, that meant something, words that embodied a kind of sincerity. Words that could give life.

I remember David Baumwoll's study, filled with what at the time seemed to me to be terribly sophisticated tape recorders and audio equipment. I remember the sense of solitude I associated with his work, the sense — which both frightened and attracted me — that it was work that took place in a world of men . . . without the kissing of hands, without the seduction of women, without *schtopping the traffic.* I remember knowing — subliminally, but clearly — that here was a man who fucked his wife, who didn't need to charm strangers or flatter women or be the best-loved man in the Fur District. I must have thought: This man is quiet. He works alone. He doesn't waste words. He loves his wife. *This* is what a man is. These thoughts intrigued and frightened me.

I must have sensed something about Molly Baumwoll as well: that here was a woman fucked and loved, motherly and intact. Here was a woman who could stand the truth. Which is why, at those moments when I was simply overcome by the truth — the truth, first, of my mother's long illness and, now, of her dying — it was to Molly Baumwoll's door that I went. From the histrionic, confused, charm-ridden, death-ridden, overeating confines of my own house — a place where a woman wasn't allowed the wildness of a cunt and a man couldn't maintain the calm, hard reticence of a prick — I went upstairs.

Molly Baumwoll answered the doorbell and gazed at me for several seconds as I stood across the threshold. There was a look of compassion mingled with respectful distance on her face. She must, I realized as I stood staring at her, have already known what had happened.

"Is Ronnie home?" I asked, in a more or less customary tone of voice.

"Yes, Martin, come in. He's in his room."

I started down the hallway toward my friend's room, past David
Baumwoll's study, where I noticed him in his usual posture of ad-
justing various knobs on the recessed wall unit of stereo equipment
and tape recorders.

"Hi, Mr. Baumwoll," I whispered.

"Hi, Martin," David Baumwoll replied. He seemed only a tad
more attentive to my presence than usual, lost in his habitual state
of revery before the tape recorders and microphones. In the back-
ground, I heard a baritone voice singing in German.

"Would you like some milk and cookies?" I heard Molly Baumwoll's voice call after me from the kitchen.

"No thank you," I replied, continuing toward my friend's room.
I suddenly realized that I didn't know, really, why I had decided to
climb the stairs to Ronnie Baumwoll's apartment. I didn't really
want to cry, I realized. Perhaps, I think now, I wanted to be pitied.

"Hi there," I said shyly.

Ronnie Baumwoll looked up from the floor, where he was gluing
together a model submarine as I entered. "Hi there," he countered.
"Wanna work on this with me?"

I wasn't really sure what I wanted. But Ronnie's proposal seemed
as reasonable as any. "Sure," I said.

So, on that late September morning of my eleventh year, while
my mother's dead body was still being transported down Fort Washington Avenue from our apartment to the busy corridors of the
Hirsch Funeral Home, I sat gluing tiny fragments of World War II
submarine hull together on the floor of Ronnie Baumwoll's sixth-
floor apartment.

3

That first night after her death, when my mother's pink nightgown
was rising toward my lips in my father's hands, what was I thinking?

Closing my eyes to the faces of hundreds of living women over
the past thirty years, I've often asked myself that question as my
face turned away from their faces, my eyes away from their eyes.

I remember the bottom drawer of the large Biedermeier chest as
it opened. I remember my father, dressed in blue flannel pajamas,
reaching down into the drawer, scooping the nightgown up in his

palms like an old Bedouin woman carrying straw through the fields. I remember him bringing it, first, to his own lips, where he planted a soft, seemingly feminine kiss against the silk, then lowering it once again.

I remember the sudden sense of dread that came over me. The image of the empty bed from which my dead mother's body had been taken that morning again flashed through my mind. I remember feeling as though I had no avenue of escape, as though I were in that room with a man who was not really a man, a lover of women who was not really a lover of women. I remember the dread and I remember the revulsion, and I remember the terrifying sight of the pink nightgown moving toward my lips in my father's hands . . .

And I remember that terrible sense of being trapped — by a man who loved his own symbolism more than he loved his son, a man who couldn't bring his whole eyes and lips and heart into contact with a living woman, a man who could only kiss the dead cloth that had once dressed a dead woman's disfigured body, a man too deprived of grief in his own childhood to allow me, his own son (though I was, without yet knowing it, *not* his own son), to grieve.

The dead are dead, and lovers love to kiss, I would write some thirty years later. Yes, the dead were dead, and I didn't want to kiss the empty nightgown of a dead woman's body. I wanted to kiss a living woman, a dying woman — yes, even the dead woman who had been secretly removed from the apartment that very morning. But what I surely didn't want to kiss was the dead woman's dead nightgown. I didn't want my living eyes to gaze into the face of such a double death.

Gib unsre Mama einen letzten Kuss. Give our mother one last kiss, my father whispered as the nightgown rose toward my terrified lips. *Gib unsre Mama einen letzten Kuss.*

But I had already been deprived of the kiss I had wanted to give the dead woman. Now, as the pink nightgown rose toward my lips in my father's hands, I was overcome by revulsion and anger and loathing and shame. My eyes wouldn't open, and my lips wouldn't utter their kiss, and — as I felt the cold silk press against my face — something in my ten-year-old heart must have vowed to avenge itself against the grief-stricken, unconscious man standing beside me. I must have secretly thought to myself that, someday, he would pay for my humiliation and shame and loss and aborted grief.

What I *didn't* yet know was that life was in no need of such modest foot soldiers as myself to carry out its oracles of revenge and retribution, to arrange for its strange lyricism of justice. I didn't know that not only were the sins of the fathers brought to bear on the lives of the sons but the rectifications of the sons might be vested, finally, on the fathers' behalf. For, as it is written: "Whom the Lord loveth, He correcteth."

It was only thirty years later — when, in hatred and revulsion and anger, I turned my face away from Laura's soft, feminine kisses — that I would realize that her kisses *reminded me* of my father's kisses, that those shy, delicate lips *reminded me* of my father's lips. Only then would I realize that my revulsion and my anger and my fear and my shame were those of a man who didn't want to be kissed by another man, a man who no longer wanted to hear the insistent rhyming of *womb and tomb*.

I was, instead, a man who wanted to look into a living woman's eyes and feel the moist, womanly flesh of her lips against my own. I didn't want, like Charlemagne, to have a charm bestowed on me that would involve me forever in a love affair with a dead woman. I didn't want to have much of anything, for that matter, to do with charm. I didn't want to gaze into a living woman's eyes ever again and see that pink nightgown rising toward my lips.

BOOK V

Shadows

———•———

What is divinity if it can come
Only in silent shadows and in dreams?
— WALLACE STEVENS,
"Sunday Morning"

CHAPTER 14

Funeral Music

The distinguishing features of melancholia are a profoundly painful dejection, abrogation of interest in the outside world, loss of the capacity to love, the inhibition of all activity, and a lowering of the self-regarding feelings to a degree that finds utterance in self-reproaches and self-revilings, and culminates in the delusional expectation of punishment.

— SIGMUND FREUD,
"Mourning and Melancholia"

Morton Gamson was depressed.

In fact, Weinstock couldn't remember *ever* having seen anyone so depressed. "My God," he said to Armitage one afternoon over at Burdick Place, "it makes his old self almost look cheerful."

Gamson, indeed, had fallen into a deep, almost catatonic depression in the months following his retirement, only intensified by the thought of Weinstock's having succeeded him. Though it was Gamson who had made the original decision to hire him, Weinstock knew that Gamson had, in the intervening years, come to think of him as an intellectual lightweight, someone who had gotten as far as he had merely by a combination of charm, reasonably good looks and a modicum of talent along whose surface Weinstock had branched out with all the speed and profundity of ground cover.

"I think he's just a little bit *too* proud of not having a doctorate," Gamson would say to Penelope about his younger colleague. "At heart, I think he considers ignorance a virtue. . . . I don't even think," he would add with no small increment of glee, "he writes poetry anymore."

Added to Gamson's convictions about Weinstock's intellectual inferiority was a more subtle dislike for the overt nature of Weinstock's Jewishness. Among the Cambridge intelligentsia at least, being Jewish was at best an ugly blemish on the smooth, homogenizing hide of intellectual achievement and high culture one tried to cover as completely as possible with the opague veneer of worldliness and good books. Gamson's well-lubricated "the year we lived in Florence," for example, was far more likely to facilitate social mobility than Weinstock's equally characteristic "in my family at Passover."

Nonetheless, Weinstock, on his way to the Gamsons' house to pick up a ceramic bowl he had bought from Penelope, was feeling a pronounced twinge of guilt at his hostile and unsympathetic attitude toward his former boss during the past months. Preoccupied with his own depression and difficulties with Laura, he had paid little attention to Gamson's worsening condition.

Penelope Gamson, dressed in a rust-colored parka, bounded down the stairs to greet him at the door. Gamson trundled out from the living room behind his wife as she opened the door leading into the foyer.

"Hi, Penelope. . . . Hi, Mort, how ya doing?" Weinstock was trying hard to sound upbeat.

"Come in, Martin. . . . Good to see you," Penelope Gamson greeted him. "Take off your coat and stay for a drink."

"How are you, Mort?" Weinstock repeated, following them through the pitch-dark living room and dining hall into Gamson's study. The house seemed to him like the home of a deceased couple the night after an estate sale. It reminded him, as he followed Mort and Penelope through the kitchen, of his father and stepmother's gloomy, darkened abode in Queens.

"Not good," Morton finally replied. "I've been having a terrible fall."

"Yeah" — Weinstock pillaged the depths of his reserves for a scintilla of sympathy — "Corliss told me you haven't been feeling all that great. . . . You must be kind of at loose ends, huh?"

"It's been awful," Penelope Gamson answered for him. "I've been afraid to leave Morton in the house alone when I've been away these past few weeks."

"Yeah, I know." Weinstock commiserated rather lamely, "I can imagine." Remembering some of Gamson's earlier kindnesses toward him, he suddenly felt a twinge of genuine empathy for his former boss's condition. "It's tough to be alone when you're depressed. I suppose you're not really working on anything either?" Weinstock noticed that his tone of voice might have passed for one of hopefulness rather than concerned inquiry. He looked over at Gamson, slouched in a stuffed brown chair not at all unlike Greenblatt's. While his former boss had never exactly been a fountain of good cheer, his present condition, Weinstock realized, was no laughing matter.

"No." Morton shuffled laconically in his chair. "I'm taking notes and doing some reading, but my heart's not really in it."

Watching the phlegmatic figure of Gamson as he spoke, Weinstock thought to himself that his former boss, too, must be working through a depressive position of sorts. He remembered something Armitage had once said after a meeting at Burdick Place. "Mort's life," he had quipped, "is one long depressive position punctuated by sleep." Weinstock wondered, gazing at the saddened, lethargic figure slouched before him, what the next step downhill might be.

"I'm sure things will get better soon, Mort." Weinstock roused himself from his own thoughts, gazing at his watch and realizing he was late for a dinner engagement with Laura. "But we have to stop for tod —— I mean, I've gotta run. . . . Thanks for the drink."

"Sure, Martin. Anytime. . . . I hope you'll come over and have dinner with us some night."

Weinstock hesitated, feeling both the terror and the attraction of the prospect. "Yes," he half-whispered, his throat tightening as he spoke. "I'd like that."

Gamson followed him into the foyer and opened the door as Weinstock headed out into the chilly December night. Hearing the door shut behind him, he breathed a sigh of relief as he walked down Bentley Place. For he had seen something as he gazed at the saddened figure of Morton Gamson in his overstuffed leather chair. Something that would leave him no peace for days to come.

In the depressed face of Morton Gamson, Weinstock had suddenly seen his own face. In the lethargic pace of Gamson's footsteps, he had heard his own footsteps. In the somber gravity of all that he hated, he had suddenly seen himself — a figure without lightness, and almost without life.

In the dark eyes of Morton Gamson, a small light suddenly flickered and revealed a face Weinstock had for a long time failed to recognize: his own.

2

"I'm soooo tremendously glad to meet you, Martin. . . . It's such a relief!"

Having never before experienced the mere making of his acquaintance described in such resuscitative terms, Weinstock stopped in his tracks to find his friend Karen Browne's sister Felicity eagerly reaching a hand out toward him. They were in the middle of the jam-packed room of friends and relatives gathered in Northampton for Karen's wedding.

"A relief?" Weinstock lamely shook Felicity's hand. "What were you expecting — the Loch Ness monster?"

"Oh no, it's not that at all." She laughed. "It's just that when I read your books at my sister's house one night I thought to myself: 'Now, that must be the saddest man who ever lived.' So, I'm glad you don't seem that way at all."

"Why, thanks." Weinstock tried smiling back. "I never really thought of myself as a walking sarcophagus before."

"Well, you certainly don't *seem* all that morbid," Felicity agreed. "But you do know that your work is absolutely *obsessed* with death — don't you?"

"Well, I suppose it mentions the subject every once in a while. . . . But I hardly think of it as obsessed." Weinstock had always been amazed at the extent to which those who read his work thought of him as a depressed and cheerless person. His most recent book, *The Possibilities of Human Existence,* seemed to have done little to dispel that consensus among almost everyone except Amanda Wayland. "I think yours," Wayland told him one day over lunch, "is actually a comic muse."

Most reviewers — at least those who had anything at all to say about the book — seemed to agree with Felicity Browne's solemn appraisal. "An encyclopedia of tristesse," a professor of contemporary poetry at Ohio State wrote in the *Omni Review*. "A bleak and unrelenting darkness masquerading as laughter," another reviewer observed in a local Boston journal. "Makes Ingmar Bergman look like Mel Brooks," a commentator chimed on National Public Radio.

"I really don't understand why people who read my work think of me as so sad," Weinstock continued to protest. "In real life, I'm a very cheerful guy."

"Oh, come on, Martin — 'The day opens like a casket door'? Why, if *that* isn't being obsessed with death, I don't know what is!"

"My God, did you *study* for this wedding?" Weinstock had never before experienced the oddly mixed pleasure of hearing himself quoted by a stranger. "What about all the cheerful and funny stuff I've written?"

"Like what? 'You smile like a corpse thinking back on its one good day'?"

"Well, you have to admit, it's a funny thought." He was beginning to feel a tad on the defensive.

"Yeah." Felicity took a large gulp of the vodka tonic from her left hand. "I could hardly stop laughing."

"Why don't we dance?" Weinstock thought the time might be ripe for a change of subject. The band starting playing "The Shadow of Your Smile." "I'm feeling kinda stuffed."

"You dance pretty well for such a sad guy," Felicity teased as he eased her smoothly across the cramped dance floor.

"Well, you know how it is — even a corpse can move if you jab a spring into it and wind it up."

"Seriously, Martin" — Felicity tried to change the tone as Weinstock steered her toward a corner of the room — "why *is* it that your work is so obsessed with death and dying? It seems someone like yourself could find something cheerful to write about."

"I have." Weinstock looked her straight in the eye, doing his best to maintain an air of complete sincerity.

"Oh? What's that?" Felicity seemed genuinely buoyed by his reply.

"What the dead will look like when they learn to dance."

3

" 'A little madness in the Spring / Is wholesome even for the King.'

"So wrote the poet Emily Dickinson, and, indeed, spring has been a subject on which poets and writers have waxed eloquent since time memorial. In order to welcome in this first day of spring, we have with us Martin Weinstock, author of two books of poems and director of the Creative Writing Program at Harvard University in Cambridge, Massachusetts.

"Welcome to *Nightwatch,* Martin, and tell us, what is it about spring that has captured the imagination of poets throughout history?"

Weinstock had been flown down to Washington as a last-minute substitute for Amanda Wayland, bedridden with the flu. Having never been on television before, he was trying hard not to seem nervous as he stared between the cross fire of strobe lights into the camera.

"Well, as Robert Frost says in his famous poem, 'Mending Wall,' 'Spring is the mischief in me,' and I think that poets, like most people, have always felt a certain mischievousness about spring — a loosening of the usual constraints, if you know what I mean."

Weinstock's host, the network's State Department correspondent, who had been "drafted" for the interview because the usual anchor was on assignment in Teheran, stared nervously at the TelePrompTer before turning to him again.

"But tell me, Martin, are the poems poets have traditionally written about spring always happy poems?"

"I'm glad you asked." Weinstock couldn't help grinning as he spoke. "As a matter of fact, most of the better-known poems about spring are terribly sad."

"Sad? How?"

"Well, if you look at the poems, you'll see that many of them sooner or later talk about death — for example, Wordsworth's poem 'Lines Written in Early Spring,' in which the poet says, quite early on: 'Pleasant thoughts bring sad thoughts to the mind.' Or Eliot's *The Waste Land,* which begins with that famous line about April being the cruelest month."

"Yes, but *why* is April the cruelest month?"

"Well, I think that, if you really take a look at the world, you'll see that poets have only acknowledged what most people intuitively realize anyway — that earthly life is really basically grief-stricken. The leaves and flowers and birds spring is just bringing to life are shortly going to die. Why, just on the way over here, I passed a cluster of freshly bloomed crocuses surrounded by a layer of last night's frost. I mean, let's face it, every little kid who's ever seen flowers bloom and die knows this, doesn't he?"

"That's really kind of a depressing thought for the first day of spring, though, isn't it?"

"Well, not really. It's only depressing if you want to think of it that way. After all, this perpetual repetition of life and death's going to go on anyway, whether we like it or not, so there's at least an argument to be made for enjoying it while we can. Why not, as Hopkins puts it, 'Have, get, before it cloy,/ Before it cloud, Christ, lord, and sour with sinning'?"

"Yes, I suppose you're right. But why do you suppose it is, if what you say is accurate, that spring, which is a time of such life and renewal and incredible beauty — rather than, say, fall — triggers so much sadness and thoughts of death on the part of poets?"

"That's a good question," Weinstock commended his host. "I think it's because — if you really stop to look at it — life and death kind of resemble each other, just the way spring and fall do. If you compare April and November, for example, you'll find that they really kind of look alike: the trees are essentially barren — 'shorn of leaves or shy of leaves' as a young poet I know put it — the temperature and sky are about the same both times of year . . . so that, if you didn't actually *know* which season you were in, it would be easy to mistake one for the other. In a way it's similar to the way sleep can be mistaken for death."

"Aren't you really saying that poets, as well as other people, have to learn to love things which — like spring — are transient and, in fact, already in the process of dying at the very moment we prepare to celebrate their blossoming?"

"I suppose so. . . . Or at least we have to learn to accept them. That's what Yeats means when he says that 'man is in love, and loves what vanishes.' " The images of his mother's blank, white deathbed and his parakeet's abandoned bird cage floated through Weinstock's mind as he spoke.

"Well, Martin, thanks to you and the other people we've had on this show — the insect man, the bug man, the head of the National Arboretum — I'm ready for spring. . . . Thank you very much."

"Thank you." Weinstock smiled into the camera. "I hope it comes."

4

When his mother's body was taken out of his house during the wee hours of that morning some thirty years ago, a fixed obsession implanted itself in Weinstock's mind, one that wouldn't leave for many years to come: *She would come back. She would — mysteriously, inexplicably — return.*

Afer all, he had never *seen* her dead body. He had never *seen* her lowered into the ground in a box. He had never actually *heard* the rabbi sing *Yisborach, v'yistabach, v'yispoar, v'yisroman, v'yisnasesh, v'yishador, v'yishalleh, v'yishalbi, sh'meh d'kudsho, b'rich nu* over her remains. No, he had only seen his mother's glazed eyes staring up at him from the bed. So why should he believe she was really dead?

He imagined it many ways, in an infinite number of venues. His favorite was his bar mitzvah: He would go to open the ark before reciting his *haftarah* and there — in place of the sacred Torah scrolls containing the Five Books of Moses — would be the living face of his mother returned to him again. Night after night, he would lie in bed weeping as he pictured this scene. When the weeping was over, a strange sense of relief would come over him, and he would fall asleep.

There were other scenarios too: He would open the apartment door one afternoon, and there she'd be — unheralded as the Fuller Brush man, discrete as the Messenger Elijah, numinous as the Angel Gabriel. Or she would suddenly be there, picking him up from school again as if nothing had ever happened, as if he were still a kindergarten student clinging to her dress. Or he would see her one day, walking down Fort Washington Avenue past Mother Cabrini High School, where — or it was rumored among the Jewish kids — the preserved head of Mother Cabrini sat in a formaldehyde tank in the lobby.

Though the venues would differ, certain aspects were always the same: first the longing, then the weeping, then the imagined reunion. Finally, the peace of fatigue and hopefulness, that elusive side door into the serenity of sleep. Though the door had been closed on the dead body of his mother, there were always hope and imagination to pry it open again.

Now, thirty years later, something about what was going on with Laura felt strangely familiar. For she, too, had finally "closed the door" to their continuing, having found the bill for Alexis's abortion on Weinstock's desk. She too — whom he had made into a womb and deprived of a cunt — had put up a sign that read DO NOT ENTER. Almost nightly, he still called her — weeping, begging, imploring . . . trying to pry the door open again. And each night after the phone call, he felt a vague relief — a hopefulness, a possibility of reunion. He felt that, at any moment, the door might open and he would find her there again.

"Hopes for reunion with the dead parent," a well-known psychologist had written, "may take one of two forms: either the parent will return home in this world or else the child wishes to die in order to join the dead parent in the next."

Weinstock couldn't exactly remember when it was that he had actually given up these hopes of his mother's returning, when the doors of the ark had finally stopped opening to reveal her face. Perhaps, it occurred to him as he surveyed the vistas of his own behavior, he never had. He knew that — at some point both undemarcated and unknown to him exactly — he had decided that, if his mother would not come and rejoin him among the living, he would go and join her in the world of the dead and the dying.

And so, with his "soulful, Keatsian eyes," his eerie ability to locate all that was depressed, sad, mournful, injured and dying, he had become "the saddest man in the world." He, too, had died.

Like a lifeguard attempting to revive a drowning swimmer he has pulled out of the sea, Weinstock looked into his own face as if for the first time. He placed his mouth against his own mouth, trying to blow the clean, revivifying air of this life into his dying lungs.

The dead are dead, he wrote as a grown man some thirty years later, *and lovers love to kiss . . .*

In the perfect justice of what isn't and what is.

CHAPTER 15

Men Weeping and Fighting

In whose name,
impoverished ones,
will they learn to love? Who
will embrace them once more
for the shaken trill
of their weeping —
their cleft, broken hearts?

— MARTIN WEINSTOCK
"The Hearts of Men"

Weinstock had always been intrigued by the fact that the obituaries and the sports pages are usually found in the same section of the daily paper. The small, dark, diminutively printed word DEATHS, it seemed, always dangled like a noose in the upper-right-hand corner just above the bright, multicolored word SPORTS.

That there was profound connection between the previous day's passages into the next life and the hitters, shooters, tacklers, jabbers and grapplers of this one, Weinstock had little doubt. He remembered, for example, his mother — who never in her life had a second's interest in sports — developing a fanatical obsession with professional wrestling before her death. Along with his blind grandmother, she would sit for hours in front of the tube, eagerly waiting for a 480-pound side of beef named Haystacks Calhoun to reduce his opponent to a wailing omelette by falling on him in the center of the ring. She would cheer wildly — among the few moments of cheer Weinstock remembered from that year of her dying — as the blubbery Flying Graham Brothers dragged opponents across the ring by their hair, or as a trim, barefooted wrestler named Antonino Roca sent a man twice his size barreling like a rifle shot into the corner with a flying dropkick, or a former football player named Vern Gagna transported opponents into a narcoleptic netherworld with his famous "sleeper" hold.

What was it about this strange ritual, these greased up, blubbery men in bikini bottoms grinding and throwing each other around a ring and breaking chairs over each other's heads, that so enticed that dying woman? Weinstock wondered. Was it that she sensed her own "fight to the death" somehow simulated, even mocked, by these jerky, theatrical displays of third-rate actors recreating some primal ritual of life and death, comedy and tragedy?

He remembered, after his mother's death, whenever he had wanted to wrestle or play rough with his father, the look of terror that came over his stepmother's face, coupled with a nearly hysterical warning: *"Heinz! Das darfst Du doch nicht mit deinem heart condition!"*

Then came that unforgettable night — in March of 1962 — when Weinstock sat dumbstruck in front of the TV as a seemingly gentle millinery designer named Emile Griffith jabbed, punched, pummeled and uppercut former welterweight champion Benny "Kid" Paret to death against the ropes at Madison Square Garden. What would his mother, he wondered, have thought of *that*?

There was yet another boxer Weinstock had known — personally, in fact: a gargantuan heavyweight from Argentina named Oscar Bonavena, whose table Weinstock once waited on at his summer training camp at Grossinger's. Bonavena, nicknamed the Baby Bull, was preparing for a heavyweight championship fight with a young champion named Cassius Clay. He would enter the hotel dining room every morning at 7:00, inhale several huge steaks and two quart pitchers of orange juice and — in the few words of English he had absolute mastery of — make his prediction for the future: *"Me heavyweight champion."*

But the Baby Bull's dream wasn't to be. Not only did he lose the fight by a fourth-round knockout, but he made his way into the *back* pages of the sports section several years later in an even more ignominious manner. Embroiled in a sordid love triangle with the madam of a whorehouse in Reno, Nevada, called the Mustang Guest Ranch (ironically enough, the one such house of ill repute Weinstock had ever visited), Bonavena met his end one afternoon through the barrel of his lover's cuckolded husband's 12-gauge shotgun in the ranch's chain-link-fenced parking lot.

Weinstock sensed — from the still memorable deaths of those two men — that there was a real connection between the man who loved and fought and the man who died — between the two powerful black men in the ring that night in 1962 and the seemingly inept, paralyzed, hyperdeliberative referee named Ruby Goldstein, who couldn't get his living body between them in time. Weinstock didn't — even at the price of death — want to be such a man. He didn't want to be a man whose weakened heart and overpensive mind kept him from the center of the ring. He wanted to be the heroic Philoctetes who went to Troy, not the wounded Philoctetes who was left stranded on Lemnos while the war went on without him.

For many years now, he had been dreaming of a man — a large, silent, powerful black man who walked out of the water one night after drinking the blood of Weinstock's dead relatives. He was the man, it seemed to him now, who had found something living to take from his mother's dead body. From his first appearance in Weinstock's nocturnal life, that man periodically reappeared in his dreams, a figure both threatening and alluring, appealing and terrifying. And Weinstock began to realize that, as a poet once wrote, it was only the dreamer who could change the dream.

It seemed to him that there *had* to be a connection between these things — between fighting and fucking and dying. And maybe, he thought as he pummeled his way through his dreams of himself, between the wounded Philoctetes on Lemnos and the Philoctetes who rose ten years later to slay Paris and conquer Troy, maybe he, Martin Weinstock, would have to fight and fuck and die too before he would really be able to live.

Maybe his mother had been trying to tell him something with that last love of hers, that final obsession with late-night wrestlers. Maybe it was a last "gift" to the ten-year-old boy who would one day, without her, have to become a man. Maybe she was trying to say to him: *Yes, you must wrestle with your father . . . you must defeat another man. You must fuck and love and fight, even if it means killing someone.*

2

The night after returning from his trip to Washington, Weinstock had a dream in which Morton Gamson was seated at a large table reading a book in Braille.

In the dream, he watched Gamson's hand glide slowly down and across the page. He saw his unseeing but curious eyes staring off into space and felt a deep, unfamiliar sympathy with the somewhat sad, patient man seated alone at the table in that large, white room.

There was, he realized as he dreamt, a certain dignity to the figure of Morton Gamson, a certain deep yet patient sadness worthy of respect. Perhaps, he was conscious of thinking to himself from deep within his dream, there was even a certain dignity, a certain nobility, to the largely undramatic lives of Gamson's "peckerless" characters. Perhaps the need for drama itself was a kind of foolish pride, nothing more than yet another aspect of Weinstock's own youthful arrogance. *"Poor Meyer."* Weinstock recalled the sad, blinded figure of an earlier dream of his — a dream in which he had been walking with his friend Trevor but suddenly went and put his arm around a blind, helpless figure named Meyer who was trying to find his way home alone. *"Poor Meyer,"* Weinstock kept repeating to the blind man in his dream, *"poor Meyer."*

In *this* dream, however, as Gamson finished reading a chapter of the book, he closed the cover and rose, walking slowly toward him. Weinstock saw, in large Braille letters, THE BOOK OF JOB printed on the cover. The book itself was huge, like the old Gutenberg Bible he had seen years before at Yale's Beinecke Library.

Gamson kept walking toward him until finally he stood inches away, directly in front of him. There was a moment of dread in which Weinstock was tempted to flee from the sad, needy figure standing before him. He could see in Gamson's face his mother's saddened face during the year of her dying, the unseeing eyes of his grandmother, the faces of two women a ten-year-old boy could neither save nor help.

Suddenly, a feeling rather the opposite of dread came over him. Almost involuntarily, he put his arms around the sad, patient, blinded figure of Morton Gamson. When Weinstock woke, trembling in his own bed, it was from the sweet, consoling sound of two men weeping.

3

"You know, Geoff," Weinstock remarked to Armitage after a game of tennis, "I really feel kind of sorry for old Mort when I think about it."

"Sorry?" Armitage could hardly hide the incredulity in his voice. "For Gamson? Jesus Christ, Martin, you haven't said a kind word about the guy in years, and now you're trying to tell me you feel sorry for him?"

"Well, yeah . . . kind of. You know, he's really a victim too, when you think about it."

"Oh. How's that?" Armitage, having spent half a decade as Weinstock's colleague, had learned by now to approach his friend's changes of heart with a willing but guarded suspension of disbelief.

"Well, picture it. You're a young scholar, not entirely sure of your talent, just back from the War with a couple of kids to feed. You've got a writerly bent too, but your heart's not really in it, and suddenly one day the chairman of the Harvard English Department calls you up and says, 'Hey, Mort, how about coming to Harvard to teach for a couple of years?' 'A couple of years?' you ask, trying to get a sense of what kind of gig this actually is, and the chairman says, 'Well, it may, of course, turn into something permanent, but we'd like you to give it a try, to see how you like it . . . and, of course, how we like you.'

"Well," Weinstock continued, "there you are, having to face the cold, competitive, heartless world of postwar American letters with what you suspect may be a modicum of talent, along with a modicum of courage. And along comes that Great University in the Sky, which offers you a great deal of prestige for the mere fact of *being* there and whispers in your ear: *Come.* . . . What the hell would *you* have done?"

Armitage, accustomed to coming to Gamson's defense in the face of Weinstock's onslaughts, seemed astonished, though not unwilling, suddenly to find himself in the prosecutorial position.

"Well, I would have taken it, of course. After all, *we* both did.

Then again, Martin, he could always have left. . . . He could have broken out of this mortuary — no pun intended — at any time and said, 'Fuck you guys, I'm a writer, not a goddamned Pirandello scholar, and I'm not going to spend one more minute of my life going to lectures entitled 'Ecclesiastical Eros in the Novels of Jane Austen.' "

"Yeah," Weinstock agreed halfheartedly, "he *could* have broken out of here, but, then again, you and I both know how incredibly hard *that* can be. After all, it's awfully inviting to substitute merely *being* at Harvard for all that goddamned doing. . . . *I'm* certainly not under any illusion that when I'm described as 'Harvard poet Martin Weinstock,' the stress isn't on the first two syllables."

"So he made a choice, right?" Armitage was now thoroughly enjoying his role on the other side of the witness stand. "He decided he'd rather be a living monument than a dead one, and that's exactly what he's become — 'Harvard's living answer to Stonehenge' is how you put it, isn't it?"

"Yeah, sure. . . . I know I've said all those terrible things about Mort," Weinstock confessed. "But sometimes when I see him meandering aimlessly around the Square, I get to thinking about what it really would be like to be in his shoes — almost thirty-five years in the place without even a vote in the Department; always regarded, for the mere sin of being alive, as second rate; knowing that you will never, not as long as you live — or aren't from some other goddamned country — have even the slightest chance of being shot out of their fucking canon."

"Now, wait a minute, Martin," Armitage interrupted. "I think your sentimental Jewish-underdog-early-New-York-Mets-fan sensibilities are getting the better of you. You know as well as I do that the main thing separating Mort from any goddamned canon isn't the Harvard English Department. It's the lack of even a *spark* of real talent, if you don't mind my sticking to the metaphor. And it's really kind of hard to feel sorry for the guy, you know. After all, he's got a rich wife, a house in Nova Scotia, a mansion in Cambridge, a happy family and all the time in the world to sit around reading *The New York Review of Each Other's Books.* What more could a person want?"

"Passion. . . . That's what more a person could want. Poor Mort may have all the security and prestige in the world, but — to put a small twist on that sign they've pasted all over the Yard — you can't fuck prestige."

"What the hell are you trying to tell me?" Armitage seemed baffled and humored by Weinstock's zealous advocacy of his new position. "That Harvard has stolen the passion from poor once-passionate Mort? Gimme a break, will you! No one's ever had their passion stolen by anyone they didn't hand it over to on a silver platter, and you know it! Dammit, Martin, you must be the most mercurial person I've ever met! One day you hate the guy's fucking guts, and the next day you sound like Clarence Darrow defending Scopes. Why the hell don't you make up your mind, for God's sake?"

"I am large," Weinstock tapped his befuddled colleague playfully on the shoulder with his racket, "I contain multitudes."

"I'll say," Armitage agreed, shaking his head in bewilderment. "By the way, I also don't think you ought to be as hard on this place as you are. . . . After all, where else could a refugee boy like yourself, who's never even read *Ulysses* and who until recently thought that a villanelle was a small castle in Spain, get to be an associate professor of English? Nowhere. Right?"

"That's my point," Weinstock conceded. "This place can get away with anything it pleases — even hiring me. Which doesn't mean we have to be so goddamned grateful that we can't have a little fun, does it?"

"Fun? You call insulting this place all the time having fun?"

"Of course." Weinstock held his ground. "It's like the photographer in this movie I saw the other night said about the Berlin Wall."

"Oh?" Armitage seemed only mildly surprised by the analogy.

"He said, 'We have to learn how to *play* with the Wall, since it's there, and not take it so damned seriously.' That's exactly the way I feel about dear old Thanatos U. I don't buy all this pompous self-regard they are trying to hand us all the time. . . . Why *shouldn't* we poke some fun at this place, have a little sense of humor about it?"

"Well, you're certainly making a valuable contribution to *that* genre," Armitage conceded. "I just wish you'd branch out. You know, expand your sense of humor into something a little more profound — what Corliss calls 'second-order narratives.' After all, you know that quote of yours about poetry being preparation for death."

"What about it?"

"Well, maybe it's something you ought to think about, since you're so goddamned obsessed with death and how death dealing and passionless this place and Gamson are. Maybe you should try a little prose. . . . Who knows? Maybe it would be a little foreplay into life — foreplay being something I know you're fond of."

"Yeah." Weinstock contemplated his half-finished novel as they walked past the Bratwurst and turned into Harvard Yard. "Maybe you're right. After all, it certainly is a helluva lot steadier work than poetry. . . . You know what Rodin said about work?"

"No . . . what?"

"He said, 'To work' " — Weinstock paused, as though to convince himself of the importance of what he was about to say. "He said, 'To work is to live without dying.' "

"That's pretty good." Armitage grinned. "Who knows? Maybe he was right."

4

For months Weinstock had been dreaming of Daniel Ortega and the Sandinistas.

The dreams came in a relentless procession of guises. Once, for example, Weinstock dreamt he was at a tennis camp on the outskirts of Managua, where Minister of Culture Ernesto Cardenal was helping him with his second serve. "Amigo, you must throw the ball up higher. Put your whole body into it," Cardenal told him. The words echoed with such vividness into his waking hours that Weinstock kept hearing them as he walked down Massachusetts Avenue to his office the next morning.

Tennis, for some reason, was a kind of metaphor for his nightly obsession with the Nicaraguan leaders. The next night, Weinstock dreamt that Cardenal and he were involved in a hotly contested game of doubles against Ortega and Interior Minister Tomás Borge. The score was 5–5 in the third-set tiebreaker when Weinstock twice double-faulted, handing the match to their opponents. Cardenal, however, was more than gracious about his folding at such a crucial time. *"Lluegaste magnífico!"* He consoled him with a big-hearted pat on the ass. *"Casi gagnamos."*

Tennis, as Weinstock came to think of it, had always been a metaphor for his deeply rooted ambivalence about competition. He remembered playing well during high school practices, only to have his game fall apart as soon as it came time for a match. "Martin," the coach confessed to him the day he was cut from the team, "there's something in you that's just uncomfortable with the idea of winning. . . . You've got the talent, young fella. But something else takes over the minute anyone starts keeping score." It seemed no accident to Weinstock that — at the crucial moment of combat with his political and philosophical heroes — he should place himself in a posture of *nolo contendere.*

Weinstock had actually *seen* Ortega once — right after the Sandinistas took power, when the newly inaugurated president was introduced to a standing-room-only crowd at Memorial Hall by Claudio Ambrosia de Madrid. "Our revolution and the revolution of our people," Ortega said on that occasion, "stands for the hopeful, life-affirming fact that the life of poetry, the life of politics, and the liberation of the people are not only not antagonistic but must be partners in the inevitable march towards the end of the oppression of one class by another . . . of men and women by their own human family."

What Weinstock so admired about the Sandinistas — in fact, about Latin Americans in general — was the way their poetry and political life seemed, somehow, of one piece, unlike the way they often seemed antithetical in academic life. "Politics," Amanda Wayland said to him when Weinstock brought up the subject over lunch, "is the death of an American poet. It turns you into a moralist."

"What about Neruda?" Weinstock replied.

"That," Wayland replied, pausing to swallow a bite of chicken curry, "was another country."

Still, the Sandinistas left him no peace. Weinstock found himself sitting up in bed one night, quaking with fear after having engaged in an arm-wrestling match with Vice President Ramírez during which — just as he was about to pin the Nicaraguan's arm to the table — Ramírez yanked Weinstock's arm out of its socket and threw it to a ratty, flea-bitten dog walking the streets.

"So *this* is what happens to you American poets when you have to fight for something." Ramírez smiled at him as he spoke. "You fall apart."

Indeed, it often felt that way to Weinstock: Having to fight, he fell apart, or at least double-faulted. He remembered Neruda's beautiful words (apt to Weinstock's own dream of failed "service," it seemed to him) written at Isla Negra: "My poetry will serve and sing of dignity to the indignant, of hope to the hopeless, of justice in spite of the unjust, of equality in spite of exploiters, of truth in spite of liars and of the great brotherhood of true fighters."

Maybe this, Weinstock thought to himself, was what he had so wanted to do in his dream — to "serve and sing." Yes, he wanted to serve and sing with the poets who were politicians and the politicians who were poets. He didn't want to be the kind of man whose arm fell off when he had a chance to fight for what he believed in. He didn't want one day to write, as a good friend of his once had, "I hate intelligence and have nothing else."

What was he to do? "Perhaps literature is the best answer to death, and each of us creates his own," de Madrid had once written. Perhaps that was the best thing to do — to go on pecking away like Sisyphus at this huge, impermeable bedrock of death's dominion. What if dust we were, and dust we were to be again? Why hurry? Why subdue himself, as the poet Mayakovsky had done, by setting his heels on the throat of his own singing?

Why not, like the poet Jaromil in his beloved Czech author's novel, find that special viewpoint that would free death of its customary aura of gloom? Why not smack the ball around with Cardenal and Ortega, with Borge and Ramírez? Why not pin the stupid bastard's arm to the table and stand up triumphant? Why not believe, with his famous Czech friend, that — in the face of death — a man can do and say whatever pleases his own self?

Why not lend his remaining hand to the outnumbered army of the living, Weinstock asked himself, and charge up the hill, singing?

5

The story of Philoctetes wasn't one that would have interested Weinstock much as a young man. Like those of most young men, his imagination was stirred by Heracles and Perseus and Odysseus and Achilles (men who fought and conquered and died and fucked) — and not some invalid banished to an island without a single woman on it.

The truth about Philocetes was that — even at the end of the play — he didn't really *want* to go off to Troy and fight. "The promise you made to me," he reminds Neoptolemus as they're about to leave Lemnos, "was to bring me home." *Home* was what Philoctetes was after, not war. All he wanted to do at the end of the play was to send one of his winged arrows flying through Odysseus's heart and get the hell off damned Lemnos and back home.

But the dogged voice of Heracles simply wouldn't let him get home that easily. "You shall go with yonder man to the Trojan city," Heracles informs our wounded hero, "where, first, you shall be healed of your sore malady. Then, chosen out as foremost in prowess of the host, with Achilles' bow you shall slay Paris, the author of these ills. You shall sack Troy; the prize of valor shall be given to you by our warriors; and you shall carry the spoils to your home."

It's a helluva long forecast, really, before Heracles finally gets to the old *locus dilecti:* home.

Weinstock, too, wanted to go home. Weinstock, too, wanted to say, *To hell with Paris, to hell with the Trojans, to hell with the prizes of valor. Just take me home.*

What, Weinstock asked himself (thinking, to his dismay, like a psychoanalyst) was *in it* for Philoctetes, spending those ten long years on Lemnos, a man unable to fight or fuck or die or believe in anything enough to get out of his goddamned cave and send an arrow flying off to anywhere? What the hell was he waiting for? What kind of miracle was he expecting?

Then the answer came: That was *exactly* what Philoctetes was expecting: *a miracle.* Philoctetes was expecting that he could sit there, whimpering and screaming and oozing into the sunlight for ten years and suddenly, one day — poof! — there would be Neoptolemus, eagerly waiting to load him onto a boat and take him home. Philoctetes was expecting what all men and women are expecting — or, at least, hoping for — somewhere deep in their hearts: *to be rescued,* to be spared from having to go to "the Troy of tears." Philoctetes didn't want, in Neruda's words, to "serve and sing." He wanted to sing, to wail and complain, and be taken home.

"Perhaps one of the reasons that you can't seem to decide *which* Troy to go to is that you don't really want to go to *any* Troy," Greenblatt suggested to him one afternoon. Weinstock had been lying on the couch again — "not," as Greenblatt suggested, "as a metaphor for powerlessness but merely as a potentially powerful tool."

"Perhaps what you really begin hoping for when you lie there — and why you find it so painful and humiliating to do so — is that someone like Neoptolemus will come and take care of you, without your actually having to rise and go of your own free will to Troy?"

"Yes." Weinstock felt his stomach muscles tighten as Greenblatt spoke. "Maybe that's what I'm hoping for."

"And yet what you resent most, it seems to me, is that sense of your own powerlessness — the feeling that you need someone to save you, to take you home, instead of being able to get there yourself. And the acompanying feeling that, if you actually let someone join you on Lemnos, they'll make you go to Troy first and fight."

"Yes . . . sometimes I don't feel the hell like fighting."

"Yet, when you don't fight, you feel humiliated and wounded and — as you so often put it — 'not like a man' — like your perpetually sick father, who was constantly being told by others that it was too dangerous for him to put up a fight, that it might cost him his life."

"Uh huh."

"What actually *happens* to Philoctetes after he goes to Troy?" Greenblatt asked.

"He gets healed by the son of the physician Asclepius, and goes on to slay Paris and become one of the heroes of the conquest of Troy, and later becomes the founder of several Italian cities."

"He doesn't actually get healed until he goes to Troy?"

"That's right."

"And does he ever actually get to go home?"

"Yes . . . he goes home. But only after having to go to Troy and slay Paris."

Greenblatt paused quite awhile after Weinstock's explanation. "It's awfully difficult to want to go of your own free will to kill another man," he said softly.

"Yes." Weinstock sighed as he spoke. "It certainly is."

6

After returning to Greenblatt's couch for the first time in over a year, Weinstock had a disturbing dream.

He dreamt he was at the beach with someone he had once worked with in Washington, a South African Jew named Russell Goldman. In the dream, Weinstock was wearing a pair of black leotards — the kind that always turned him on when worn by women — and no underwear. Russell and he decided to stop and sleep on the sand for a while before leaving the beach.

As they lay there, Russell began moving his head down Weinstock's body until, finally, Weinstock's penis was in his mouth. At first, Weinstock resisted, but it felt good. Russell placed a towel over his body so they wouldn't be discovered. But, a few minutes later, two policemen came by, ripped the towel away and threatened to arrest them. Weinstock felt terrified, humiliated. He awoke, nervous and fitful, and spent the rest of the day ill at ease, unable to focus on anything.

When the time came for his appointment with Greenblatt the next day, something in him absolutely couldn't lie on the couch again. He sat in the brown, overstuffed chair, alternately meeting and avoiding Greenblatt's gaze as they spoke.

"What do you *make* of that dream?" Greenblatt insisted, after Weinstock glibly revealed its contents, then moved quickly to another subject.

"I don't know. . . . It's not the kind of dream I usually have. And I'm not sure why I would have dreamt of Russell Goldman. I haven't seen him in fifteen years."

"What comes to mind when you think of him?"

"Well, we worked together at this foundation in D.C. called the Close-Up Foundation."

"The Close-Up Foundation?" Greenblatt's hand fell from his chin as Weinstock spoke.

"Yes. . . . The name *could* be somewhat symbolic, I suppose," Weinstock confessed sheepishly.

"Yes." Greenblatt smiled. "I suppose."

"Well, anyway, I don't frequently have homosexual dreams, so I was kind of wondering what brought this one on."

"And then, today, you shoot right up into the chair again."

"What does *that* have to do with anything?"

"Well, first you come in and lie down on the couch for the first time in months, and that same night you have a dream in which you are seduced by a man you worked with at a place called the Close-Up Foundation. The next day you come in here and head right for the chair in a kind of panic. . . . What do *you* make of all that?"

"Well, I suspect it must have aroused some kind of fear or memory I had about my father being so seductive with me — about all that romantic energy he always directed at me instead of at the women he was married to. I was thinking, as a matter of fact, of this cruise to the Bahamas he took me on when I was fourteen — when boys my age were wanting to go hunting or fishing or something like that with their fathers."

"Or wrestle with them?"

"Yes . . . that too."

"So, instead of taking you to war — to Troy — he took you on a kind of "Love Boat?" Weinstock could always tell by his ever-so-slight change in tone when something really piqued Greenblatt's interest.

"Yes. . . . That's right."

"And now — when what you're consciously thinking of is how you can learn to fight with and defeat other men, of how you can get to Troy and finally have a *woman* put your penis in her mouth and look her in the eye — what your unconscious is dreaming about, on the night after you lie here on the couch in front of me again, is of being seduced by a *man*. . . . As if it is telling you 'Make Love, Not War.' Or like that bumper sticker that was prevalent during the Vietnam War: 'WOMEN SAY YES TO MEN WHO SAY NO.' "

"Yes. . . . I suppose that's too coincidental not to make some sense. It also reminds me of something I once heard about men who are writers."

"What's that?"

"That men who are writers, instead of confronting their fathers in Kansas, attack them long distance from typewriters in New York and Hollywood."

"Or from typewriters in Cambridge . . . instead of going to fight them on the plains of Troy," Greenblatt added.

"I'm not so sure the couch is any improvement over the typewriter." Weinstock was still unable to resist any opportunity to question his own treatment.

"Particularly if it's a place where you're likely to get seduced, or overpowered — where you can't get either your pen or your sword up."

"Yeah. . . . So what's the point of my lying on the couch then?"

"If you hadn't lain there, you wouldn't have had the dream and been able to experience your own helplessness again."

"Why the hell would I *want* to experience my own helplessness again? I think once is more than enough."

"Because this time you may be able to understand it and *do* something about it."

7

"It occurred to me," Weinstock said to Greenblatt at the beginning of their next session, "while reading this book by a Jungian analyst about *Tristan and Isolde,* and after our talking about my being seduced by various men, that being at Harvard makes me feel like Isolde of the White Hands."

"How do you mean?"

"Well, in the legend, Isolde of the White Hands is the one who — no matter how beautiful she is, or how much love she offers Tristan — can't get him to desire her the way he desires Isolde the Fair, with whom he has drunk the magic potion and who remains always somewhat unavailable to him."

"How does that apply to being at Harvard?"

"Well, you know, there's this way in which the only way you can be appreciated at Harvard — no matter how many books you pub-

222 🦃 MICHAEL BLUMENTHAL

lish or how good a citizen you are or how many awards you get for your teaching — is by seeming to be disinterested in being there, by being somehow unavailable . . . or dead. If you show the slightest actual desire to be or stay there — if you're not someone who's constantly threatening to leave or actually leaving — you're thought of as needy, somehow, and therefore not worth paying attention to."

"It's a bit like the way you've never been able to make your father and stepmother entirely happy either — no matter how devoted you've been to them, or what kind of woman you were with — Jewish or not Jewish, rich or poor — or what kind of success you've had in your work. It's never seemed quite enough."

"Yes. . . . I suppose it's a bit like that." Greenblatt's words filled him with such a profound sadness that it was suddenly difficult to speak.

"I wonder if you remember from the story how Tristan got his name — from the French word for sad, *triste.*"

"Well" — Weinstock paused for a moment, as though blocking out a knowledge he knew he possessed — "yes . . . in fact I do. It was because his mother died giving birth to him — leaving him to a life of sadness and unrequited longing."

"Just like someone else you know."

"Yes . . . like my father."

"Someone else who seems to prefer, as Harvard does, the love of those who are unavailable to him — or dead — to those who are available and living."

"Yes." The horrible coherence of all this seemed suddenly irrefutable — and deeply painful.

"So you seem to be faced with a kind of no-win situation — a kind of Scylla and Charybdis — in your life."

"Scylla and Charybdis?" Unable, momentarily, to focus on what Greenblat was getting at, Weinstock could do no better than repeat his analyst's words.

"Yes . . . between remaining, on the one hand, Isolde of the White Hands to those whom — like Harvard and your father — you will never *ever* be able to satisfy, or, on the other hand, going back to your previous posture of being Isolde the Fair to those who, like your friend Laura, actually desire you and offer you their love . . . and whom you perpetually reject."

"Yes." Weinstock felt a certain heaviness enveloping him, making his body feel like a lead weight in Greenblatt's chair. "I suppose those are basically the ways I've been."

"Of course," Greenblat added after quite a long pause, "there's yet a third option."

"Oh?" Weinstock suddenly felt himself sit up in the chair, as though lightened by possibilities he hadn't considered. "What's that?"

"You might" — Greenblatt inhaled and paused momentarily — "you might — as I think you're beginning to do — decide you've had enough pain from both those alternatives and do something entirely different."

"And what's that?"

"You might decide to change."

CHAPTER 16

At Heart

In the incoherent babble of the child,
I return to my childhood.
And in the sharp, unfeeling syllables of betrayal,
I renounce my betrayals.

— MARTIN WEINSTOCK
"Tongues"

In his heart of hearts, what Weinstock had always been interested in with women was a kind of "spiritual fiddling," serious play that involved life and death, pleasure and pain, laughter and weeping, the ridiculous and the sublime, the throbbing flesh and the beckoning dust.

Not only did *womb* rhyme with *tomb*, he realized, but *fiddling* with *diddling*, *cunt* with *stunt* . . . *death* with *breath*. At heart, he knew, there was nothing as intoxicating — nothing as serious — as a man and a woman in search of the playfulness that can weep.

"Sometimes I think you only believed that I loved you when you were able to make me sad," Laura told him one night on the phone. "It was as if my happiness wasn't as credible to you as my sadness."

"Yes," he admitted, "I hate to think so, but maybe it's true."

"It was almost as if you had to make me sad in order to believe I loved you."

Weinstock had to admit to himself that Laura's habitual cheerfulness, much as he envied it, had always seemed somehow inauthentic. It was only in her moments of sadness — in their shared moments of weeping — that he could let himself feel close to her.

"Yes." He paused. "I wonder if that could be true. . . . I need to think about it."

Weinstock had always thought of himself — as he had tried to convince Karen Browne's sister Felicity — as a cheerful sort of guy, a man for whom laughter was the first foretaste of a deeper happiness, someone for whom the cheerful and the profound were, ultimately, one. But when he now thought back to Felicity's appraisal of him as "the saddest man who ever lived," when he remembered the reference to his "soulful, Keatsian eyes" Amanda Wayland made, when he remembered his friend Claudia saying to him that "until recently, I always thought of you as a tremendously depressed person," Weinstock had to gaze with a cold eye upon himself. He realized that Laura's cheerfulness perhaps had seemed inauthentic to him because he had no real cheerfulness of his own with which to engage it.

"You need to find yourself a woman who's had a happy childhood," Trevor had once told him. Yet it seemed to Weinstock that whenever he found himself such a woman, he did whatever he could to make sure that her adulthood contained a compensatory unhappiness, instead of trying to compensate for his own unhappiness by sharing her joy.

What was this "spiritual fiddling" he was after? Where was the wild justice, the perfect equilibrium, the balance between lightness and heaviness, the cunt and the womb, he so longed for? Must a person always, as Camus suggested, recognize his homeland only as he was about to lose it? Wasn't it, as Camus had also written, impossible to discover the absurdity of one's own desires without being tempted to write a manual of happiness?

So maybe it was Weinstock's novel — and not his longed-for life with a woman — that was his avenue into the world of "spiritual fiddling," his "manual of happiness." Maybe he had turned to art, as Nietzsche suggested, "in order not to die of the truth," in order to find for himself something that would be the equal of a happy childhood, that would not have to make a woman weep in order to convince him of her love. For even a crushing truth perishes from being acknowledged. Even a sad face smiles when it looks into the mirror of its own sadness.

2

Dear Martin:

As your letter indicates, you feel it is unfair and painful for me to have seen in your little "innocent" affair with your student Alexis (how was it you used to describe her — "Joan Baez with a nose job?") something reminiscent of your behavior when we were lovers. In truth, that behavior had nothing to do with what you call "ambivalence" in your letter — We both, like *all* lovers, felt "ambivalent" about each other.

What it *had* to do with, though, was a pattern of asking for trust, and then, when you got it, pulling the rug out from under me. Your lies and cruelties were in no way a necessary result of "ambivalence," as you must know by now from how other lovers (including your own) behave.

It would, even, have been different had you at least had the courage to tell me about it yourself, rather than have me learn about it by finding that bill from the abortion clinic on your desk. (Why, I ask myself, would someone as determined to live a "secret" life as you be so careless about concealing it?) Knowing the past complications of your life and your fear of intimacy, I certainly would have done my best to be compassionate and understanding, as I always was in our relationship. Then again, I suppose anyone with as complicated a relationship to the truth as you have had in your life can't be expected to be much good at it.

Either you are right that your "innocent little affair" and your leaving the bill on the desk where I would so easily come across it (Didn't you once tell me a story, by the way, of your father always asking you to write to him "in secret," and then leaving the letters around the house where your stepmother would find them?) didn't predict an intent to hurt me, and I responded un-fairly, or I am right that there *was* such an intent. In either case, what appears to have happened is that, in coming not to trust you as a lover, I also have come not to trust you as a friend.

Either the injustice of that mistrust or its accuracy requires that I break off contact with you. You certainly don't need friends who don't trust you, and I don't need friends I'm unable to trust. So I'm not going to write or phone you, and I ask you not to write or phone me. Although I'm not able to be a friend to you, if we do meet by chance someday it will be with joy that I remember the good times of the past with you.

I very much hope that our breaking off contact will be of little consequence to you. All your friends in Boston and whatever new lover I am certain you will in a short time find will be sustaining to you, and I wouldn't be able to sustain you as well as those friends even if I were there.

I'll always remember the many happinesses we had together — some of them even amidst the worst unhappiness — and your wonderful voice, your love of words, your endearments and kindnesses, and all your funny, wonderful names. You have so much desire and such capacity for self-knowledge that — when you are ready — you will surely find happiness and peace with someone.

Adieu — love —

Laura

Weinstock opened the letter, which arrived a week after Laura's hasty departure, with a sense of doomed foreknowledge.

He had tried, in the six months since Laura had first left Boston, to maintain a genuine friendship with her (something he had rarely succeeded, for reasons he still couldn't fathom, in attaining with previous lovers). So it was with an even deeper than usual sense of disgust and disappointment that, after inviting her to come visit over the Fourth of July "just as friends," he returned to his apartment from running some errands that weekend to find her staring at the bill for Alexis's abortion he had so carelessly left on top of a pile of papers while cleaning out his desk.

Within forty-five minutes, all his weeping and imploring and begging for forgiveness notwithstanding, Laura was on a plane back to Wisconsin, and Weinstock's only existing platonic friendship with a former lover was over. With a sense of utter dejection, he rolled a piece of paper into his typewriter carriage and started typing:

Dear Laura:

You're right: I didn't deserve you as a lover, and it doesn't seem that I deserve you as a friend either. As my friend Trevor said, I don't seem to be someone who can let kindness into my life without my mean, lustful, frightened, death-seeking self getting in the way.

Maybe courage simply isn't a thing I have much of . . . or goodness for that matter. Maybe all that desire and capacity for self-knowledge you so generously mentioned in your letter is nothing more than that — a desire for *knowledge,* but not necessarily for *improvement.*

The fact is that your breaking off contact with me, much as I understand your reasons for it, *will* be of great consequence, because — in my own stupid, bumbling, ineffectual way — I have loved and treasured you.

Maybe, I think at times, I should give up on my great moralistic program of oracle-revision and self-improvement. Maybe I should just learn to love and accept the mean, cruel, lying, lustful animal I seem to be and make for myself, like my old hero Henry Miller, a happy, ass-grabbing life of *yahoo!* and *yippee!* in which I could simply say, as he did, "for me the book is the man and my book is the man I am, the confused man, the negligent man, the lusty, obscene, boisterous, thoughtful, scrupulous, lying, diabolically truthful man that I am."

Oh hell, Laura, who knows? I sure don't. I did the best I could, however little that must have seemed to you. And I'll always remember you too — your kindness, your sweetness, your generosity, your intelligence, your capacity for forgiveness . . . the latter which, I suppose, it took only a dumb Weinstock like myself to finally exhaust.

With love and gratitude,
Martin

Weinstock unrolled the letter from his typewriter and sat, blank-faced, staring at its contents. The truth, he realized, was that he had grown so adept at his own eloquence and self-scrutiny that he no longer knew *what* he meant or didn't mean, what he knew or didn't know.

"Interest in oneself," he remembered Bertrand Russell having written, "leads to no activity of a progressive kind. It may lead to keeping a diary, to getting psychoanalyzed, or perhaps to becoming a monk. But the monk will not be happy until the routine of the monastery has made him forget his own soul."

It seemed to Weinstock, as he sealed the envelope and lay down to take a nap, that he just wasn't capable of forgetting his own soul.

3

Dear Martin,

At 6:15 this morning I woke up, thoughts of you popped into my head, and I felt this compulsion to write you. As you may well know, I always listen to my inner voice — so here I am writing you a letter even before the sun is fully up.

As the letterhead attests, after spending two years getting a Master's, I'm now a college professor, sort of. I'm an instructor at St. Catherine College, a lovely and wonderful Lutheran school in Northern Minnesota. We have 3400 students, 80% of whom are Lutheran, many of whom are blonde and blue-eyed. It makes me chuckle to be here in the heartland of Scandinavianism after summers on that kibbutz. You may not know that I have a deep and long-abiding faith in God. At the time you knew me, I was pissed at him/her/it because of the state of my life, and I was ignoring h/h/i. As time went by, that passed. I am now not at all unhappy, even as a Jew, to be on the faculty of a Christian school.

Now don't misunderstand and think I'm oh-so-holy. Hell no. Most people here are as human as the next guy. I'm always amused that the public seems to think religious folks have no fun, don't talk dirty, don't drink booze. Well, they ought to get to know some of my clergy friends here! I haven't yet been able to write a poem that would make any of them disown me. And I've tried.

I suppose the reason I'm writing you is that I feel the need to say some things to you now. I think of you quite often and think small prayers for you. You moved me deeply from the first time I met you. *You are so lost, Martin.* I recognized that from the first minute. And, given the state of my undergraduate life, I was open to your sort of need.

I know you've denied any sort of complicity in our "misunderstanding," but I still don't accept that. You knew I was lonely and hurting in some way, and I suspect you saw I was vulnerable. I was also safe because I was young and a student. There was no serious chance I might expect something from you. You hurt me deeply when you denied leading me on in subtle ways, when you would only call me when you were horny or lonely or cheating on some other woman like Laura whom you were "really" involved with. Many people saw it. Which is why I didn't really want you with me the day of the abortion, and why I didn't return any of your calls or notes after that either: I always sensed that I was really nothing more to you than a quick lay, some way of fending off your middle-aged, menopausal male fear of dying.

But all of that is water under the proverbial bridge. I've long ago forgiven you. I've even forgiven me. In some way, you have been a blessing to me. I learned a lot about myself and about the world through you. I learned how sad it is when people are untrue. Will you admit that there was a lot of untruth? It's so destructive, Martin. It's lonely enough in this life, without bricking ourselves in further.

So Martin, I hope you're well. One day you could write me if you felt like it, but you needn't. I respect your need to remain private and apart. If you ever feel the urge to see Northern Minnesota, I have an extra bed. It's really quite lovely here — flat, big sky, windy. Not quite Manhattan, but with its own charm. If you ever leave Harvard (do you *still* call it "Thanatos," or have you finally started to see that some of that deadness is inside *you*?), will you please at least let me know where you're going? Otherwise how am I going to be able to write you when the universe tells me to? Part of my religious belief is mystical. I've had enough weird experiences to pay attention when the cosmos speaks. I guess it's why I write poems, too. I really don't think I write them alone.

Take care of yourself, Martin.

With affection,
Alexis

Weinstock opened Alexis's letter with a certain trepidation. The word **PERSONAL** was boldly typed on the face of the envelope, and he was certain that the contents, like all the epistolary outbursts of Alexis Baruch, would make him more than a tad uncomfortable.

Alexis, indeed, *had* been an extremely vulnerable young woman during her semester in his workshop. And Weinstock had to confess that he had found himself rather naively surprised by the fact that his usual offhanded flirtatiousness toward all but his most unattractive female students had evoked such an intensity of response. "That young woman," Armitage, who had taught Alexis in his fiction seminar, warned, "is obsessed with you."

Rather typically, Weinstock was abetted in his dismissal of Alexis's attention by denying any complicity in its arousal. "She's absolutely wacko," he would say whenever Armitage teased him about her visits to his office. "I don't know where she gets the faintest idea I'm interested in her."

Sitting at his desk now, Alexis's freshly opened letter in his hand, he had to admit to himself that maybe he *did* have an idea how he had aroused his student's interest. Maybe he *had* noticed her vulnerability and led her on in subtle ways. "Why do you always come on to me in impossible situations and then disappear?" a fellow writer had once scrawled in his notebook at a conference in Vermont. "You are a lover of the *Verboten*."

Looking down at Alexis's letter still trembling in his hand, Weinstock reread the lines that reverberated with an aura of absolute truth in his lonely life. "*You are so lost, Martin. . . .* It's lonely enough in this life, without bricking ourselves in further. . . . I respect your need to remain private and apart."

Those words, he realized — though he was almost forty and a professor at probably the world's finest university — were still the most accurate with which to describe him: *lost . . .* a lover of the *Verboten*.

4

Dear Martin,

When you called again after having called and left that message about your problems with Laura and with that former student of yours, your voice was filled with disappointment that I hadn't gotten your message or at least responded in the proper, sympathetic way (whatever that is). I felt that I had let you down in some way. I felt guilty. And then I realized that I was *tired* of feeling that I am your friend when you are in need and want someone to share your burdens with.

You're a needy guy. Well, we're all needy and we call on our friends to help us over the rough spots. But, between us, it's your pain and discouragement that I feel most of the time. From what you tell me, your life is dragging you down and is depressing. Your life as an academic doesn't suit you and you resent it. When you published your last book — usually a joyful, sharing event for friends and family — you chose not even to celebrate that fact with your friends, but to let it pass as if it were something that made you feel ashamed, rather than proud. It felt that way, and it felt selfish.

It's hard to get on board and invest love, time and caring in someone who always seems unhappy and doomed. Whenever you call, I expect to hear another chapter in the saga of Martin's torment. Yet I've never known someone who has more going for them and is as unhappy. You have spent years in therapy and psychoanalysis and licking your wounds, but you still project this woeful Martin persona, this man who was badly wounded and will spend his whole life changing his bandages . . . at least that's the side of you *I* get to see.

We've *all* been wounded, don't you see? We grow up and get beyond it because death's just around the corner, and life, for all its troubles, is a good time and worth the effort.

I love you and want to keep our friendship alive and well. I don't want to be your brother only in pain. I don't want to keep hearing the sad tale of a man who has had more than his share of advantages and cannot see the bright side . . . of a Martin Weinstock who is always among the dying.

Sometimes I have wanted to say to you: "For Christ's sake (or Moses's), Martin, stop this whining and woe-is-me shit and get on with it. You have milked your childhood story — your two fathers and two mothers, your eggs and your furs — for all it's worth and now it's time to put it behind you. You're a grown-up now. Act like it."

I am not a fair-weather friend. But I expect more from you than what you have so far allowed yourself to have . . . and you *can* let yourself have it! (But it might mean giving up some old scripts.)

So there I am.

I *am* your friend, and I feel I have let you down by not saying these things earlier, as friends are supposed to do.

Love,
Trevor

5

"You're getting better, though I know it must be difficult for you to believe it."

Weinstock was seated in Greenblatt's stuffed brown chair, shaking with sobs as Greenblatt spoke.

"I feel" — he stopped crying for a moment as he spoke — "as if I'm in one of those *New Yorker* cartoons. The patient's on his deathbed dying, and this physician is sitting next to him saying, 'You're getting better, Mr. Weinstock, you're getting better.' Why, in one week I've gotten letters from my ex-girlfriend telling me I'm a no-good louse, a former student half my age calling me a lost soul, and my best friend telling me I'm nothing but a temple of doom — and you have the *nerve* to sit there with your stupid Freudian boilerplate of transference and resistance and tell me I'm getting better."

"Yes." Greenblatt evinced a heartfelt sympathy as he spoke. "It must feel that way . . . it must feel as if, everywhere you turn, you're failing and dying. But perhaps it would help if you merely thought of yourself as in mourning."

"I've *been* in mourning for thirty years. Don't you think that's enough?" Weinstock was losing his capacity for disguising a certain rage he felt toward Greenblatt.

"Yes," Greenblatt replied in the same, reassuring voice. "You've been sad for a long time, haven't you?"

"Yes." Weinstock began sobbing again as he spoke. "For a very long time."

"Yet you've also wanted so much to escape the sadness, to avoid being engulfed by it."

Weinstock shook his head.

"Well" — Greenblatt paused, seeming to measure his words as he spoke — "I think that, if you can bear it for a little while longer, the sadness will finally abate and you'll feel stronger again."

"Well, I'm certainly not feeling any stronger now."

"No, you're not. And you probably won't be . . . for a while at least. But if you can just manage to *inhabit* your sadness and pain awhile longer, I believe it will pay off for you."

"And what if it doesn't? What if I just keep getting sadder and sadder and weaker and weaker until there's nothing left of me?" This was Weinstock's greatest fear — that he was about to fall into an abyss of sadness so deep he would never be able to extricate himself again.

Greenblatt paused once more, as though seriously considering Weinstock's question. "I don't think that's likely to happen," he said. "But you may need to do a bit more dying before you can truly enter the world of the living. Philoctetes, I'm sure you remember, spent ten years stranded on Lemnos before he got to Troy."

"Yes." Weinstock wiped his tears on his sweater sleeve. "I remember."

"Perhaps you're feeling anxious," Greenblatt suggested, "because these many discrete sessions we have had over the past five years — these many poems we have been writing here — haven't yet taken on a final shape, haven't yet become a book. Perhaps they seem to you more like a series of vignettes that haven't yet been ordered — into, say, a novel."

"Yes," Weinstock agreed with unusual rapidity. "I feel a bit as though I'm doing these things — coming to these sessions, writing my book, living my life — in a way that's totally random."

"Just as your book seems at times to be totally random."

"As if the entire contents had somehow been shaken up and disordered —"

"And now need to be reordered." Greenblatt, not usually one to interrupt, completed the sentence.

"Yes, I suppose so. Isn't that what they say about psychoanalysis? That it's like taking a house down brick by brick and then having to rebuild it?" A slight, almost imperceptible smile trickled over the corners of Greenblatt's mouth as Weinstock spoke.

"That's been said occasionally. But I think it's difficult for you to have faith that the house *can* actually be rebuilt, that the apparent disorder actually contains an order."

"Yes. It's hard for me to have faith."

"Yet I think that — if you can continue writing your book, if you can continue coming to these sessions, and not feel that you need to impose a false order on all of this before the actual order is revealed — you'll be much better off. . . . Who knows" — Weinstock thought he detected a faint sigh in Greenblatt's voice as the analyst spoke — "but that you might even get well?"

6

Weinstock had first met Ida Lou Hart on the Eastern shuttle while on his way to what he thought was his stepmother's deathbed at Mt. Sinai Hospital, where she was being treated for cancer. This time, he consoled himself, even as he contemplated the death of the woman he had hated and who had hated him from the moment she entered his life almost thirty years before, there would be no dying without his presence. . . . There would be no removing anything without his being there.

It was a bright, sun-drenched morning. There was somehow an erotic tinge to Weinstock's thoughts, and to the fragrant, colorful dyings of late October, which must have lent him a special vulnerability and openness as he sat in the Logan Airport waiting room staring at an exotic-looking woman in lavender boots reading Colette's *Chéri*.

"Are you a fan of Colette?" he ventured, as she turned toward him.

"You bet! Why — are you?"

Weinstock had to admit that he had never actually read Colette. "But lots of my women friends really admire her," he quickly added.

"Oh yeah. . . . I just *love* how unashamed of her sexuality she is . . . especially for a woman writing at the time."

Weinstock didn't really want to change the subject but thought it might be a good idea. "What's your name?" he asked politely.

"Ida Lou. . . . What's yours?"

"Martin — Martin Weinstock. Great to meet you, Ida. You live in Boston?"

"Well, I *have* been. I'm just in the process of moving to New York."

"That's too bad." He felt gratefully distracted from his mission of that morning. "Didn't know you were going to meet me, huh?"

Ida Lou smiled. "Yeah — kind of. I need to move to New York for my work."

"What's that?"

"I'm an actress and singer, and there's not much of that kind of work in Boston. . . . It's kind of a dead town when it comes to theater, if you know what I mean. . . . Come to think of it, it's kind of a dead town, period."

"Yeah, I think I know what you mean," Weinstock agreed. "What are you going to be doing in New York. . . . Kind of tough to break in there, no?"

"It is." Ida Lou put away her Colette and moved to the empty seat beside him. "But I've got this pretty good job waitressing three nights a week and an agent who's gotten me gigs singing at funerals until I can start auditioning."

"Funerals? Sounds like fun."

"Well, believe it or not, it's not a bad thing. I can do two or three funerals on a typical Sunday at somewhere between fifty and a hundred dollars each. That's pretty good money — and the work's easy."

The thought of this Liza Minnelli–like figure in black tights and wide-looped earrings singing Kaddish seemed mildly humorous to Weinstock. "What kind of funerals do you do?"

"Oh, the whole bit — Jewish, Catholic, Unitarian . . . you name it."

"What do you sing — Alban Berg's greatest hits?"

She chuckled. "Not really — just a little bit of everything you'd expect — sections from Mozart's *Requiem* or some Goethe *Lieder*. Last week I sang "Kumbaya" at this terrific Unitarian funeral in Westchester for a man who founded a Waldorf school. And I sang some Billie Holiday songs at this black jazz musician's funeral on Staten Island a couple of weeks ago."

"Well," Weinstock said, "if you feel like practicing your Wagner, I may have another gig for you soon."

Ida Lou paled, uncertain whether or not he was joking. "What do you mean? Is someone in your family dying?" Her look of genuine concern only endeared her to Weinstock further.

"Almost always."

"Seriously . . . is someone you know sick? Is that why you're going to New York?"

"My stepmother. She's got cancer."

"That's awful. . . . I'm really sorry."

"It's not so bad." Weinstock didn't want to put too much of a damper on their flirtation. "Someone in my family's usually doing some bad imitation of the dying. . . . She'll probably outlive both of us," he joked.

"Well, I hope you're right," Ida Lou joked back, as a voice came over the loudspeaker asking them to board. "It's a lot more fun to do funerals if you don't know the person involved."

"I'll bet." Weinstock's tone must have turned suddenly serious, because Ida Lou gazed pityingly at him. "Want to sit together?"

"Love to."

Weinstock's stepmother hadn't, in fact, died on that occasion. Nonetheless, he and Ida Lou managed to have a brief, passionate affair before she officially moved to New York several weeks later and married her boyfriend, a tap dance instructor from Long Island City. They had kept seeing each other periodically over the years since, so that — on this particular evening as they sat drinking Absolut martinis at a dimly lit Cambridge bar called the Commonwealth Café — there was a sense of long-standing famliarity between them.

"Well, Ida, you might say that by now we kinda 'go back,' don't you think?" Weinstock lifted his glass. "So here's to old friends."

"I'll drink to that." Ida Lou was dressed in a short black skirt over green tights and a sequined see-through top. She lifted her glass toward his. "And to your stepmother — who made it all possible."

Weinstock clicked his glass against hers and slowly poured the warming liquid into his gullet. "It's really kind of spooky, don't you think — the way we met?" he said.

"Spooky? Why spooky?"

"Well, the fact that I thought my stepmother was dying that day when I left for New York, and that I felt so attracted to you in that waiting room, when I probably should have been thinking more serious thoughts."

"More serious thoughts? Why, what could *possibly* be more serious than being attracted to someone?" Weinstock had always liked Ida Lou's sense of priorities.

"You know what I mean — after all, my stepmother seemed like she was going to die at any minute."

"What in the world does *that* have to do with anything, Martin?" Ida Lou seemed to be getting a tad irritated. "After all, we all are.

"You know what I think, Martin?" she continued. "I think you take all this stuff about death and dying and all those stuffy-faced, sad-eyed old boys at Harvard too seriously. You ought to lighten up a little bit. After all, it's *all* a tragedy, if you want to look at it that way. . . . It's just a matter of how you get through it. And I think that the most interesting way to get through it is to say, 'I can't help it, I'm full of passion, and I'm going to die this moment!' Why, it's the one sure way of pretending you're really alive."

Weinstock kept sipping his second martini as Ida Lou spoke. There was always something about being with her that made his sadness ebb, something that made him think of a line he'd once read in a poem: "Love is a mouth." There was something about her singing "Kumbaya" at that Unitarian's funeral, something about those lips trembling their songs into the light as bodies were lowered into the earth, that still excited him. He always felt, making love to her, that he was on the cusp of life and death, of sadness and happiness, of his dark, death-filled past and some brighter, more life-affirming future.

"I guess," he said, gazing intently at her in the bluish light, "that I just have this sort of obsession with coincidences . . . the weird justice and injustice of it all."

"Oh, Martin." Ida Lou's large, bedroom eyes moved to within an inch of his face. "Pleasure's the only justice. Don't you know that by now? . . . And you know what a pleasure pig I am."

"Yeah . . . I know." Weinstock felt his heart begin to beat rapidly and pulled Ida Lou toward him. "Let's drink up and go over to my place," he whispered. "Let's go home and pretend we're really alive."

7

The night after spending his first and last full weekend with Ida Lou Hart, Weinstock dreamt he was being attacked by a band of gorillas.

It was a terrifying dream, the gorillas tearing at him with their sharp nails, pummeling him with their fists, the tightly wound, dark hair of their faces reminding him of something he couldn't quite put his finger on.

"You are both my cunt and my womb," he said to Ida Lou after making love the night she arrived in Cambridge. "Much as I love fucking you, sometimes all I want to do is rest my head between those big, gorgeous breasts of yours and go to sleep."

Ida Lou, indeed, *was* both a cunt and a womb — playful, erotic, independent, nurturing, serene. There was, in fact, only one thing wrong — or, perhaps, right — with her from Weinstock's distorted perspective: She was now married and living in New York.

From that moment of their first meeting in the airport lounge, the ease between them had made remaining lovers natural, though somewhat inconvenient. Yet they had never, until the past weekend, actually *slept* together. So it was Ida Lou's finally being in Cambridge again for a theater conference that made it possible for Weinstock to realize his long-simmering fantasy of spending an entire night with her.

"Sex," he had often remarked to Trevor Johnson, "is the place of the cunt. But sleep is the place of the womb. It's like the kiss and the fuck," he added. "You can fuck a turtle if you have to, but a kiss — a kiss is the most intimate act in the world. When you kiss a woman, it means you have to look her right in the eye and say: *you.*"

It wasn't, indeed, easy for Weinstock to look a woman right in the eye and say *you,* so that these two days and nights spent with Ida Lou — reading aloud, jogging, making love, gripping her tongue between his teeth as he gazed into her eyes and ran his fingers over her forehead and hair — felt like an entryway into a place he had rarely, if ever, known . . . and had found so difficult to locate with Laura.

"She simply refuses to be a cunt," he had once complained about Laura to Trevor, "except in private, where it doesn't really count."

"Oh?" Trevor seemed startled. "I always thought that in private was the *only* place it counted. It's like this writer I once read said — what every man really wants is 'the good whore who resembles his mother.' "

That, in fact, was what Ida Lou Hart was — an unabashedly erotic lover who was by now also the mother of a two-year-old son by her tap-dancer-turned-public-relations executive husband, Rick. To accommodate her own divided desires, she had been involved with a series of long-term lovers, Weinstock among them, since her marriage. "But I'll never," she confessed, "leave my husband."

"So, what do you make of this dream of yours?" Greenblatt asked after Weinstock recounted his nightmare.

"Well, I don't exactly know." Weinstock sat in the stuffed chair, thinking. "It occurred to me that I was thinking about traveling again — to Indonesia — and I started to remember what you said about my not being nearly as interested in journeying to the exotic places *within* me as to exotic places on some other continent. Maybe what the dream was about is my fear of the dark and terrible animals inside myself."

"Yes, perhaps." Greenblatt seemed lost in thought. "What night did you say it was that you had that dream?"

"Sunday night."

"That was the night your friend Ida Lou left, wasn't it?"

"Uh hmm." Weinstock felt his usual caution about Greenblatt's interpretations begin to overtake him. "What does that have to do with anything?"

"Well" — Greenblatt scratched his black beard as he spoke — "I was wondering why you would have such a violent dream about being attacked right after a weekend in which you experienced — as you put it — 'the cunt and the womb in the same place.' I wonder if you feel, somehow, that it's prohibited to have that kind of pleasure."

Weinstock was thinking hard as Greenblatt spoke. "Well" — he hesitated — "I suppose that would make a kind of sense. . . . After all, my father would always find some way to attack me or start dying whenever I experienced any real sexual pleasure with a woman."

"Yes." Greenblatt shook his head in agreement. "I wonder if the gorillas in your dream remind you of anyone." He scratched lightly at his beard.

"Well . . . come to think of it" — Weinstock still hesitated — "they probably remind me of *you* — I mean, with your black beard and all your goddamned Freudian orthodoxy that reminds me of my father's orthodoxy. Like a real Hasid, if you know what I mean.

I think that's what I remember best about those gorillas — their terrible blackness."

"So that you might think — very much as your father threatened you with his *own* death whenever you showed up with a cunt and a womb in the same place — that *I* might threaten you with death after a weekend in which you experienced a womb and a cunt with the same woman."

A chill flooded over Weinstock as Greenblatt spoke. "What a stupid, shallow, typically asshole Freudian move," part of him wanted to say.

"Yes," he agreed, "I might think that."

"Well" — Greenblatt took his hand from his face and smiled ever so slightly, "you might want to think some more about why you feel it's so dangerous to have both passion and comfort with a single woman — why it threatens you, even, with death. And why" — he paused — "it seems you can only find it with a woman who is married to somebody else."

8

Dear Martin,

What an incredible time I had with you this past weekend — in *and* out of bed!

I'm lying here reading Baudelaire in bed (where else?). I had just put down Italo Calvino and was still thinking about lightness when I read this, with the wondrous line "The sweetness that enthralls, the joy that kills."

I was also reminded of one of my favorite parts of *Paterson* (enclosed). They couldn't have been talking about the same woman, could they?

Just three weeks until I get to see you again. I kiss you all over your delectable body —

Love,
Ida Lou

Weinstock unfolded the sheet of paper bearing Ida Lou's scrawled note, with a Xeroxed copy of Baudelaire's poem "To a Passer-by" folded inside it. The second and third stanzas of the poem read:

Noble and lithe, her leg was sculptural.

And I myself, with wild intensity,
Drank in her eyes, a sombre, stormy sky,
The sweetness that enthralls, the joy that kills.

A lightning flash . . . then night! Love passing by,
Whose sudden glance bestowed new life on me,
Shall I not see you till eternity?

But it's too far! Too late! Never, maybe!
I know not where you are — you, where I go,
You whom I should have loved — and felt it so!

He lifted the page. Beneath it was a second sheet of paper, on
which was Xeroxed a section of William Carlos Williams's *Paterson,*
describing

> a woman in our town
> walks rapidly, flat bellied
> in worn slacks upon the street
> where I saw her.
>   neither short
> nor tall, nor old nor young
> her
>   face would attract no
>
> adolescent . . .
>
> if I ever see you again
> as I have sought you
> daily without success
>
> I'll speak to you, alas
> too late! ask,
> What are you doing on the
>
> streets of Paterson? a
> thousand questions:
>
> intelligent woman

have you read anything I have written?
It is all for you.

Weinstock felt a wave of sadness come over him as he gazed at the two poems side by side. He stared out the window, then rolled a sheet of paper into his typewriter.

Dear Ida Lou:

No, they couldn't have been the same woman — since the strange, the unknown, the unattainable, the one always "passing by," is forever beautiful and desirable to Baudelaire, who himself is the "adolescent" Williams speaks of . . . and for whom, of course, all joy is something that "kills" — since it can't last forever.

But for Williams, who lives on the earth like a real, terrestrial creature unafraid of his own dying, this woman — plain, ordinary, earthbound, actually *seen* instead of imagined — is the one of whom he can say, "I have sought you/daily" (*daily* being the big word here, since Williams constantly affirms dailiness), of whom he can say of everything he has ever written: "It is all for you."

The problem between us, I've come to realize lately, is that maybe you want me to play Baudelaire, while I finally am ready to play Williams. *You* want me to be a man in love with the unattainable (therefore, in love with you, in love with death), while *I* want to enlarge (not reduce) you to a kind of dailiness, and make you — make us — part of living.

Maybe it's easy — since it's actually impossible — for me to pretend that I want you, embellished by distance and longing and lost opportunity. Maybe it's easy for me to imagine that I could roll every centimeter between New York and Cambridge into a ball and throw it away and nothing would be reduced for lack of longing. Maybe I flatter myself by thinking that I would want you without plane trips and assignations and phone calls and dark hotels.

The truth is I've played Baudelaire too long, with its enthralling sweetnesses and flesh that's "sculptural" instead of living . . . with its quick joy that "kills," instead of the long happiness that grows patient and endures. The truth is that I'm tired of sweetnesses that enthrall and joys that kill, tired of being the man who can only open his eyes and say *you* when what he is looking at is about to disappear.

Send me a poem, love, any time the thought crosses your mind.

Just don't make me into something like Baudelaire's "too far! Too late! Never, maybe!" when every syllable I've ever uttered is for the one — pray God she comes — who'll be mine without absence or infidelity or longing or more than a merely human distance . . . plain as she could ever grow in her worn slacks and imperfect body, more beautiful with every diminished mile.

Happy New Year.

Love,
Martin

CHAPTER 17

A Yacht in Search of God

So he goes, nightly, down to the docks
To wave at the glorious ships. He goes

Down to gaze at the prows and the deckhands
And the sails that hang blowsy in the channel.

Because they have gone somewhere, anywhere,
Without him, because his life is an ongoing yelp

Against the singular self, because the shore
He lives on is never as lovely as the shore,

In another life, he might have sailed to.
He goes down and waves at the lives he could

Never have lived, so as, somehow, to make them
His own, because the grief of the never-taken roads

Is the grief of all men . . .

— MARTIN WEINSTOCK,
"A Man Grieves Always for
the Ships He Has Missed"

Seized by the all-too-familiar panic that seemed to find him whenever he was in a foreign country, Weinstock had just finished, at a cost of 870 sucres per minute, telling Laura how much he loved her and trying to talk her into giving their relationship yet another shot. So he was really in no mood for meeting another woman, he told himself, as he sat down to have a *café con leche* at an outdoor café on the Avenida Amazonas in downtown Quito.

He hadn't, in fact, told *any* woman he loved her for quite some time now. Liking, against all the accumulated evidence, to think of himself as someone for whom the word and the deed were more or less identical, he now sat rather self-consciously at the café, trying to convince himself what a relief it was not to be looking for romance in a foreign country.

So (he would maintain later, when recounting the episode to friends) he hardly noticed the two rather European-looking women — one with long, black hair wearing a red poncho, whom he might easily have mistaken for Portuguese or Italian, the other with curls of gray and white hair and an unmistakably French nose, whom, had he been in the mind for making such comparisons, he would no doubt have found the less attractive — who sat down at the next table and began speaking what he mistook for Spanish.

He had decided to leave his tour group — arrived in Quito the night before at the midpoint of a three-week trek through the highlands and tropical rain forests of Peru and then the Galápagos — to spend a night alone in the Ecuadoran capital. He had tired both of being paraded from attraction to attraction like a herd of sheep and of the cacophonous vocal cords of one of his fellow travelers, a computer programmer from Delaware.

"That jerk's vocal cords," he confided to his one friend in the group, a geriatric nurse from Los Angeles, "are loud enough to make every living thing into an endangered species. If I have to listen to him for one more day, I'm going to have to spend the rest of this trip in an Ecuadoran jail."

So Weinstock felt relieved, on this particularly sunny Sunday in Quito, to find himself alone, having had his usual separation anxieties quelled by the consoling, once-again-forgiving sound of Laura's voice.

"Don't worry," she said to him in the jerky, delayed syllables of international telecommunications, "I'm not even going out with anyone else. We can talk it all over again when you're calmer and back home. You know how you get when you're traveling, don't you? Just try and relax and have a good time. After all, you've wanted to go on this trip for years — remember?"

Weinstock did remember, so he concentrated on quietly sipping his *café con leche* and studying the street map of Quito to plan his day's perambulations. He knew that the bright, sunny morning would soon turn into the cold, rainy midafternoon of Ecuadoran winter and thought he would take advantage of the impending inclemency to visit Quito's Modern Art Museum. The museum, their guide had informed him, was located in the Casa de la Cultura, not far from the hotel.

Never having had much of a way either with maps or with solitude, he turned to the two women seated at the table to his right. "*Esculpa me, señoritas,*" he asked in his rapidly improving Spanish, "*posiblemente ustedes pueden ayudarme.*"

"*Posiblemente.*" The black-haired woman in the poncho looked up from reading a letter. "*Qué quieres?*" Weinstock detected what was clearly not a Latin American accent.

"*Ustedes no son Ecuadoreñas?*" he asked, somewhat disappointedly.

"*No,*" the twosome's spokeswoman, who introduced herself as Veronique, answered, "*Somos francesas.*"

Her companion, who had been compulsively addressing postcards since the pair sat down, looked up and smiled shyly. "*Y usted?*" she asked.

"*Soy norteamericano,*" Weinstock answered.

"*Hola, un gringo!*" she half-teased. "The gringos are everywhere."

"*Habla inglés?*" Much as he loved speaking Spanish, the prospect of a few moments of easy communication wasn't all that unappealing to Weinstock.

"Yes . . . a little." Veronique's suddenly animated companion introduced herself as Beatrice. "Would you like to sit with us?"

The two women, Weinstock soon learned, had been traveling in Ecuador for a month and were planning to spend several more months in Quito doing volunteer work at a *guardería* for poor Ecuadoran children administered by a French relief organization.

"That's noble of you," he said, lapsing easily into English once more. Weinstock's own penchant for social action had rarely ventured beyond the fantasy stage.

"We don't like this feeling so useless," Beatrice explained in her slightly idiosyncratic English, "even if we can only change the statue quo a little bit."

It was almost noon. Weinstock's destination, he reminded himself, had been the art museum.

"*Ahora*" — he saw Veronique glancing at her watch — "*vamenos?*"

"*Sí,*" Beatrice replied somewhat hesitantly. Weinstock sensed the two women had been discussing him while he went to the rest room. "But I don't think the museum is open until August."

"*Hola! Qué lástima!*" Weinstock felt very proud of himself for remembering the word for shame.

"Yes," agreed Beatrice, somehow unconvincingly. "If you would like, we're going to Otavalo for the night . . . you're welcome to come with us."

The prospect of spending a day and night wandering around Quito alone, now that he had decided to follow Laura's suggestion and try having a good time, suddenly seemed no longer all that inviting. His group, he rationalized, wasn't leaving for the Galápagos until Tuesday morning. There was really nothing to lose, he told himself, by spending a day and night in the nearby Indian town with two obviously friendly, and not unattractive, French women.

"*Por qué non?*" he answered rhetorically.

"Great." Beatrice, suddenly no longer shy, smiled as they paid the check and prepared to go their separate ways down the Avenida Amazonas. "We'll meet you at your hotel at three-thirty."

2

The bus from Quito to Otavalo, as usual on Sundays, was crowded with jet-black-haired Otavalans returning from selling their wares on the streets of Quito. Heading north, it passed a monument consisting of a large, circular globe indicating the *mitad del mundo* directly on the equator.

"Here we are, at the center of the earth" — Weinstock turned to Veronique, seated in the window seat beside him — "two Frenchies and a gringo in Ecuador." Beatrice smiled slightly from across the narrow, fruit-and-vegetable-strewn aisle, where she was reading her mail.

The bus climbed on, deep into the scenery of the Andean mountains, dotted with shining white churches set in small villages with names like El Quinche, San Antonio and Tabacundo. To the right, the snow-capped peak of Cayambe, Ecuador's third highest volcano, jutted out over a collar of drifting clouds.

"It's beautiful, isn't it?" Beatrice interrupted her concentration on the mail, smiling at Weinstock. "I love it."

"Yup," he agreed, suddenly noticing how beautiful she herself was, possessing what he sensed to be an air of great kindness and calm. "Gorgeous. . . . By the way, what were you doing in France before coming here?" It suddenly dawned on him that he knew nothing at all about the two women he had so readily agreed to spend the night with.

"I'm a homeopath."

"A homeopath?" Weinstock had always thought of homeopaths as slightly overweight, middle-aged gay men who had flunked out of dental school.

"Yes. . . . It's what I was studying in Los Angeles for five years. It's a wonderful way to make a living here. . . . There are only five in the whole country."

"You mean you're actually thinking of *staying*?" Weinstock was astonished at the thought of anyone, on their own, considering something as adventurous as emigrating to a tiny Latin American republic bordering on the combat zones of Peru and Colombia.

"Por qué non?" Beatrice turned toward the window as she spoke, staring at the snow-capped peak of Cayambe. "It's so beautiful."

"Yes." Weinstock had always liked hearing English spoken with a French accent. "You're right . . . it's a beautiful country," he said. Still staring out the bus window at the snow-capped volcano, they lapsed into a long, somehow very consoling, silence.

3

"We have only two rooms left," the innkeeper at the Residencias Santa Ana, a blond-haired Belgian from Brussels, told them when they inquired at the desk. "How many do you need?"

There was a long silence as Weinstock, who himself had been pondering the answer to that question during the last hour of the bus trip, stared first at Veronique, then at Beatrice.

"Well." Beatrice, somehow no longer the shy girl at the café, broke the silence. "We're not sure. . . . We only met this morning. Can we see the rooms?"

"Of course." The cheerful Belgian grabbed two sets of keys, marked 7 and 18, from behind the desk and headed up the stairs to the balcony of the two-story structure. She unlocked Number 7, revealing a modest but well-lit room with a sagging double bed and cot, informing them that "this is the nicer of the two." Weinstock thought he saw Beatrice smile slightly at Veronique as the woman spoke. "I'll show you the other one, just in case."

They followed her downstairs to a dark corner of the lower floor, where the number 18 was faintly scrawled on a peeling, red-painted door. She unlocked the room to reveal a double bed covered with a tattered dark brown bedspread. A small wooden table in the corner was the only other piece of furniture in the room. The bar-covered window faced out on a stuccoed wall some three feet away, admitting only a slash mark of light.

"I think we should take them both." Beatrice, who was standing behind Weinstock, spoke before anyone else could. The idea of spending a merely platonic night with the two of them in the upstairs room, originally rather appealing, had rapidly been replaced in Weinstock's mind by other possibilities.

"That's fine," he concurred. "We'll take them both."

4

By the time they returned to Room 7 at Residencias Santa Ana from dinner, carrying a bottle of vodka and a can of grapefruit juice, the faint drizzle had abated, revealing a star- and cloud-studded sky and a perfect half moon above the hills of Otavalo.

Beatrice and Veronique seated themselves like bookends in the wide window, staring out onto the abandoned street, while Weinstock sprawled on the double bed, nursing his drink. It was 10:30, and he was feeling tired after the eventful day.

"The moon is beautiful, isn't it?" Beatrice gazed across the room at him, smiling. Her shyness of that morning seemed to have been entirely converted, in his eyes, to a kind of engaging sweetness, not at all diminished by the allure of her accent.

"Yes." He edged toward the end of the bed, craning his neck to see a bright sliver of moon out a corner of the window. "It's beautiful."

Veronique suddenly swung her legs from the window ledge and walked over to the chair in the corner, slipping her pink and blue down vest over her sweater and taking the key to Room 18 from the dresser. She dangled it briefly but purposefully in front of Weinstock, as though voicing some secret code he was not yet familiar with.

"Where are you going?" Weinstock's naiveté, in retrospect, would astonish him.

"To bed," Veronique replied, as though stating the obvious.

"I have to go to the bathroom." Beatrice suddenly inserted herself into the conversation, leaping down from the windowsill. "I'll be right back." She walked out, leaving Weinstock and Veronique alone in the room.

"You want to sleep here with her tonight, don't you?" Veronique turned to him with what seemed like a bit of previously rehearsed English as the door closed behind Beatrice. Weinstock felt a sudden sense of embarrassment at not having caught on earlier. He was trying hard to forget the sound of his own voice on the phone less than twelve hours earlier, telling Laura how much he loved her.

"Why — uh, yes . . . sure," he stammered, suddenly forced to admit that his own half-formulated plan to lure Beatrice downstairs by borrowing her toothpaste has been rather amateurish by comparison. "Sure I would."

Veronique again twirled the key around her finger and smiled. *"Alors,"* she said, opening the door as she draped her daypack over her shoulder. *"Hasta mañana."* She smiled coyly, closed the door behind her and disappeared down the stairs.

5

"Oh, Frenchie." Weinstock opened his eyes and gazed up from the large double bed in Room 7 of the *hostería* La Cienega near Mount Cotopaxi. Beatrice was standing naked in front of the large mirror before the double French doors that opened onto the eucalyptus- and light-buttressed path leading from the hotel grounds. "You are *sooooo* cute."

"Oh, Gringo" — she laughed, throwing herself on the bed on top of him — "you are very cute yourself." She paused, flicking a quick series of kisses at him from on top of the covers. "*Especially for a gringo.*"

It was ten days after their first night in Otavalo, and Weinstock, in the rare instances when he bothered to think about it, didn't feel that he *ought,* given his panicked phone conversation and frantic love letters to Laura, to be feeling as happy, as unambivalently comfortable, with Beatrice as he had been since returning from the Galápagos.

Yet that was how he felt — how he had felt since that morning walking around Lago San Pablo after their first night together in Otavalo. Why not, he said to himself, enjoy it? Laura, after all, ought to know better by now than to trust him, or to believe a single word he said when spoken more than fifty miles from his own front door.

"I think, Gringo" — his reveries were pleasantly interrupted by the sound of Beatrice's voice — "that I am starting to fall in love with you." She kissed the back of his neck as she spoke, running her warm hands down the small of his back. The room suddenly grew terribly silent, as rooms do when someone is waiting a long time for an expected response.

"Never speak in heat." Weinstock suddenly remembered his now long-standing injunction to himself from the end of his first marriage. A feeling of terror welled up inside him. A tightness took hold of his chest, making it difficult for him to breathe. He was so tired, he thought to himself, of the endless continental drift of his soul, the words uttered in hope, then quickly transmogrified to terror and retreat. But there was something about *this* woman, the calm and kindness in her face, the consoling quietude of her touch, that had opened him once more — quick though their coupling had been — to love's relentless, ever-hopeful refrain: *This time will be different.*

He turned his face toward the window and gazed out into the late-afternoon Ecuadoran light. "If I love you" — he suddenly remembered one of Trevor's favorite aphorisms (was it Emerson or Nietzsche?) — "what business is it of yours?" Yes, he thought, what business was it of hers?

"*Moi aussi.*" The foreign syllables came slowly, like the last gasp of an electrical appliance that had already been unplugged, or an engine whose ignition had been turned off, but that kept humming of its own will.

"I think I love you too."

6

They were lying in bed. He was gazing into her eyes. With his right hand, he traced a path around the tight little crow's-feet on the side of her eyes. With the other hand, he parted the snippets of gray hair that fell flat against her forehead, wanting to see more of her face, to know her more deeply.

He realized that she reminded him of no one in particular, yet of something close, personal, familiar. She reminded him of life, and of death. Of the mother into whose living face he had once gazed, and the mother into whose near-dead, glassy eyes he had stared hours before she was carried from his life forever. He felt, in their bed, very much at home. "Home" — he remembered a line of Robert Frost's — "is the place that, when you want to go there, they have to take you in."

He felt her shudder with pleasure as he rose, pressing himself more deeply inside her. *"Te amo,"* he whispered, *"te amo mucho."* "Never speak in heat" — he heard his own advice reverberatng again. But he now realized that heat might be the *only* place from which men and women spoke of the true longing in their hearts — of wishes as deep and fundamental as the wish for cure, or the wish for a happy ending.

"Te amo también," she answered. There was a long moment during whch they gazed silently into each other's eyes.

He moved his right hand along the wide curve of her hip, felt his scent mingling with her scent. Outside, there was a rustling in the treetops, the summer breeze and the scent of honeysuckle coalescing in the bright morning light. It sounded to him, in the narcissistic haze new lovers are prone to, like applause, a benificence of light and air that had gathered entirely for their benefit. *"Que bonita es la luz en los árboles,"* he whispered, circling Beatrice's mouth with his hand. *"Que felicidad."*

"Sí," she agreed, puckering her lips against his hand, kissing his fingers, *"que felicidad."*

Though it *was* a genuine happiness he felt, it was a sadness as well. He had wanted, for so long, to write a book with a happy ending, to make his own manual of happiness. But the wish for a happy ending — like love itself, he realized — could be an illusion, since there was only one possible ending, and that not necessarily a happy one. In the interim, there were merely moments of happiness — moments that could pass, temporarily, for love. Everything else, as Karl Wallenda had once said about walking the high wire, was waiting.

Sometimes, he even thought to himself that this, in fact, was all love *was* — life's strange little piece of bait, the lure it dangled at the end of its sociobiological line like the tiny, scrumptious-looking fly certain spiders wove into their webs to attract insects. Maybe love was merely life's way — deceptive, alluring, yet fundamentally impersonal — of calling out, with Flaubert, "Life! Life! To have erections!" of making us part of its relentless, ongoing web of living and dying, rebirth and extinguishment.

He looked again into Beatrice's face. He felt a familiar tingling in his loins, a near numbness at the tip of his cock. "I'm not sure it's safe," he heard her say halfheartedly as he closed his eyes and gave in to the feeling of pleasure and sadness that drew his entire body toward its center. He felt her, too, submit, giving in to some force larger than will or control or foresight or rationality, a force both transcending and including them.

Soon, they were moaning their separate languages into the morning air. He felt a sudden loss of himself, of the tangible world in which there was so much struggle and pain and pleasure and mystery between the days of living and dying.

Then — both knowing and not knowing what he was about to do, led on by a force larger than thought, more generous than reason, more dangerous than hope, more naive than experience — Martin Weinstock shot a wet, warm stream of seed high up into that dark, womanly place (the place of the egg) where the yearning for light first meets its maker and begins to dance.

7

Back in Cambridge two weeks later, he felt his hand trembling as he dialed Laura's number. He hadn't spoken to her (indeed, he had to confess, he had hardly *thought* of her aside from periodic pangs of guilt and self-loathing) since his awful phone call from Quito.

Even now, he would have preferred not to call, but for his sense of shame and his certainty that there was, ultimately, no avoiding the uncomfortable, humiliating words he was about to hear.

"Coming not to trust you as a lover, I also have come not to trust you as a friend." Laura's words — stinging, painful, accurate — reverberated through his mind as he heard the phone ring on the other end.

"It's Martin," he finally muttered, seemingly minutes after hearing Laura's familiarly cheerful "hello."

"Well, well, if it isn't my desperate, passionate Ecuadoran lover. . . . What's new? Has your new girlfriend dumped you already?"

Weinstock couldn't remember Laura's voice *ever* having sounded so sardonic, so intending to wound, and it was only the fact of Beatrice's being in the next room, of his at least *not* calling from the usual sense of loss and desperation, that fortified his self-respect enough to allow him not to hang up.

"No" — he swallowed hard as he spoke — "no one's dumped me . . . and that's not why I'm calling."

"So why *are* you calling?" Laura paused, as though expecting an answer. "If it's not panic, then I suspect it must be remorse, no? You're calling to invite me to your wedding?"

"Listen, Laura" — he spoke mainly to interrupt the onslaught — "I'm calling because I just got back and wanted to hear your voice."

"Just got back? According to your dozen love-torn postcards and ten desperate phone calls from Ecuador and Peru, you've been back for three days and can't *wait* to hold me in your arms again. . . . Listen, Martin, why don't you cut the bullshit and tell me what's up? You don't really think, after all that's happened between us, that I would take all that desperate crap of yours seriously in the first place. . . . Those panics of yours are *way* too transparent to anyone who's known you more than two weeks."

There was a long pause as Weinstock, unable to find either the will or the words to come to his own defense, merely turned the receiver away from his ear, checking to make sure Beatrice was still on the other side of the closed bedroom door.

"So tell me about her already, Martin — What's her name? American or Ecuadoran? Another shiksa or a nice Jewish Peace Corps volunteer? A darkie, or another blond, blue-eyed innocent like me?"

"What makes you think I met someone else?" Weinstock asked lamely, as if feeling obliged to cling to the role of someone wrongfully under attack.

"Oh c'mon, Martin, give me a break. Don't you think I *know* by now that the only times you come running to me, full of passion and high rhetoric, are when you're off in some foreign country feeling rootless and abandoned? And that all it takes is some other woman, some naive little student of yours, and — whammo! — you're gone again? Why the hell do you think I wrote you that good-bye letter in the first place? To practice my penmanship?"

"Listen, Laura." Weinstock's refusal to take responsibility for what he had done was, by now, only serving to prolong his agony. "Yes, I met someone else, and I'm terribly, terribly sorry for what I've done to you, and for the miserable way I've behaved . . . really I am."

There was a long silence, during which he felt like a wounded animal waiting for a hunter to reload his rifle.

"You know what, Martin?"

"What?" Weinstock felt himself barely capable of uttering a monosyllable.

"You utterly disgust me. In fact, you sicken me, even though I must admit I kind of pity you. Though you may yet luck out some-day, Martin, and find someone patient and loving and generous and, yes, *stupid* enough for you to finally get over your miserable child-hood and stop betraying everyone who's ever cared about you — if it ever *does* happen, it won't be because you deserve it. And, in the meantime, Martin dear, you could at least do me one last favor."

Weinstock felt the rifle cocking, its barrel aimed straight at him.

"What's that?"

"You could stay the fuck out of my life and find someone else to call next time you're in one of your crazy panics in some far off Bolivia or Tierra del Fuego, OK?"

"OK, Laura. I'm really sorry about what happened."

"I am too, Martin. So long."

Weinstock felt the line go dead just as the bedroom door opened and Beatrice emerged, putting her arms around him and kissing him on the forehead.

"You may yet luck out someday, and find someone patient and loving and generous enough . . ." Laura's voice still resonated in his ear as he returned the receiver to its cradle and put his arms around Beatrice.

"I love you, Gringo," she whispered softly.

"I love you too," he answered, feeling, despite himself, like someone who meant what he was saying.

8

Weinstock parked his car, as he had done four or five times a week for six years, on the maple-lined street in front of Dr. David Greenblatt's office on Perry Street in Brookline.

It was a bright, already-dewy day in early September. As Weinstock walked around the house, a middle-aged man in a blue raincoat surfaced from the back door and walked past him. They exchanged brief smiles and scarcely audible grunts, like two members of a secret society passing near its headquarters. From a small forest of rhododendrons and oaks in Greenblatt's backyard, Weinstock heard the repeated high peeping of a cardinal and the persistent voice of a robin, calling *cheer-up, cheer-up*.

He entered, as was his habit, hanging his jacket on a hook inside the door and taking a seat in the round-backed wooden chair beside the end table, on which sat copies of last Sunday's *New York Times* and *Boston Globe* magazines, and a two-week-old *New York Review of Books*. From inside the double doors, he could hear the familiar sound of Greenblatt's answering machine clicking on and off, then the muffled sound of the psychiatrist's voice returning his patients' calls. At exactly ten minutes past the hour, he heard the customary few short footsteps as the double doors opened and

Greenblatt, dressed in the usual deepbrow, sartorial symmetry, stood at the cusp of the office and waiting room.

"Hello." Greenblatt greeted him with an unusual degree of expressiveness, reaching out to shake his hand. "Nice to see you again."

It had been several months since their last meeting, Greenblatt having been off to the usual unrevealed destinations, and Weinstock just back from spending the summer in Ecuador with Beatrice.

"Good to see *you* too," Weinstock agreed, not certain he wasn't allowing good manners to triumph over conviction as he followed Greenblatt into his office.

Greenblatt took his usual seat in the stuffed brown chair behind the couch. Weinstock hesitated a moment, stopping to gaze at the brown- and rust-colored fabric of the couch, its small head cushion still deflated by the head of the man he had passed on the walkway. Smiling, he took a seat in the stuffed chair opposite Greenblatt. He crossed his legs, mimicking Greenblatt's posture, and clasped his hands in his lap.

"Well." Weinstock exhaled slowly after a long silence during which Greenblatt and he simply sat looking at each other. "I think this is going to be my last time here." There was a twinge, but only a twinge, of sadness in his voice, which he was not quite certain was for Greenblatt's benefit or his own. "I think I've had about enough of exploring my inner Borneo."

Greenblatt smiled, lowering his right hand from his chin and placing it in his lap. "Yes," he said, "you've worked very hard here for a long time." Again, there seemed to be a long silence before Greenblatt continued. "I believe you said you *think* this is going to be your last time. . . . Does that mean you're not sure?"

"I suppose it means that I *want* it to be my last time here. I've wanted that for some time."

"Yes." Greenblatt nodded. "It's difficult for you to say good-bye."

"Yup," Weinstock agreed, forcing back tears. "It is."

"Even if it's to someone, like myself, who in many ways you don't even *like* all that much — someone you feel you haven't freely chosen."

"Yup," Weinstock agreed again. "I have trouble saying good-bye to a cold. . . . And I don't really think," he added somewhat mournfully, "that I've ever really chosen *anything*."

"But I think this process has been helpful to you" — Greenblatt spoke with the air of someone simply stating a fact — "though it's up to you to eventually decide that. You seem to me, at least, not nearly as anxious or uncentered as when you first came here. . . . In fact, you seem actually like someone who knows who he is."

"He has no self." The line from Keats came to him again. "Yes," he admitted, "I suppose I do. I've certainly spent enough time thinking about it."

"In any event," Greenblatt continued, "I've very much enjoyed working with you. I've learned a lot from it."

Weinstock couldn't resist taking one last jab at the now-smiling man seated across from him. "Well, that's one of the more convincing things I remember reading about this process years ago."

"What's that?"

"That the one sure outcome is that the *analyst* is going to learn something."

"Yes." Greenblatt laughed out loud. "And sometimes the patient too."

"Yes." Weinstock could no longer restrain the outward drift of his cheeks into a slight smile. "Sometimes the patient too."

"I have a sense," Greenblatt said, "that perhaps now you feel, in your new relationship, that you can actually *trust* someone, that you can be held — the way Dylan Thomas feels at the end of "Fern Hill," when he says, and correct me if I'm wrong —

> *I was young and easy in the mercy of his means,*
> *Time held me green and dying*
> *Though I sang in my chains like the sea.*"

"Yes." Weinstock was impressed (perhaps, it occurred to him, *too* impressed) by Greenblatt's academiclike outburst of quotitis. Yet the lines themselves somehow saddened him. "And look," he said, after a long pause, "what happened to him."

Greenblatt paused. "Yes. . . . I suppose you're right. He probably didn't really *believe* those lines . . . or, at least, he may only have believed them when he wrote them, and not have been able to actually *live* them."

"Frankly" — Weinstock gazed directly into Greenblatt's eyes as he spoke — "I'd prefer not to be quoted."

"Yes. . . . I think you'd rather be held 'green and living.' "

"I sure would."

"I suspect that that's now possible for you. . . . And I hope you'll let me know from time to time how you're doing." Greenblatt rose from his chair, extending his right hand toward Weinstock. It was still many minutes short of their customary fifty-minute hour. "I'd appreciate that."

Weinstock rose, grasping the hand extended toward him. "Sure," he said, looking straight into Greenblatt's eyes. "Who knows, maybe we'll run into each other some time . . . maybe even in Borneo."

Greenblatt smiled without answering, staying in the middle of the room as Weinstock turned and backed toward the door.

"So long." Weinstock turned his head once more toward the center of the room, gazing for a moment at the couch and the chair, then at Greenblatt. "Have a nice fall."

"You too," Greenblatt replied, repeating the words to no one in particular as the door closed behind Weinstock. "You too."

BOOK VI

Returning

————•————

And if this life grows old without clarity,
you look forward to the next, twisting
small wisdoms to your own purpose, only
a turn of words, perhaps, but sufficient,
you tell yourself, certain that whatever wants
to look forward must eventually look back.

— MARTIN WEINSTOCK,
"Looking Forward"

CHAPTER 18

Again Through New Eyes

Yes, this too shall come, at some difficult turn,
and, when you emerge from it, it shall seem
as if the body of flesh were the metaphor of all light
on which the dark bird of love has come home to roost,
and the city of angels shall be the city of dust,
and the dreams of the young child who flew
and the man who fell from the uprootedness of air
shall be one, and nowhere will be somewhere
and the *else* a *you*.

— MARTIN WEINSTOCK,
"Somewhere Else"

The night I returned to my aunt and uncle's now overgrown, eggless New Jersey chicken farm, I slept in the same bed that, twenty-three years earlier, my grandmother had died in.

She had died tragically — blind, lamed by a stroke, following her daughter into the grave by seven years in that terrible inversion of the life cycle in which a mother survives to bury her own child. I remembered the day she died, a week after suffering a second, severe stroke, when I — a boy of sixteen eager to be a man — had taken my driver's test in Queens, rather than go to the place of the egg and watch an old woman die.

Now, a grown man, I was sleeping in her bed. I was sleeping in the room my adopted father — the father of fur — had built for her almost thirty years ago, after she had been evicted from my parents' house by my stepmother. I realized, as I lay there gazing up at the ceiling, inhaling the long-gone scents of my grandmother and of chickens and of eggs, that — for my grandmother, at least — the place of the *egg* had been the place of death, and the place of the *fur* had been the place of life.

I realized that it was the life of fur, not the life of the egg, that had rescued her from Nazi Germany, that it was the life of fur that had nourished and given her a family and a home and a place of light until that fateful morning when her daughter's dead body was taken from that room.

I realized, as I lay there, that — for the old woman who had died in that same bed twenty-three years before — the place of the egg had been a place of darkness and loneliness, not a place of life. And now I was there — at the crest of my life's curve, the midway mark — lying in her deathbed, in that place where, until the time of my mother's passing, the lives of my two star-crossed families had intersected.

I was lying, in fact, on the cusp of life and death. So when I dreamt, that night, that the birds had all descended from the trees and were walking along the ground eating from my hand, I knew I was dreaming the dream of life and death, of Icarus descended and Philoctetes risen, and that I, too, might survive that bed of death to rise once more into the light of some real and conquerable Troy.

I remembered the first time I had ever mentioned my dreams of becoming a bird to anyone. I was sitting in my Jungian analyst's office in Washington, describing how I had taken off from the ground and flown toward an owllike creature sitting on a wire. The dream had felt good, light and transcendent.

"It seems to me it's a dream about not being grounded," my analyst had responded, puncturing my bubble of contentment. But who, in his right mind, I thought at the time, would *want* to be grounded? After all, didn't people *fall* to the ground (as they *fell* in love)? Didn't things *grind* to a halt? Wasn't a thing that had run *aground* something broken, defective?

Over the years, the bird wishes of my dreams had diminshed. The animals had all turned terrestrial, becoming foragers and ground dwellers. The world became populated by trees, where once only birds had lighted on telephone wires strung between poles. Just days before arriving in New Jersey again, I had dreamt of walking with Beatrice in some African savannah, looking for a tree to name after myself — a tree named Martin Weinstock. . . . Maybe, I realized, it wasn't a man's place to resemble a bird. Maybe it was a man's place to resemble a tree.

Sitting in my aunt and uncle's living room that night, sitting on the sofa where I had once spent so many nights nestled between the bookends of my two families, I looked around at the photographs on the walls and cabinets. There were my biological sister, her husband and their two teenage daughters, then my biological brother and his wife and their two adopted children. There was a picture of my dead mother and my dead grandmother, while my actual mother — the woman from whose living, intact body I had slid into the world — sat in the green upholstered chair beside me. But I, Martin Weinstock, was nowhere to be found on those walls or cabinets. I was the missing link, the one who had been given away, the one who — even now, at almost forty — continued to reverberate between the fur and the egg.

"I have always wanted another father," I had once written in a poem. "You *have* another father," Greenblatt reminded me. Sure enough, I did — sitting right there, on the rocking chair in front of me, that sliver of bullet still embedded in his arm. The truth was, I had had two of everything — two mothers, two fathers, two siblings, two versions of manhood, two homes. And all I wanted now was to have them both in a single place.

2

My parents were coming to visit me for the first time since I had left home for college almost twenty-five years ago.

"Why don't you come see *me* for a change?" I had said to my father when, for the umpteenth time, he asked, in a tone suitable for addressing a twelve-year-old, "When are we going to see our dear son again . . . for your daddy's birthday?"

For some reason, it seemed a good idea to have my parents, for the first time, on my own turf. "It's another typical parental power fuck," Trevor had said. "If parents never come to visit you in *your* home, they never have to acknowledge the fact that you've grown up."

My parents' home, indeed, *had* always been a focal point for my stepmother's relentless, neurotic power. Throughout my late adolescence and early adulthood, whenever I would come to visit, she would cover all the furniture in plastic, then fasten a Christolike wrapping of tattered white sheets to the wall (lending a worse-than-funereal pallor to their already bleak and lifeless abode) because, as she put it, "you get the walls dirty when you lean against them." What's more, there was never quite enough hot water for a shower ("the hot water is sooooo expensive"), my stepmother habitually followed me around the house turning off the lights ("doesn't the glare bother you?") and it was virtually impossible to have even a moment's uninterrupted peace to talk on the phone ("Martin, it's time for dinner") or read a book ("Can you please read the stock market listings to me? My eyes are so bad."). So the idea of having my parents finally come to a place where *I* had some control of the choreography seemed not at all bad.

Apart from their getting on the wrong flight and my being unable to find them when they arrived at Logan Airport, the three of us spent a relatively pleasant weekend, eating at restaurants, walking in the Boston Garden, and meeting some of my Cambridge friends.

"Such a pleasure to meet you, Miss ———," my father would say to every woman to whom I introduced him, kissing her hand as he spoke. "God loves you, and so do I."

"Your father," Nourit Goldman whispered to me after being subjected to this treatment, "is the cutest man who ever lived."

"I know," I agreed cynically. "God loves you, and so does he."

By the time I went to take my parents back to Logan Airport for the return trip to La Guardia on Sunday night, I therefore felt that a relatively benign, if not downright successful, weekend was drawing to a close. When we arrived at the airport, I decided to walk my parents — whose penchant for making the wrong turn,. getting on the wrong plane or attending the wrong funeral was by now legendary — directly onto the shuttle. As I escorted them to seats 10D and 10E near the front of the wide-bodied 707, I recognized several Cambridge acquaintances, including Leonard Hapgood, already seated on the plane. ("My parents," I whispered almost apologetically as we passed. "Up for the weekend.")

"Well" — I kissed them both on the cheek as they reclined into their seats — "I better get going before the plane takes off. . . . Thanks so much for coming." I started toward the exit, feeling a bit like a young boy who had set off a firecracker and wanted to split the scene before it exploded.

"Ein moment." I suddenly heard the familiar sound of my father's voice and — to my chagrin and amazement — turned to see him standing in the aisle, reaching into his jacket pocket. Before I could utter a syllable in protest, out came the familiar, cologne-soaked white handkerchief and Hohner B-flat harmonica.

"Dad!" I frantically tried to abort what was about to happen. *Not here. . . . Please!"*

There was no stopping my eighty-four-year-old father. To the delight and amusement of the 200-odd passengers aboard the shuttle and the near hysteria of Leonard Hapgood, he raised his white, cologne-soaked handkerchief in his right hand, placed the harmonica against his mouth with the left and — waving the handkerchief wildly at me as I fled toward the cabin door — began playing *"Auf Wiedersehen."*

Flushed with embarrassment, I walked out the terminal door and toward my car, thinking about my unappeasable hunger for travel and light. I, for one, didn't want to be pronounced dead before my time had come. I didn't, like Lotte Baumgartner, want to be welcomed prematurely into the dark while a light still burned within me. I realized that — though I, too, wouldn't mind one day being an eighty-four-year-old man who played the harmonica — I didn't want the only song in my repertoire to be *"Auf Wiedersehen."*

3

For the first time since her death some thirty years earlier, I decided to visit my mother's grave, located about an hour from New York in Westwood, New Jersey's Beth-El Cemetery.

I drove through the cemetery gate and, after asking directions to burial plot F-11, parked my car and walked up the hill toward where the guard had directed me.

Soon I was standing near her grave, the one I had never visited as a child. But now I was in a man's body. I looked out over the low hills of New Jersey, over the vast valley of stone slabs . . . white as her empty bed had been white, white as the pail into which she began to pour back her life. In all directions, the names of my childhood — Heilbronn, Schoenbach, Marx, Meyer, Hirsch, Guttman, Dingfelder, Katzenstein — called out from their cold litany of stone, old *daveners* reunited once more in a synagogue of hedges, a vast democracy of marble and flowers.

Suddenly — off to my left, in an aisle seat — I found her:

BETTINA WEINSTOCK
nee Loeb
1907–1959

I found her, mother of no body, mother of affections but not flesh, right beside my grandmother, her mother, who had followed her here:

JOHANNA LOEB
nee Neumark
1878–1966

Suddenly, I understood why I had become what I was: a man who needed to bear himself anew into the world each day by speaking his life. I saw how the tidal surge of grief needed to come ashore, how the force that drove no water for so long needed to well up inside the tangible body of flesh until a new wave could rise behind it. I saw how, for almost thirty years, I had dipped the wafer of my life into her dying and partaken of it; how, left in the world to save her, I could save no one, not even myself.

I placed my black prayer book against her headstone. Something much like speech rose from the water behind her. I recited the words I had never had the chance to speak in her name: *v'yishalleh, v'yish-allol, sh'meh d'kudsho . . .*

4

In the dream I stood again at the threshold to my mother's room.

Once more, I could see the high bed in the corner, her body lying on it. I could feel my own body turn once more into the body of a young boy. I saw her wide eyes staring up at me from the high bed, her head that could move no more, her lips that could speak no more.

I stood there, in the place where I had once been kept from going farther, and looked in at her. It seemed like years of my life passed before me. I raised my too-long-hampered legs and stepped over the threshold. I stepped from the long corridor of grief into the room, and stood beside her.

I placed my fingers against her face. I looked into the deep, unseeing wells of her eyes and stared Death in its literal face. *Hello, Death,* I said, *I have come for you now. Hello, Death. I have come for you for real.*

Thirty years of my life congealed into that single instant. Hundreds of women I couldn't kiss, hundreds of women I couldn't see, merged into the light of this dying woman's eyes. I lowered my face toward her face. I lowered my lips toward her lips and planted on them, finally, that long-belated kiss —

The kiss of death, the kiss all life comes from.

5

I was just a few days shy of my fortieth birthday, asleep in my parents' house in Queens. I was sleeping in the basement, in almost the exact spot where my stepmother's mother had fallen down the darkened stairway from the upper floor of the house and died some twenty-five years earlier.

Suddenly, I woke in the middle of the night, hearing a commotion in the bedroom above. I turned on the lamp on the night table beside the bed and looked at the clock. It was 4:00 A.M. I had always hoped (and, at least partially, feared) that — on one of those rare nights when I found myself again sleeping in my parents' house — the inevitable would happen. But, this time, I would be there for the death.

Naked, I ran upstairs toward the faint light in my parents' bedroom. A small old man in a blue bathrobe was standing beside the bed. He was cradling his wife's head — a toothless head with caved-in cheeks and closed eyes that hardly seemed among the living — against his body with one arm. In the other hand, he held a blue pail. My stepmother was retching into the pail. *"Ach, es ist mir so schlecht,"* she moaned, as she heaved over the pail. *"Ach, es ist mir so schlecht."*

I stood for a moment, staring transfixedly at the two old people before me. For a few seconds, I couldn't move. "What's the matter?" I finally asked my father.

"Ach, mir ist es soooo schlecht," my stepmother repeated the words. A torrent of vomit flew from her, missing the pail and landing on the bed sheet. *"Ach, mir ist es so schlecht."*

I walked over to the side of the bed beside my father and cradled my stepmother's head in my hands. It felt like a dead weight against my palms. As she continued retching into the pail, small rivulets of spittle flowed down the sides of her mouth and over the lip of blue plastic.

"Let me hold her. She's too heavy for you," I said to my father. The old man, trembling in his blue bathrobe, backed away. I picked my stepmother up in my arms and set her in a chair beside the bed so that she could sit upright. I noticed that her green nightgown had risen over the tops of her legs, revealing mounds of sagging blue and red flesh, reminding me of my grandmother's body. The air around her limp body had the faint odor of rotten apples. Though she was a dead weight in my arms, she seemed light to me now, as though not even the weight of the dead and the dying could over-power me any longer.

My father, meanwhile, had gone into the kitchen to make tea. When he returned, I knelt beside the limp old woman, feeding her the tea in spoonfuls. She inhaled, making loud slurping sounds. Still naked, I stood in the center of the room watching the two old people. I felt a sense of calm coupled with disbelief, a sadness bordering on detachment. I reached behind the closed door to find my father's other bathrobe. It was too small, and, when I tried to put it on, the sleeves reached only two thirds of the way down my arms, just past the elbow.

Finally, my stepmother stopped vomiting and fell into an almost comatose sleep. "Why don't you go lie down? There's nothing more you can do now," I said. My father, wearing a light blue flannel pajama bottom beneath his bathrobe, did as I told him. I stood at the foot of the bed and gazed at the two helpless old people sprawled before me. I suddenly thought again of the dream I had had. *"Poor Meyer,"* I had said, putting my arm around the blind man walking toward me on the street. *"Poor Meyer."*

My stepmother was starting to snore in the chair. Her head had fallen entirely to one side. Beside her on the radiator stood the blue pail. The only other sound in the room was the faint humming of the fluorescent ceiling light. Slowly, I walked over to the chair where my stepmother was sleeping. I placed my left hand gently below her head, my right arm below her thighs, and lifted her almost lifeless body of flesh and bones back onto the bed. Then I propped the head of this woman who had never wanted to call me *son* against a pillow. I placed the down comforter over her and turned out the reading light mounted on the headboard.

"Go back to sleep," I said to my father, who lay on the bed, nervously gazing at the nearly lifeless body of his second wife. "She'll be better in the morning."

"Jawohl," my father said limply. "Was ein blessing that our son is here on this night . . . like the Messiah, our Savior. God loves you, and so do I."

"Yes," I murmured under my breath. "Like the Messiah, your Savior. . . . God loves you, and so do I." I turned off the light and backed out of the room toward the basement stairs. Slowly, I closed the door behind me and went down to bed.

I gazed once more at the clock beside the bed. It was 5:20 A.M., March 1, 1989. I turned off the light on the night table beside me. I drew in a deep, almost mournful breath, which I didn't release for a long time. I felt a strange sense of relief, of almost calm, as I closed my eyes.

Then I fell asleep.

CHAPTER 19

Paper Things
and Flesh Things

Little bird,
small sacred flake
that has fallen from the heat
of my longings . . .

— MARTIN WEINSTOCK,
"A Prayer for My Son"

"I don't think we should go through with it."

It was a Sunday afternoon in late September, and Beatrice and I were sitting at the café of Boston's Museum of Fine Arts, where we had finally decided to have *the* talk concerning what to do about our pregnancy. Some two months had now passed since that morning in Quito when we had gone to the clinic north of the Old City, opened the tattered envelope with Beatrice's name on it and read the words *"positivo para embarrasada"* scribbled on the scrap of paper inside.

"I think," I continued, "that we would be better off waiting until we've known each other a bit longer — until, you know, our relationship is on a more solid ground and we're really able to *choose* whether or not to do something this dramatic and irrevocable." I noticed that the word "choose" made me feel nervous and uncertain, as though I was talking about something I didn't really know the meaning of.

"After all," I continued, trying to evade the look of sadness and disappointment on Beatrice's face, "we've hardly known each other four months. . . . "We must in fact," I went on, trying to make a kind of joke, "have one of the shortest meeting-to-conception times in the history of romance."

"Yes." Beatrice was looking into my eyes as she spoke, slowly and thoughtfully. "But the fact is, Gringo, that this child already *exists* . . . there's no changing that, or pretending it's not true."

I, by now a veteran of three abortions, knew she was right — there *was* no pretending that this child, or whatever it now was, didn't exist . . . or that there would be no cost to me, or to life, in putting its tenuous existence to an end. Didn't it seem, after all, that there was something in me that *wanted* to be born, that wanted to give life? And here, at this very moment, seated before me in the shape of a flesh-and-blood woman — not an Iseult the Fair, but an Iseult of the White Hands — it was.

"It's not *that*," I continued stubbornly, "or that I wouldn't want to have a child with you when a better, more reasonable, time comes. It's just that we hardly know each other, to be perfectly hon-est . . . and we haven't exactly been having a great time of it since we got back here again." Beatrice and I, since returning to my "real" life in Cambridge, had had our share of arguments and uncom-fortablenesses, Beatrice having not found the situation of suddenly being pregnant and in someone else's life and country a particularly easy one.

"Yes," she agreed, "that's true. But the truth also is that there may *never* be a 'better' or a 'right' time — especially for someone with a past like yours." Though we hadn't known each other for long, I had, of course, told Beatrice the story of my splotched and confused heritage — and been touched, from the beginning, by her seeming compassion for my ambivalence and confusion.

"So what do *you* want to do?" I finally asked, fatigued by my own unconvincing ruminations on the subject.

There was a long silence, as Beatrice continued to gaze into my eyes, slowly stirring her yet untouched cup of coffee.

"It's a child of passion," she finally said, slowly but firmly. "He was conceived in a moment of real love."

"What does *that* have to do with anything?" I asked, already knowing the answer. I was trembling.

"It's a good omen for someone's life." Beatrice, for the first time in our somber conversation, smiled slightly. "*You*, for example, would probably have had a happier life if you had been a child of passion." She paused for a long time before continuing. "So I'm ready to have it."

2

She had grown so heavy with the weight of what had been growing inside her that she couldn't get in or out of the bathtub without my help.

"I've become a totally dependent creature," she said as I half-lifted her over the edge of the tub. "I have to count on you for everything these days."

I put my arms around the huge girth of her waist, felt her give herself over entirely to my arms. *"Poor Meyer."* I again heard the voice of my earlier dream as I stared at my all-but-helpless wife. *"Poor Meyer."*

"It's nothing," I said, surprised by the seeming sincerity of my own words. "I'm happy to be here."

"I think he already knows the sound of your voice," she said, suddenly smiling. "He can even hear you from the womb."

"How could he miss?" I joked, gazing affectionately at her distended belly. "I talk so damned much."

Falling asleep that night, I thought to myself that it could be my last as a son who wasn't also a father, the last time I could ask the question, "Which father would you kill?" Tomorrow, perhaps, there would be a child — *my* child — who wouldn't have to face the confused paternity of two fathers, who wouldn't need to live his life in a chasm between blood and feeling. Tomorrow, perhaps, the sins of the fathers would no longer be visited upon the sons. By tomorrow, perhaps, I would have lived in my own wound so long I wouldn't need to pass it on to someone else. . . . I would finally be able to leave Lemnos.

Thinking these thoughts, I allowed myself to be eased into a deep, consoling sleep by the sound of Beatrice's breathing beside me. It seemed like only minutes later when I woke to a gasping sound from beside me on the bed, and a calm but firm hand on the back of my neck. I turned to watch Beatrice heaving with convulsions that shook the entire bed.

"It's happening," she stammered as her body quieted itself momentarily.

I felt immediately alert, intensely alive. "Just relax," I said, jumping from the bed. "I'm going to call the midwife."

As I headed toward the living room, Beatrice grasped her hands tightly around the wooden bed frame and stared over at the digital clock on the night table. *Three minutes.* She timed the space between the contractions that shook her entire body upward and almost off the bed. *Just three minutes.*

As I reentered the room, I heard a popping sound coming from beneath her abdomen. Water suddenly began pouring out of her, soaking the bed in a bath of amniotic fluid.

"It won't be long now," she whispered as I went to cover the plastic pad we had put on the bed with a new set of sheets.

"No," I replied, feeling my breath come short. "It won't be long."

The words were hardly out of my mouth when what now seemed to have been only mild contractions were transformed into all-consuming reverberations. ("The most intense feeling of my life, Gringo, except maybe for death," Beatrice would say to me later. "It was like a shuddering of my entire being.") Seeing her face turn a near crimson as she gasped for breath, I dropped the sheets and ran over to hold her.

"Let's go," I said, firmly but calmly. "I think I'd rather not have this be a home delivery."

By the time we got to the car and were heading toward the hospital, the contractions were almost every minute. I looked at my watch for the first time. It was 6:45 A.M. Beatrice was squeezing my right hand so intensely I couldn't feel the blood circulating in my fingers.

The midwife was waiting for us when we arrived at the hospital and led us to a spacious room on the first floor. "Relax," she whispered. "It's no big deal. . . . You're going to have a baby."

The sun was starting to rise. A wash of yellow light poured into the room as we entered. A nurse followed us, carrying a tray of apple juice and ice cubes.

"Don't push," the midwife kept saying to Beatrice, who was soon lying on her back on the bed, both knees in the air. "Don't push — you'll hurt the baby."

My hand starting to become unnumbed from the force of Beatrice's squeezing, I stood near the foot of the bed and gazed at her. More blood than I had ever imagined could be produced by a single living human being was now pouring out of her. In the midst of it all, I thought I saw a small, fleshy tuft of hair moving toward me.

"He's starting to crown," the midwife, in a remarkably calm voice, said. "You need to start pushing now." The nurse, meanwhile, was holding a mirror over the side of the bed between Beatrice's legs so she could see the baby's emerging head. Her eyes seemed to be leaping out of her skull, like those of a fish gasping for oxygen.

"I can't do it! I can't do it! I can't push anymore!" she screamed, as I stretched my right hand out to stroke her hair. But for the fact that I knew who this woman was, I would scarcely have recognized the seemingly possessed creature whose otherworldly moans now filled the room.

"Now's the time to think of our secret place," I said, whispering the name of the Ecuadoran volcano we had climbed the previous summer. I hadn't eaten for some twenty-four hours, but felt as if I was in a complete warp of time and space. In a kind of controlled stupefaction, I gazed at the emerging mass of pinkish skull and hair that was about to slide out of Beatrice's body. As my two hands reached, almost of their own volition, forward, I noticed it was 8:15 A.M. — almost the exact time at which, more than forty years ago, I myself had been born.

Then, like a small, greased piglet shimmering out into the air of its own being, a tiny, breathless body — covered in blood, slime, mucus and other effluvia so unmentionably grotesque and beautiful that I could never find the words to describe them — slid into my waiting hands. Then, through the descending haze of my own tears and my own mute voice, in a motion so sweeping and natural, so organically whole as to seem planned and executed by the gods themselves, I, Martin Weinstock — the man of the impotent father and sad, dying mother; the man of the long-festering wound and the relentless yearning toward some Troy of my own making — arced the body of my blood-born child upward toward the waiting arms and intact breasts of its living mother, its life.

CHAPTER 20

Kafka's Father

> I look into the forest of my father's eyes.
> The trees, dark and threatening,
> look back. And I say *oh father*
> *why does the forest frighten me so,*
> *and what shall we do*
> *about these terrible fleas?*
>
> — MARTIN WEINSTOCK,
> "Fleas"

A few weeks after the birth of my son, I flew to New York to visit my parents, both of whom weren't doing well physically, to help with some personal details and shopping. My father had been diagnosed with cerebral arteriosclerosis, which seemed to render his always scattered and repetitive mental functioning all the worse, and my stepmother, whose lifelong osteoporosis had, in recent years, made her spinal column resemble a camel's hump rather than a human back, had broken yet another vertebra and was flat on her back.

My parents had greeted the birth of my son with a funereal sobriety, so I was, as usual, prepared for the worst when I passed through my usual point of entry — the basement — into the customary darkness of my stepmother's house.

The first day of my visit included a fruitless session with a social worker, through whom I was attempting to secure some domestic help for my parents. I was hoping, ever cautiously, to flee the premises without any further tragedy the next afternoon when, to my shocked amazement, a small spill of water I caused while taking a shower threw my father into a tirade of abuse and invective ("you bring nothing but unhappiness into our life . . . and then you marry another poor *goyische schmatte*") so deranged and inexplicable that

I resolved merely to use the "duck's back" approach Greenblatt had advocated and drive him, as I'd been asked, to the wholesale kosher butcher's on the Lower West Side before catching the two o'clock train.

We drove in silence across the Triborough Bridge and down the East Side Highway, I trying with all my power to keep my eyes directly on the road and ignore the deranged verbal geyser seated on my right. When we finally arrived at Chambers Steet, my father got out of the car, where he was enthusiastically greeted by a small cluster of overweight men in bloodied smocks, with whom he shook hands as though preparing to address a state troopers' convention.

"Shalom, Mr. Yarmolinsky. Shalom, Fred." My father serenaded the two men, as he followed them into the warehouse. "God loves you, and so do I." He returned some fifteen minutes later, this time with two younger butchers in tow, carting four large bags of kosher steaks, lamb shanks, soup bones, brisket and calves breasts.

"God bless you, *Landsmann*," my father said, kissing the larger of the two men on his bloodstained hand as he got back into the car. "God loves you, and so do I."

A moment later, we were driving silently up Ninth Avenue when my father suddenly turned to me. "Let's stop and have a coffee," he suggested, his voice exuding a thinly disguised animus. Our last such stop, in that small coffee shop in Pine Hill before my marriage, was an event I didn't particularly want to repeat. "I don't have time," I replied coldly. "But I want to warn you," I added, momentarily losing my grip on the "duck's back" approach, "not *ever* to talk about my wife that way again."

Whatever modicum of self-control my father was still capable of now went out the window. "Aren't you ashamed of yourself?" he railed. "To talk to your sick old father that way?"

"And aren't *you* ashamed," I countered, straying even further from my limited Buddhist training, "of the way you behave toward me and my family?"

The words "my family" must have only set him off further.

"You are cursed by God," he said, taking his white handkerchief from his breast pocket and placing it over his face. "You will never find happiness.

"No one ever loved or wanted you" — he began sobbing — "not

even my sisters. I was the only one . . . you were my million. I don't have anyone else but you. . . . I never loved Ilse. I never loved anyone else. Sex," he said, suddenly getting to what I agreed with Freud was the root of the problem, "sex, it never worked for me . . . not with our mama, not with Ilse."

I was trying to keep my eyes on the road, to concentrate on the traffic, on not responding. He put his face in his handkerchief again, heaving with sobs. I realized that what this man so badly needed — what he had *always* needed — was to be loved, to be hugged, to be told that he no longer needed to "schtop the traffic," to kiss everyone's hand and bless them. But by now I had been too hurt and wounded, too often turned against and betrayed. All I could do was keep driving, keep trying to remain silent.

"I was born to death" — he suddenly looked up again — "and now I am going back to death." I was amazed at how quickly he seemed able to move between weeping and railing.

"You should have waited until I was dead and rotted — until I was *verreckt* — to marry," he continued. "I would have bought you a house — we would have lived downstairs, and you could have lived upstairs."

At any other time, the thought of sharing a house with my father and stepmother would have thrown me into convulsions of laughter. Now, I merely struggled to maintain my silence, to work my way as quickly as possible back to the Triborough Bridge.

"What did I do to deserve such a son?" he went on. "I was always so good to you." He paused, sobbing again. "And you were only intrested in sex . . . sex and women."

I was thinking to myself: *This is not really happening, this is a dream, keep driving.*

"You don't know what you are saying," I finally mumbled. "You've suffered too much."

"It never worked for me, sex, never. I never loved her . . . you were my million. I sacrificed everything for you," he went on. "You are damned, cursed. . . . *Der lieber Gott* will never let you find happiness."

He began sobbing into his white handkerchief again. "Forgive me," he said, taking my right hand from the steering wheel and covering it with kisses. "Soon I will be dead. Let us go apart in peace."

I kept silent. We were almost over the bridge.

"Be good to your stepmother when I am gone," he said. "She is all I have — without her cooking, I would have been dead years ago.

"Forgive me," he said again, kissing my hand. "I don't know what I am saying. Please don't say anything to Mama."

"Yes," I whispered quietly, as though to myself, "you don't know what you are saying."

I realized as I spoke that — right there before my eyes — something had finally happened that I had been waiting for all these years, something that would allow me, finally, to stop telling stories, something that would allow me to stop thinking about which father I would kill. For me at that moment, the man I was sitting beside as I made a sharp right onto the Triborough Bridge was already a dead man.

❖

We arrived back at my parents' house in Jackson Heights. I carried the meat in from the car and began packing my bags.

"You're not staying for lunch?" my stepmother asked.

"No," I said, trying to keep the conversation to a minimum. "I've got to get back. . . . I have a small son."

"I'll pack up some steaks and some challah for you and Beatrice," my father said, behaving as if the past three hours had never happened.

"That's fine," I said politely. "We have plenty of our own food at home — and, as I've told you a thousand times, we don't eat red meat." I had only one desire: to get out of their house.

"Here," my father said, handing me a small foil-wrapped package with a note Scotch-taped to it and kissing me on the hand, "at least take the challah. . . . Your mama made it fresh for Shabbos."

"OK," I said. "Thanks."

Ten minutes later, still feeling as if I had been stabbed with an ice pick, I was on the Eighth Avenue subway, headed for the train station and the consoling arms of my wife. Feeling too defeated to either read or think, I simply peeled the Scotch-taped note from my stepmother's challah.

"For our dear daughter-in-law, Beatrice," it read in my father's nearly illegible scrawl. "May you enjoy it in good health and with *guten appetit*. . . . God loves you, and so do we."

2

1 May 1992

Dear Father,

You will never read this leter, it being in neither your language nor your idiom. But greater writers than I — writers with equally damaged and damaging fathers, like Kafka — have written letters to their fathers that were never really intended to be read. So why should it stop me, a mere Martin Weinstock trying to work his way back among the living?

For I think the old Yiddish proverb is true — "Troubles overcome are good to tell." But you, unlike myself, weren't blessed with the talent to make a song of your troubles. Through no fault of your own, there was little else you could do than pass them along through the exits and entryways of demons never addressed, darknesses never entered.

Yet yours, too, ought to be a story without blame, a story without enemies. Given the fact that some strange God gave me a voice — where he gave you only charm, a harmonica, and an aborted wish for singing — it seems I ought to say something about your part in the story, your own claim for pity and compassion and dignity and coherence.

What a terrible beginning it must have been! Opening your eyes that first day in the light of the world to find yourself the child of a dead mother, the brother of six motherless sisters, the speechless infant of a widowed butcher with eight children! Had you had the sense or the capacity, or the tragic foreshadowing of your own future, you might simply have crawled back in and followed her to the next life.

But there you were — brought into this life by the cold, ambiguous hand of death, and having to make of that dark maternity a kind of living. And then, as if that first abandonment weren't enough, your father apprenticed you to that second, great teacher of longing and unrequitedness — a stepmother who neither loved nor wanted you, but forced you to spend the rest of your childhood in a state of exaggerated goodness and martyrdom aimed at securing her niggardly affections. *"Am Ende, hat sie gesehen was ein guter Sohn ich war,"* you would say to me a half-century later — "In the end, she saw what a good son I was." But only in the end.

Then, just a few years later, your only brother Irwin — the one man in your life not yet so overburdened by his own tragedy that he might have taught you how to be a man — died in the War and you became a young boy (*"Bube,"* as your sisters would call you all your life) in a world overwhelmingly female, a world that perfectly prepared you for the charming, flattering and kissing of women that would become your livelihood.

What did you do then — you who really wanted to be a cantor, who wanted to live in a world of singing? You who were blessed with a father unable to support you, a stepmother whose love you would forever be trying to earn without succeeding? You went and apprenticed yourself to a profession whose life came from the same source as your own: the world of the dying. At an age when most young boys were apprenticing themselves to learning and lust and the vague passages into young manhood, you went and apprenticed yourself to Meyer und Vogel, GmbH. . . . You went and apprenticed yourself to the life of fur.

Again, you found yourself — this time as a handsome, charming, chauffeur-driven Don Juan — surrounded by women. Kissing, flattering, seducing them into your life of quick sales and departures, *schtopping* the traffic. Like some Pavarotti of the chinchilla cape and the mink boa, you whipped from town to town, *von Dorf zu Dorf,* leaving behind the scent of cologne and an armada of women so flushed with flattery that they almost forgot you were already long gone down the road toward some remoter Dangensdorf, some lovelier Tübingen.

I look at photographs of you then, and can see what a great salesman you must have been — what an engaging peddler of transmogrified hides and pelts! There was something so soft — so downright womanly — about your face, a Jewish Mario Lanza of androgyny and longing. Longing, indeed, must have been your métier — you who had reached out your hungry lips in search of a mother's breast to find only a cold world of death and disappearance. And what else could possibly have become your

motto vis-à-vis women than that line from Nietzsche you ultimately chose — *"Wenn Du zu dem Weibe gehst, vergesse nicht die
Peitsche"*? (When you go see a woman, don't forget your
whip.)

For the *better* part of a possible life with women — the nurturing
and sustenance — never came cheaply, never came without a chorus of longing and deadened passion. So who else could possibly
have become the love of your life, the one woman with whom you
might possibly have found the womb and the cunt in a single place,
but Claire Haas — the young, beautiful, vivacious Aryan opera
singer from Regensburg whom neither your father nor your times
nor your limited sense of manhood would ever have allowed you
to fully possess? (With the added convenience of something as
brutal and daemonic as the Nazis to make it impossible . . .
something to send her fleeing to some far-off Chile, where she
could remain forever a symbol of the unattainable, the impossible,
the unrequited.)

No, dear father, the Nazis were within you as well: the dark
Kristallnacht of their gaze, and their brutal whips that kept you
from possessing the one thing that might have kept you from
needing to pass on to me your dark legacy of impotence and dying.
For, as the psychologists have long told us, the best thing a man
can do for his son is to love his mother . . . to love his mother's
warm, nurturing, life-giving womb, and her playful cunt. There
was something in you, I think, that would have had to *invent* the
Nazis if they hadn't been there, that would have had to find some
dark *Polizei* of impossibility, some macabre Julius Streicher prowl-
ing the streets of Frankfurt with his storm troopers and whips.
Anything in order not to have to look a woman — to look your
dead mother — in the eye and say: *you.*

And who did you marry instead? — The sad, fatherless girl
whose blind mother was the keeper of the cemetery keys in Georgensgmünd. You married someone you would call *Mama* all her
life, so that the womb you had always been in search of could
finally be yours, and the cunt could remain off in some distant
Chile, some wild Santiago of passion and longing. Because *you*
were the kind of man who would always choose to kill the king
instead of the father, who would always return to that first source
of betrayal and abandonment, instead of grabbing the bright scep-
ter of his possible manhood and power. Because who can possibly

afford to kill his father when his father is — as yours was, as mine was in turn — the only living thing between him and the orphanage?

What else could that poor woman have ultimately become to you but someone already dying? That woman whom you left unfucked and unfertilized, whom you loved the way an infant loves his dead mother instead of the way a man loves his living wife? That woman whose breasts — because you wouldn't let them become a source of life — had to become the source of her own dying? What else could she possibly have become but someone for whom you could play the one song in your repertoire, your long, mournful *"Auf Wiedersehen"*? What could you do in turn but replay the broken record of your shattered life and adopt into that dying woman's arms this one son of the rectifying heart, willing to kill any father he has to in order not to repeat him?

And when that woman finally died — when you were finally left with the same motherless son you yourself were in Frankfurt fifty-four years earlier — what was there left for you to do but complete the cycle? You had no other choice — you who didn't understand your own life, and so were destined to repeat it. You found for him the same loveless stepmother your father had found for you. You held "auditions" for the one who would love him least — the one about whom he, too, would be able to say, some thirty years later, *"Am Ende, hat sie gesehen was ein guter Sohn ich war"* — "In the end, she finally saw what a good son I was."

So you — you who were born to dying and who made a life of dying, who couldn't understand your own life and so needed me to understand it for you — you made a perfect circle, you created a kind of divine order of coherence and *Auf Wiedersehen*, a kind of poetry. Who can blame you? Who, for that matter, can blame anyone for anything? Because always, in the end, there is some comprehensible story of pity and rage and fate and misunderstanding. Because always there is some wild oracle of destiny and breathtaking powerlessness. Because always there is a Philoctetes who — through some dark accident of fate and misfortune — was abandoned on Lemnos, and a Philoctetes who — through some noble passion for justice — is trying to find his way back home.

Theodore Roethke said it about Yeats (a kind of father to him), and I say it to you:

I take this cadence from a man named Yeats.
I take it,
And I give it back again.

I took this story from you. I had no choice. Now I give it back. With sadness and compassion, with rage and forgiveness. I took it, and now I give it back.

Your son,
Martin

3

10 May 1992

Dear Berthold and Meta,

I am writing to you today about a serious matter, which seems particularly appropriate since you are about to meet my son — who, as you know, is your own biological grandson — for the first time.

I have realized for many years — and even more so now that I have my own family — how painful it has been for me that neither (or both) of you, nor anyone in my "other" family, has ever fully explained to me the circumstances surrounding my birth and adoption. At the same time, I have had to live with this imperfect knowledge — and you have had to live with the pain of keeping the "secret" of it — and with all it has cost us psychologically and personally, for the past forty-three years.

It seems to me that now — while we are all still alive — it is high time that someone told me the *whole* truth . . . or at least what you know and can tell of it. I deserve to know. My son deserves to know. My wife deserves to know. *You* also deserve a chance to tell me, and to bare yourselves of what I know must be a painful and complicated burden.

While I have never spoken of what has been obvious to all of us, I have long known that — at least as a matter of blood — I am your son. I want, and deserve, to know more of what occurred during that strange time now almost half a century ago. No one should have to go through his entire life, as I have until now, with the story of his birth and adoption so much a mystery.

Why was I given away to Heinz and Bettina? Whose idea was it? Why did they never have any children of their own? What was my mother's life like before she met Heinz? (Only Berthold, I think, can answer this.) My father's long-delayed and seemingly dishonest explanations of all this have never satisfied me, nor seemed entirely true. (You both know, of course, how painful and difficult his own birth and mother's death were, how panicked and confused a man he is.)

So, it would mean a great deal to me — now, before it is too late — for you to help me clear up some of these "mysteries." No one ought to be so much "in the dark" about his own origins, and I can assure you that — were the same thing or anything like it to ever happen to my own son — I would, as a father, make sure he knew the whole truth.

It would mean a great deal to me if you would finally tell me: How was this "arrangement" made? Whose idea was it? Why was I never spoken to or told about it? How sick was my mother already when I was adopted? When did you first know that she had cancer? When was her second breast removed? It is unbelievable to me, and to those I know, that no one ever bothered to tell me the answers to these questions. Now — with your other grandson (also, I might remind you, adopted) about to be bar mitzvahed — I think may be a good time to try and repair these wounds.

I know it will not be easy for you to speak about, or have to remember, these matters. No doubt, it was also a painful and difficult time for you, having just arrived from Israel with two young children. But I, personally, would be grateful to you both for anything you can do to clarify these too-long-clouded answers. In the meantime, we all send you our love, and look forward to seeing you soon.

Love,
Martin

4

Millville, N.J. 5.26.92

Dear Martin,

we thank you very much for your sincere letter! — You wrote "it is high time" — but thank G – d, not too late, to answer all the questions you have to get, you deserved and no secrets! — Only the truth! — you can tell and trust me; *from our part no Secrets — never!* — Without complaining, I am not in good health anymore, but still around and asking myself, what was holding you up solang, to ask us many years earlier? — You had all the right to do so. — From our side, it was and still is my belief, that we would not "talk" behind "others"! —

And now answering your questions so good I can: My sister was always a great lady — loving, caring, faithful, true and dear to our family. — She never was sick, so lang I can remember at home. — Before I left my homeland, we met Heinz; 1936 our Father died and two years later Omi and my sister Bettina visited me in Palestine; Heinz and Bettina were engaged and going later on to the USA, where Heinz had his family members. — 1947, after all this years, we visited here. Once again, we were happy in the family! — Also 1947 Bettina had her first Operation; she recuperated and she was later on again aktiv and happy. — 1948 we settled on the farm and started a new beginning; new surrounding, language, hard working and trying to fulfill our Obligations; there it came, unexpected: Meta was pregnant! — As a family, "all 5" (Omi included) we had not a "Idea" but in good intention that it was done, what we don't can change anymore, but we fulfilled my sister's longtime wish, to raise her child. — Which fault it was that they had not any children of their own, I can not answer. — Unfortunately it came different as we all were wishing for. 1958 the second Operation. —

It is hard for me to explain, maybe much harder for you, dear Martin, to understand, but this are the facts! — Hopefully, this letter will help not to mistrust us, but that *you never will change our belonging together in the future!* — If you need more Answers — we are ready every time! — We are looking forwards to see you all on 6.16, but that is not the right time to talk about this problem — this day belongs to Jonathan! —

Give our love also to Beatrice and Isaac! —

Love,
Berthold and Meta

CHAPTER 21

Endings

He wrote the words: THE END.
And it was the end.

— MARTIN WEINSTOCK,
"The End"

"Now stand just a little closer to your aunt and uncle — there . . . that's it! Now — all together when I say three: CHEEEEZ!"

I'm smiling for the photographer, my face wedged like a ball lodged in a metal fence between the aged, sickly-looking faces of my aunt and uncle . . . my mother and father.

"OK, now. . . . Let's have Cousin Martin over here a bit closer to the bar mitzvah boy's father, OK? Let's see you all hunker right in there. . . . *Thaaat's* it. . . . A *big* smile now from everybody, OK? Nice and luvvy duvvy now, let's all *squeeeeze* right in there together and — when I count to three — say *CHEEEEZ*."

My cheeks are starting to feel as if they're going to crack under the effort of all this smiling, but smile I do. It's my cousin's — my *brother's* — son's bar mitzvah, and — as I stand behind these four people who are, in reality, my blood — I realize that I, quite literally, tower over the others, that my own body — that once childish figure that now towers over these four smaller, more fragile-seeming bodies — might be thought of as testifying to what a certain writer I know calls "the moral immensity of a single soul."

It has been only a month since my uncle — my father — at the age of eighty-six, had his cancerous left breast removed, a rare kind of condition, I'm told, for a man. His face and expression, already, reveal a kind of ghostly air, as if he knows that his time here among the living is drawing to a close. His daughter, Rachel — my sister —

is also a jeopardized creature: Fifteen years ago, in her early thirties, she too — in what is beginning to feel like a macabre family tradition — had a cancerous breast removed, and now, at nearly fifty, her hands are so wracked by pain caused by nerve damage from the radiation that she can no longer work . . . can, in fact, no longer dress herself without help. To her left, her mother — *my* mother — sits in a wheelchair, her left knee so severely shattered in an auto accident thirty years ago (in which three of her best friends died) that she has progressively lost the ability to walk. Beside her, below my chin, stands her other son — my brother — whose own son, according to Jewish law, is about to become a man.

What, finally, is blood? I ask myself as I again force my cheeks apart at the photographer's request. Who are these people to me, and I to them? What force, what inexorable claims of destiny and blood, has brought us together once more — no doubt for the last time — in the gaze of this photographer's lens?

When the session is finally over, my cousin — a lawyer in suburban New Jersey who looks, as I once described him to my wife, "a bit like a band leader in a second-rate Cuban nightclub band" — puts his arm affectionately around me. "I'm really glad the three of you could make it," he whispers into my ear. "It's great to have you here." It's only been of late that I've taken either my cousin or his life-style, so different from my own, all that seriously, perhaps hiding my jealousy of his material comfort and cheerful good nature behind a smug sense of intellectual superiority — the kind of superiority, I now remind myself, that I hate. But today — indeed, the last several times I've seen him — he strikes me as an extraordinarily likable, good-natured, generous sort of guy.

Even his sister — *my* sister — whose trailer-park life of financial struggle, sentimental homilies, bowling leagues, store-brand ketchup and frozen fish sticks I've often looked down on — seems to me this morning to embody a certain nobility, as I observe the grace and good cheer with which she refuses to draw attention to her many burdens, the obvious warmth and affection that exist between her and her family.

We enter the synagogue, where, within minutes, in the first two rows are assembled — for the first, and no doubt last, time since my grandmother Johanna's funeral twenty-five years ago — all the living members of my two families, the confused and confusing cast of blood and acquired affections and hatreds that has brought, and raised, me into this life. In the second row, our small son, Isaac, wearing a checkered shirt, suspenders, and a black bow tie, is seated on Beatrice's lap; she is just to my left; my father and stepmother noisily whisper to each other on my right. The rest of my family — the blood part, that is — is seated in front of us in the first row.

Suddenly, roused out of my own revery of amazement and mixed feelings, I hear the rabbi call out my uncle's and cousin's and nephew's names — *"Will Berthold Loeb, Aharon Loeb, and Jonathan Loeb please rise and stand in front of the ark"* — and then my own: *"And would Mr. Martin Weinstock please mount the podium as well."*

"These Torah scrolls," the rabbi continues, opening the ark and handing the first of the ornately embroidered scrolls to my uncle, "are herewith being passed along from generation to generation to signify the passing of our laws from generation to generation. We trust that you, Jonathan, who will now read from the Holy Torah that has been passed to you by your own father, and received by him from his, will take seriously both the obligations and the rights which this coming of age as a man signify, and that you will enter into the Covenant which we are here today to celebrate with a sense of seriousness, purpose, honor and reverence."

A few minutes later, my nephew/cousin Jonathan's *haftarah* and the accompanying blessings having been completed, the rabbi — with the help of Jonathan's father — lifts the heavy scroll from the podium, carrying it over to where I am seated, to the left of the ark. From where I am sitting, I can look down, now, at the aged figures of my parents and aunt and uncle, the somewhat amused faces of my cousin Rachel's two daughters; the proud face of my cousin Aharon's wife, Barbara; at my own lovely wife and son seated beside my parents in the second row. As the rabbi places the embroidered satin cover and silver pointer over the scroll which I — the one odd piece in this jigsaw puzzle of fate and reunion — am holding, I gaze out at my son and swear I can see his still-infant face break into a wide, unambivalently joyful, smile.

2

15 June 1992

Dr. Paul Weitzel, Chairman
Department of English
Harvard University

Dear Paul:

There comes a time, even in the life of Iseult of the White Hands, when she (or he) has had enough of patience and devotion (or, to put it in the present context, of trying to be the so-called "Best in the World") and wants, as this writer does, merely to be loved for his flawed, human, imperfect, less-than-Best-in-the-World self — a mere mortal in the world of the living.

And so it now is with me — your merely human Weinstock of the occasionally unscanning verse who has not (why not finally say it?) ever read *Ulysses,* and frankly doesn't intend to, no matter how many times he may hear an angel speak its name into some realm of the ought-to-have-read or the canonical.

Why, in the end, just not say what happened? I got here, and was miserable, and — from the first day my mortal, imperfect self walked through these lofty portals — have felt like a life-starved wanderer in the realm of the dead and dying. *Somewhere in the middle of my life I went astray,* as the Good Book says, and now, still somewhere in the salvageable middle, I intend to fix it.

T. S. Eliot (at whose expense I confess I've had my share of laughs) said it better than I can (but I'll paraphrase anyway, being a classic profaner of what others hold sacred): *The end is often the beginning, the beginning the end.*

And why shouldn't I, Martin Weinstock, begin again by ending here? I was sick, and then, right here at good old Thanatos U, my sickness grew worse, and now I'm — if not restored — then at least better enough to say, in the immortal words of my adoptive father Heinz, *Auf Wiedersehen.*

So, Mr. Best-in-the-World Chairman at this Best-in-the-World institution, this is a formal *adieu* from your lesser but wiser Weinstock, wishing you, as the old song goes, bluebirds in the spring and all sorts of other fine things too.

And the fire and the rose, as the old dead bard said, are still one.

Your not-so-obedient servant,
Martin Weinstock

3

June 18, 1992

Mr. Martin Weinstock, Director
Creative Writing Program
Harvard University

Dear Martin:

I assume from your letter that what you wish to convey to me is your decision not to proceed with submitting your name to the Department for promotion next fall, a wish I most certainly intend to honor. I realize, of course, the difficulty and bravery of your decision — as well as, I must confess, its wisdom, given the realities of life at this University and the undeniable fact that permanent positions for those with such unorthodox credentials as yourself are, indeed, few and far between.

I want to make clear, however, that we in the Department, and the University as a whole, are deeply in your debt for the fine work you have done here — not only as a teacher and administrator, but as a poet (and, I understand, an incipient novelist) during a unique and formative part of your own career. You not only served as an important source of continuity after Morton Gamson's retirement, but, even more importantly, as an inspiration to such students as Melissa Wainwright, whose success and public acclaim are such an important aspect of this University's mission and continued prominence.

I am most certain that — and we in the Department plan to be helpful in any way we can in that endeavor — you will soon be able to locate another university worthy of your talents, energy, and honesty, and where you will be able to continue making the same sort of unique and generous contribution you have made during the last ten years here. In the interim, I wish you every success for your future career, and thank you again on behalf of all those in the Department for your fine work, for which you will be remembered long after your actual presence here is past.

With great admiration,
Paul Weitzel

4

June 21, 1992

Dear Martin,

I wanted to tell you how very moved, and of course deeply troubled, I was by your letter to Paul. You certainly did the right thing, if I have reconstructed your previous conversations with him correctly — the noble thing, the self-respecting thing.

The important point is to realize that these bastards have nothing on you, that you don't need them or their approval, that your esteem is self-generated, that you did good work and know it, and no more needs to be said. It is appalling for me to think that Harvard is letting you get away from them, but then I say to myself that it's logical in a way. You were always too true, too honest, too libidinous (in your work) for these false and phony and cas-trated nonentities. You showed that beautifully and movingly in your letter. They know it and shudder at the thought.

Whatever the difficulties it may bring you, you should realize that the authentic and honest path was the one you took. I've thought about it quite a bit. It seems to me that what must have been the motivating factor, aside from the apparent justifications of no tenure position or whatever Weitzel told you, was the fact that you never pretended: Never pretended to be more than we all are, never pretended to coincide with some overriding Harvard destiny, never faked being something other than a guy who wrote some poetry, read some books, loved this or that about life, had these anxieties and these hopes, came from this or that back-ground.

What all these characters can't face is just that — their mediocre humanness, their nonimportance, their ephemerality. My guess (though I don't really know for sure) is that you mirrored some-thing to them that they couldn't afford to acknowledge, and that Weitzel's defense — like every good German's — was his officious-ness. Maybe that's all wrong. But it's the way I imagine it. And I guess I imagine it that way because you are one of the few people I really admire, and admiringly love. It's that existential honesty I admire and love which, I suspect, so threatened our overly im-portant colleagues.

Above all, and entirely selfishly, I will miss your presence here — your sunny disposition, your zest for life, your relentless honesty with both yourself and others, your unwillingness to distort your zeal for life itself into a postured obsession with what's mostly dead and dying. Harvard or no Harvard, you and I are "tenured" for life — in those moments of affection and truth which friend-ship, uniquely, offers to us all, and which will endure.

Ever-affectionately,
Siggy

Epilogue

Am I a bad man? Am I a good man?
— Hard to say, Brother Bones. Maybe you both,
like most of we.

— JOHN BERRYMAN,
The Dream Songs

It was late at night in the small Provençal village of St. Étienne-
les-Orgues, where my family and I were spending the summer.
I hadn't been able to sleep for days, so I told Beatrice I would
take Isaac, who had been up crying for hours, for a walk to town
and be back shortly.

Our small house was some two kilometers from the village, and
I must have walked for ten minutes or so, carrying my son in my
arms beneath the full moon, the air thick with the scent of freshly
harvested sage and lavender, the bent heads of the *tournesols* nodding in the breeze like a battalion of old men. In the bright moonlight, I could see his face staring up at me, and it seems to me now
he must have sensed that something was about to happen, for he
wailed and contorted his little legs and arms in a way I had never
seen him do during the six brief months of his life. As we walked
along the road, above the deep, unpunctuated silence of Provence,
the only sound you could hear was my son, Isaac, wailing in the
night.

I don't know what exactly I was feeling as I left the house. As I
looked down at my son's small, contorted, weeping face, it occurred
to me that I felt virtually *nothing at all* for this still unformed being
I had half-ushered into the world. In fact, it seemed to me at that
moment that I had never felt *anything*, that whatever it was inside

a human being that was able to feel had, inside me, never been born . . . or else had died.

I didn't, of course, realize exactly what I was doing. I merely felt an irrepressible rage well up inside me as Isaac wept, a complete inability to feel anything beyond hatred and self-pity, a deep, almost desperate, wish for him to stop. At first, I merely shook him hard with both my hands, trying to make the crying stop, hoping the sounds of his wailing wouldn't be heard in the otherwise eerily silent summer air.

By the time I put him down, still crying, at the edge of the lavender field, I still don't think I had much of an idea what was going to happen. I simply went down on my knees and started digging into the dry, light earth at the field's edge with my hands, pulling out an occasional mallow weed or dried poppy as I went. Within what seemed only minutes, I had made a hole almost the size of Isaac's cradle. Out of the corner of my eye, I could see his head turn violently from side to side, as though he was trying to see, to understand, what was happening around him.

All the while, he kept wailing and screaming. After I placed him rather gently in the hole, and began covering his small, wrinkled arms and legs with dirt, it seemed for a moment, as his pear-shaped eyes gazed up toward the moonlit heavens, that a look of great tranquillity came over his face, much like the look I had seen that first second when I caught him entering the world and brought him to feed at his mother's breast. At one point, I even stopped for a moment in the utter stillness, trying to feel something for this being I had fathered, watching the big, elephant tears run down his cheeks into the parched sand of the hole I had dug.

But nothing came. Nothing, that is, except this terrible wish to have him be silent, this desire not to have to look into his weeping, contorted, tear-splayed face again. And when, finally, I scooped the last handful of dirt over the now silent shape of my son and woke from my horrible dream, all I could feel were the first shards of morning light slanting over the poppy- and lavender-strewn fields of Provence, entering our bedroom to announce the day.

2

We are sitting on the train between Paris and Avignon. My wife is in the window seat, looking out at the Monetlike landscape covered with fields of *coquelicots* and lavender, sage and mallow weed. Our son nods peacefully against her breast, his small, pink lips half-encircling her nipple. Every few seconds, he opens his eyes, as if to make sure we are still with him, and takes her nipple into his mouth, making intense sucking sounds that mingle with the steady hum of the train and our own shallow breathing.

Sitting in my seat gazing at them, I feel — despite all the evil and anger and rage that is within me, and that I cannot disavow — as if all that is good and decent and ordinary and right in the world is contained in their being, a conjunction of which I am part maker, part participant . . . and part merely spectator. For I know already, half sadly and half contentedly, that part of this simple, perhaps divinely ordained *rightness* — part of this calm and contented peacefulness that is the coming together of a mother and child — is forever closed to me, open only to my imaginings and longings.

I also know, as I gaze at these two beings whom I — for lack of a better word — *love,* that I have done something large and difficult and, if I might say so, in its own small way, *heroic.* I know that — by some, perhaps, nearly negligible but significant increment — I have taken my single soul at least one step closer to a world the dead and living can occupy equally. Despite all the ambivalence, terror, fear, confusion and melancholy in my heart, I have taken the chance of life.

And I can't help but think, as I gaze down at my son's six-month-old face, already so much like my own — as I see his wide, helpless, curious eyes gaze back at me — that a poet I once admired (and who was unable, like so many poets, to lift his own sad soul out of the tragedy and confusion he saw as his destiny) was right when he wrote, "The child is the meaning of this life."

That, it seems to me, may well be what this child — and this woman who offers me, so relentlessly and forgivingly, her love — are: *the meaning of my life.* Not something that will bring a long-dead woman back to life, or allow a long-grown man to become a ten-year-old boy and bid her adieu, but something that may allow *this* grown man to do the one thing life allows us by way of reprieve: *to forget, and to go on.*

And what of the wish for a happy ending? Well, there are *many* possible endings, some far worse than others, but none of them entirely happy. Because the wish for a happy ending, when you get right down to it, is also a kind of childishness — like the wish to undo your own history, or to return to your mother, like the hatred of rabbis. It is, after all, a divinely mixed world, neither heaven nor hell, neither all yin nor all yang, and the only sure thing is that some form of living and dying, in the end, will come to us all.

I've often thought of how it might have gone for Oedipus had he just stayed home (like, say, Philoctetes on Lemnos, or a patient on an analytic couch) and accepted his oracle, instead of trying to hard to escape it. Maybe he still would have killed his father, but his mother would merely have gone on and married a stranger. Maybe he would have married his mother anyway (don't we all want to?), but no one would have given a damn about it. Maybe some small victory might yet have been his — say, the birth of a son or some beautiful night with some bright piece of cuntliness and womb who never bore him. Who knows?

"You had the wrong parents," Amanda Wayland once said to me over lunch, meaning, I suppose, all four of them. And, indeed — in terms of "some overriding Harvard destiny" like my friend Siggy mentioned in his letter — maybe I did. Maybe I would have been better off, happier no doubt, with a father who *really* fished, a mother who read Keats, an aunt and uncle who drove something more interesting than eggs along the New Jersey Turnpike between my two homes. Then again, I had the *only* parents who could have allowed me to write this story, the perfect characters for this book that has lived so long inside me.

"Through these sufferings of yours you shall glorify your life," says Heracles to Philoctetes at the end of Sophocles' play. "You shall sack Troy; the prize of valor shall be given to you by our warriors; and you shall carry the spoils to your home." What more could a man ask of his own story? What more could he want to do than add some small increment of hope and forgiveness to the world's landscape of mixed luck and dreaming? What better thing could he ask than to be someone who occasionally looks out into this wild domain of living and dying, of order and chaos, of freedom and necessity — someone who can look a dead woman in the face and say, without shame or apology, without guilt for his own being: *"Isn't life wonderful?"*

And, as I gaze at my son, at my wife, at this mixed kingdom of happiness and sadness, it seems to me clear that we won't know till the end what our victories are; whether, dead as we may once have seemed, we will yet survive to emerge — a living Weinstock in some small, happy kingdom of weeping and singing.

Acknowledgments

I wish to thank the John Simon Guggenheim Memorial Foundation for a grant in poetry during the 1988–89 academic year, when work on this book began, which—like any self-respecting writer—I turned to my own devices. I can only hope that this "infidelity" to my original genre will prove, in that generous foundation's eyes, a forgivable transgression.

Though Martin Weinstock was not *always* blessed by the company of his colleagues, his creator *has* been blessed with true and devoted friends, without whom I could not possibly have sustained the commitment and energy to keep working on this book. Above all, I want to thank Ross McElwee and Melanie Thernstrom, who read the manuscript and offered me detailed comments and suggestions, not once but more times than pride allows me to acknowledge. I would also like to thank Rob Moss, Tina Feingold, Marilyn Levine, Laura Cunningham, Lorrie Moore, Carol Bolsay, Twig Johnson, Elizabeth Arthur, Julie Graham, Margie Smigel, John and Lilly Engle, Jack Estes and Shannon Gentry, all of whom read the manuscript at various stages and offered helpful advice and encouragement.

I am also deeply grateful to David Wellbery, both for his long and devoted friendship and for the (perhaps unintended) "gift" that helped me to end this book. And to Sacvan Bercovitch, Helen Vendler, Seamus Heaney and Monroe Engel for innumerable kindnesses and generosities over the years, and for embodying—each in his/her own particular way—all that seems to me best about academic life. And my deep gratitude to Roland Pease and Zoland Books for believing in this book at the outset.

The text includes quotations, either literal or distorted, from, among others, Dante Aligheri, Jorge Luis Borges, John Bowlby, Joseph Brodsky, Albert Camus, E.L. Doctorow, Stephen Dunn, Ralph Waldo Emerson, Carlos Fuentes, Randall Jarrell, James Joyce, Milan Kundera, Primo Levi, James Logan, Robert Lowell, Howard Nemerov, Delmore Schwartz, William Shakespeare and Ellen Bryant Voigt, to all of whom I am grateful for their life, work, and inspiration.

Finally, I owe perhaps the greatest debt of all to my wife, Isabelle, whose love, devotion and patience provided me with some of the calm with which to finish what I had begun . . . and some of the courage to end what I wanted to end. And to my son, Noah, for acquainting me with the better, and happier, part of the life cycle.

Books from *Pleasure Boat Studio: A Literary Press*

(*Note:* Caravel Books is a new imprint of Pleasure Boat Studio: A Literary Press. Caravel Books is the imprint for mysteries only. Aequitas Books is another imprint which includes non-fiction with philosophical and sociological themes. Empty Bowl Press is a Division of Pleasure Boat Studio.)

UPCOMING: *The Shadow in the Lake* • Inger Frimansson, Trans Laura Wideburg • **a caravel book**
UPCOMING: *Immortality* • Mike O'Connor
UPCOMING: *Working the Woods, Working the Sea* • **an empty bowl book**
UPCOMING: *Listening to the Rhino* • Dr. Janet Dallett

The War Journal of Lila Ann Smith • Irving Warner • $18
The Woman Who Wrote King Lear, and Other Stories • Louis Phillips • $16
Dream of the Dragon Pool: A Daoist Quest • Albert A. Dalia • $18
Good Night, My Darling • Inger Frimansson, Trans by Laura Wideburg • $18 • **a caravel book**
Falling Awake: An American Woman Gets a Grip on the Whole Changing World—One Essay at a Time • Mary Lou Sanelli • $15 • **an aequitas book**
Way Out There: Lyrical Essays • Michael Daley • $16 • **an aequitas book**
The Case of Emily V. • Keith Oatley • mystery • $18 • **a caravel book**
Monique • Luisa Coehlo, Trans fm Portuguese by Maria do Carmo de Vasconcelos and Dolores DeLuise ISBN 1929355262 • 80 pages • fiction • $14
The Blossoms Are Ghosts at the Wedding • Tom Jay • ISBN 1929355351 • essays and poems • $15 • **an empty bowl book**
Against Romance • Michael Blumenthal • ISBN 1929355238 • 110 pages • poetry • $14
Speak to the Mountain: The Tommie Waites Story • Dr. Bessie Blake • ISBN 1929355297 / 36X • 278 pages • biography • $18 / $26 • **an aequitas book**
Artrage • Everett Aison • ISBN 1929355254 • 225 pages • fiction • $15
Days We Would Rather Know • Michael Blumenthal • ISBN 1929355246 • 118 pages • poetry • $14
Puget Sound: 15 Stories • C. C. Long • ISBN 192935522X • 150 pages • fiction • $14
Homicide My Own • Anne Argula • ISBN 1929355211 • 220 pages • fiction (mystery) • $16
Craving Water • Mary Lou Sanelli • ISBN 192935519X • 121 pages • poetry • $15
When the Tiger Weeps • Mike O'Connor • ISBN 1929355189 • 168 pages • poetry and prose • 15
Wagner, Descending: The Wrath of the Salmon Queen • Irving Warner • ISBN 1929355173 • 242 pages • fiction • $16
Concentricity • Sheila E. Murphy • ISBN 1929355165 • 82 pages • poetry • $13.95
Schilling, from a study in lost time • Terrell Guillory • ISBN 1929355092 • 156 pages • fiction • $16.95
Rumours: A Memoir of a British POW in WWII • Chas Mayhead • ISBN 1929355068 • 201 pages • nonfiction • $16
The Immigrant's Table • Mary Lou Sanelli • ISBN 1929355157 • $13.95 • poetry and recipes • $13/95
The Enduring Vision of Norman Mailer • Dr. Barry H. Leeds • ISBN 1929355114 • criticism • $18
Women in the Garden • Mary Lou Sanelli • ISBN 1929355149 • poetry • $13.95
Pronoun Music • Richard Cohen • ISBN 1929355033 • short stories • $16
If You Were With Me Everything Would Be All Right • Ken Harvey • ISBN 1929355025 • short stories • $16
The 8th Day of the Week • Al Kessler • ISBN 1929355009 • fiction • $16
Another Life, and Other Stories • Edwin Weihe • ISBN 19293550117 • short stories • $16
Saying the Necessary • Edward Harkness • ISBN 096514139X (paper) • poetry • $14
Nature Lovers • Charles Potts • ISBN 1929355041 • poetry • $10
In Memory of Hawks, & Other Stories from Alaska • Irving Warner • ISBN 0965141349 • 210 pages • fiction • $15
The Politics of My Heart • William Slaughter • ISBN 0965141306 • 96 pages • poetry • $12.95

The Rape Poems • Frances Driscoll • ISBN 0965141314 • 88 pages • poetry • $12.95
When History Enters the House: Essays from Central Europe • Michael Blumenthal •
ISBN 0965141322 • 248 pages • nonfiction • $15
Setting Out: The Education of Lili • Tung Nien • Trans fm Chinese by Mike O'Connor •
ISBN 0965141330 • 160 pages • fiction • $15

Our Chapbook Series:

No. 1: *The Handful of Seeds: Three and a Half Essays* • Andrew Schelling •
ISBN 0965141357 • $7 • 36 pages • nonfiction
No. 2: *Original Sin* • Michael Daley • ISBN 0965141365 • $8 • 36 pages • poetry
No. 3: *Too Small to Hold You* • Kate Reavey • ISBN 19293505x • $8 • poetry
No. 4: *The Light on Our Faces: A Therapy Dialogue* • Lee Miriam WhitmanRaymond •
ISBN 1929355122 • $8 • 36 pages • poetry
No. 5: *Eye* • William Bridges • ISBN 0-929355-13-0 / 24 pages / chapbook / $8
No. 6: *Selected New Poems of Rainer Maria Rilke* • Trans fm German by Alice Derry •
ISBN 1929355106 • $10 • poetry
No. 7: *Through High Still Air: A Season at Sourdough Mountain* • Tim McNulty •
ISBN 1929355270 • $9 • poetry and prose
No. 8: *Sight Progress* • Zhang Er, Trans fm Chinese by Rachel Levitsky •
ISBN 1929355289 • $9 • prosepoems
No. 9: *The Perfect Hour* • Blas Falconer • ISBN 1929355319 • $9 • poetry

From other publishers (in limited editions):

Desire • Jody Aliesan • ISBN 0912887117 • $14 • poetry (an Empty Bowl book)
Deams of the Hand • Susan Goldwitz • ISBN 0912887125 • $14 • poetry (an Empty
Bowl book)
Lineage • Mary Lou Sanelli • No ISBN • $14 • poetry (an Empty Bowl book)
The Basin: Poems from a Chinese Province • Mike O'Connor • ISBN 0912887 206 •
$10 / $20 • poetry (paper/ hardbound) (an Empty Bowl book)
The Straits • Michael Daley • ISBN 0912887044 • $10 • poetry (an Empty Bowl book)
In Our Hearts and Minds: The Northwest and Central America • Ed. Michael Daley •
ISBN 0912887184 • $12 • poetry and prose (an Empty Bowl book)
The Rainshadow • Mike O'Connor • No ISBN • $16 • poetry (an Empty Bowl book)
Untold Stories • William Slaughter • ISBN 1912887 249 • $10 / $20 • poetry (paper /
hardbound) (an Empty Bowl book)
In Blue Mountain Dusk • Tim McNulty • ISBN 0965141381 • $12.95 • poetry
(a Broken Moon book)
China Basin • Clemens Starck • ISBN 1-58654-013-0 • $13.95 • poetry (a Story Line
Press book)
Journeyman's Wages • Clemens Starck • ISBN 1-885266-02-2 • $10.95 • poetry (a Story
Line Press book)

Orders: Pleasure Boat Studio books are available by order from your bookstore, directly from
PBS, or through the following:
SPD (Small Press Distribution) Tel. 8008697553, Fax 5105240852
Partners/West Tel. 4252278486, Fax 4252042448
Baker & Taylor Tel 8007751100, Fax 8007757480
Ingram Tel 6157935000, Fax 6152875429
Amazon.com or **Barnesandnoble.com**

Pleasure Boat Studio: A Literary Press
201 West 89th Street
New York, NY 10024
Tel: 2123628563 / Fax: 8888105308
www.pleasureboatstudio.com / pleasboat@nyc.rr.com

CPSIA information can be obtained
at www.ICGtesting.com
Printed in the USA
BVHW030249230421
605713BV00006B/60